THE
YOUNG
WIVES
CLUB

THE YOUNG WIVES CLUB

a novel

Julie Pennell

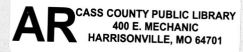
EMILY BESTLER BOOKS
—
ATRIA

New York   London   Toronto   Sydney   New Delhi

ATRIA PAPERBACK

An Imprint of Simon & Schuster, Inc.
1230 Avenue of the Americas
New York, NY 10020

First Emily Bestler Books/Atria Paperback edition February 2017

EMILY BESTLER BOOKS / ATRIA PAPERBACK and colophons are trademarks of Simon & Schuster, Inc.

For information about special discounts for bulk purchases, please contact Simon & Schuster Special Sales at 1-866-506-1949 or business@simonandschuster.com.

The Simon & Schuster Speakers Bureau can bring authors to your live event. For more information, or to book an event, contact the Simon & Schuster Speakers Bureau at 1-866-248-3049 or visit our website at www.simonspeakers.com.

Interior design by Bryden Spevak

Manufactured in the United States of America

10 9 8 7 6 5 4 3 2 1

Library of Congress Cataloging-in-Publication Data has been applied for.

ISBN 978-1-5011-3646-7
ISBN 978-1-5011-3648-1 (ebook)

For two of the strongest southern women I know,
my mom, Sandy, and my sister, Jill

prologue

TWO THOUSAND, ONE hundred and fifty-four people live in my town. There are ten restaurants, two stoplights, one grocery store, and three schools—Toulouse Elementary, Toulouse Middle, and Toulouse High. Not the most creative names, I know, but that's Toulouse for you.

Life here is simple. All we need is a nice white dress for church on Sundays, and a shaded porch on a hot summer day. For us, heaven on earth is a run-down restaurant with a sticky floor that serves crawfish and sweet tea.

After all, just like on the Upper East Side or in Beverly Hills, every girl here is hoping for her happily ever after—only she won't be trotting down the aisle in Louboutins or toasting her wedding day with Dom Pérignon. Hell, she probably isn't even old enough to legally drink. Because in my little corner of Louisiana, finding your one true love happens sometime around high school. If you're lucky, he might just be the man you thought he was. But not every girl has luck on her side. . . .

1

laura

"COULD YOUR LIFE *be* any more perfect?" the short brunette squealed, hugging Laura Landry. They'd run into each other while waiting in line for hot dogs during halftime at Tiger Stadium, where they'd briefly caught up on the last few months of their lives—in between an ongoing debate about whether they should be bad and get the chili.

Laura felt terrible, but she couldn't for the life of her remember the girl's name, even though they'd spent all of last year's gym class complaining to each other about running laps in the humid Louisiana weather. Perhaps it was because Laura had other, more important things to pay attention to back then, like when Brian's papers were due (she wrote them for him) and how he liked his locker decorated for game days (school colors, but not too over-the-top).

"We miss you at school, but you definitely did the right thing. I mean, Brian's doing awesome out there! He's gonna win this one for sure." The brunette squeezed Laura's arm encouragingly.

Laura smiled. She knew her husband was amazingly talented—it was why she'd dropped out of school after her junior year and married him, following him to LSU—but it was still reassuring to hear other people say it. "Still half the game to go, don't jinx it!" she teased, but secretly she knew Brian would pull off the win.

It was LSU's second home game of the year, playing rival Ole

Miss. Because Brian was a freshman, his coach had been hesitant to start him when they played Auburn, only putting him in at the end of the third quarter. But Brian hadn't been recruited on a full scholarship for nothing: two touchdowns and zero interceptions later, Coach Perkins had decided Brian deserved to start the next game. At the rate he was going today, he'd be starting *every* game, for years to come, until two decades from now when he'd retire from the NFL (just like his uncle Bradley, a football legend who was a commentator on ESPN, and the most famous person—make that the *only* famous person—to come out of Toulouse). And of course Laura would be by his side through it all.

After saying a quick good-bye, Laura made her way back to Brian's parents, Rob and Janet, in the stands. Rob had made up his own chant for the tenth time that day: *"Cracklins, boudin, crawfish pie . . . come on, Tigers, kick it high!"* The sea of purple and gold around them cheered. To her left stood a line of beefy frat boys with floppy hair and backward baseball hats, the letters GEAUX TIG S spelled out on their shirtless chests. The *E* and the *R* were nowhere to be seen, perhaps a casualty of heavy tailgating.

"Can't believe all of this is for my baby," Janet said, fidgeting with her purple and gold Mardi Gras beads. She then let out a roaring "Who dat!" For such a tiny little woman, it was always a mystery where Janet's booming voice came from.

Laura took a bite of her hot dog and glanced around the stadium, taking it all in—the manicured field edged with ESPN cameras, the coiffed cheerleaders stretching on the sidelines, the deafening roar of nearly a hundred thousand people. It was a far cry from the tiny field with rusted bleachers she grew up with eighty miles away. But this was *it*. She always knew she belonged in a place like this; it was in her blood. Her mom was originally from Dallas, and as soon as Laura married and moved out of town, her parents had hightailed it to Arlington, Texas, bought a condo, and never looked back. No one in Laura's family had visited tiny Toulouse in the months since. They weren't meant to be small-town people.

The crowd roared as halftime ended and the players returned to the field. But Laura had eyes for only one of them. She zeroed in on number seven, enjoying how cute Brian's butt looked in his spandex, how powerful he seemed as he arranged his players around him. She smiled, appreciating her man. She took a quick picture of the field and posted it on Instagram, tagging it with #blessed and #luckygirl. She still couldn't believe she was really here, that this was really her life. It had all started on a seemingly ordinary day less than six months ago. . . .

On a scorching spring afternoon right before prom, she and Brian lay sprawled on his dad's fishing boat in the middle of Darby Lake. They had just rubbed each other down with baby oil, and every page she flipped in her *Cosmo* was sticky from her fingers.

Brian shifted his body into hers and gently grabbed the magazine out of her hands. "There ain't nothing you can learn from that article that you don't already know," he said, grinning.

Laura lowered her cat-eye sunglasses and blushed.

"But you sure as hell can practice," he said, glancing down at his swim trunks.

Laura grinned and looked around the lake to see if anyone was nearby, but all she spotted were a few birds pecking around in the water. As she hovered over him in between kisses, she caught her reflection in his Oakleys. She liked the girl she saw—the girl he made her feel like when she was with him. Hot. Fun. Loved. Their lips touched and she slipped her tongue into his mouth. He pulled her closer and kissed her harder. And then he grabbed her hand and guided it down his shorts. As she explored him, she felt something hard, round, and . . . metal?

"What's this?" Laura asked as she extracted a dainty diamond ring, tied to a string inside his trunks. Brian just sat there, his head propped up on his strong arm. "Brian Hunter Landry. What the hell is this?" Laura's stomach filled with butterflies. His smile only grew deeper. "Is this for me?"

"No, it's for my other beautiful girlfriend . . ." he teased. "Yeah, it's for you." He sat up and pulled her in close. "Laura Lynn Har-grave, will you marry me?"

Her heart, already pounding hard, stopped in her chest, and she started to cry. "Um, you better get your ass down on one knee." She laughed through the tears. "I'm already gonna have to edit out parts of this proposal when we tell people, so you sure as hell better do some of it the right way."

"You're really gonna make me do this, huh?" he said, taking off his purple baseball cap and lowering his two-hundred-pound body into a kneel on the floor of the boat.

Laura nodded, wiping away the tears. She'd fantasized about him proposing to her ever since he gave her a heart-shaped promise ring on her Sweet Sixteen, but the moment still took her by surprise. She'd imagined everything would feel like it was happening in slow motion, but in fact it was the opposite: it was all going way too fast. Her head spun as he placed the ring on her finger.

"Time to celebrate!" Brian had shouted, grabbing his new fian-cée's bare waist with one hand while untying her hot pink string bikini top with the other.

"GET 'ER DONE!" Her father-in-law's loud chant, resounding in her ear, brought Laura back to reality.

The second half of the game was starting, and Brian and his team went swiftly into action. He swung out to the right on a quarterback sweep, and she watched him react quickly as a line of blockers formed in front of him. He collided with a mammoth defensive lineman, but there was no way for him to prepare for the safety coming in low from his blind side, plowing into his left knee. Brian flailed through the air, landing hard on the ground as the crowd collectively gasped.

"Brian!" Laura screamed, standing up quickly on weak legs. She had seen him get hit plenty of times on the field, but never so violently.

"My baby!" Janet cried out at the same time.

They watched as a trainer rushed to the field and kneeled down next to Brian, who was still lying on the ground, his face twisted in pain. After a few minutes, the trainer waved over another player and they propped Brian up between them, slowly helping him rise to his feet. Even from a distance, it was obvious: Brian couldn't put any weight on his knee.

Laura watched in horror as her future limped to the sideline, disappearing off into the distance, amid a smattering of shell-shocked applause.

• • •

"HOW ARE YOU still so sexy even when you're lying in a hospital bed?" Laura whispered into Brian's ear. It wasn't entirely the truth. After two days in the hospital, he still hadn't showered, and his blond hair was curly with dried-up sweat and grease. But at this point, she'd say anything to make him smile. She put her hands delicately on his cheeks, feeling the roughness of his stubble. "You feeling okay, baby?"

Brian just sat there, staring intently at the old TV mounted on the wall. Laura resisted the urge to walk over and turn it off. Whenever *SportsCenter* was on, she might as well be wearing a cloak of invisibility.

"Do you need any more painkillers?" she prompted, feeling as though his pain was hers.

"Dammit, Laura—I don't need any more painkillers!" Brian snapped, finally taking his eyes off of the screen. "I need my knee to work again." His eyes lowered for a moment before returning to the TV.

Her stomach twisted at his tone of voice, but she reminded herself that he was upset at the situation, not her. "It will. I'm sure you'll play again in no time," she said soothingly, even though she couldn't get the hushed words the doctors had used in the hallway out of her brain: *"He'll be lucky to walk after this."*

Brian glanced up at the ceiling, looking almost as if he was going to cry. She had never seen him shed a tear, even on their wedding day when she was bawling, the mascara running down her cheeks.

"What did the coach say?" she asked. A few of the coaches and trainers had come by to check on Brian earlier that day, along with some of his teammates.

"Nothing much," he said in a flat tone. "He says they'll honor my scholarship, but I don't know what the point is if I can't play."

"It's so great they're supporting you," she said brightly.

He didn't answer. She could tell he wanted to be alone, and for some reason that made her sadder than the thought of him in pain. "I'm just gonna leave you right here for a minute," Laura said, forcing a smile and turning toward the door. As soon as she walked out of the room, a flood of tears streamed from her eyes, tears she didn't want Brian to see. She had to be strong for him. That was something she had learned from her mom—she was her dad's rock, and Laura always wanted to emulate that in her own marriage.

Making her way into the dimly lit hospital cafeteria, she spotted Rob and Janet tucked into a table in the corner. "Mind if I join y'all?"

Rob was eating a ham and cheese sandwich that looked almost as sad as his mood. Janet was knitting, her go-to stress relief. Sophomore year, when Brian was learning to drive—and showing reckless abandon around stop signs—Janet would sit in the passenger seat, knitting furiously so she didn't have to look at the road. Needless to say, everyone got scarves that year for Christmas.

"Oh, Laura, this ain't good. This ain't good." Rob cleared his throat. The noise echoed throughout the quiet room.

"It'll be fine," Laura said adamantly, leaning back in the uncomfortable metal seat. "*He'll* be fine."

"I know my baby," Janet said, looking up from the pile of blue yarn in her lap. "You tell him he can't play football, and all hell's gonna break loose." She frowned and then went back to knitting.

"He'll play again," Laura said firmly, picking up one of their used napkins and shredding it into tiny pieces. "He will."

She wasn't sure who she was trying to convince.

2

madison

THE WOODEN PORCH swing creaked every time it went up and down, and Madison Blanchette found the repetition therapeutic. She puffed on her cigarette, watching the mosquitoes float through the evening air. One landed on her arm. Her first instinct was to squash it; she never thought twice about killing one. But today, for some reason, she couldn't. Did it really deserve to die? It was just doing what it was supposed to, trying to live. Who was she to take its life? *Dammit.* She watched as the mosquito positioned its stinger into her pasty skin.

As Madison exhaled, the smoke engulfed her. She could practically feel it seeping into her long, wavy brown hair. She knew it was weird, but she would often smell her hair throughout the day, the scent of smoke calming her. She hadn't always been a smoker; after learning about the dangers of cigarettes in elementary school, she would hide her parents' packs to try to make them quit. But they learned to keep them out of her reach, and *she* learned that smoking made her feel cool, and that was the end of their hide-and-seek game.

"Put that damn thing out," her father said as he opened the sliding glass door, joining her on the porch. "You wanna be like me when you grow up?"

"Well, yeah, actually . . ." Madison said, tapping the cigarette with her index finger and watching the ashes fall to the concrete.

"Don't be smart with me, young lady," he said, crossing his thin arms as he sat down next to her on the swing. She couldn't help but notice how much weight he had lost. Her throat tightened. "You know damn well what I mean."

"How was the doctor?" she asked, even though she didn't really want to know. She'd prefer to pretend that her dad was healthy, that everything would be okay.

He looked at her with heavy eyes. "Same ol', you know."

She nodded, accepting the lie. Her dad sipped from his blue plastic tumbler. Anyone who saw it would think he was drinking ice water; anyone who talked to him would know that it was vodka. Her father had promised his family and doctors he'd quit smoking after the lung cancer diagnosis, but there was steel in his eyes when he told them they'd have to pry his vodka soda from his cold dead hands.

After a lengthy pause, he said, "I gotta quit working. Doc says I can't be offshore anymore. Too risky."

Madison looked up sharply. Her dad's job as a crane operator on an oil rig was their family's main source of income.

"What are we going to do?" she asked, feeling flushed. "Mama doesn't make enough." Her mom earned some money cleaning houses for the well-to-do folks in the next town over, but there was no way it would support them.

"We're gonna need you to help out more," her dad said, clutching his drink with his rough, pale hands. "You need to get a job."

Madison glanced down and sighed. "I'm looking, you know that," she said, smashing her cigarette on the ground with her black Chuck Taylors. Madison had graduated from Toulouse High that spring. Ever since, she had been trying to find a job, applying for every admin position in town, but there wasn't much out there, and no one seemed to want to hire her.

"You can't be picky right now," he said. "We just need a little bit extra to stay afloat, okay? Maybe you can get a job as a maid like your ma."

Sometimes Madison would go with her mom to help, and she'd sneak away and sift through the women's closets, touching all the fine fabrics and trying on the expensive jewelry. But she shuddered at the idea of scrubbing soap scum off of rich peoples' porcelain tubs. The tired and desperate look in her father's eyes told her this wasn't the time to be dramatic, though. "I'll get something this week, Daddy. I promise."

He put his drink on the concrete below them and leaned over to pat her knee. "Thanks, darlin'," he said, his voice shaky.

"Who knows . . . maybe I'll win the lottery," she said wistfully. She and her dad had scratched off lottery tickets once a week for as long as she could remember. In the promising moments before she put the coin down to paper and revealed her results, they would each say what they'd use the money for if they won. Over the years, all her fantasies had a travel theme—Disney World when she was little, Paris when she started taking French in school, Amsterdam after reading about their "coffee shops" online—but they all remained just that: fantasies. Now her only fantasy was that her dad would get through this. "I'd give every cent to you," she added.

"Is that before or after you bought all the things you wanted?" he asked, shaking his tumbler, the ice cubes hitting each other in an uneven rhythm.

"After, obviously." She chuckled. "So, let's see. If I won twenty-five million dollars, after the vacations, new house, clothes, car, and party—because we'd definitely need to celebrate—you'd have a cool five hundred thousand for sure."

"Wow, that's actually higher than I thought it'd be," he said.

"You raised a very generous girl, Daddy." Madison flashed him a smile so wide, she revealed the gap between her two front teeth, a view she normally tried to hide. He smiled back.

The mosquitoes were getting bad, swarming the yard. It had rained the night before, and small puddles of water collected on the blue tarp covering their scratched-up fishing boat.

Madison stared out at the boat. "Do you remember that time you tried to reel that catfish in for me, and ended up falling in the water?"

Her dad chuckled. "That sucker wasn't no catfish. It was ten foot long and mocking me with a mouth full of fangs."

"Wasn't it five foot the last time you told the story?"

"Nah, it's always been fifteen." They both burst into laughter.

Madison's mom poked her head out the sliding door, a wan smile on her face. In the months since Allen had gotten sick, gray streaks had shot through her short brown hair and she had stopped wearing makeup. "What's all the fuss out here?"

"Just reminiscing about our fishing trips," her dad responded.

Connie turned to Madison. "You've got company."

She jumped off the swing and ran inside the house, making a beeline for the front door. "I don't know why that boy never comes in . . ." she heard her mom say under her breath.

"Must be scared of us," her dad replied.

In the driveway, Cash Romero sat on his Boss Hoss motorcycle, revving the engine. His shoulder-length black hair fell into a messy swoop as he removed his helmet. He shook his head, the strands immediately falling where they belonged. Madison's eyes trailed his tattoos from his wrists to the top of his large biceps, peeking out from his snug black T-shirt. Heat pooled in her stomach.

His dark brown eyes caught hers. "Like what you see?" he called out with a smile.

"I didn't know you were gonna stop by today," she said, giving him a kiss. "Why are you here?"

Cash brushed a strand of her hair away from her eyes. "Just wanted to see how my girl was doing. Come to my show tonight," he said, grabbing her waist. "I want you right up front." His face was so close to hers, she could feel his warm breath on her lips.

"I'm kinda in a mood right now," she said, lowering her eyes. "Put me down as a maybe?" She hated to say no, but after the conversation with her father, she knew she couldn't afford the ten-dollar cover, or the bar tab. Cash would be onstage most of the night, so he couldn't buy her drinks, which meant she'd need at least forty bucks for the night. Money was too tight for that.

"I'm in a mood, too," he whispered, pulling her closer, moving his hand from her waist to her butt. He nuzzled his face into the crook of her neck and nibbled on her earlobe, sending a spark of pleasure down her body. She hoped her parents weren't looking out the window, but it felt so good, she didn't want him to stop. "I want you," he said, finally kissing her and biting her bottom lip.

She could taste his last cigarette, and he could probably taste hers. He slid his hand up her neck into her hair, tugging at a few of her ever-present knots, and probably causing a few more. She moved her hand under his shirt slowly, feeling his stomach. It was smooth, save for the line of hair that led to his belly button. She knew exactly where that trail ended.

Cash slowly pulled back, pecking her on the lips. "I'll see you tonight. Ten p.m. at the Sea Shack."

Madison just nodded. Before she could form words, Cash and his motorcycle were already out the driveway and down the street.

3

claire

@Pastor_Gavin: "Today's a new day. Show gratitude for the joyful things in your life & seek God's strength. You got this!"

CLAIRE THIBODEAUX SQUINTED at her iPhone, rereading her tweet to make sure she hadn't misspelled any words. Last week, one of their church's youth group members had replied, "Don't you mean 'MESSAGE?'" to Claire's tweet about the importance of God's *massage*. It still made her blush.

Claire held her phone out to her husband, Gavin, who was sprawled across their navy sectional couch. "Do you like this one?"

Gavin glanced up from his iPad. "Love it, hon. Thank you." He smiled at her, his blue eyes crinkling adorably behind his thick-rimmed glasses, and went back to typing away. She glowed with pride.

Managing Gavin's personal Twitter account was just one of Claire's many jobs at the church—*their* church. She worked behind the scenes, building up Pastor Gavin's national following and bringing his message to the tens of thousands of fans he had on social media. The demand for her—er, *Gavin's*—words of wisdom was so huge that she was even writing a book in his name. Well, it was an ebook, but still, she had been staying up until midnight every night working on it.

She pressed TWEET and waited for the notifications to start rolling in; with their large following, each missive from @Pastor_Gavin got tons of retweets, favorites, and replies. Though she knew it was prideful, Claire couldn't help enjoying the flurry of activity.

Her phone buzzed and she picked it up excitedly, but it was just a text from her cousin Madison:

Take a break from ur perfect life and come out w me tonite? 10pm Sea Shack?

Claire frowned, the words "perfect life" rubbing her the wrong way. When Claire was Madison's age, she was already engaged to the love of her life and working a full-time job at the church. Her cousin, on the other hand, seemed to take a more impulsive approach to her future—oftentimes, to her own detriment. Claire didn't want to encourage that kind of behavior.

C: It's a school night sweetheart.
M: Since when are u in school? :/
C: You know what I mean . . .
M: Boo . . .
C: How's your dad doing BTW?
M: :(
C: So sorry, Mads. Praying for him.

Claire placed her phone down on the beige carpet and sighed. "Uncle Allen isn't doing well," she said, fighting a wave of sadness. Her uncle was practically her substitute dad. He was the one who had taught her the important things in life, like how to ride a bike and suck the head of a crawfish. "We need to send prayers to him and Madison and Aunt Connie."

Gavin looked up from his iPad, his eyebrows furrowed with concern. "Of course."

Sadie started whining, flailing on her fleece blanket in the middle of the living room. She wasn't crawling yet, but she seemed determined to try. "What's wrong, little girl?" Claire asked her daughter in a soft voice, scooping her baby into her arms.

Claire rocked Sadie. "I just can't imagine what Mads is going through right now. She's so close with her dad. Like you and Sadie. What you have with her just stops my heart."

Gavin's eyes lit up. "This is good," he said.

"Good?" Claire's voice cracked with confusion.

"I'm writing my sermon on family matters," he said, setting his iPad down. "What you're saying—it's really interesting to think about. Why does it take these life-altering moments to look at what you have and appreciate it? If your dad was dying, would you feel differently about him?" He picked up the device from the side table and started typing furiously.

Claire's father was only fifteen miles away, but he hadn't seen her more than five times in the last year. She resented him for walking out on her and her mom when she was six. Resented him for forgetting her birthdays, for never coming to her school plays when she was younger, for not coming to see Sadie very often now. But at the thought of him dying . . . "I'd be devastated," she admitted. It made her wonder if she should make more of an effort.

Gavin typed something. "Do you think that sometimes we take what we have for granted? Family-wise, I mean."

"Of course," Claire said. "But you'd never do that to me and Sadie, would ya?" she teased.

Gavin missed her playful tone. "Never." His head was still down as he continued to write.

Claire stood up, bouncing a now-fussy Sadie on her hip. It was her bedtime. After putting her daughter down, Claire lingered in her bedroom, staring at the collage framed on the wall. It was filled with pictures of Claire and Gavin before they had Sadie. Her eyes went immediately to their wedding picture, the two of them standing under the arch of two large oak trees on Gavin's family's property. They looked like bride and groom cake toppers—she in a heavy, poufy white gown from David's Bridal, Gavin in his freshly pressed suit. She could just hear the Ziggy Lou Zydeco Band performing at the barbecue reception. Gavin had insisted that an accordion would go better with brisket than a cello would. She'd been skeptical but had to admit he was right . . . as he usually was.

That day was incredible, although their beaming smiles in the picture hid just how nervous they were about that night. It would be the first time they would see each other naked, or do more than kiss. Claire had secretly researched what to do, Googling until she came across a Christian relationship blog that gave her some vague tips:

1. *Ask your husband or wife what pleases them. Just like in your relationship, communication is important in the bedroom. This is a surefire way both of you will have your wants and needs met.*
2. *Be creative and have fun! Keep things spicy and playful— it's important for both of you to enjoy this special time. Maybe you can even buy some books on techniques or classy lingerie that will liven up the routine.*
3. *Focus on your spouse and not your supposed flaws. Be confident in the body God gave you.*

Claire had always been sheepish about the idea of Gavin seeing her naked, but from the look on his face on their wedding night, he liked what he saw. And she liked how it felt. As he discovered new parts of her body, he greeted each one with a kiss. Each time his lips touched down, she felt even more confident and sexy, much to her surprise. Within the first few minutes of their getting-to-know-each-other session, her body began begging for more, quivering with pleasure. It was a spiritual experience. She took him in slowly. It hurt, but the pain felt good. Each movement they shared made her body fill up with a power she couldn't explain until it finally overflowed and burst. Afterward, they lay together side by side on their backs, breathing heavily.

"I love you," she had told him, in between gasps. At that moment, she'd felt closer to him than she ever thought she could.

Now, as Claire gazed at her wedding photo, all she could think was that the nineteen-year-old girl staring back at her was so beautiful. She missed that long flowing brown hair—it had been cut into a short bob when a crying baby made long showers and primping impossible. And she missed that svelte frame—the extra twenty pounds of baby weight were not going anywhere, no matter how hard she tried. But Claire was sure that she could recapture that powerful feeling of being sexy, of being wanted.

In the bathroom, she brushed her hair and put some makeup on. Her tired eyes popped once she applied black eyeliner and mascara. Her pale lips transformed into a sexy pout with the swipe of a red lipstick. Her colorless cheeks had life in them again after a smear of cream blush. Finally, she traded in her gray hoodie for a fitted black V-neck. It wasn't anything special, but she always felt seductive in black.

In the living room, Gavin was still working on his sermon.

"She's asleep," Claire said, walking over to him and taking his iPad out of his hands. Before he could say anything, she sat on his lap, trailing kisses down his neck, reaching lower and lower. "Let's be bad," she said in a husky voice, unbuttoning his jeans.

Gavin placed his hands on hers to stop her. "I've got to finish this sermon, honey."

Claire sat back, searching. "But you've got all night. C'mon. We finally have some time. Please?" Was he really going to make her beg?

He kissed her forehead. "I'm so sorry, babe, but I'm in a groove right now. I really need to get this done while I'm inspired."

She pouted and wrapped her arms around his neck. "Don't you find me attractive anymore?"

He took off his glasses. Without them, he looked as tired as she felt. "Of course. Why would you say that?"

"It's just been so long. . . ." It had been weeks since they'd had sex. It seemed like life was constantly getting in the way these days—if Gavin wasn't busy with work, Claire was exhausted from taking care of Sadie. There was no more time for *them*.

Gavin sighed. "I know. Maybe your mom can take Sadie next weekend and we can have a date night?"

Claire slid off his lap and averted her eyes, trying to fight back tears. It somehow felt personal, like being unable to balance their marriage with their lives meant she was failing as a wife. "Sure."

Gavin buttoned his jeans and grabbed the iPad from the side table. "I love you," he said, already starting to type again.

Their small, orderly living room suddenly felt stifling. Claire stood, a decision forming in her mind. "I have to take Madison to her boyfriend's show tonight. I'll be out late." She walked out of the room without waiting for Gavin to say another word.

• • •

IT WAS ALREADY midnight, and Claire couldn't stop yawning. Madison was sitting on Cash's lap in a dark corner of the bar; they hadn't come up for air in a while. Ricky Broussard, the restaurant's owner, slid into the booth next to Claire. He always made her uncomfortable, with his bushy mustache and leering gaze. Back when she was in high school, he'd try to hit on her despite being a decade older. "I'm gonna marry you one day when you're older, Claire Guidry," he'd once whispered into her ear. "You just wait."

"I just got myself a new shotgun rifle," he told her now, smoothing his thick brown mustache out with two fingers. "I work hard, ya know? Gotta blow off some steam out there on the hunt. And this baby's a powerful one."

Claire nodded, repressing the urge to roll her eyes. A group of women in their late twenties were starting a dance party a few feet away from the table. She had watched them all night trying to pick up guys: Purple Crop Top had made out with an overweight bearded man for a free gin and tonic earlier in the evening, while Ed Hardy Dress had finally convinced a Toulouse High senior to dance with her . . . until his girlfriend showed up. At this point, they seemed perfectly content buying their own drinks and dancing by themselves.

They were now collectively jumping up and down screaming to celebrate "The Cupid Shuffle" coming on the speakers. With their longneck beer bottles in hand, the women started moving in tune to the lyrics. These women were at least five years older than she was—how did they still have so much stamina at this hour?

Ricky sucked on his cigarette and gave them a weak round of applause when it was over. "I've gotta go talk to those there ladies," he said, standing up and straightening out his plaid button-down shirt. "You'll be okay here?"

"Actually, I need to go," Claire replied, checking the clock on her phone. "I've got church in the morning." She silently thanked God for that perfect excuse.

"Come back around more often," Ricky said, with a final smoothing of his mustache. "Bring the husband and baby for lunch on me one of these days."

"Sounds good," Claire replied with a smile, thinking, *that will never happen*. She put her cardigan on and grabbed her bag. "Bye!"

"Bye now," Ricky said. He walked toward the dancers, greeting them with his go-to line. "That was great! Now, who wants shots?"

Claire made her way toward Madison and Cash, who had been making out since his band sang their last song—a cover of Nirvana's "I Hate Myself and Want to Die," which was, ironically, how Claire felt when she listened to them play. Madison was sucking Cash's face with the strength of a Hoover, their bodies—and whatever else they were doing—thankfully concealed by a wooden table piled with bottles and dirty glasses. Claire cleared her throat, hoping that would force them up for air, and finally shouted over the music, "Mads, we have to go."

Madison looked up at her cousin and smiled beatifically. "I'm going to stay with Cash tonight," she slurred. "I told my parents I was staying with you."

"Seriously? You could have told me that an hour ago," Claire said, frustrated.

"Sorry!" Madison laughed and went back to kissing Cash.

Claire drove home alone through the winding back roads, the streets lit only by her headlights. By the time she got back to her pretty little house, which sat at the end of a cul-de-sac, all of her anger from earlier in the day had drained away. So what if she and Gavin were having a little rough patch physically? She thought again of the dark bar and its sticky floors, the girls half-dressed and desperate for attention, Ricky Broussard and his leering gaze, and practically shuddered. Who would want that kind of life?

She tiptoed into their bedroom, her movements masked by Gavin's loud snoring, and slipped on her favorite Lilly Pulitzer-esque pink-and-green floral pajamas from Target. For a moment, she considered seducing her husband in his sleep—Gavin waking up to the feel of himself inside of her. But remembering the scene in the living room earlier, she slid silently under the covers instead. Looking at Gavin sleeping peacefully next to her, she reminded herself that she was perfectly happy with the life she had.

4

gabrielle

"WE'RE THE YOUNGEST people in here by fifty years!" Gabby Vaughn yelled to her boyfriend, Tony Ford, as they two-stepped and twirled their way around the dance floor of a wood-paneled restaurant.

Tony grinned and kissed her on the cheek. "But their fried crawfish is *magnifique!*" He spun her again so quickly that she barely noticed when an elderly man in a plaid shirt and red suspenders swooped in and grabbed her hand.

"Well, hello there, young lady," the man said, bouncing to the upbeat rhythm of the piano accordion and washboard coming from the zydeco band onstage.

"Uh, hi!" she said, laughing. To her right, Tony was now carefully bopping up and down with a short grandma in a long floral dress, probably Suspender Man's wife.

The white-haired man clapped his hands to the beat. "I may be old, but I got better moves than your boyfriend."

Gabby spun on his lead. "You *are* good at this. Do you come here a lot?"

"Well, yeah." He swung her arms from side to side to the music. "Every Friday. Whole group of us." He pointed to all his aged friends dancing around them.

"I hope I'm as cool as you when I'm y'alls age," Gabby shouted over the music. She could just see her friends growing old together like that. Claire would be the old lady in the corner cheering every-one on. Laura would be the one at the bar getting her man another beer. And Madison would be the one with the rose tattoo on her arm, flirting with all the widowed guys on the dance floor.

"Key is to dance every day," the old man said, clapping his hands as the song finished. "My wife and I do it in the living room . . . in the kitchen . . . in the bathroom. Keeps you young."

Gabby looked at him, eyes wide, hoping he was talking about dancing. "Well, thank you for the dance," she said, shaking the man's liver-spotted hand.

"Thank *you*, my dear," he said as Tony came over to exchange partners. The old man turned to him. "You got a good one, son."

Tony slid his arm around Gabby's waist. "I am well aware, sir."

She looked up at him and smiled. She still had to remind her-self sometimes that this wasn't a dream. Tony—smart, kind, well-mannered Tony—was unlike any of the guys she'd dated in Toulouse. In fact, he was the complete opposite of her last boyfriend, Russell Stevens, who'd left her crying on the side of Main Street after a stupid debate over an Adam Sandler movie they'd just seen. Before that was Klepto Connor—she had a feeling her Sweet Sixteen neck-lace was still in his possession. Freshman year, there was Jimmy Hill, who was so high all the time that he forgot 90 percent of their plans. Her track record with guys was so bad that sometimes, she couldn't help wondering: Were they the problem . . . or was she?

But then Tony came along four months ago. From their first date, Gabby felt like there was something different about this relationship. He was serious—about his life, and about her—but balanced it with a dashing smile and witty personality. They always made each other laugh. Although she knew it might be impossible, Gabby hoped that this relationship was the one that would last. . . .

"Let's go eat!" Tony said, snapping her out of her thoughts. A waitress led them to a table by the window that overlooked the lake.

"This is perfect," Gabby said as Tony pulled her plastic chair out for her.

"The table, or your life?" He grinned as he sat down in his own seat.

She giggled. "Both."

Tony grabbed her hands from across the table. The red-and-white-checkered vinyl tablecloth was still a little sticky from someone else's gumbo. "You look amazing tonight."

She felt a blush bloom across her cheeks. "Thank you."

Her fitted burgundy dress was a hand-me-down from Claire. Though Gabby felt bad her friend was still struggling to lose her baby weight, it admittedly wasn't terrible to benefit from it. Each week, it seemed like Claire was discovering some nearly new item that wouldn't fit her anymore, and Gabby was more than happy to take the clothes off her hands.

Tony unlocked his fingers from hers and looked down at his menu. "What are you gonna get?"

"It all looks so good," she said, scanning the laminated paper. So far, all of Tony's restaurant picks had been amazing, but the grainy photos next to the menu items secretly worried her.

"I know this place is a little cheesy, but seriously, babe, the food is awesome." He glanced at her over the top of his menu. "My family used to come here all the time. The couple who owns it has been running it since my parents were our age."

She looked around. The room was packed with families and groups of older people, like their new friends from the dance floor. The whole restaurant had a slight shabbiness to it, like a grandparent's house—the result of being loved for decades. "It's great."

He leaned closer to her. "I told my ma we were coming, so she gave me a five-dollar bill and said I had to order the stuffed mushrooms for you."

Gabby laughed. "Why the stuffed mushrooms?"

"Because they're her favorite and no one else in my family eats mushrooms. She got excited when you ate yours when you came over for dinner." He put his menu down and looked at her slyly. "That means you're in."

"Don't jinx it. Still haven't met your dad." The idea of meeting Mr. Ford made Gabby nervous. Tony looked up to his dad so much; she worried his approval would make or break their relationship. Every time she went over to Tony's family's house, the patriarch was at work or out of town. A high-powered career politician, he was currently serving as a Louisiana congressman. A snarky DC blog once gave him the nickname "Smokey," not only because of his chain-smoking habit, but also for the pace at which he fired staffers. He was well connected in DC and Louisiana; the governor was Tony's godfather.

"He's gonna love you," Tony said, waving his hand as if to wave away her doubts.

The waitress came up and pulled a blue pen out of her silver bun. "Are y'all ready to order?"

Gabby quickly scanned her menu again. "Yes. Let's see . . ." She twirled her short red spiral curls with her finger. "I'll do the seafood platter."

"I'll have the same," Tony said. "And let's start with the stuffed mushrooms." After the waitress walked away, he reached back over the table to hold her hand. "So how are classes going?"

Gabby's stomach lurched. "Amazing." Could he feel her palm sweating? She pulled her hand away to squeeze lemon into her water. "I'm on track to get straight As right now."

A huge smile grew on his face. "That's awesome, babe! I'm so proud of you. I'm sure your mom would have been, too, if she were still with us." Gabby averted her eyes from his earnest gaze. "Have you given any more thought to those master's programs we talked about? You probably have to start your applications soon, right?"

"Mmmhmm," she replied, noncommittal.

"Not that you need any help with it, but I have a book about writing personal statements, if you want to borrow it. I used it for my law school apps." He leaned back in his chair.

"Sure," she said, flashing a tight smile. "That sounds great." Tony had just graduated from Tulane Law in the spring. He was currently working at a local firm but confessed that he didn't really like it. His true passion was politics.

"I'll give you the book the next time you come to my place," Tony said, taking a sip of his water. "I'm glad you're applying. You're one of the smartest people I know."

Gabby squirmed a little in her seat and rested her elbows on the table. "Well, I guess I just love school."

"I would hope so, Miss Education Major!" he teased.

The waitress returned, saving Gabby from responding. She slid a plate of large mushroom caps stuffed with crab and shrimp as well as a side dish of corn bread onto the table.

"Oh my goodness, this looks delicious!" Gabby said.

"Mushrooms are all yours," Tony said, wrinkling his nose. "Corn bread . . . all mine!" He brought the plate closer to himself, shielding it with his strong arms.

She laughed, grabbing one of the mushrooms and holding it up. "To us."

He held up a piece of the bread and tapped her food with his. "To us, babe."

• • •

"ARE YOU SURE I can't come up?" Tony asked, nuzzling her neck under the entrance archway of the girls' dorm at the University of Louisiana in Lafayette.

"I told you . . . my crazy roommate doesn't like guests." She sighed as his kisses made their way to her collarbone. "Besides, it's a total mess."

"And you're sure you don't want to stay with me tonight?" His warm breath sent a delicious thrill down her spine.

Her body quivered. "I really want to . . ." she whispered. "But I have a stupid study group early tomorrow morning. It's better if I stay here."

Tony slowly eased up on the kissing and brushed her hair behind her ear. "You are an amazing woman."

"You're an amazing man." She stared into his dark brown eyes.

He pulled himself away from her and lifted her chin softly with his hand. "I just . . ." He stood silently for a second, studying her.

She could feel her heart beating faster. *Did he suspect . . . ?*

"I love you, Gabrielle. You just make me so damn happy." Gabby felt fireworks exploding inside her as Tony caressed her cheek. He *loved* her. She'd never heard a guy say those words before.

Her knees felt weak and her head began spinning. She grabbed his face with her hands and kissed him hard, completely swept up in the moment. "I love you, too." They both stared at each other with goofy grins. "I never thought you were gonna say it," she teased.

"Hey . . . you could've said it first!" He nudged her arm playfully.

She laughed. *Maybe*, she thought, but even in any other circumstances, she probably wouldn't have. After all, that was the one thing her mom had taught her about love: guys scare easily.

Tony left a few moments later and Gabby lingered in the entranceway of the dorm, watching him get into his BMW and drive away. Her heart swelled with love, but underneath that warm feeling was a pit of anxiety. Once she was sure he was long gone, she walked back into the parking lot and got into her own car, a beat-up 2007 Nissan Versa. Then she started the long drive home down I-49.

Her mind reeled as she drove. She'd fallen so hard for Tony, but it wasn't supposed to happen this way. When she pulled up in front of her actual residence, a shitty apartment building in Toulouse, Gabby burst into tears. Coming home to this awful little studio apartment—the best she could afford on her day care worker's salary—was a reminder that her unbelievable happiness with Tony had a shelf life. She'd spun a fantasy for both of them, but her lies were unsustainable, and sooner or later they were going to catch up with her.

Her cell phone buzzed as she opened up her creaky front door. It wasn't a number that she'd programmed into her phone, but she knew it by heart. Taking a deep breath and wiping the tears off her face, she answered it. "Hello?"

"An inmate at the Barton Correctional Facility is trying to contact you," the automated voice relayed. "Press one if you would like to accept this collect call. Press two if you wish to decline."

Gabby pushed one, waiting for the call to connect. She sat down on her bed and looked at a framed picture of her and her mom. In the photo, she had been a high school freshman with an unfortunate lopsided haircut, thanks to her mom's effort to save money by doing it herself. They were still living in the Rydell neighborhood where Gabby felt so unsafe that she worked out a deal with the school bus driver to drop her off right at her house, even though it wasn't an actual stop. In the picture, their eyes were tired, their smiles forced.

A few months after the picture was taken, everything started turning around. Her mom got a job at the dentist's office and moved them to that cute little house on President Street. Elaine even got Gabby a hairstylist who actually knew how to cut her curls properly. Her life changed completely. She became happier and more confident, and felt like she had been given another chance. She wasn't that poor, sad girl anymore—she had a future, and it included college at Tulane, her dream school. Gabby could tell her mom was happier, too, as they were able to buy the things they wanted and needed.

Of course, Gabby didn't know at the time that most of the money her mom was using didn't actually belong to her. She found that out the day Elaine was arrested—the day her entire life fell apart. Elaine had been embezzling money from her employer for years. Her mom went to jail, and the money went away, leaving Gabby with no way to pay for college; it was too late to apply for scholarships. Tulane became just another thing that was taken from her.

Not that Tony knew any of that.

The phone line clicked through. "Gabby?"

"Hi, Mom." She sighed after greeting the woman on the other end.

As it turned out, they were both frauds.

5

laura

"THEY REALLY GOTTA keep the air conditioner on when it's sixty degrees outside?" Laura whined. The orange faux leather chair in the doctor's examination room was smooth and cold, and she was shivering.

Brian fidgeted on the raised exam table. "I'll warm you up," he said with a grin, motioning for her.

Laura walked over to him, her boots clacking on the tile floor. She nestled into his arms, enjoying the heat emanating from his body. He hadn't held her close like this since the accident; these days, he held his beer bottles more tightly than he did her. He even moved her hand away from his boxers when she started seductively exploring down there. But finally, he was holding her like he used to. Laura breathed in his musky scent. His hands moved up and down her body, from her shoulders to her thighs, warming her up with a friction that made her body go from frigid to hot in moments. He kissed her neck. She kissed his. She wanted to take him right there but knew she couldn't. It made his touch all the more thrilling.

Knock, knock. The door handle turned slowly, and Laura quickly composed herself. She turned to see Dr. Carter, the LSU team doctor, smiling in her green scrubs and white lab coat.

"Hello," she said, looking down at the clipboard with an embarrassed expression.

Laura, realizing the doctor had seen, turned bright red and returned to the orange chair.

Dr. Carter began examining Brian. "So, how's the pain?" she asked chattily, palpating his knee.

"It's fine," Brian said shortly. "Am I going to be able to play again?"

Dr. Carter scribbled something in his chart and took a moment before looking up. "As you know, Brian, your injury was quite severe," she said briskly. "You're going to need surgery, but I just want to be up front about your expectations. We can repair some of your ligament damage so that you can walk again, but even with physical therapy, your knee won't be strong enough to withstand stress—or sustain another major hit. It's likely you won't be able to play again."

Laura's gasp echoed throughout the quiet, sterile room. Brian remained silent.

"At this point, your options are very limited. There is one surgery that I would recommend, but it's new and not widely practiced. I can refer you to a specialist in New Orleans and have him take a look. The surgeon has worked with some of the Saints players, and he's very well regarded. Of course nothing is guaranteed, but it's your only option if you want to play any kind of sport again. I called and he's agreed to see you, but unfortunately he doesn't take your insurance, so you'll have to pay out of pocket."

"Doesn't the school need to pay?" Laura asked. So far, the school had covered all their costs because Brian had been hurt on the field.

"They would if the doctor was in network," Dr. Carter explained. "But the surgery is experimental, and even if the doctor were in network, they might still refuse to cover it, especially since Brian has other options available to him."

"Not playing again is not an option," Brian said. "I don't want some surgery that just helps me walk again—I want to *play.*"

Laura sat up in her chair. "How much would something like that cost?" she asked.

"A lot," Dr. Carter said sympathetically. "My advice is to go for a consultation and learn more." She turned back to Brian. "I know football is a big deal to you, but I want you to seriously weigh your decision before you leap into this surgery. There are a number of risks, both physically and financially. "

Brian's gaze remained calm. "If I don't do it, will I ever be able to play again?"

"Most likely not." She pulled out her notepad and twisted her pen. "I'm sorry."

"I'm going to do it." He held his shoulders back, confident with his decision.

Laura knew the look of determination in Brian's eyes. It was the same one he had worn when Toulouse High had been down a field goal against their toughest opponent, Port Arthur, during the last game of his high school career. She had cheered her heart out for him that night, and she had every intention of doing it again this time around.

Dr. Carter nodded and jotted down the contact info on a page from her notepad. "Good luck." She bid them good-bye before walking out of the room.

Once she was gone, Brian hung his head. "I can't believe this."

"Hey, I'm feeling pretty optimistic," Laura said, rubbing his arm encouragingly. "We'll find a way to pay for the surgery, and everything will be fine. You'll play again. You'll see."

He huffed as he stood, and he hobbled toward the door on his crutches. Laura looked down at her watch. "Do you want me to drop you off at your three o'clock class? You'll be a little early, but at least you won't have to walk all the way there on those things."

"I'm not going," Brian said flatly. He didn't wait for her as he made his way to the car.

• • •

IT WAS A beautiful sunny fall day. Not that you could tell from the inside of Laura and Brian's small on-campus apartment.

As she opened the front door, fresh from her morning shift at the Magnolia Coffee House, Laura sighed. Brian lay supine on the couch, watching ESPN in the dark. At least he was awake; over these past few weeks, he had pretty much been sleeping all day.

"Hey, baby," she said, dropping a pile of mail on the kitchen counter. "What'd you do all morning?"

Silence.

"That cute old lady came in today," Laura continued, opening the blinds. Sunlight streamed into the room, lighting a trail of dust motes. "You remember me talking about her—Mrs. Stratton? Well, she asked how you were doing. She read about the injury in the paper and told me she's praying for your speedy recovery. Oh, and she gave me a fifty percent tip. I love that woman."

Brian still hadn't stirred from the couch. "Hey, babe?" he finally croaked. "Can you bring me another beer?"

Laura paused. *Another?* "It's only eleven thirty. How many have you had?"

"Just one," he said.

"Should you be drinking before your class today?" She walked over to him and put her hand on her hip.

He looked at her blankly. "Who cares?" he said with a shrug, letting out a burp that echoed through the apartment.

"Brian Hunter Landry, that's disgusting." Laura headed to the fridge and grabbed him a Natty Light. "My shitty salary isn't going to support this drinking habit for long," she added, handing it to him.

"I won two hundred bucks today on online poker," he said opening the can. "I deserve to drink."

Laura raised her head. "Really? That's amazing! I didn't even know you were playing." Brian sat in silence for a minute. Uncle Bradley was on ESPN, talking about the upcoming Florida/Alabama game. A thought occurred to her. "How many times have you played before?"

"A couple." He chugged a few sips. "I just started."

Her eyebrows furrowed. "So, how much money have you *lost*?"

Silence.

"What time are you heading to class?" Laura called from the

kitchen as she started to prepare lunch. She was making red beans and rice for the third day in a row, trying to save money for the surgery. Their consultation with the surgeon had gone well. He'd said Brian was a good candidate for the surgery, and with intense physical therapy, he could even be ready to play as soon as next year. But first they had to come up with $40,000.

"I need to make money," he said, focused on his laptop. "So I'm not going."

Laura frowned. Brian hadn't been to class in over a week. "I understand that, but don't you think it's important to stay in school?"

He chuckled slightly. "That sure is rich, coming from you."

Laura threw him the middle finger. "In case you've forgotten, I dropped out to *marry* you." The decision hadn't bothered Laura too much at the time; they were getting married, and Brian was starting at LSU. It didn't make any sense for her to stay in Toulouse and finish high school when her whole life was waiting for her elsewhere. But it didn't help her case now. She dried her hands on a dish towel and walked out into the living room. "If you want to play for them when your knee is better, don't you still have to pass your classes?"

"Nah." He cleared his throat. "I talked to Coach. He says if this surgery works, they'll take me back. I'm the best they've got."

"But can he really guarantee that if you aren't enrolled?" Laura asked. "Not to mention that you'll lose your scholarship and your health insurance. . . . What if something else happens to you? What if you decide you want the other surgery, the one they will cover?" The water from the pot started boiling furiously and spilled out onto the stove. She grabbed a ratty dishrag and began cleaning up the mess.

"I've got this game down," he said, glancing up. "I'll take care of us. And I can go on my parents' insurance; it's not a big deal."

She twisted the towel in her hands anxiously. "I just don't think you're thinking this through, Brian. We're going to have to move out of this apartment."

"So, I've been thinking about that. . . ." He closed his laptop. "My parents said we can stay with them rent-free to save some money for the surgery. As much as I don't want to do it, it makes sense."

She paused for a moment, processing what he'd just said. Then a sinking feeling hit her stomach. "No. No, no, no. I am not going back to Toulouse, *and I sure as hell am not going to live with your parents.* What, are we in high school again?"

Brian ran a hand through his messy blond curls. "We stay with them for a few months—tops—and I'll dedicate myself full-time to this poker thing, and I promise we'll have enough money for the surgery in no time. Don't you want me to play football again? Don't you want me to play in the NFL like we planned? You're not gonna get that mansion or those damn shoes with the red soles on them if I don't do this. You know you want this as much as I do."

Laura leaned her hip on the cabinet, shaking her head. She stirred the food, allowing the smell to wash over her. The scent reminded her of her mom's cooking, except that her mom's meals were always homemade, and Laura was lucky if she could make a successful dish from a box. She'd even screwed up a Zatarain's mix; the rice had come out gummy the night before. She wanted to call her mom and ask for advice—about the food and about Brian—but she reminded herself she was an adult and quite frankly should be able to figure out what to do. "There's got to be another way," she finally said, an edge of desperation in her voice. "We can't just go from living alone to having chaperones twenty-four seven."

"Oh please . . . You know they're not like that. You seem to be forgetting the long periods when they left us alone to do all that stuff on the living room couch," Brian said with a laugh.

"Brian, this isn't funny!" Laura yelled. She threw the wooden spoon on the Formica countertop and stormed into the bedroom.

She had been staring at the ceiling for a few minutes when Brian calmly limped into the room. "I'm sorry," he said, leaning down to kiss the top of her head. "I know this is really hard for both of us, and it's not fair to you. I'm just asking you to make this one sacrifice for me."

Just this one? she wanted to say. Instead she wiped her wet cheek dry. "I refuse to be stuck in that house with them every day."

"I'm sure Ricky'll give you your old job back," Brian said, patting her head like a puppy. Back in high school, Laura had worked for Ricky Broussard at the Sea Shack. It wasn't such a bad job because it was where all of her friends hung out.

"I never thought we'd be going back to Toulouse, that's for sure." She intertwined her fingers with his.

"You and me both," he said, sinking onto the bed beside her.

She sat up and shifted her body toward him. "Be serious with me. How long do you think this is going to last?"

He propped his head up with his muscular arm and leaned into her. "If I have the surgery, I can be back on the field next year. That means we'd be back in Baton Rouge in the summer for training."

"I guess that's not so bad," Laura said, silently weighing the pros and cons in her head.

Pro: Saving money more quickly, and being able to pay for the surgery sooner.

Con: Going back to that Podunk town.

Pro: Being on track for Brian to play professionally and never having to worry about money again.

Con: Going back to that Podunk town.

"So, what do ya say?" Brian asked, his gorgeous blue eyes pleading with her.

"Fine." She took a deep breath and grasped his hand. "But only because I love you."

6

madison

MADISON ROLLED HER mud-splattered blue pickup into the parking lot of Gary's Fuel Depot. She hoped the weird rumbling noise it was making didn't mean anything serious; the last time it sounded like this, she wound up stuck on the side of I-10, hyperventilating at the idea that someone could come plowing into her at any moment, killing her before she lost her virginity. That very night, she gave it up to a friend of a friend she met at a bonfire party. Nothing like a brush with death to make you frisky.

She turned off the ignition and sat for a second as the rumbling turned into a clacking sound. *Hopefully it'll turn on again*, she thought as she opened the creaky door and hopped out onto the concrete parking lot. A busted truck was the last thing she needed right now.

Madison looked down as her phone buzzed with a text from Laura:

> Looks like I owe you $5. Back in town on Saturday. Maybe u can use it to buy me a drink to drown my sorrows :(

Her heart sank a little. On Laura's last night in Toulouse, Madison had bet her that she and Brian would move back to Toulouse one day. But she had been teasing; she hadn't actually wanted to be right. She knew how excited Laura had been to leave.

In theory, Madison and Laura should never have been friends. Madison was always making fun of the cheerleaders in high school, and Laura was too busy rooting for the team (and Brian Landry) to notice. But they bonded one night over a joint and a bucket of Smirnoff Ice at a house party. Madison couldn't believe someone so popular would want to talk to her all night, while Laura couldn't believe someone so cool would want to hang out with *her*. The rest was history.

Madison paused in the parking lot to quickly send a reply.

Ugh. I'm sorry, love . . . Call when u get here!

As much as it pained her to hear that Laura was going through a hard time, it was kind of refreshing to know that she wasn't the only one. As Madison opened the door, jiggling the metal bell hanging on the handle, the store's smell of ICEEs and beef jerky washed over her. Mr. Gary looked up from the newspaper spread before him on the checkout counter.

"Hello, my dear," he said, shuffling the sections together and folding the paper back up. Strands from his thin gray comb-over were going every which way, and his Hawaiian print shirt had a glaring mustard stain right on the front. Madison couldn't decide which was more tragic.

"Hi, Mr. Gary!" she said, walking up to the counter.

"How's your daddy?" he asked, looking concerned.

"Can't we just talk about me instead?" She flashed a cheeky grin.

The old man chuckled. "You're definitely your daddy's daughter."

"Thank you for confirming that. I was starting to get worried," she teased but then grew serious. "He's doing okay. I don't know if you heard, but he had to quit working."

"I didn't," he said, taking off his thick plastic-framed glasses and cleaning them with his shirt. His specs were so old that they were actually on trend again. "I'm sorry to hear that."

"It is what it is, I guess," she said, leaning her elbows on the counter. "I'm actually looking for work right now, so I can help out."

She made her voice soft but strong, a trick she learned when she was little. "You don't happen to have anything available, do ya?"

Mr. Gary stroked his patchy beard for a second. "I'm sorry, Mads. I ain't got nothing right now."

She sighed and flashed a smile. Coming here had been a last-ditch effort; if even Mr. Gary wouldn't give her a job, who would? "No worries. If anything comes up, you'll call me, won't ya?"

"Yes, dear."

Madison quickly changed the subject, trying to ease the sting of rejection. "Well, while I'm here, can I get a scratch-off? One of the lucky shamrocks, please."

He nodded and turned his back to her, moving slowly as he grabbed the lottery ticket behind the counter. Madison put her bag up against the candy display in front of her and shoved a few Snickers bars in it. She had been doing this for years. She loved the thrill of taking something and knowing she'd gotten away with it.

"That'll be two dollars," he said, finally turning back around with the ticket in hand.

She reached into her bag for her wallet. "Thanks, Mr. Gary!" she said, putting the exact change on the counter. "Have a nice day." She walked back to her beat-up truck, praying it wouldn't die on her way home. At least she'd have some Snickers bars to survive on if it did.

The truck continued to make the rumbling noise on the six-minute drive back to her house. She pulled into her driveway and got out just as the front engine started smoking. The last time this happened, it had meant a six-hundred-dollar mechanic bill and a week of bumming rides from her friends. *That should make the job hunt even more fun*, she thought bitterly to herself.

Inside, Madison followed the smell of coffee through the foyer, past the living room, straight to the kitchen, where her parents were sitting with a man she didn't recognize. He put down his red HANDSOME DEVIL mug—a present from her mom for her dad's birthday one year—and looked up at her with striking green eyes. Madison was just relieved they hadn't given this guy the MY DAUGHTER IS A

GENIUS mug she so humbly made in middle school art class for Father's Day.

"Hi, honey," her mom greeted her. "This is George Dubois. He works with your dad." She paused. "*Worked*."

The man ran his fingers nervously through his neat brown hair and stood up. "Nice to meet ya," he said with a thick southern drawl, shaking her hand with a firm grip.

"You, too." She gave him a once-over as their hands met. He had to be in his early thirties at most, but dressed like he was already someone's embarrassing dad. His jeans were high-waisted—and not in a cool retro way—and he'd tucked in his ill-fitting red button-down shirt. But his shirtsleeves were rolled up, and Madison's eyes lingered on his tan, muscled forearms . . . and the gold and silver Rolex glinting on his wrist. She cleared her throat as they let go of each other's hands.

"George is the CEO of your dad's company." Her mom took a sip of coffee.

Madison watched as he sat back down at the table. So *this* was the "youngun" her dad was always griping about. . . . "Young spoiled rich kid gettin' the company from his daddy . . ." he'd say.

"He just came to pay a visit to your dad to see how he was doing," her mom continued. "Isn't that nice?"

"Sure is," Madison agreed, voicing the extent of her thoughts on the subject.

"I was tellin' your daddy the crew really miss him." George tapped his fingers awkwardly on the table. "Some guys are even raising extra money for him with a Ping-Pong tournament next week."

"Did you know I was the Ping-Pong champion over there?" her dad asked with a proud, goofy grin.

"You learn something new every day," Madison said, grabbing a Coke from the fridge.

"So, I heard you just graduated from Toulouse High," George said, turning to her.

"I did—a few months ago."

"Congrats." He shifted his eyes from Madison, to the kitchen sink, to her dad, back to Madison in the span of one second. "Heard that's a mighty fine school."

She paused. *Was he being serious?* She was able to pass all her classes despite skipping approximately one-third of them. Her teachers didn't even notice she was missing. "Um, thanks," she said, opening the can.

"Why don't you have a seat, sweetie?" Her dad pulled out the chair next to him.

"Just for a minute," she said, plopping down reluctantly. She knew the visit was important to her dad. "So, where do you live?" she asked George politely.

"I used to be in Lafayette, but I just bought a little place over here on Darby Lake." He took another sip of the coffee. "I needed some fresh air."

"Fresh air?" She chuckled. "You know there's a paper mill five miles away? Smells like fart all the time in this town."

Her mom shot her a disapproving look.

George let out a nervous laugh. "You know, I actually like the smell of paper mill. I smell the pine . . . not the poot." His smile turned into an awkward wince, as if he were silently yelling at himself for saying that.

She grinned. "Well, to each his own, I guess. So you just moved here, huh? My cousin Claire's in-laws live on Darby, too. Sometimes we go over when they're out of town and have bonfires and parties. They have a really awesome pool . . . do you have one, George?"

Her mom shot her another look.

Madison shrugged her shoulders and shot her a "What?" look. This was a very important question.

"I don't." George shook his head. "Do you think I should get one?"

"I do," she said, matter-of-factly. Madison locked eyes with him and held his gaze, trying to see if she could make him blush.

"Well, we'll all have to go fishin' one day," her dad said, quickly changing the subject.

"I sure would like that." George turned his wrist to check the time. "Geez, it's already five. I better get going. Got a Mardi Gras krewe meeting tonight in New Orleans."

"You're driving *all the way there* just for a meeting?" Madison couldn't grasp that concept. In the nineteen years she'd been alive, she had never once made the three-hour drive to the city. Her idea of getting out of town was driving forty miles to Cash's grandfather's hunting lodge in New Iberia to smoke pot. In fact, she was looking forward to their date there tomorrow.

George chuckled as he stood to leave. "Well, yeah. It ain't that bad. I make that drive about every week."

"Why?" she asked bluntly.

"That's where all the action is! Sometimes I have meetings, other times I just want some beignets from Café Du Monde."

Jealousy overcame her. George grew up only miles away, and yet his life was so different from hers. He got to travel while she was left to dream about far-flung places while reading the *National Geographic* subscription she'd been forced to buy during a school fund-raiser. He had black-tie parties, she had blacked-out friends. He had everything handed to him, and dammit, she wanted that, too.

"Pleasure meeting you," he said, reaching for her hand.

"I can walk you out," she said, standing up. An idea had just occurred to her.

"Sure thing." After hugs and handshakes were exchanged with Madison's parents, George joined her on a walk through the house, grabbing his briefcase and slipping on his brown leather loafers, which were sitting by the front door. *How odd that he took them off . . .*

Outside, his silver Porsche was parked across the street, practically gleaming in the late-afternoon sun. How had she missed it on her way in? She could almost smell the new-car scent just by looking at the clean, crisp leather interior. She'd never seen anything so nice.

George caught her staring. "Wanna sit in it?" he asked, unlocking the door with a remote control.

"Obviously," she said, smiling. He opened the door, and she crawled into the driver's seat. She rested her right hand on the stick shift, her left hand on the steering wheel, and imagined herself speeding out of town. "Maybe one day you'd let me take it for a spin? I've always wanted a car like this." It was a little white lie; she didn't necessarily want a Porsche, just a car that worked. And she didn't necessarily care about riding around in it; she just wanted to see George again—not because she liked him, but because she liked the *idea* of him. She liked the idea of his easy life, and the idea that maybe he'd share some of it with her.

"I'd love that," he said, resting his arm on the open door. She flashed a smile.

"Let me see your phone. I'll put my number in it for you." He handed it to her, and she added herself as a contact. "See you soon I hope," she said, getting out of the car and tossing her brown wavy hair back in what she hoped was a sexy swoop.

"You have a good day now, Madison." George got into the car, and she watched as he drove away.

Back inside, her mom and dad were washing the coffee cups. "Meant to ask you, did Gary have any work for you?" her father asked.

"No, unfortunately not," Madison said, leaning against the countertop. Her mind returned to George for a moment. She grinned. "But I got a backup plan."

7

laura

ROB AND JANET'S house still reeked of mildew from Hurricane Sebastian, a Category 5 that had passed through with a vengeance a year before. The new tile floors shone with polish, but otherwise, the place hadn't changed much since Laura first started dating Brian in eighth grade. The pictures and trophies had only grown more cluttered over the years.

In the hallway leading to Brian's side of the house, an eight-by-ten prom photo hung beside their wedding picture. Laura was the same age in both, and thanks to that updo tutorial in *Seventeen* magazine, she had the same hairstyle. If only someone had told her to get rid of those curly tendrils. Though she was only a year older now, she felt much more sophisticated—probably a result of living in the big city.

The rest of the pictures were a shrine to Brian: Brian as a baby in a tiny version of his uncle Bradley's jersey, Brian as a peewee football player, Brian as a middle school football player, Brian as a high school football player. Framed news clippings: "Landry Named MVP at Toulouse," "Landry Leads Toulouse to State Victory," "Toulouse Football Players Share Their Favorite Recipes." That last one always made Laura laugh. The *Toulouse Town Talk*, a newspaper created and edited by a bunch of bored local housewives, asked some of the players to participate, and Brian had shared Janet's recipe for crawfish soup. It had more cream cheese than tails in it, but he loved that stuff.

Laura had attempted to make it last winter for him, but after using milk instead of cream ("They're basically the same thing, right?"), he had politely suggested that maybe it should just be his mom's thing.

"Now, do you hang these or put them in a drawer?" Janet was currently standing at the foot of Brian's bed, holding up a pair of his khakis. He lay sprawled on the blue plaid comforter.

"Hang," he responded, and immediately returned to text messaging.

"Brian, you are one lazy boy if you're gonna make your mama unpack for you," Laura declared as she entered the room.

"Oh hush. I wanna do this for my baby." Janet waved her away. "Besides, he can hardly do anything with that brace."

Laura blushed. *If she only knew what he was capable of doing with that brace two nights ago. . . .*

"You really don't have to do that," Laura said, walking over to the suitcase and grabbing a polo shirt to put away.

"Stop it right this second, Laura!" Janet said with a steely look in her eyes. "This is *my* home, and I'm gonna take care of *my* boy."

Laura recoiled and glanced over at Brian, desperate for some sort of reaction from him, but he was still looking down at his phone. She let go of the polo shirt and walked out of the room. She'd made it into the kitchen before her eyes began welling up with tears of frustration. *So much for feeling like an adult,* she thought.

Rob looked up from the copy of *Garden & Gun* he was flipping through at the kitchen table. "I was just gonna go outside. Join me, sweet girl."

She knew her eyes were wet and her face was probably red, but she nodded and walked onto the porch with him.

"You did the right thing," he said as the two of them settled into the padded porch chairs. "I know comin' back here wasn't in the plan, but life ain't always perfectly mapped out, ya know?" Chewing tobacco was wedged under his lower lip and he spit into his infamous Styrofoam cup. "Twenty years ago, I thought for sure I'd be playing ball too at LSU, but instead I got Brian. Best thing that ever happened to me, don't get me wrong, but definitely didn't see that comin'.'" His right cheek bulged from the wad of dip. He spit again. "Whatever happens, you'll be all right."

"I know," Laura said, trying not to think about what was in that cup. "Thanks for taking us in."

"Our pleasure, darlin'. Just be careful. Janet's not gonna want to let y'all go." Laura could feel the truth of that statement weighing down on her, suffocating her.

It's only temporary, she reminded herself for the thousandth time.

"Babe," Brian shouted from the back door. "Kenny's here. We're goin' out. See ya later!"

The door slammed shut before she could even form words. Was he really going to leave her alone with his parents? Anger festered in her stomach.

She looked back over at her father-in-law. *Spit.*

• • •

"I JUST DON'T know if I can do this," Laura whined to Madison, Claire, and Gabby as she dipped her greasy french fries in ketchup. The girls were at Meryl's Diner, a small fifties-themed restaurant on the outskirts of Toulouse that made its waitresses dress like they were at a sock hop. "I mean, they're so nice for letting us stay, but I'm already losing it. Janet hogged the TV all day to watch a *Southern Kitchen* marathon. And Rob. He's so sweet, but oh my god— I picked up his dip cup thinking it was my tea, and wanted to die."

"Oh, sweetie," Claire said sympathetically. Claire, out of anyone, could most understand what Laura was going through, having to balance in-laws with her own family life. It was part of why Laura loved being around her. Getting advice from Claire was almost like getting advice from a future version of herself.

"I mean, what if you guys weren't around tonight?" Laura pointed her fries at her friends. "Was he just gonna leave me alone with Dip and Doo Da?"

"Oh, please tell me you call them that to their faces," Madison said with a wicked grin.

Laura rolled her eyes and dipped the soggy fries in ketchup again. "Did I make a mistake, y'all?"

"Hell no," Gabby chimed in. "First off, we get you back, so there's that. Second, this is something you needed to do. And girl, you know Brian is worth it."

Laura nodded. Gabby was right—she and Brian had spent years fantasizing about their future together. They had to get that surgery for him. They just had to.

"So, did you get your old job back from Ricky?" Claire asked.

Laura sighed and pushed the empty fry basket away from her. "Yeah, he has me working four nights a week right now. Luckily he had just fired a waiter for giving free boudin balls to all his friends. I start on Friday."

"You'll still give *us* free food though, right?" Madison grinned.

"Ha." Laura leaned her head back on the vinyl booth. When she worked at the Sea Shack in high school, she constantly gave her friends free appetizers and Cokes. *How did I keep that job for a whole year?* Regardless, she was gonna have to be more careful this time. As strange as it sounded, her future—and her husband's—depended on it.

Madison nudged her arm. "So, what are you gonna do during the days? Doesn't Janet stay at home?"

"Seriously, Mads, how is it that you always know the *worst* thing to say at any given time?" Laura joked, throwing her crumpled-up straw wrapper at her friend.

"Years of practice." She smirked. "But for real, what are you gonna do?"

Laura shrugged. She liked Janet . . . in small doses. But the idea of hanging out with her on a regular basis filled her with overwhelming dread.

"You'll find something to keep you busy. You know"—Claire paused, as if an idea was suddenly occurring to her—"you could always go back to school and finish your senior year."

Laura sat up. In truth, the idea of going back to Toulouse High had crossed her mind, but she hadn't entertained it seriously. After all, she couldn't very well return to the school that she'd acted so high and mighty about leaving . . . could she? "That'd be weird, right?"

"Why?" Claire asked, her blue eyes focusing in on Laura's face.

"I don't know." She squirmed in her seat. "It'd just be strange to be back there and not be with Brian." All of her best high school memories were tied to Brian: cheering for him at the football games, walking together hand in hand down the halls, sneaking into closets in between classes to make out.

"You're still *with* Brian," Gabby reminded her.

Laura rolled her eyes. "You know what I mean."

"Oh, I think it'd be fun!" Claire said with cheery excitement. "You never experienced high school without him right there next to you. It'd be good for you. Besides, don't you want to finish? What if . . ." Her voice trailed off.

"What if what?" Laura's skin prickled. Claire had always been the voice of reason, almost to a fault. Her honesty was sometimes as hurtful as it was helpful.

Claire took a deep breath. "All I'm saying is that Brian might not be able to support you the way you always thought. What if he can't play football again?"

Heat rushed through Laura's veins. "He'll be able to play again," she said coolly. "That's why we're here, so he can get the surgery."

"I'm just sayin' . . . nothing bad can come from getting your diploma."

Claire's tone reminded Laura of her mother's, when she had tried to convince her not to marry Brian just yet. "*I'm just sayin' . . . nothing bad will happen if you wait,*" she had said. But then Laura reminded her that Brian could meet someone new at college, break up with her, and live the dream life—the one she'd worked so hard to help him get—with some other girl on his arm.

Laura tapped her phone and saw that it was after ten. "I gotta go, you guys."

"Look, I'm sorry. Forget what I said," Claire begged.

"Seriously, I'm not mad at you." She shook her head and pulled out her wallet, throwing some dollar bills on the table. "I'm fine. I just really need to go. Brian's gonna be home soon."

The girls all looked concerned as they watched her stand up and swing her bag over her shoulder.

"We love you," Gabby said softly as Laura waved good-bye.

Laura paused and smiled tightly. "I love y'all, too."

• • •

AS SHE PULLED into the driveway, Laura noticed Brian's bedroom light was on. Either Brian was home or Janet was in the process of doing a turn-down service and leaving chocolates on their pillows. Laura wouldn't put it past her. When she got inside, she saw her husband lying on the bed, texting.

"Hey, babe! How was your night?" She greeted him with a kiss on his lips. He tasted like liquor. When he didn't answer, Laura sat on the edge of the bed. "What did y'all do?"

He looked up from his phone with bloodshot eyes. "Drank too much."

"Was it just you and Kenny?" She finger-combed his messy locks and pushed them away from his eyes.

Silence. Groping. Kissing.

"Oh, someone's feelin' good," Laura said as he moved her onto the bed. He unbuttoned her jeans and began lifting up her shirt. "Wait," she said. "I'll be right back." She hated to stop him, but she'd drunk two Cokes at the diner and needed to go to the bathroom before they did anything more. She hurried down the hall; when Brian drank like this, there was a fine line between amazing sex potential and well, *nothing*. He was either a lion in bed . . . or passed out like a kitten.

Unfortunately, this time he was the latter. She returned to find him face-planted on the bed, snoring. "Good night, babe," Laura said, kissing his forehead and turning out the light.

• • •

EARLY-MORNING SUN PEEKED in through the blinds. Brian was sprawled out on top of the comforter, wearing nothing but his boxers. His stomach was looking a little softer than it usually did, Laura noticed; he hadn't worked out since the injury, and it was starting to show. Perhaps a result of too many Natty Lights. *Low calorie, my ass*, she thought. At least the black graphic tattoo he'd gotten when he was sixteen still wrapped snugly around his arm muscle, hugging one of her favorite parts of his body. Her other favorite part of his body was just waking up. She decided to kiss it. *That'll get him movin'*, she thought. Brian continued to snore as she leaned into him. He woke up immediately as she gently tugged on his boxers, pulling them down.

"Oh, *hello*," Brian said in his scratchy, sexy morning voice.

"We didn't get to play last night," Laura said with a purr.

Even though he was sluggish, he wasted no time lifting up her tank top and kissing her breasts. His rough hands glided down her smooth skin, waking up each part of her body. He began kissing her neck, then moved to her stomach. She always felt self-conscious about that area, but it felt way too good to worry about right now. His kisses moved south, stopping at the inside of her thighs.

"I want you," she called out, clutching his arms tightly. She rolled him over and positioned herself on top. The buildup was so intense, she wanted nothing more than to have him inside her, right that second.

Knock, knock. "Morning, kiddos!" Janet yelled from outside the closed bedroom door.

"Shittttt," Brian whispered, whimpering with frustration.

"I've got beignets and coffee ready. Come 'n' get it!" The sound of footsteps drifted off in the distance.

Laura glared at the door. "Did that just happen?" she asked as her body slowly lost all the heat they had just created.

"Forget about it. Let's do this," Brian said, pulling her close.

"No way," she said angrily. "I've completely lost the mood." She got off of him and put her tank top back on. She didn't know who to be mad at—Janet for not giving them their space, or Brian for putting them in this situation.

"Are you *kidding* me?" He glared at her.

"I can't do this, Brian. We are *married*. We should be able to have sex anytime we want without your mom interrupting." She got out of bed and put her pajama pants on. "I don't want to be here. I don't wanna be stuck with your parents while you go off and get drunk with your friends. I don't wanna stay at home all day with your mom. This wasn't the plan. This wasn't how I pictured our first year of marriage."

"And you think *I* did?" Brian asked, his voice raised. "Do you seriously think I wanted this? I'm the one who this affects the most. I'm the one who can't do what I love right now."

She paused in the middle of the room. "And you think I love working at the Sea Shack?"

"How is that any different from what you were doing at Magnolia?" He was still sitting in bed naked, making it harder to take him seriously.

"Well, for one, when I was off from Magnolia, I didn't have a forty-year-old woman force-feeding me breakfast and hoggin' the TV." She grabbed her paddle brush and started stroking her hair with it furiously.

"You're being a bitch."

"*Excuse* me?" Laura fumed. He had never called her that before.

"My parents are giving us a place rent-free right now. They're paying for all our food. Why can't you just suck it up for now?"

"We may be saving money, but I swear I'm gonna lose my sanity." She threw her brush on the desk.

"I don't know what to tell you," Brian said, finally putting his clothes back on. "Suck it up. This is our life right now."

Laura didn't want to be under the same roof as him—or Janet—at that moment. But there was nowhere else for her to go. Or was there? She glanced at the framed picture of Claire and the girls on the desk, remembering the conversation they'd had the night before. She contemplated it for a moment more.

"I'm going to get some breakfast," Brian said.

She turned around and looked at him. "And I'm going to go back to school."

8

claire

MRS. DEBORAH, THE church's sweet silver-haired secretary, had brought in a homemade praline pie so rich that one tiny sliver had to have been about a thousand calories. But Claire brushed that thought aside as she took bite after bite of the decadent dessert that was quickly turning into her lunch. She had been in the church library all morning working with Beau, one of their youth group members and their current media intern, to develop a reel of Gavin's best sermons for the church's website. Now it was almost two o'clock, and the video was finally turning into something they were both excited about.

"Oh, this would be a great place to put that part where he talks about being forgiven for sins," she said, pointing at the computer screen.

Beau nodded and dragged the clip across the screen, inserting it between the sections on "feeling blessed even in difficult times" and "the importance of forgiving others."

"I feel like this is it," she said, taking a deep breath, proud of what they had accomplished. "Send me the video, and I'll add it to the website." She stood to leave and grabbed the half-full pie tin. "You don't want this, right?" Beau shook his head.

As she made her way back to her office down the hall, she felt inspired. Gavin's sermons always had a way of making her feel like she had just come from counseling. And given how quickly their congregation was growing, she wasn't the only one who felt that way.

Gavin's dad had started the church in the nineties and had gathered about three hundred loyal followers from the surrounding area, but when Gavin joined him two years ago and began preaching, they soon ran out of pews for congregants.

One newspaper called him a visionary. People around town buzzed about his fresh ideas and commanding stage presence. His dad even admitted Gavin was better than him, stepping aside to allow his son to take the spotlight. This was no surprise to Claire—from the moment they'd met, she'd been drawn in by his devotion to God and ability to inspire others.

The first time she saw him, he had been onstage leading Youth Worship Night, a monthly Friday gathering for the fifteen to twenty-one crowd. His orange shirt read JESUS, but it was written in the Reese's peanut butter cup logo. She thought it was genius. Gavin strummed the guitar, a couple of leather bracelets wrapped around his wrist, and sung about faith. His deep soulful voice rocked her to her core. They locked eyes during "God Gave Me You." He smiled at her. She blushed and continued swaying to the music, but she was pretty sure her moves had become robotic by that point.

"What's your name?" were the first words he ever said to her.

Her witty response? "Claire."

It was still her favorite conversation to this day.

Her phone buzzed on her desk, bringing her back to reality.

From Madison:

I'm outside. Come take a break with me?

Her cousin never stopped by the church except on Sundays, which meant she must have needed something . . . probably money. She knew that Madison's parents were struggling right now. "Charity begins at home," Claire recited to herself, grabbing her wallet and walking outside.

"Hey!" Madison sat on the edge of a large concrete flower pot at the entrance, fiddling with her packet of cigarettes.

"Hey, Mads. What brings you around?" Claire sat down with her.

Madison scowled. "I'm supposed to clean a house down the street in a half hour."

"Oh my gosh, you're working? I'm so proud of you." Claire put her hand on her cousin's shoulder.

Madison rolled her eyes. "Save your excitement. I'm still holding out for the role of professional groupie. I told Cash my starting salary needs to be a hundred thousand dollars."

Claire chuckled, though she wasn't entirely convinced it was a joke. "So then you just came by to say hi? That's so sweet."

"Well, actually . . ." Madison shuffled her feet, clearly uncomfortable. "There's something I need to talk to you about."

Claire decided that she wouldn't make a big deal about the money when she asked. The poor girl looked so distraught, and she was family, after all.

Madison lowered her eyes. "I don't know how to say this, so I'm just gonna say it, okay?"

Claire nodded. *Here it comes . . .*

"So, last night I was going past The Saddle . . ." Madison paused, lighting a cigarette, and Claire jiggled her foot impatiently. Why was Madison telling her about a run-down strip club thirty minutes outside of town? "And, well, I saw Gavin's truck parked outside of it." Madison brought her cigarette back up to her lips and inhaled.

"Wait . . . what?" Claire shook her head, laughing. "Oh, bless your heart. He was at Bible study last night. Could you even imagine Gavin at The Saddle?" She patted her cousin on the shoulder. She was clearly mistaken.

Madison frowned. "I swear, Claire. Me and Cash were on our way back from New Iberia—"

"Wait—you and Cash?" Claire's eyes narrowed. She knew what that meant. "Madison, had y'all been drinking when you saw this?"

"Well . . ." Madison dragged her foot back and forth across the pavement guiltily. "I wasn't *completely* sober."

Claire shook her head. "Did you even check to see whether it had the Ron Paul bumper sticker on the back?" She took a deep, frustrated breath. "Madison, I swear . . ."

"Look, I saw what I saw." Madison tapped the ashes from her cigarette to the ground. "Maybe you're in denial."

"This is ridiculous." Claire couldn't help her voice becoming shrill. A knot was forming in her stomach. "You come to *my* job and tell me my husband *might* be going to a strip club behind my back, and *then* you insult me?"

"I was only trying to help." Madison crushed her cigarette into the concrete, putting it out. "You think it was easy for me to come here and tell you this? You think I wanted to deliver this news? God, Claire! I've been up all night debating what to do."

"Next time, before you accuse my husband of adultery, maybe make sure it's true." Claire stood up from the planter and straightened out her skirt, trying to calm down her rage. It was just like Madison to stir up trouble for no good reason.

"I didn't accuse him of anything. I just said he was there. That's for you to deal with however you want." Madison stood up, too, patting the butt of her jeans for dirt.

"I have to go back to work." Claire moved for the door, leaving her cousin behind without a second glance.

Back at her desk, her stomach began turning. She convinced herself it was the praline pie—she knew she shouldn't have eaten all of those slices. *But maybe . . . no . . . it couldn't be?* she conversed with herself internally. *Maybe I'll just go talk to Gavin—prove that there's nothing to worry about.* After a few minutes of cooling down at her desk, she knocked on his open office door.

He looked up from his computer. "Hey, hon, what's up?"

"Nothing, just wanted to come say hi." She plopped down in the chair in front of his desk. "How's your day goin'?"

"It's fine," he said, looking back at the screen.

"That's good," she said, taking a brief pause. She wondered if she should just let it go. It was all a big misunderstanding anyway, she was sure about that. But there was still a gnawing at her stomach that needed to be put to rest. "Oh, I meant to ask, how was Bible study last night? Who ended up going?" She crossed her leg and leaned in toward the desk.

Gavin looked back at her. "It was good—a small group."

"Were Tyler and Blake there?" She cocked her head to the side. He shook his. "Aren't they always at those things?" she asked, trying to sound nonchalant.

"Not this one." He paused. "Sorry, babe, I have to get back to work. We'll talk later tonight?"

Claire stood up. "Ah, okay." She walked toward the door and looked back at him, typing furiously on his keyboard now. "I love you."

He glanced at her and smiled. "I love you, too, hon."

When she returned to her office, her head was spinning. She glanced down at her wedding ring set. It fit snugly—almost too tight—on her finger and shone dully back at her. When they first got married, she'd cleaned it at least once a week. Gavin would make fun of her, but she knew he secretly loved how much pride she took in it. "One day when I make more money, I'm gonna upgrade it," he'd say. But she loved the quarter-carat diamond more than anything, and it bothered her when he fantasized about replacing it.

"This ring means more to me than any other one you could ever put on my finger," she'd say, holding her hand in front of her as she admired the tiny sparkle. "It will always remind me of who we were when we got married."

"Young, poor, and desperate to have sex?" he'd say, laughing.

She'd blush. "Oh stop it, Gavin." He'd kiss her to let her know he was joking. She'd kiss him back to let him know she loved him.

They'd had fewer moments like that since Sadie came along. It was hard having a baby, sure. But not hard enough that he should be running off to a strip club. *It's not true. It can't be*, she thought as she opened up Gavin's Twitter account. The words "What's happening?" stared back at her. *He would never do that.* The cursor blinked. *Would he?*

Of course not.

"Listen to your gut as often as you listen to God," she typed. *"Both will give you the right answers."* TWEET.

9

gabrielle

GABBY POPPED AN aspirin in her mouth and downed it with a glass of water, saying a hallelujah for naptime. Most days, she felt lucky that Claire had hired her to work at the church day care, but today had been a new level of exhausting. Three of the toddlers had colds and were dripping snot everywhere, one of the infants projectile vomited all over her colleague, and Gabby had spent the entire morning trying to calm down Carter Montgomery's tantrum over a stuffed dragon. Now, with the kids finally slumbering on red and blue mats scattered around the room, she lowered her head and sighed. *Is this really my life?* She'd always dreamed of working with kids . . . but as a teacher, not some glorified nanny.

The day care door creaked open, and Claire popped her head in. Gabby held a finger over her lips, angling her head toward the sleeping kids. Claire crept toward her, an oversize knit scarf wrapped around her shoulders.

"Just came to say hello to my Sadie," Claire whispered, scanning the room. "But if everyone's napping . . ."

Gabby was shocked by her normally tidy friend's appearance. Claire's mascara was smudged under her eyes, and if Gabby wasn't mistaken, there was some sort of food smeared on her blouse. "You okay?" Gabby asked, nodding at the stain.

"Oh." Claire blushed and wiped at it. "Yeah, just a busy day. I ate pie for lunch, clearly a little too enthusiastically." She looked up from her shirt. "Hey, do you want to come over after work?"

Gabby grabbed a red Twizzler from the staff candy jar and bit into it. "I can't—I'm meeting up with Tony."

"Ooh, the mysterious Tony . . ." Claire grabbed a Twizzler out of the jar, too. "When do we get to meet him?"

"Um . . ." Gabby lowered her head. She wanted to say soon but didn't want to lie. She had been doing enough of that already—precisely why she was in this mess in the first place.

The night she had met Tony, she was at a bachelorette party in Lafayette, draped in plastic penis necklaces. Tony came up to her at the bar and asked her if she liked his jacket. When she shot him a confused look, he said, "It's made out of boyfriend material," then flashed her a smooth grin.

Gabby rolled her eyes and walked away, uninterested in cheesy pickup lines. Her ex-boyfriend Russell had opened with something similar, and it was all downhill from there. *Not doing that again*, she thought as she joined her friends back at the table. But the other girls at the party admitted they put him up to it; it was a challenge on the bachelorette party dare sheet. A bridesmaid bought Tony a drink for playing along, and he in turn gave it to Gabby as an apology.

"Do you like Guinness?" he asked her.

"Yeah," she said, accepting the drink. (Lie number one.)

"It was a pretty suave line, right?" he asked as they huddled at a high-top table in the corner.

She shook her head. "Please don't ever use that on another girl."

"Because you'd be jealous?" He smiled, his cheeks dimpling, and Gabby realized how cute he was.

She smiled back. "Because you sound like an ass."

When he asked her about her family, she told him what she told most strangers: "My parents aren't around anymore."

"Oh, I'm sorry—they passed away?" he asked, looking genuinely sad for her.

She nodded. (Lie number two.) To her, it was easier and less embarrassing than having to admit she didn't even know her dad and that her mom had gone to prison for embezzlement her senior year of high school—a ten-year sentence that she was now only four years into.

"What school do you go to?" Tony had asked her, his TAG Heuer watch peeking out from his blazer.

"U.L.," she'd said, thinking of the closest school in the area: University of Louisiana at Lafayette. (Lie number three.) Gabby hadn't even applied there . . . but to be fair, she'd gotten into an even more prestigious school: Tulane. After her mom was arrested, she hadn't been able to afford college—any college—so it was kind of a moot point. But it was fun pretending she was still that girl for a moment. So when he asked her major, she continued living in her fantasy and said education (lie number four), just like she had always dreamed about. And she left out the part about living in Toulouse and working at a day care (not a *lie*, per se . . . just a pretty big omission). In her head, it was fine. This was just a fun night out with the girls; she'd never see this guy again, anyway.

The more they talked, though, the more she realized all the things they had in common. Like how they both secretly loved courtroom TV shows—not the dramas, but the petty small-claims reality shows. And how their playlists consisted of both Lil Wayne and Wayne Newton. He was even helping his dad with an education reform bill and asked if he could get her ideas.

"Maybe we can go for a drink one night, and I can pick your brain," he said, running his fingers nervously through his hair as they were saying good-bye. She'd *meant* to tell him the truth about her life when they met for drinks a week later, but the outing was less education reform talk and more flirty banter. And then there was that sweet good-night kiss . . . the kind where she could feel sparks in her stomach. She decided to wait to tell him. If her dating history was any indication, he'd probably ghost on her soon enough anyway.

But as the weeks passed, she began to see that he wasn't like those jerks she had dated before. Even though she kept bracing herself for him to catch her in a lie or confront her about the truth or just plain old stop calling, it never happened. Tony was so wonderful and so trusting, and as each date blissfully came and went, Gabby started to feel like it was too late—she was in too deep, and it never seemed like the right time to tell him the truth. If Gabby was being totally candid with herself, she wasn't sure she even wanted him to know the truth. She was ashamed that her life had turned out the way it had.

Gabby was the one person in her group of friends who was supposed to make it. She was driven—perhaps a result of growing up with so little—and had planned out her whole future: she'd get a degree in education, meet an incredible man, become a teacher, and maybe even go on to be a principal or superintendent someday. But then her mom was arrested and Gabby's dreams, and her whole life, imploded. She hadn't applied for scholarships or student loans. . . . Suddenly, Gabby was back to being a poor girl with no hope of escaping Toulouse.

When she was with Tony, Gabby could forget about the four disappointing years she'd had. It was almost like she had found a shortcut to the life—and the man—that she was always meant to have. But since the *I love you's* were exchanged a couple of weeks ago, there had been gnawing in her stomach that wasn't going away.

"I'm not sure how much longer we'll be together," Gabby said to Claire now, snapping back to reality. Though she'd had the thought before, it was the first time she'd admitted it out loud. Unbidden, her eyes filled with tears.

"What?" Claire gasped. "But you're so happy with him."

Gabby sniffed hard, trying to keep the tears from flowing over. "He's so different from the other guys I've dated—"

"Isn't that a good thing?" Claire said, shaking her head. "What are you not telling me?" She'd always had an uncanny ability to read people.

"It's a long story," Gabby began, realizing she had to talk about it with someone. She couldn't keep carrying this alone.

But right as she was about to tell Claire everything, a three-year-old redhead sat up on his mat and shouted, "Miss Gabby, I'm hungry!" Before she knew it, the whole room had woken, eager for snack time.

Claire shot her an understanding smile, rising to leave. "I want to hear about this later, all right?"

After the fruit snacks were successfully distributed and Gabby got everyone settled to watch a cartoon about Noah's ark, she sat in one of the tiny plastic chairs and took a deep breath. Claire was right—she *was* happy with this guy. It was a shame it could never last. Gabby vowed to herself to finally tell him the truth . . . tonight. She silently prepared herself for the impending heartache.

• • •

"SO, GABRIELLE, TONY tells me you go to U.L.," said Rebecca, a girl with glasses who towered over her. "My friend Daisy Jones is a junior over there. Maybe you know her?"

Gabby sipped her vodka soda and shook her head. "Name doesn't ring a bell." Her stomach turned into knots and she hoped there'd be no more discussion about her college experience. She looked around the cute coffeehouse–art gallery and tried to change the subject. "I had no idea this place even existed," she said. "What a great concept." The whole scene—the expensive coffee, the sleek art, the cultured partygoers—was indicative of the kind of girl Tony thought she was . . . a girl who could fit in here.

Tony put his arm around her waist. "And can you believe all of this is for my boy?" He put his other arm around the shoulders of his childhood friend LaMarcus, who was being honored as the café's local artist of the month. His paintings, all of which had a dreamy expressionist vibe, hung around the brick-walled room. Gabby could envision the people who would buy them: smart and sophisticated, just like Tony's friends.

"Oh, Tony," said Jeremy, a short guy wearing an unflattering turtleneck. "I was at an event the other night at the bookstore downtown and guess who I ran into: Stephanie Brown! Remember her from college?"

Tony's eyes lit up. "Oh yeah! What's she up to now?"

"Workin' at freakin' NASA. Can you believe it? Engineer or something like that." He shook his head. "Always knew she'd be doing great things."

"Seriously, man." Tony looked at Gabby. "We had a couple of classes with this girl," he explained. "She was so smart. Ran some very intense study groups."

Gabby nodded her head. People used to say that about *her* in high school. She wondered if anyone still talked about her like that. More likely, the conversation went something like: "*Oh Gabby Vaughn—she sure is living the life. I hear she's working at a day care and changing diapers like a champ.*" She shuddered.

"That's amazing," she said to Tony.

"Maybe when you're a teacher, she can come and speak to your class for career day," Tony suggested.

"It's really awesome that you're gonna be a teacher," Rebecca interjected. "We need smart people like you in the system. Just think of how many lives you're going to change." She looked at Tony and Gabby appraisingly and grinned. "Education and politics. What a power couple!"

Gabby smiled back and took a sip of her drink, trying to hide her embarrassment. If only Rebecca knew the truth . . .

"Okay, now that you've made both of us blush," Tony joked, "we're gonna go look at the other paintings." He grabbed Gabby's hand and began leading her toward the far wall. "We'll be back!"

They stopped at a painting colored in bold blue, red, and gold hues. The brushstrokes were distorted, but Gabby could make out the scene: a couple dancing cheek to cheek on an empty dance floor. "Gosh, this is beautiful," she said, stepping back and admiring it.

"Look, she kind of has red hair like you." Tony nudged her playfully.

Gabby focused in on one of the figures. He was right. "Oh, and look, the guy has dark hair." She giggled. "It's us!"

Tony put his arm around her waist. "Maybe we were his inspiration? If so, he should give us a good deal on this painting."

"Seriously," she said, thinking how fun it would be to be the kind of person who bought original artwork . . . the kind of person like Tony. She felt that painful, sad twinge of regret again that this life was about to slip through her fingers.

"I'm gonna see how much he's asking for it," Tony said, walking over to the small white piece of paper taped next to it on the wall. "Wow," he said, leaning in closer. "You've got to see this!"

Gabby wondered what could possibly make Tony's mouth drop like that. Was LaMarcus asking thousands of dollars for paintings already? She braced herself for the figure as she leaned in to look at it. But there wasn't a number on it.

LaMarcus Rogers
"Gabrielle, will you marry me?"—Tony
OIL ON CANVAS

She put her hand over her mouth as she tried to process what was going on. She swiftly looked over at Tony, who slowly dropped down on one knee and held out a sparkly diamond ring.

Her heart beating out of her chest, Gabby looked around the café, expecting someone to tell her that she was being pranked. But here was Tony, down on one knee, asking to be hers forever. All the party guests mingling at the front had gone quiet and turned their attention to the two of them. This was, without a doubt, the most romantic thing that had ever happened to her. Tony stared up at her, his beautiful brown eyes looking eagerly into hers. Her body began to feel weak—the good kind of weak. The kind that told her he was the right guy for her.

All plans to tell him the truth flew out of her mind. She said the only thing she could think of: "Of course I'll marry you!"

laura

THE SCHOOL BELL rang, and the students scurried into their respective classrooms like crawfish into their burrows. Laura kept her eyes on the gray tile floor as she followed Mrs. Walker, the school's guidance counselor, through the dim hallway to her new homeroom. It felt so strange being back at school—everything from the lockers to the students seemed smaller to her.

"So, what's Brian gonna be doing while you're here?" Mrs. Walker's shoes squeaked with each step. "I've never known y'all not attached at the hip." She smiled innocently.

"Oh, uh, he's got plenty to keep him busy." Laura ran her fingers through her hair nervously. "But I'm excited to be back." Actually, now that she thought about it, *excited* might not be the right word— more like *anxious*, or *terrified*.

"You are?" Mrs. Walker looked up with a confused expression. "Golly, I woulda thought you would've been so done with this place after movin' to the big city." She laughed. "I probably woulda never come back."

Laura's stomach twisted with misgiving. She could see the outside door about thirty feet from where they were, daylight peeking through the cracks, and wondered if she should just sprint toward it. If she could make her way out the door, she'd keep running down the street, along the main road, past Benji's Bait and Tackle, and end up in the Landrys' living room, where she'd hide her face in one of Janet's floral couch pillows.

"Here we are," Mrs. Walker said with a wink. They were in front of Mr. Leblanc's door. A poster was taped to the outside that read, COME TO THE NERD SIDE, WE HAVE π. She glanced back at the outside door—only five feet away now. *It's now or never*, she thought to herself. Then, Mrs. Walker swung open the classroom door. *Too late*.

Her eyes darted around the room. There were even more posters: GEOMETRY KEEPS YOU IN SHAPE, KEEP CALM AND DO MATH, and MISTAKES ARE PROOF THAT YOU ARE TRYING.

"Look who's back," Mrs. Walker announced proudly as she presented Laura to the class. Eighteen faces turned in unison to stare. One second felt like an eternity as her face became as red as her top. "Hey y'all," she said, sheepishly raising her right hand a little and waving to her former—now current—classmates.

"Oh. My. God." A girl's voice squealed from the back row, breaking the awkward silence. Even though a stocky football player's head blocked her face, Laura instantly recognized cheer captain Riley Cavanaugh from her high-pitched voice and signature satin ribbon tied around her bouncy ponytail.

"Welcome back, Laura," Mr. Leblanc said, his pencil disappearing into his thick gray hair as he tucked it behind his ear. "There's an open seat right there." He pointed to the second-to-last desk on the front row, sandwiched between Ridge Maclin, the biggest stoner in town, and a guy she'd never seen before.

Laura shuffled over to the desk. Feeling the eyes of everyone watching her and hearing a couple of snickers in the back of the room, she could barely remember how to walk. Her arms swung at an odd pace. Her legs stumbled as if she were about to trip. What was only a few feet from the front of the class to the desk felt like a mile.

Finally she got to her seat and slunk down in her chair.

Mr. Leblanc placed a textbook on her desk with a loud thud. "Vince, could you share your most recent notes with Laura so she can catch up before our pop quiz tomorrow?"

Moans filled the room.

"Hey, be thankful. I wouldn't have even said anything had it not been for our new student. All right, let's break off into pairs and work on the equations on page one hundred thirty." Mr. Leblanc leaned down and whispered in Laura's ear, "Vince can help you out if you need it."

She turned to the stranger sitting next to her and smiled politely.

"Nice to meet you," he said, grasping her hand with a firm grip. He had warm brown skin, close-cut hair, and hazel eyes.

"You, too." She smiled nervously.

"So, you used to go here?" he asked as he flipped through the pages in his textbook.

"Yeah." She nodded. "You're new, I take it?" She unzipped her army green messenger bag and pulled out a pencil, noticing it was indented with Brian's teeth marks from when he borrowed it last year.

"Yep." Vince began twirling his pencil around his fingers. "My family moved here over the summer from Atlanta. My dad's a contractor, and he's helping rebuild some of the places destroyed by Hurricane Sebastian."

"Cool . . . I've never been to Atlanta. How does it compare to Toulouse?" she asked.

He flashed a smile, showing off his straight white teeth; he probably wouldn't put those babies anywhere near a wooden pencil. "I still haven't found a place that doesn't sell crap coffee, but other than that, it's not too bad here. The people are cool at least."

"Ooh, they have fancy coffee in Atlanta?" she joked. "Well, la dee dah . . ."

He playfully hit her arm. "Oh, shut up. What's your story? Why'd you leave and come back?"

"I was in Baton Rouge for a few months." She put her elbow on the desk and starting twisting her hair. He wasn't the only one from a big city, Laura reminded herself.

His eyes got bigger. "Oh. Why?"

She sighed and gave him a sly grin. "Shouldn't we be working on this assignment?" She scratched her pencil on the wide-ruled paper in front of her. It felt weird holding it in her hand; she hadn't written with one in months. Even at the coffee shop, she'd memorized her customers' orders.

Vince leaned in closer. "Does someone have a secret?" He smirked.

"Not really." She shook her head and could feel her face turning red. Why didn't she want to tell him the truth? "My husband and I moved so he could play football for LSU, but he got hurt so we're back for now"—she paused—"until he can have surgery."

Vince whistled. "Well, I'll be darned. Landry, huh? So, your husband is Brian Landry?"

She looked up. "You know him?"

"I've heard about him. I'm on the team here." He put on his own stuffy accent. "Everyone talks about the 'legendary Brian Landry.'" Vince puffed out his chest.

"Oh. You play?" She glanced at his body. She should have known he was on the team.

"Yeah. I reckon not as good as Brian, but yeah." An awkward pause fell over them. "Anyway, I guess we better do these problems." He pointed to the book and started scribbling some numbers down on his notebook. "So, we need to find the factors of this equation."

Laura looked down at the numbers, fractions, exponents, and parentheses jumbling together in her vision. But she focused in and began separating everything out on her paper.

"We have a common factor of three right here," Vince said, pointing the tip of his pencil to the two numbers listed. "So, you—"

"You could make it . . ." Laura said, interrupting him and pointing at her scribble: $3(y2+4y)$.

He looked up at her, surprised. She could feel her face turning red again. She hadn't meant to blurt it out, and she certainly wasn't a know-it-all, but it had felt so good, just for a moment, to figure something out on her own. It had been a while since she'd done that.

"I'm impressed," Vince said. "You could even take it further, you know?" He began making some notes of his own on the paper in front of him.

Laura leaned in closer to his desk. Her head was so close to his, she could smell spearmint and feel the warmth of his breath.

His pencil began flying across the paper. "Since they both share the variable of y, you could do something like this, too." He showed her: $3y2+12y = 3y(y+4)$. He looked at her, his hazel eyes looking into hers to make sure she understood.

"I don't think I would have caught that," she said, suddenly feeling defeated after her silly moment of triumph. Had she made a huge mistake, coming back here and trying to catch up with everyone?

"Nah. You got this. What you did was right. Mr. Leblanc just wants to see you thinking about every option. It just takes some practice. Here," he said as he clicked open his three-ring binder and took out a few sheets of loose-leaf paper. "Take my notes for the quiz tomorrow." He scribbled across the top page. "There's my number. Call me if you need anything. But I'm sure you won't have any problems."

"I really appreciate it," she replied, tucking the papers into her bag. Her mom had always told her to use the word *appreciate* around guys: *You can get them to do anything you want with that word*, she'd say. Laura didn't know what she wanted to get Vince to do but figured it couldn't hurt to say it.

The hour went by quickly as she and Vince raced each other on every problem. "You can't tell anyone we did this," he said, after they agreed it'd be funny to time it. "This is about the nerdiest thing I've ever done."

She burst out laughing. "Well, I have a reputation to uphold myself. Secret's safe with me, I promise." Laura playfully locked her lips with her fingers and pretended to throw away the key. The bell rang, and the sound of eighteen metal chairs scraping the linoleum floor filled the room. Before Laura could say thank you to Vince, Riley and a couple of the other girls from the cheer squad, Rory and Emma, ran up to her.

"What the hell are you doing back here?" Riley exclaimed, a bubbly smile on her face.

"Miss Cavanaugh . . . *language*," Mr. Leblanc called out from his desk.

Riley giggled. "Sorry, Mr. L!" She turned back to Laura. "But seriously, we all thought you were gone for good—at least that's the way you made it sound." The other two girls nodded their heads, though Laura caught an almost-unkind glint in Riley's eye. "Does it have something to do with Brian's knee?"

Laura swallowed, embarrassed that she'd made such a big deal out of leaving in the first place. "Yeah, we're back while Brian waits for surgery. It's temporary, of course." Laura immediately wished she could take the words back—she sounded *so* snobby.

Emma crossed her arms. "Of course," she said, her tone icy.

Riley ignored her and grabbed Laura into a bear hug. "Well, we just can't believe you came back—I'm so happy!"

"Me, too, actually." She glanced at the clock on the wall. "But I should really get to my next class."

They followed her out the door. "What lunch period do you have?" Riley asked as they began to part ways in the hall. "I have second. We should talk about you rejoining the team." She flashed a thumbs-up sign.

Laura twisted her mouth as she pondered what to say. Jumping, tumbling, and cheering for the Toulouse Gators had been a huge part of her high school experience for the past three years. But did she really have time, between catching up at school and working to save money for Brian's surgery?

"We'll talk!" she yelled as she turned in the opposite direction.

The next three periods were just as overwhelming as Laura expected. Besides all the history she had missed, the literary classics she hadn't read, and the French that she didn't quite know (*la catastrophe!*), she was also being bombarded with questions.

"When do we get to see Brian?"

"How's he doing since the injury?"

"You mean to tell me y'all have to stay with his folks right now? Bless your heart."

Laura tried her best to answer them without sounding super pathetic.

"I'm sure you'll see him around. You know he'll be at the games and parties."

"He's doing just fine. You know him—he's strong. Doctor says he'll be back to normal in no time."

"It's just temporary. We didn't want to go to the trouble of finding a new place, since we're only here for a little bit."

When the second lunch bell rang, Laura headed to the bathroom before going to the cafeteria. Just as she was about to exit the stall, three familiar voices came in.

"So, do you really think she's going to join the team again?" Rory asked over the sound of a makeup bag unzipping. "Can we even have her? I mean, all of our routines are planned out—it'd be kinda hard to add another person."

"I really don't think it's fair to let her back on," Emma added. "We've already done tryouts—what message does that send to the girls who didn't make the squad?"

Laura listened quietly, her heart pounding so hard she was almost afraid they'd hear it.

"Listen, I know it's so weird that she came back, but she was one of the best we had." Riley smacked her lips together, as if she'd just glossed them. "Plus she's our friend."

Some of the tension left Laura's body.

Riley's voice lowered in a whisper. "Besides, don't you guys kind of feel sorry for her? How embarrassing to have to come back here after all that 'I'm going to be a trophy wife' crap." She let out a laugh that echoed in the tiled bathroom.

Laura suddenly felt ill.

"Wait—did she really say that?" Emma asked, spritzing on a pungent Victoria's Secret body mist.

"Well, she might as well have, with how she acted when she left." Riley switched her voice to imitate Laura's: "'Oh, I'm getting married; Oh, I'm leaving this small-ass town. My life is perfect.'" She switched back to her normal voice. "It's actually pretty funny when you think about it. Now that she's come crawling back."

The girls burst out laughing and closed up their makeup bags before heading out the door.

Laura stood there, frozen as her mind processed everything that was just said. Sure, maybe she'd been excited to leave, but it wasn't like she rubbed it in anyone's face. And why would they think it was funny that her life didn't go according to plan? These people were supposed to be her friends.

She grabbed her bag and headed out the door. The girls' comments replayed over and over in her head, making her angrier with each second that passed.

"Hey, you," Vince said as she ran into him turning the corner. "The cafeteria's this way. I thought you'd know that?" He shot her a teasing grin.

"Oh sorry, yeah." She looked up at him with a forced smile, trying to hold back her anger. "I'm actually gonna do some stuff in the library instead. I didn't realize how much I would need to catch up on." *Or how much my former teammates hated me.*

"I hear ya. I feel like every teacher is giving a quiz or test this week. Do you mind if I join you, actually?" He tucked his thumbs between his chest and backpack straps, waiting for her answer.

"In the library?" she asked, flustered.

Vince looked confused. "Yeah."

"Sure, yeah. Okay." Even though she would have preferred to be alone, she tucked some stray pieces of hair behind her ears and led him to the room.

The library felt like a time capsule from the seventies. A green shag rug sat beneath four dark wooden tables in the center of the room. A mural, painted by the class of 1975, hung above the tall cases filled with musty old books. Laura and Vince were the only two people inside. Even Mrs. Eleanor, the sassy old librarian who had worked there for thirty years, was at lunch.

"Did you spend your lunch breaks in here before?" Vince asked, unpacking his books from his bag.

"No actually. I never came in here." It was true. Brian didn't even know where the library was, and Laura was usually right next to him. "I just figured it'd give me some peace and quiet to study."

"I see. What are you studying?" He looked over at her books as she unpacked them from her bag.

"Umm . . . everything?" Laura spread her notebooks across the table and sighed at the sight of all her notes from just that day.

"You're in AP chemistry?" Vince asked, eyeing her textbook.

"Yeah, why?" She clicked her pen.

"It's just . . ." Vince trailed off.

"It's just what?" She tightened her grip on her pen.

He ran his hand across his short brown hair and looked at her as if weighing her.

"You're obviously smart. Why'd you drop out?"

Her eyes widened. "Um, I told you. Brian was heading to LSU, so I went with him." She could hear herself sounding defensive.

"Yeah, but why? You could have waited."

Laura felt like she'd been slapped. Vince wasn't the first one to make this argument with her, and she was sick of hearing it. She felt embarrassed and, quite frankly, a little angry. He had just met her. Who was he to judge? "I did what I needed—make that, *wanted*—to do," she said sternly. "We had our future all planned out, and there was no need for me to have a high school diploma."

"So what made you come back then?" He leaned back in his chair. "Not to Toulouse, I mean. To school."

"I don't owe you any explanation, do I?" she huffed.

"Not at all," he said with a genuine look. "I was just curious."

"No offense, but I just want to study in quiet, okay?" She opened her notebook to a clean page and shifted in her chair slightly so she was facing away from him. Staring down at the paper, she prayed that she could just get through the rest of the day without appearing as weak as she felt.

Vince raised his hands in a peace-making gesture. "I'm honestly sorry if I offended you in any way," he said, standing and packing up his books. "I didn't mean to, I swear."

"It's okay," Laura said guiltily. She hadn't meant to take her stress out on him. "I'm just really on edge right now."

"Good luck," he said, slinging his backpack over his shoulder and walking out.

The door slammed shut behind him, the humming of the exhaust fan the only sound audible. Laura sighed as she silently replayed their conversation in her head. *You're obviously smart*, he had said. Sure, she did well in school, but Brian was the one going places. It was never even a question of whose career they would pursue.

There was a hollowness in her stomach that she chalked up to hunger; she had refused Janet's offer to make her scrambled eggs for breakfast and had opted instead for a chocolate chip granola bar. But even after she ate the sandwich she'd brought with her for lunch, the feeling remained. She couldn't stop thinking about what Riley and Emma had said. Were they right? Should she not have come back to school? And what Vince said . . . had she *needed* to drop out of school after they were married? *Was Brian's dream really hers?* She'd asked herself these questions before, of course. So why did hearing them from Vince, someone she barely knew, make the questions ring in her head? She blinked and stared down at her French homework.

"Translate the following phrases and match them to the common English saying."

D'autres fois d'autres manières.

Laura pulled out her pocket French dictionary and began translating, trying to lose herself in work. "Other times, other manners," she wrote, scanning the right-hand column for the English phrase that matched it. She drew a diagonal line to the words *"Times change."*

She looked up at the clock in the library and let out a deep breath, chasing away an image of Vince's slow smile. *They sure do.*

11

madison

"CHARLIE WELLINGTON, YOU should really buy a girl a drink first!" Madison had barely sat down on George's back porch when his golden retriever had put his paws on her shoulders and licked her face. She laughed and kissed his furry forehead.

"Now, how come that doesn't happen when I slobber on girls?" George laughed at his own joke.

"Well, you're not as cute as he is," she said, petting Charlie's ears.

"I appreciate the honesty," George said wryly.

The two sat on a brand-new rattan couch, eating peanut butter cookies. Her mom had made a batch as a house-warming present, and Madison offered to deliver them, eager to check out George's new house. He'd bought the place right next door to Claire's in-laws; the previous owners were going through a bitter divorce. Word around town was that Mr. Allen found Mrs. Allen between the sheets with the gardener—which explained all the destroyed flower beds around the property. Flowers aside, the property was huge and beautiful.

"Do you want something to drink?" George asked.

Madison perked up; a guy like George probably had a fully stocked home bar. At the very least, he had to have something better than the Southern Comfort and Mountain Dew that she and Cash usually went for. "Sure!"

He stood and headed inside. "Milk?"

She deflated. "Oh, um, no I'm good."

He came back out with two large glasses of it anyway. "You can't have cookies without milk—it's criminal."

Madison raised a brow. Being a grown man who preferred milk to booze was what was criminal. She put her feet up on the large metal table. "How do you like living here?"

"So far so good," he said, staring distractedly at her shoes on the table.

Was this guy for real? She immediately took them off.

He relaxed and leaned back into the couch. "The potholes in the driveway are going to be the death of my car and it looks like I'm in the market for a new gardener, but other than that, I like it."

"Still loving the smell?" she asked with a wink.

George grinned. "Can't get enough of it."

A gust of cool wind blew off of the lake, sending Madison's long hair flying. As she pushed it out of her face, their eyes locked. She was surprised again by how very green his were, like freshly mown grass on a hot summer day. He flinched nervously and looked away.

"How's your dad doing?" He'd asked that every time they'd talked over the past two weeks—a couple of calls where Madison didn't know what to say (she usually only texted with guys) and the afternoon he'd let her test-drive the Porsche. She cringed every time he asked her about her dad, though. As thoughtful as it was, it just made her sad.

"About the same as the last time you asked," she remarked, leaning her head back on the white cushion. "Honestly, I don't really want to talk about it, okay? I just feel like that's all anyone asks me, and the answer is never good." Talking about it wouldn't change the situation, so what was the point?

"I understand," he said, awkwardly patting her knee. "So . . . I went to go look at pools yesterday. I think I'm gonna get one."

"Oh, great," she said. "I'm probably going to need a new place to swim." She gestured to the house next door, a sour feeling in her stomach. "I doubt I'll get invited there anymore. Claire hasn't talked to me in two weeks."

George's brow furrowed. "What happened?"

"I told her something about her husband, and she refuses to believe it. She has her head in the sand about her marriage. She can be so naive sometimes." Though she was trying to sound casual, it stung that Claire didn't listen to her. Did her cousin really think so little of her?

"Family drama's the worst, ain't it?" George stared out over his lawn, his gaze settling on a copse of cypress trees that divided his property from the Thibodeauxs'. "I'm actually dealing with some of my own."

Madison glanced sideways at George, taking in his neatly pressed khakis and the striped dress shirt that he'd buttoned up to the very top. The chairs on his porch were arranged at perfect right angles to the couch, and he'd put his glass of milk on a coaster. It was hard to imagine something out of place in George's orderly existence. "Oh yeah?"

"My brother and sister stopped talking to me when I took over my dad's company." He frowned. "He left me in charge of it when he passed away, and they've never forgiven me. It's been a whole year and not a word. . . ."

"Damn, I'm sorry to hear that." This two-week silence was the longest Madison and Claire had gone without talking, and her stomach sunk at the idea of it stretching into next year.

"What's funny is they got the better end of the deal anyway— a huge payout without having to do any work." He let out an ironic laugh. "I'm left with insane hours and the weight of an entire company on my shoulders."

"But you love your job, right?"

He looked out toward the lake, squinting in the afternoon sun. "*Love* is a strong word."

"Well, it has to be better than scrubbing mildew off of shower walls." Madison put her hand on her heart. "I win this pity party, hands down."

George raised his glass. "To us," he said. "The pathetic duo."

"I can definitely drink to that," Madison said, raising her glass. She winced. "But not with this, because frankly, I find milk disgusting."

He laughed and put his head in his hands. "This is why I don't ever have company."

"Because people are afraid you'll force-feed them milk?" She cocked her head to the side.

"Something like that," he said, standing up and smoothing his pants. "What do you want—for real?"

"Let me see what you have." She got up and walked to the kitchen with him. Beautiful mahogany cabinets lined the walls and a marble-topped island stood in the center of the room. An oversize stainless steel refrigerator was covered in postcards from all over the world: Bangkok, Berlin, Paris, London, New York City, Moscow, Athens, Dubai, Marrakech.

She stared at a picture of Ben Big at night. "Have you been to *all* of these places?"

"Yeah," he said, walking over to her.

A whisper of jealousy stole through her. She plucked a scene of a market in Venice and flipped it over. It was stamped but blank, as if he'd mailed the postcard to himself. It was sad to think that he'd traveled all over the world and hadn't had someone to share it with. "Which place did you like the most?"

George pointed to one showing a crowded street lined with buildings and long balconies. BOURBON STREET was spelled out in green, purple, and gold letters on the bottom of the image. "Hands down my favorite place in the world," he said.

"I've never been," Madison confessed, turning to him. "I even joined this stupid club my senior year because they had a field trip there. I had to sell about a hundred candy bars to all of my friends. But then Hurricane Sebastian hit, and the club donated the money to the victims instead."

He leaned against the counter. "Well, that was nice of y'all."

"I guess. . . ." Madison trailed off, thinking of all the people who'd lost their homes and belongings. Her home hadn't been damaged by a hurricane, but she couldn't help but worry that her family's existence teetered precariously on the edge. "Honestly, though, and I know how selfish this sounds, but I was bummed that I didn't get to go."

George's eyes widened, and for a moment Madison thought he was going to scold her, but then he walked over to the other side of the fridge and pulled a piece of parchment paper out from under a magnet.

"What's this?" she said as he handed it to her. She read the words out loud:

Krewe of Celio Mardi Gras Ball
Saturday, the Eleventh of February
At Half Past Seven in the Evening
Archer Ballroom, New Orleans

He smiled. "Wanna go with me?"

"Seriously?" She gripped the thick card stock, staring at the intricate tendrils of gold foil.

George bit his lip. "I mean, if you think it's weird, that's fine." He took a step back, as if to ward off her imminent rejection. "It's just that I have an extra ticket, and you've never been to New Orleans. . . . Could be a win-win for both of us?"

Madison grinned, trying to hold back her excitement. "Yeah. I'm in." She was suddenly acutely aware of her Chuck Taylors and her chipping black nail polish. If she was going to go to a *ball*, she would need to clean herself up.

George held his hand out to high-five her, and Madison chuckled, slapping his hand with her own. He was *such* a nerd.

He cleared his throat. "We have to stay the night. But I'll get you your own hotel room, of course."

Madison raised an eyebrow, amused by how embarrassed he was. "So you're not expecting some *Pretty Woman* scenario, right?"

"No, ma'am," he said, shaking his head.

She tucked her hair behind her ears and glanced over at George, who was straightening the postcards on the fridge, his cheeks bright red. She knew what she wanted out of their relationship—some good meals and maybe some expensive gifts, since all the money she earned these days went to helping her parents. Not to mention that it was sure to make Cash jealous when he found out. But she still wasn't sure what *he* wanted, if not sex. He was new in town and clearly didn't have many friends. Was he lonely? Or was it something else entirely?

Her phone buzzed and she grabbed it out of her pocket. It was a text message from Cash.

Fat Pat's at 6?

Madison hit her lock screen, feeling slightly guilty that she was leaving already. "I gotta get going."

"Thanks for coming out today," George said. "And tell your mama thanks for the cookies."

"I will," she said, opening the front door. Outside, the sun was beginning to fade away, and a cotton candy sky hovered over the trees. She turned back to George before heading to her truck. "See you soon." Her words hung in the air, stretching out between them as they stood there. She didn't know the protocol for this sort of situation. Should they hug? Kiss on the cheek?

Finally they moved toward each other awkwardly and ended up doing a sort of half-hug, half-shoulder pat. "Get home safe," he said with a laugh.

As she started her truck—the engine rumbling and exhaust smoke spewing from the underside—she looked back at George. He waved eagerly at her from the front porch of the grand Victorian, Charlie lying by his feet.

She blew them a kiss and smiled to herself. Only a few weeks in, and already she'd snagged herself a trip to New Orleans. She couldn't wait to see what George would offer up next.

12

claire

"HOW LATE DO you think you'll be?" Claire asked as she scribbled down the WiFi password on her "Fixin' To" notepad. Her mom would be there in a couple of minutes to watch Sadie while Claire and Gavin went out with their respective friends. Her mom's only stipulation for coming over was that she have good Internet access—she was addicted to her Mahjong with Friends app.

Gavin poured his glass of water down the sink and left the dirty dish on the counter. "I'm not sure. The game starts at seven, but the guys and I were talking about practicing a couple of songs for the church talent show after, so it might be kinda late."

"I'm sure Becky'll love a jam session in her living room at eleven o'clock on a Friday night," Claire said, sticking the piece of paper to the fridge.

"She's out of town this weekend, so sadly for her, she doesn't even get to hear us play." He pushed his glasses up with his finger. "How long you gonna be?"

"I think we're just having dinner, so it should only be a few hours." She grabbed Gavin's glass and put it in the dishwasher.

"All the girls are going?" He moved behind her and wrapped his arms around her waist, his breath warm against her cheek.

Claire nuzzled his cheek with hers and turned her head to kiss him. "Yep."

Her heart began to beat faster, but it wasn't from the kiss. Madison would be there tonight, and things hadn't been the same with her since she had accused Gavin of going to a strip club last month. Claire still couldn't believe that Madison had been so thoughtless, and so *wrong*.

Claire and Gavin had been working harder on their relationship recently—taking breaks together at the church, setting aside time to eat dinner together as a family, and even going on a few romantic dates. Marriage was hard work, something Madison couldn't possibly understand. The girls had made up last week and texted a few times. But Madison was being the most cordial and polite she had ever been in her entire life, and quite frankly, it scared Claire a little.

Gavin disentangled himself and walked over to the breakfast table. He sat down, tying his brown shoes. "And you still haven't met Gabby's fiancé yet?"

"No . . . weird, right?" Claire pulled up the chair next to him. "She said he's out of town this weekend but she's going to bring him around next week. I still can't believe they're engaged—it happened so fast. I think she's in shock."

"That happens." Gavin looked up from his shoes with a smile. "Remember how surprised you were when I asked you?"

Claire's lips curled up as she thought about that night. They had been celebrating their one-year anniversary, which fell on the same night as the church's youth choir concert. Gavin promised he would take her out for a late dinner after the performance. They sat in the front row, and Gavin held her hand throughout the entire show. The last song just happened to be their song. As the kids belted out "God Gave Me You," chill bumps started covering her body. The singers then pointed to her in a coordinated move. She blushed and looked over at Gavin, who squeezed her hand and kissed her cheek. When she looked back at the stage, the kids were holding out letters that spelled out "Will You Marry Me, Claire?"

Gavin gently let go of her hand and got down on one knee. Totally shocked, she nodded, tears rolling down her face, and the entire audience cheered. Their families—even her dad—popped out from behind a door to congratulate them. "This is the happiest day of my life," she had whispered in Gavin's ear. "It'll only get better," he had whispered back.

The doorbell chimed, shaking her out of the memory, and Claire stood up. "Mom's here!" She ran to the foyer and opened the door, welcoming her mother into the house. "Thanks so much for doing this, Mama."

Jillian swept into the room, tucking her short golden hair behind her ears. She was in her midforties, but people often asked Jillian and Claire if they were sisters, and not in a fun, joking way. Claire liked to tell people it was a blessing that her mom looked so good—it meant she'd age well, too.

"Sure thing, sweetheart," Jillian said, pulling a bottle of wine out of her canvas bag. Claire tried not to look at it in disapproval; she wasn't about to lecture her free babysitter. The silver bangles on Jillian's wrist clinked together as she set the wine on the coffee table. "Sadie and me'll be fine. Now, where are y'all going again?"

"Gavin's going over to his friends to watch the LSU game," Claire said, putting her jacket on. "The girls and I are going to the Gumbo Fest."

"Oh yeah. Went last night." She began uncorking the bottle. "It's a real good time."

Gavin entered the room. "Thanks for watching Sadie for us," he said, giving his mother-in-law a hug and kiss on the cheek.

"You kids have fun," Jillian said, pouring her first glass of wine as Claire and Gavin headed to the door. "Don't get into too much trouble!"

• • •

CLAIRE PULLED HER car into the packed festival parking lot and found the girls in the tent, sitting at a long table near the bandstand. The Gumbo Fest was an annual tradition where almost everyone in town—from the drunks to the rich folks who lived on

Darby Lake—mixed and mingled over good food and live music. The gumbo cook-off was just as popular as the line-dance contest, and the funnel cakes were the best in the world, according to an unscientific poll developed by Madison and Claire when they were kids.

The girls greeted her, but Claire noticed her hug with Madison was a little stiffer than the others. As she sat down in the plastic seat they'd saved her, she saw that they'd already ordered food and gotten her a big bowl of gumbo.

Claire nodded to Gabby's left hand, where the two-carat princess-cut diamond glimmered. "Is your arm sore yet from carrying that gigantic thing around?"

Gabby blushed and put her hand down in her lap. "It's not a big deal, really."

Claire frowned. The day after Gabby's engagement, Claire had stopped by the day care and her jaw dropped when she saw what was on Gabby's finger. Hours before, Gabby had been claiming that she was going to break up with this guy, and now here she was, *engaged*. And when Claire made a big deal about it, Gabby downplayed everything. She'd known Gabby her whole life and the girl had been planning her dream wedding since she was eight. She couldn't figure out why her friend was suddenly being so evasive about it.

Madison held up her ringless hand. "And then there was one. You guys are dropping like flies."

"I'm sure if Cash gave you even a Cracker Jack box ring, you'd be on your way to the chapel in a heartbeat," Laura said with a laugh.

"I highly doubt it'll happen anytime soon." She frowned. "Cash and I are only hookup buddies. He's made that loud and clear. 'Band comes first, babe,'" she said, mocking his deep voice. "But whatever. I'm having some fun with someone else."

Claire leaned in across the sticky table, intrigued. Normally, Madison told her everything about her romantic entanglements.

"Well . . . who is he?" Laura asked eagerly.

"My dad's boss." Madison took a sip of her Coke and gave the girls a measured look, waiting for their reactions.

Claire's initial thought was that someone needed to slap some sense into her cousin. But screaming, *Are you out of your damned mind?* might go over poorly, so she went with: "Um, how old is this guy?"

"Thirty-something, I don't have his birth certificate. But I'm not like *into* him, you guys." She shrugged. "We're just friends, and he happens to be a nice distraction when Cash is too busy with his dumb band." She held her hand up, rubbing her thumb, middle, and index fingers together. "Plus, he's rich."

Claire sat back in shock. "So, you're using him for money?" she asked. The words came out far more judgmental-sounding than she'd meant.

Madison looked away, her cheeks reddening. "Whatever. He's taking me to a Mardi Gras Ball in New Orleans. I get to go to New Orleans and stay at the Ritz freakin' Carlton!"

"So you're using him for money," Gabby repeated.

Madison held her head up, her eyes narrowing. Claire knew that look—it was the same one Madison had worn when she was twelve and had snuck bottles of beer for her and Claire at a family reunion. It meant she was scheming. "And to make Cash jealous."

"Is it working?" Laura asked, blowing on a spoonful of gumbo.

"Well, you shoulda seen the look on Cash's face a few weeks ago when George and I pulled up next to him in the Porsche on Tilley Road. . . ." Madison leaned back in her chair and smiled slyly. "I've never seen Cash Romero look so insecure in his life. He's been texting me like crazy this week, and we're going to his family's cabin tomorrow."

Madison could handle herself, and if this was what she wanted to do, nothing Claire could say would stop her, but still . . . "Don't you feel a little guilty playing this guy?"

Madison huffed. "Not at all—he's using me, too. He's nice enough, but he's so socially awkward, it's not like he's got girls flocking to hang out with him." She grabbed the corn bread and tore a piece off. "If I can bring some amount of happiness to his lonely life, then don't you think it's worth a trip and maybe a few gifts?" She popped the corn bread into her mouth.

"Just be careful," Claire insisted. This whole thing sounded like a bad idea, and she didn't want her cousin to get hurt—or hurt someone else, for that matter.

Madison rolled her eyes. "Okay, *Mom*."

Claire hid a smile. *Finally. She's back to her old self.* Maybe she didn't totally agree with Madison's plan, but she didn't want to strain their relationship again. She put her arm on Madison's shoulder. "But . . . if you want to pick me up in the Porsche one day, I'll have no objections," she joked.

"Deal." Madison grinned.

Claire and Laura hit the funnel cake stand while Gabby and Madison held the table, the delicious smell of fried food thick in the air. The line, which was moving at a glacial pace, snaked back through booths full of vendors selling knickknacks.

"So, how's Brian doing?" Claire asked. They hadn't had much time alone since Laura had been back, and Claire was worried about her friend—and how her relationship was holding up under all of that stress.

"Um, you know . . ." Laura said, edging forward in the line.

The girls sidestepped a wobbly man in a cowboy hat who was holding a bottle of Bud. "No, I don't," Claire said slowly. "What's going on?"

"It's just been really hard living with his parents," Laura said with a sigh. "They're so nice, but. . . ."

Cowboy Hat Man took a drunken stumble and fell to the ground. The girls jumped out of his way just in time. Claire shot him a look of disgust and turned her attention back to Laura. "But what?"

"I'm going batshit crazy," Laura confessed. "They're just always there. Brian and I are never alone." She paused. "We haven't had sex in, like, two months."

Claire's eyes widened. "Really?" Well *that* certainly put her dry spell with Gavin in perspective. She and Gavin had a somewhat disappointing quickie the other week after one of their date nights. It wasn't the crazy, passionate lovemaking of the early days of their marriage, but at least it was something.

Laura bit her lip and frowned. "I swear it's like Janet knows when we're about to do it or something. She always comes knocking, hollering about breakfast or coffee or some dumb report on the news."

"I'm sorry, sweetie," Claire said. "It's just for another few months, right?"

"Yeah." Laura paused at a booth selling glass paperweights and grabbed one with a crawfish design in the middle. Claire noticed for the first time how tired Laura looked. Her long blond hair— normally shiny and curled—hung lank around her face, as if she'd been too exhausted to do anything with it. "Would it be weird if I bought this for Ricky Broussard?"

Claire made a gagging sound. "Why the heck would you buy something for Ricky?"

"I decided I'm gonna ask for a promotion to manager at the restaurant," Laura said, putting it back down on the table. "I'm over being a waitress."

Claire put her hand on Laura's shoulder. "You don't need a suck-up gift. You're worthy of a promotion even without a twenty-dollar piece of glass."

Laura stood in silence for a moment, looking as if she was trying to convince herself of her worthiness. "Maybe," she said, like she didn't quite believe it.

Claire squeezed her arm encouragingly. "You got this. Besides," she said playfully, grabbing the paperweight, "I'm going to get this for Gavin's office, and there's only one."

• • •

AS THE GIRLS finished up the last piece of the funnel cake, Claire checked her watch. "Y'all, I hate to do this 'cuz I'm having so much fun, but I gotta go." She wiped her hands with the paper napkin and stood up. "My mom's at home with Sadie right now, and I've got to relieve her."

She gave all the girls a hug and kiss on the cheek. When she got to Madison, she held her a little tighter. "Love you," Claire whispered in her ear. Madison gave her a squeeze back.

As she walked back to her car, she thought about Madison's odd new relationship, Gabby's awkwardness about her engagement, Laura's difficulties with Brian, and even the issues she struggled with in her own marriage. She pulled out her phone and opened Gavin's Twitter account. *"The only one who should judge is God,"* she typed. *"You never truly know what's going on, so use your energy to lift others up, not tear them down."*

During the drive home, Claire turned on the radio, tapping her fingers to cheesy love songs as she drove down Main Street. A few teenagers were hanging out by the gas station, smoking and skateboarding around the parking lot. She rolled her eyes at them but then noticed a familiar truck pulling out of the station ahead of her. The bumper sticker read: RON PAUL.

Well I'll be darned, she thought. Gavin must have gotten done with the guys early. A smile grew on her face as she thought about pulling up behind him in the driveway. "You were there this whole time?" he'd say, greeting her with a kiss.

She wondered if he realized she was right behind him. It was probably too dark for him to tell. They drove through two stoplights and Claire thought about giving him a call. Maybe they could pull off somewhere. . . . Claire felt a rush of desire and reached for her phone, but then Gavin's truck turned onto the highway on-ramp. She leaned back, confused. That wasn't the way to get home. . . .

Her mind raced. *Keep following him or go home?* She turned her blinker on and the next thing she knew, she was headed south on I-49. She was immediately filled with regret. A wife was supposed to trust her husband, and she always trusted Gavin. Following him down the highway was *not* a way to show her faith in him. She almost turned around—once, twice—but Gavin kept driving, and with each passing mile, a little voice in the back of her head whispered, *This is the way to The Saddle.*

Finally, they neared the infamous strip club, the neon lights clear even from a distance. Through the darkness, a flashing sign showed a sexy woman riding a bull. *Keep driving,* she willed the truck in front of her. *Go past this. You wouldn't do this to us.*

She groaned as Gavin's truck pulled into the gravel parking lot and cozied up between two beat-up cars. Several potbellied, grizzled men stood against one wall, chain-smoking. All of the building's windows were blacked out. Claire pulled over to the highway's shoulder, feeling dizzy as she watched her husband get out and walk into the dilapidated building. *What the hell is he doing in a place like this?* She hadn't felt this angry with a man since her dad walked out on her and her mom.

Tears started to flow down her face, and soon she was sobbing, her head pressed against the steering wheel. Gavin was supposed to be a *good* guy. What had she missed? She grew angry with herself, too, for being as naive as Madison thought. She resisted the urge to get out of her car, storm into that horrible place, and confront her husband. Instead she rolled down her window and threw the glass paperweight on the sidewalk, shattering it into a million pieces.

13

madison

"SO, WHAT'S THIS guy's deal?" Cash asked, lighting his cigarette.

He and Madison were sitting on the rotting wood bench outside his parents' cabin, which was set back in the woods about thirty minutes outside Toulouse. They were having a smoke, and she had just casually mentioned hanging out with George at the Paradis Coffee House, a newly opened café that catered to Toulouse's artsy and sophisticated crowd.

"I met him through my dad. He's the CEO of my dad's old company." Madison took a sip of her beer, trying not to smile.

He raised his eyebrow. "A suit, huh? So, are y'all, like, dating?"

"Not exactly." Madison ran a hand down his arm, the muscles hard beneath his shirt.

Cash paused for a moment, a rare look of consternation on his face. "So . . . that means we can still do it, right?"

Madison rolled her eyes. "You sure do know how to make a girl swoon." She stared at him for a second. "So, you're cool with this?" This was clearly bothering him, which made her want to grin in victory.

He took a swig of his beer, squinting in the sun, finally saying, "Why wouldn't I be? You can do what you want."

The words took her by surprise. A piece of her had hoped that he'd be so overcome with jealousy that he'd scoop her up and declare his love for her right there. "I guess I just don't understand what we are . . . what this is," she blurted, immediately regretting it. She sounded like those girls she made fun of—the clingy ones like Claire and Laura, desperate to define the relationship.

Cash sighed, smoke filling the air. "We talked about this already, babe. You know I'm not in a place for something serious."

Madison looked at the muddy ground, fighting back an inexplicable sadness. She was usually okay with their relationship—hell, she wasn't the type to settle down either—so why did this bother her?

Cash nudged her with his shoulder, and she looked back up, her body tingling at his touch. "You know I think you're cool," he said, "and I care about you—that's why I don't want to hurt you."

You just did, she admitted to herself.

She and Cash had been hanging out for three years now, ever since they began hooking up sophomore year. Every so often, she'd wonder if he was getting serious about her, like when he'd invited her to his parents' house for his birthday dinner last year. She had met his cousins and uncles and even his PawPaw at a family barbecue, and he always called her "his girl." But every time she started to feel like this could be something real, he'd do something to remind her that it wasn't, like drop her home early to go to a house party without her or not call her for three weeks. He continually managed to find subtle ways to keep her in check.

Oddly, it wasn't the romantic rejection that hurt Madison the most . . . it was how stupid she felt every time he did this to her. But it worked; every time he made her feel like she couldn't have him, she wanted him more.

A hummingbird buzzed in front of them, stopping at the recycled bird feeder Cash's mom had made out of Heineken bottles, and a cool breeze gusted through the trees. Madison shivered and pulled her sweater tighter around her.

"I understand," she lied. "It actually works out better for me, too—if we're not, you know, exclusive." She sucked her cigarette and then blew the smoke out hard.

Cash glanced up quickly, a satisfying look of concern on his face.

"I was kinda feeling guilty about the whole George thing. But it makes me happy—relieved, actually—that you're so cool with it." She stroked his knee. If he was going to play games, she was, too. "We're actually going away together for Mardi Gras."

Cash cleared his throat. "You just said it wasn't anything?" His voice had an edge to it now.

"Oh, yeah . . . it's probably nothing," she said, waving smoke away from her face. She could sense she was getting a rise out of him, and it made her happy.

"'Probably?'" He angled toward her, finally giving her his full attention. "Whatever . . . fine, go with him. But you know you're gonna come back here beggin' for me."

"'Begging?'" Madison teased. "All I have to do is this, and *you'll* be begging for *me*." She crushed her cigarette into the ground and straddled him. He groaned in pleasure and pulled her body close to his. He smiled and ran his hands through her hair, sending a tingle down her spine. She kissed him, breathing in the taste of cheap beer and cigarettes. She knew it was silly but it turned her on because it tasted like Cash.

"Let's go inside," he whispered in her ear.

They left their drinks outside and hurried into the cabin. He ripped her sweater off as soon as they got inside, her shirt and bra following suit. She shivered in the cool air and ran her hands along his abs. Cash guided her to the black futon in the front room and lowered himself over her. His every move made Madison feel bad, but in a good way. He grabbed her hips so hard that the line between pleasure and pain vanished. Madison flipped on top and ground into him, both of them moving so vigorously that the futon creaked dangerously beneath them.

This was hands down the hottest sex they had ever had. Hotter than the first time, when Madison went dry-mouthed at the sight of his body. Hotter than the time they were both high and did it in her parents' shed, laughing and moaning at the same time. Even hotter than the Halloween when she wore the purple wig and pretended to be a stranger. Something was different about this time, but she couldn't quite put her finger on what.

After it was over, they lay quietly for a few minutes, staring at the ceiling.

"You okay?" he asked, brushing her sweaty bangs off her forehead.

She smiled. "You just took it outta me, that's all."

Cash propped his head up with his arm, his brown eyes narrowing. "I make you happier than him, don't I?"

Madison smirked. "Is someone jealous?" *It was working. . . .*

"No way," he said defensively, pushing himself up. "Why on earth would I be jealous of some old loser?" He swung his legs over the edge of the futon.

"Right . . ." She sat up, grabbing her black bra off the floor, and clasping it back together.

Cash walked over to the minifridge, his long, dark hair falling over his shoulders, and grabbed another beer. "Let him take you to New Orleans, that's fine," he said, popping the top off. "Just wait until I go on tour, though. Baby, I'm gonna take you places you've never been before."

A thrill ran through Madison. Cash had been talking about going on tour for months, but he'd never once mentioned bringing her. That hadn't stopped her from imagining what it would be like, though—her man, the open road, cool clubs all over the country.

"Any news?" she asked, sitting back down on the futon.

"Max is working it out right now." Cash sat down next to her and put his arm around her. "With any luck, we'll be heading out in a few months."

"Nice. Maybe George and I can come see you play." She looked over at him innocently, knowing that would eat at him.

Cash's lips curled and he shook his head. "Not cool, Blanchette. Not cool."

She burst out laughing. "Too soon?"

Cash teasingly punched her arm and started tickling her.

"Stop!" she screamed, laughing uncontrollably. "I surrender! I surrender!"

He finally stopped and stared at her as if he wanted to say something more. Instead, he unhooked the bra she had just clasped and started kissing her again, harder and more passionately than before. Madison's mind went blissfully blank. Every problem in her life— her dad's cancer, her family's money issues, her miserable job cleaning houses—all of it was forgotten as Cash made her focus on other things, like how good it felt when he did *that* or touched her *there*.

Madison surrendered to the moment, drinking Cash in. He made her feel better than any drug she had ever done, even though she knew he was just as bad for her, if not worse.

14

gabrielle

GABBY KNEW SHE had to tell Tony the truth the second he placed the ring on her finger, but it had been a month, and every time she tried to tell him, something came up. The night of the engagement, he'd covered his whole apartment in roses and candles and she couldn't bring herself to ruin that moment. The next day, he'd found out his granny had suffered a stroke, and Gabby didn't want to hurt him with more bad news. And a week later, he found out his work was sending him to DC for a monthlong stay. As frustrating as it was to have this hanging over her head, she also felt relieved, like she'd been granted a reprieve.

But Tony would be back the following week, and she'd been thinking about every possible approach to telling him.

She could try nonchalance, prefacing the whole conversation with, "So, I have a funny story. . . ." The only problem with that scenario was that every time she pictured it in her head, Tony did not actually laugh. *Scratch that one.*

Another option was to skip over the awkward conversation and surprise Tony with a visit to her mom. While there was a chance he'd be so confused that he would just accept everything, there was a much bigger chance he'd dump her on the spot. *Scratch.*

Out of all of the scenarios in her head, not one of them actually ended with Tony saying, "It's okay, babe. I forgive you."

Gabby's cell phone rang, jolting her from worries. *Tony*.

"Hey, babe," she answered with a smile. Her mom once told her people could hear your expression on the other end. "How's DC?"

"Hey, baby," he said, the sounds of a city in the background. "I'm just checking out the Washington Monument and wishing you were here with me."

Gabby pictured him elbowing his way through throngs of tourists. "Me, too. I'm excited to see you next week!" Excited . . . nervous . . . those were the same, right?

"Actually, that's what I'm calling you about. My mom wanted to make sure you knew you were invited to Thanksgiving dinner next week—I've been so busy with work, I completely forgot it was even coming up."

Gabby grew silent. *Turkey with a side of heartbreak?*

"It's just going to be me, my mom, my brother, and my sister. Unfortunately my dad won't be there—he's going to be helping the governor pardon a turkey."

She paused, thinking about the invitation. "Sure, I'll join," she said reluctantly. While it would be nice to spend the holiday with a family—she usually went to Claire's and felt like she was intruding—this meant she would have to wait until after Thanksgiving to tell him. She didn't want to embarrass him in front of his family.

"Great! I gotta run, babe. I'm meeting up with an old law school buddy for lunch."

"Okay, I love you," she said softly into the phone, but he'd already hung up.

• • •

CLAIRE OPENED THE front door with a crying baby on her hip and flour on her cheek. "Hey," she said, sounding tired. "Come on in."

"You sure now's an okay time?" Gabby asked, peeking into the house. "You seem busy."

"Girl, I'm a working mom," Claire huffed. "I'm always busy. Get in here and take off your shoes. I just vacuumed the living room."

Gabby obeyed her friend and followed Claire and the sounds of Sadie's screams into the kitchen, which looked like it'd been turned into a cookie factory.

"I'm putting you to work," Claire said, throwing her a floral apron. She put Sadie down in her high chair and slid a bowl of Cheerios to her. "I signed up to make six dozen cranberry cookies for the Thanksgiving potluck at church tomorrow and am definitely regretting that decision right now."

"Well, how many have you made so far?" Gabby looked around.

"One batch." Claire opened up the oven and pulled out a baking sheet covered with twelve perfect cookies. She frowned. "It's gonna be a long day."

"Well, I'm here, don't worry." Gabby tied the apron around her waist and started mixing some of the ingredients together in the stainless steel bowl.

"Thank you," Claire said. "Sorry I was so short with you on the phone. I'm just—" She paused and threw her hands up in the air. "All of this, you know?"

Gabby nodded. "No need to explain." She often wondered how Claire did it all—it was impressive, albeit a bit stressful, to see her in action sometimes.

"So, what did you want advice on? I'm all ears—well, one of my ears might be busted thanks to screamin' Sadie over there. . . ." The girls both looked over at the baby, who was beginning to calm down as she picked at the cereal curiously. "But let's hear it."

Gabby grabbed some of the dough and began rolling it into a ball in her hands. "Claire, I'm in a big ol' mess."

Her friend looked up from the measuring cup of flour, her eyes widening. "What is it?"

Gabby braced herself; she still hadn't said these words aloud to anyone yet. "I may have lied a little to Tony."

"What do you mean? What did you say?" Claire put the measuring cup down on the table.

Gabby began furiously rolling the dough in her hands, unable to look at her friend. "So, he thinks I'm a senior at U.L. about to apply for my master's in education, and that my parents are . . ." She dropped the ball of dough back into the bowl. "Dead." She shook her head in disgust, and tears began rolling down her cheeks. As if on cue, Sadie knocked over her Cheerios and began screaming again.

Claire gasped and put her hand over her mouth. "Why in the world would you have said that?" This was the first time Gabby had ever seen Claire ignore her baby's cries.

Gabby lowered her head. "It just happened. . . ."

Her friend pulled out the two chairs from under the table and sat down in one of them. "This is major," she said, shaking her head in disbelief.

Gabby sat down next to Claire, wiping away the tears with the back of her hand. "I'm going to lose him, huh?"

"I just don't understand why you said all this to him in the first place. . . ." Claire swept the Cheerios off the table and back into their bowl, and put it back on Sadie's tray. The little girl calmed down again.

"He just was a guy in a bar—I never thought anything would come of it, so when he assumed I was at college, I just went along with it." She put her head in her hands. "It was nice to pretend for a second that I actually got to live out my dream. There hasn't been a day that's gone by in the last four years where I don't feel ashamed of how my life has turned out." She sniffled and looked up. "But when I told him my parents weren't around anymore, he took it to mean they were dead. Once we started dating, I wanted to correct him, but that would've meant explaining everything with my mom, and I just . . . I just couldn't."

Claire raised her right eyebrow but thankfully withheld judgment.

"He would have never asked me out if he had known the truth. There's a reason I haven't dated anyone seriously since high school." She sighed, fidgeting with her fingers. "I know I sound like a crazy person, but when I'm with him, I feel like I'm finally living the life I was always supposed to have." Her heart ached. "He's the only guy I've ever met who appreciates my ideas—he tells me I'm smart all the time, and I swear, Claire, I *feel* smarter when I'm with him. When we're together, he looks at me like I'm perfect."

"Because you *are,* Gabs." Claire put her hand on her shoulder. "And I'm talking about the real you."

Gabby rolled her eyes. "You have to say that! You're my best friend. But we both know there are things in my life that are awful." She shook her head. "You don't know how hard these last few years have been for me, Claire. Tony makes me forget all of that bad stuff. He makes me feel happy, and if—I mean *when*"—she corrected herself—"I tell him the truth, he's going to leave me and I'm going to be alone again, with nothing."

As Sadie happily tossed her food around, Claire leaned over and rubbed Gabby's back. "Even with the little hiccups in your life, you've managed to stay strong and you haven't lost what makes you *you.* Tony didn't fall in love with you because you're in college; he fell in love with you because you're smart and he likes hanging out with you. And if you're worried about him judging you for your mom's situation, then quite frankly, I don't think he's worth it."

Gabby shook her head. "I don't really think it's a coincidence that the one I don't tell ends up proposing to me. Every guy I've told previously has run away." The words were painful to say aloud.

Claire's voice sharpened. "It doesn't matter. You have to tell him, Gabs. Your mom's eventually gonna get out of jail, and then what? You're gonna cut her out of your life? You know you can't do that. And what if you really do want to go to school one day? Isn't he going to wonder why you're getting your degree twice?"

"I know all of that! I know I need to tell him," Gabby said. "I just don't know how."

Claire cocked her head to the side. "You just have to be honest with him. Promise me you'll do it the next time you see him."

Gabby nodded, sniffling. As awful as the truth was, the viselike grip around her chest was finally beginning to lessen. She'd been carrying this lie alone for so long. "I will. After Thanksgiving."

"Okay, good." Claire patted her on the back. "And I know you're nervous, sweetie, but I truly believe that everything goes according to God's plan. If Tony doesn't want to be with you after this, it wasn't meant to be." Sadie began to fuss again and Claire stood up, grabbing her out of her high chair, and bouncing her on her hip.

"But what if he's my soul mate, and I screwed it up?" Gabby asked, standing up and going back to work on the dough.

"Well, worst-case scenario, you learn from this. Just remember, if he can't handle the truth, then he's not worthy of you. You deserve the best, Gabs. Don't settle for anything less."

Those words echoed in Gabby's head as she rolled the dough between her hands. "*You deserve the best. Don't settle for anything less.*" She could only hope that Tony didn't live by that mantra.

15

claire

AFTER GABBY LEFT, Claire's own advice to her kept repeating in her head. *"You deserve the best. Don't settle for anything less."* It hurt that her husband had been going to a strip club, yes. But what was worse was that he'd been lying to her. She didn't deserve that.

When she finished baking the final batch of cookies, she packed Sadie in her carrier and drove a few miles up the road, turning into the Sunnybrook apartment complex where her mom lived.

Her mom looked worried when she opened the door. "What are you doing here? Is everything okay?"

With Sadie's carrier in hand, Claire brushed past Jillian and made her way to the floral couch. It was the same one that she had cried on through her parents' divorce, two high school breakups, one fight with Gabby, and the slight panic attack over a catering snafu before her wedding.

"I'm a total wreck, Mama," she confessed, setting Sadie's car seat on the ground.

Jillian sat down, her forehead wrinkling in concern. "What happened, sweetie?"

As she told her mom about seeing Gavin at The Saddle last night, she felt disgusted with him, with herself, with their marriage. She could taste the salt from her tears by the time she finished.

"Just tell me it's gonna be okay," Claire pleaded between sobs.

Her mom hugged her tight. "I'm sure it's all just a big misunderstanding."

"How could it be a misunderstanding?" Claire said, pulling away from Jillian. She put her feet onto the brown leather footrest that used to be in her granny's house before she passed away. She and Madison would use it to build sheet forts as kids. Life was so much easier when the biggest drama was Granny yelling at them for playing with her good bed linens. "I saw it myself. What am I supposed to do?"

"You've gotta talk to him," Jillian said, thrusting a quilted Kleenex box at Claire. "Find out what's really going on."

Claire blew her nose and glanced over at the bookcase, where a framed photo of them on their wedding day sat. Gavin had seemed so sincere when he said his vows in front of God and all their family and friends. What had changed? "What if he's just . . . bored with me?" she asked, voicing her worst fears.

Jillian stroked her daughter's hair. Her hands smelled like lavender and eucalyptus, the lotion she'd been wearing all of Claire's life. "Take control of your marriage. It isn't easy. You've gotta work at it all the time."

Claire's chin started to wobble again and she swallowed, fighting back more tears. "How? What can I do?"

Jillian paused, as if debating whether or not to say something, and then stood up. She walked over to the bookcase and opened the cabinet, pulling out a DVD. "Here's my favorite aerobics video. Start with this," she said, handing it to her daughter.

Claire bristled and handed the DVD back to her mom. Was Jillian telling her she was . . . fat? "I highly doubt that a workout video made fifteen years ago is gonna save my marriage. And maybe I'm naive, but doesn't being in a committed relationship mean loving your partner regardless of how they look?"

"Honey . . ." Her mom sat back down next to her and grabbed Claire's hands. "I'm not saying he's *stopped* loving you. I just wish someone would've given me advice like this—before it was too late."

Claire shook her head, confused. "What do you mean? Daddy didn't go runnin' off to a strip club. . . ."

Jillian pursed her lips. "No, he just ran off with Nancy Martin instead."

"Wait—Daddy had an *affair*?" Claire's stomach went into free fall. When her dad had left, her mom had told her he couldn't handle the responsibility of being part of a family anymore. The fact that he'd chosen someone else over them made her feel physically ill.

Jillian brushed her blond hair off her forehead, her cheeks reddening. "You were too young to know the truth, and as you got older, I didn't want to color your opinion of your father. And honestly, I was embarrassed by it. I'd been so focused on raising you that I completely neglected our marriage."

"So, it's *my* fault you got a divorce?" Claire suddenly had a vision of her and Sadie having this same conversation twenty years in the future. She buried her face in her hands.

"Oh my goodness, no!" her mom quickly said. "Don't you ever think that." She took Claire by the shoulders and gave her a steely look. "It was my fault, it was your dad's fault, but it was *definitely* not yours. All I'm saying is that if I could do things differently, I'd have made more of an effort. Gavin's just going to a strip club, not having an affair. You still have time to turn things around. You can change things."

Claire took a deep breath and rested her head on the back of the couch. Maybe her mom was right. Maybe she could be making a better effort. If she was being honest, she hadn't tried all that hard to lose the baby weight. And, though Sadie was her heart, she knew she spent more time thinking about her daughter than she did thinking about her husband. Suddenly, the events of the last twenty-four hours felt exhausting.

"Is it okay if I stay here for just a little while longer?" Her eyes fluttered closed. Claire felt her mom's gentle kiss on her forehead, heard her trail of footsteps heading toward the kitchen, and let herself drift, feeling at peace for the first time in days.

The next thing she knew, she was woken up by the sound of her cell phone vibrating on the table by her head. She reached for it groggily. Somehow, it was seven already, and Gavin was calling.

"Hello?" she said wearily.

"Where are you?" He sounded panicked.

Claire sat up halfway and rubbed the sleep out of her eyes. "My mom's."

Gavin sighed in relief. "I was so worried about you—I thought you said you'd be home at five." His voice wasn't accusing but filled with genuine concern.

Claire smiled. A man who worried this much about his wife couldn't be cheating on her. Was it possible that she had misunderstood Gavin's actions? Could there be some explanation for what she saw?

"Is everything okay?" he asked.

"Yeah, of course. Just came over to say hi and ended up falling asleep on the sofa. We'll come home right now."

"Drive carefully," he said. "I love you."

"I . . . okay," she said. "Me, too." She ended the call and stood up too fast, her head going dizzy.

"Mama!" she yelled.

Her mom walked in from the kitchen, carrying Sadie. "Yes?"

"Why didn't you wake me up?" Claire grabbed her bag and her keys. "We gotta go."

Jillian followed her to the front door, handing off the baby. "Good luck, my love." She kissed Claire on her cheek.

Claire put Sadie in her car seat and drove home in the dark. When she'd driven to her mom's house earlier, she was furious with Gavin, but now she couldn't help feeling a little guilty. Maybe her mom was right. There were two people in this marriage and it was up to her to make it work.

16

laura

NO MATTER HOW hard she tried, Laura couldn't stop smell-ing boiled crawfish as she drove home from work Sunday night. Granted, she loved crawfish, but after an eight-hour shift of working at the Sea Shack's first annual Bowl and Boil, Laura never wanted to eat another in her life.

She was proud of her idea, though. When she was a kid, she and her neighbors would fill soda bottles with water and line them up in the middle of the street like bowling pins. Then they'd take turns trying to knock them over with a soccer ball. She'd suggested host-ing a similar event at the bar to bring in new business, hoping Ricky would recognize her managerial potential.

He'd been skeptical at first. "No one's gonna order crawfish just 'cuz you arranged two-liters filled with colored water in the middle of the restaurant," he said. "But I'ma let you try it out." Thanks to Claire posting the event on the church bulletin board, everyone and their mama came to the Sea Shack after church that day to "bowl" and eat crawfish.

"Told ya it'd be a success," Ricky said at closing time, counting the cash at the register as Laura picked up crawfish heads from the floor.

She rolled her eyes and laughed. Then with her heart racing and palms sweating, Laura walked over to Ricky. "Can I ask you some-thing?" She put her dirty rag on the counter.

"Yes, ma'am," he said, closing the machine.

"I've been working here for a while now. . . ." Laura fiddled with a piece of receipt paper. "And you know how much I love it," she lied.

Ricky nodded and leaned his elbows on the counter.

"I've been taking on a lot of extra hours and responsibility lately, and I think I've gone above and beyond the duties of a waitress. I'd really like to be promoted to manager." She'd looked up from the receipt, trying to gauge his reaction.

He scratched his dimpled chin. "You're one-a my best employees. I just ain't got an open position right now for that." He nudged her arm. "But the second anything opens up, you my go-to girl."

She stifled a sigh and cracked a smile. "Thank you for considering me," she said, standing up and taking off her apron. "I'm gonna go home now."

"Good job today," he yelled to her as she opened the door. "You're a bright one."

As she drove down Main Street, sadness rooted in her chest. She'd really needed that promotion—not just for the money for Brian's surgery but also for herself. She felt like she needed to prove to herself that she could do more than just serve food and drinks. Hell, she was smart—even strangers like Vince could see it. But lately, she had been feeling like she was destined for something more, and this time it was up to her—not Brian—to make that happen. Granted, it was a tough balance. All that schoolwork she was juggling . . . like the science paper on climate change due tomorrow (even though Mr. Myers insisted under his breath that global warming wasn't actually a thing) . . . and the French participles exam on Wednesday . . . and the limits test in math on Thursday. . . . It gave her the sweats just thinking about it.

Brian often asked her why she worked so hard at school. "You have me. You know I'll take care of you," he'd say. And she didn't really have an answer. But tonight as the stress of school and work pressed down on her, she tried to let all of that worry go and instead fantasized about the future he'd promised her.

The setting: an extravagant NFL banquet. They'd be seated in a glimmering ballroom, eating steak with warm rolls and those little butters shaped like seashells. Brian would be next to her, unable to keep his hands off of her, because she'd look like a knockout in her silky floor-length designer gown. A really expensive one, from one of those flamboyant French guys named Christian or Jean-Paul.

Her hair and makeup would be professionally done—no more doing it herself from a *Cosmo* guide—and when Brian got up onstage to accept an award, she'd dab the tears from her eyes with a linen napkin. He'd say something like, "I wouldn't be standing here tonight if it weren't for my beautiful wife who has been by my side through it all. Baby . . ." Even though there were a thousand other people in the room, his eyes would focus only on her. "Thank you for being *you*." Everyone in the ballroom would smile at her and everything they'd gone through to get there would be worth it.

Honk! Honk!

Laura snapped out of her fantasy and realized she was sitting at a green light. "Sorry!" she yelled, as if the driver of the truck behind her could hear.

When she pulled into the Landrys' driveway, she noticed Rob and Janet's car wasn't there. "Sweet," she said to herself, imagining all the things she and Brian could do to celebrate this rare occurrence.

Laura opened the front door and yelled her husband's name. The house was dark and silent. She walked to the back of the house and noticed the light was on in their bedroom.

"Brian?" she called out again.

A moan responded.

Panicked, she ran toward the door and found Brian lying on the floor. "What the hell? Brian! Are you okay?" She dropped her bag and kneeled down next to her husband.

Brian's blue eyes fluttered open, looking unfocused. "I'm jus' *turd*," he slurred.

"*Turd?*" Laura asked, confused.

"Tie-errrred," Brian enunciated, using all the energy he could muster up.

Laura lifted him up and propped him against the white bed frame. "What happened?"

"Jack," he said, his lips puckering.

"Who's Jack?" she asked, gently pushing his hair off his forehead. She glanced around, half-expecting some guy name Jack to jump out of their closet.

"*En* Coke."

Her eyes narrowed. "Jack and Coke?" She felt as though she were in French class, trying to interpret what the hell was being said.

Brian nodded in an exaggerated way.

Laura looked around and realized there was an empty handle of Jack Daniel's sitting on his desk and Coke cans scattered all over.

"Get up and get in bed," she said, sighing. She tried to lift his body off the floor, but he weighed twice as much as she did. Brian grunted and managed to flop onto the mattress.

"I'll be right back," she said, heading straight to the kitchen to brew him a cup of coffee. She returned quickly and handed him the mug carefully. "How did you get this drunk?" she asked as he took a sip.

"Kenny," he said, not looking at her.

Laura tried to force away her irritation, but it was just so typical that she'd spent her whole night working her butt off for nothing while Brian sat around drinking with useless Kenny. "So, Kenny force-fed you Jack and Coke? Way to own up to your own mistakes," she spat. This was *her* room, too, that he'd trashed. She grabbed the empty handle and cans. "What were y'all doing in here anyway?"

"Jus' chillin'," he said, taking a sip of the coffee.

Holding three cans and a bottle, Laura started to head out the door when Brian yelled out, "Missed one!" and threw an empty aluminum can toward her. It flew just a few inches past her head and landed on the floor.

"Oh my god!" she screamed. "That could have hit me!"

He put his hand over his mouth, as if knowing just how much trouble he was about to be in. "Sorry . . ."

Laura huffed and walked out of the room into the kitchen, where she tossed the cans and bottle into the trash and stomped her foot in a rage. *There's nowhere to go!* she thought to herself. All she wanted to do was slam a door, but Brian was taking up the bedroom, and going into the bathroom just wouldn't have the same effect. She noticed the back door to the porch, stomped over, and slammed the door shut behind her. It made a satisfying echo in the house.

She sat on the glider, her anger festering inside of her. A little while later, Brian finally opened the door and joined her.

"I'm really sorry, babe," he said, sounding a tad more sober now. She didn't know if it was the coffee or her rage, but at least he was forming complete sentences.

Laura crossed her arms and looked off into the yard, where a rope swing dangled from a giant oak tree. When they were younger, Brian used to push Laura on the swing. It always made her feel like she could fly. But now, this whole house made her feel stifled. "I'm so pissed at you."

"You have every right to be," he said, lightly touching her shoulder, as if uncertain it was welcome.

She didn't turn to acknowledge him. "You've got to get it together," she said, resolutely staring into the distance.

"I will," he said softly.

She snapped her head toward him and glared. "*Now*, Brian." She was tired of all of this.

"Okay, jeez," he said. He leaned his head against the back of the chair. Laura could tell he was having trouble keeping it up. His eyes were glassy, and he looked out of it. "I'm basically sober now."

"Right," she said sarcastically. Then she sighed. "You've got a problem, Brian. I'm worried about you." She braced herself for him to get defensive, to say that she couldn't understand what he was going through, to push her out like he'd been doing over the last few months.

Instead, Brian took a deep breath, and said: "I'll quit."

Laura's eyebrows shot up. "You'll quit drinkin'?"

"Yeah, why not?" Brian said. His head was still resting drunkenly against the yellow floral chair cushion, but he actually sounded like he meant it.

"Can you write that down so you'll remember it tomorrow?" she asked.

"I'm for real," he said. "No more, I swear. Promise." He held out his pinky. They had been doing the pinky promises since they first started dating five years ago. Usually Laura used it in ways, like, "Promise you'll call me every night while you're stayin' with your granny for Christmas?" and "Promise you'll still love me even if I don't make cheer captain?" This was the first time Brian initiated it, and it was the first time it involved anything serious.

She extended her right hand and grabbed his pinky with hers.

"I can't tell you how much I'm looking forward to going back out on the field," Brian said, shifting his hand to interlock their fingers. His palm was warm and strong against hers, and for the first time all night, Laura felt calm.

"I know," she said, squeezing his hand.

"Everything that we worked for, it's gonna happen," he assured her. "We're going to save enough money and I'm going to get this surgery, and all of our dreams are going to come true. I promise that, too."

A knot of tensions felt like it was slowly unraveling in Laura's chest. "Have you talked with Coach Perkins lately? Didn't he tell you to keep him updated on things?" Keeping after Brian about stuff like this sometimes made her feel like his assistant.

"He called me last week. Tried to talk me into just going with the surgery they'll pay for, the one the doctor said probably wouldn't help me. I said no." He laughed. "And Coach said, that's why he admired me. He liked my determination."

"He probably feels a little guilty that they can't cover the operation, but you know he wants you back on the team." *God, I hope he can play again*, she said silently to herself. She barely recognized Brian these last few months. All he did was drink and mope around; what would happen to him if he could truly never get back out on the field?

"Don't worry, babe," he said. "We'll make it happen."

Laura bit her lip. She believed that Brian meant what he said . . . but how long would it take them, between her waitress salary and his poker? "Wait," she said, an idea popping into her head. "I was watching this show about doctors with your mom the other night." Truthfully, it was a weight loss reality show on TLC, but Brian didn't need to know that. "And one of the patients appealed to their insurance and they actually came back and paid for the whole surgery." If that insurance company on TV had paid for someone's gastric bypass, maybe theirs would reconsider Brian's surgery. His whole future was on the line.

"I don't know, babe," Brian said, looking skeptical. "Don't you think that's just . . . TV?"

Laura shrugged. "Maybe. But if there's a chance that it could work, shouldn't we try? At least we'll have given it a shot."

Brian nodded slowly. "Why not, I guess? I don't know how we even go about doing that, though. It sounds complicated."

It was so nice to hear Brian sounding hopeful for once. "I'll figure all that out," Laura said, starting to feel excited. This was what they *both* needed—a little bit of hope. "We'll get through this, and it's all going to happen, just like you said. Then you'll go back, play for LSU, get scouted by the NFL, and be a famous quarterback."

Brian wrapped his arm around her shoulder, pulling her close. "And we'll buy a mansion," he said, burying his head in her hair. His breath was warm against her neck, and she felt a happy tingle down her spine.

"Can it have a Jacuzzi?" Laura asked, fantasizing about the bathrooms she and Janet drooled over during their HGTV binge-fests. The type of person who had a bathroom with two showerheads and his and hers sinks would never have to clean up a million crawfish heads to try to impress their boss.

"It can have *five* Jacuzzis," Brian said, pulling away and flashing that confident smile that made Laura fall in love with him in the first place.

"We'll be such a power couple," she said, grinning back at him. Her mind flashed back to the banquet she had envisioned just a few hours before on her drive home. "You really think it'll happen?"

"I promise," he said, leaning back and putting a hand over his stomach. His eyes fluttered closed.

"How are you feeling?" she asked. "Still *turd*?'"

He chuckled and hung his head in shame. "I'm an ass, huh?"

"Yeah, but for some reason I keep puttin' up with you," she said with a small smile.

They fell into a comfortable silence. Janet's wind chimes jingled in the cool evening breeze and a neighbor's dog barked nearby. She stared up at the sky, where the stars seemed to shine brighter than usual. Laura felt like they were on the precipice of something great. They couldn't be working this hard for nothing.

She blinked as she saw a light streak across the sky. "Oh my god, do you see that?" she said. "Is that a shooting star?"

"Huh?"

"I swear I just saw a shooting star!" Laura squealed. She had never seen one in real life before.

Brian squinted at the sky. "You sure it wasn't an airplane?"

"I don't think so," she said, refusing to let doubt creep into her mind. "I'm gonna just say it was one. It went by so fast!"

"Cool," Brian said, his eyes fluttering closed sleepily.

"You can make a wish on those, right?" Laura asked. He shrugged his shoulders. "Well, I think that's what you're supposed to do. I'm gonna do it, okay?"

She closed her eyes tight and tried to think of the biggest wish she could make. There were so many things she wanted—make that *needed*—at this moment. How was she supposed to choose? Then, it hit her. There was one wish that would cover everything. She quietly recited to herself, "*I wish for Brian to keep all of his promises.*"

gabrielle

GABBY COULD HAVE sworn that the Fords' cast-iron gargoyle doorknocker was leering at her. She'd been standing in front of their wooden front door for too long, shivering in the November chill. She knew she needed to knock and go inside, but something about the gargoyle stopped her. It was like it was staring her down, judging her for all her lies. *Stop being silly*, she told herself, trying to shake off the feeling. With a deep breath, she knocked, and moments later, Tony appeared, greeting her with a wide smile and sweet kiss on the lips.

"You look amazing," he said, guiding her into the foyer of the Fords' massive Victorian home. "Happy Thanksgiving!"

He looked like a J. Crew model in his khaki pants and a cozy burgundy sweater, his sleeves pushed up slightly. He casually held his glass of bourbon in his right hand.

Love rushed through her. "Gosh, I missed you," she confessed as she hugged him again. She inhaled his scent, trying to take all of it in—his signature Polo Black cologne, the hint of Tide lingering on his soft sweater—never wanting to let go. She planned on telling him everything tomorrow; this might be their last day together, and she was going to make it count.

"I have a surprise for you," he said with a big smile.

She looked up at him, wondering what in the world he could have for her this time. "You and your surprises . . ."

He laughed. "This one isn't a ring, I promise! It's a person. Guess who's here. . . ."

"Is this my future daughter-in-law?" a deep voice greeted her. A giant bear of a man with salt-and-pepper hair walked over. His deep brown eyes—just like Tony's—squinted, assessing her. He was much taller and more intimidating than the pictures Tony had showed her.

Gabby forced a casual smile, trying not to look nervous. "Hi, Mr. Ford! It's so nice to meet you." She held out her hand, hoping neither of them would see it was trembling. She was even more nervous about meeting him than she was about meeting any of the rest of his family. It was probably the way Tony talked about him, like he was hard to please.

He walked over to her and stopped. "None of this handshake business," he said, waving her away. "We do hugs around here." He swooped in and squeezed her tight. "Welcome, sweetheart."

She let out a sigh of relief, surprised and soothed by the man's warmth. For a moment she forgot she was supposed to be nervous about coming clean to Tony tomorrow.

"Gabrielle, Tony tells me some great things about you. In fact he won't *stop* talking about you." Mr. Ford chuckled as the three of them walked through the mansion, the old hardwood floors creaking beneath them.

"Oh, lovely—you're here!" Mrs. Ford said as they entered the kitchen. She was wearing a forest green silk top, black pants, and a strand of pearls. Her hair was twisted into an elaborate updo, reminding Gabby of Laura's hair during the pageant phase she went through sophomore year. "Come here, darling," she said, walking over to Gabby with open arms.

The two hugged, and Gabby stayed in her arms just a little longer than she probably should have. The motherly embrace was so comforting. Whenever she visited her mom at the prison, their hugs were quick, under the cold stare of a guard.

"Thank you so much for having me," she said, finally letting go.

"Well, I would have been offended if you *didn't* come!" she said, holding Gabby's cheeks with her hands. "I just can't believe you two are engaged! We need to toast this properly as a family. That's why I called Raymond and said, 'You better get your butt over here and meet this wonderful future daughter-in-law of yours. The governor can pardon that turkey himself!' So he came home a little early.'" She took Gabby's hand and led her to the bar cart in front of the bay window. The setup looked like it was straight from the pages of *Southern Living*. "Champagne?" Mrs. Ford poured some Veuve Clicquot in a crystal flute and handed it to Gabby.

"This is just Mom's way of making sure you're not knocked up," a voice from behind added. "Y'all got engaged so fast, after all."

Gabby choked on her champagne and turned to see Carter, Tony's seventeen-year-old brother, coming down the stairs.

"Oh stop," Mrs. Ford said, swatting at his shoulder. "It's not too late to ship you off to boarding school, you know."

He laughed and walked over to Gabby. "Congrats," he said, greeting her with a sweet hug. "You're like the sister I always wanted."

"*Excuse* me!" Tony and Carter's twenty-two-year-old sister, Willow, came down the stairs, popping her brother on his shoulder. She walked over to Gabby and hugged her. "It's so good to see you again!" She grabbed Gabby's left hand and studied the diamond. "Beautiful! Did he tell you he picked this out all on his own? Boy's got some serious taste."

Gabby laughed. "Yes, he does," she agreed.

"Good taste in jewelry, good taste in girls . . ." Mrs. Ford squeezed Gabby's shoulder. "I'm just over the moon that all of us could be here together to celebrate this happy occasion."

That sick, nervous feeling came back, knotting Gabby's stomach. How could she pretend to be happy today, when tomorrow her heart might be broken?

Tony whispered in Gabby's ear: "She's on her second glass of champagne. She'll be saying stuff like this for the rest of the night—just a warning."

"To Tony and Gabrielle," Mr. Ford said, raising his glass high. "Welcome to the family, sweetheart."

She raised her flute to him and smiled. *If only.*

• • •

"SO, HAVE YOU guys talked about a date yet?" Mrs. Ford asked, passing the cranberry sauce. The wine had been flowing over the course of dinner, and they'd fallen into one enjoyable conversation after another. It was inevitable that wedding talk would come up at some point, but now—maybe it was the wine, or the comfortable presence of Tony's parents—it didn't really bother Gabby. She just let herself soak it in and enjoy the little time she had left.

"Not yet. Just taking it one day at a time." *As in, one day from now, we might not be engaged anymore.* She scooped some mashed potatoes onto her plate.

"Do you know what kind of wedding you want?" Willow asked from the other end of the table.

"Um, we haven't really talked about it yet," Gabby said, pushing her turkey into her cranberry sauce.

"You must have some idea," Willow said, taking a sip of wine. "Heck, I'm not even dating anybody, but I've got my wedding already planned out."

Gabby laughed, but she understood. She and Claire had been playing "bride" since they were eight. They'd found a couple of old bridal magazines in the local library's giveaway box, and each built a dream book. Gabby's was filled with everything she could possibly want for her wedding day: a lace sheath dress, a cake with multiple levels, and of course a handsome groom in a tux.

"Yeah, we haven't discussed this yet," Tony said, wiping his face with his napkin. "What's your fantasy wedding?"

She thought back to those magazine tear-outs, to the day she'd planned down to the littlest details. "Well . . ." she said softly, feeling a twinge of excitement. "I've always pictured a classic southern wedding. Magnolias everywhere . . . maybe an outdoor ceremony at an antebellum mansion covered in oak trees?"

"Gorgeous!" Mrs. Ford said enthusiastically.

"Have you set up your Pinterest board yet?" Willow chimed in. "There are so many great ideas for DIY projects. I'll help you with anything you need. If you want to go shopping for a dress or need help planning or making chalkboard signs, I'm your girl."

"Ooh! Me, too," Mrs. Ford said, her third flute of champagne in her hand. She and Raymond exchanged a knowing glance, then smiled at Tony and Gabby. The loving look they were both giving the couple was so . . . parental. For the first time in her life, Gabby could imagine what it would have been like growing up in a normal family. "Also, we want you both to know that we're planning to foot the bill for this whole event, so there's no need to stress about money, okay? I know Tony's got a lot of student loans to pay off and your parents . . ." She cocked her head to the side and smiled softly, her eyes tearing up a little. "Well, this is just something we want to do for y'all."

Gabby gasped, about to protest, but Tony spoke before she could.

"Thanks, Mom," he said, putting his arm around Gabby's chair. "We really appreciate it."

Gabby's eyes began to water just like Mrs. Ford's, though for another reason. She looked around the table at all the love surrounding her. Tony, his family . . . they were all so wonderful. They really made her feel like she was one of them, and she could want nothing more. An irrational thought crossed her mind and she latched onto it. Maybe she didn't have to tell Tony the truth after all. It'd been six months and he hadn't found out yet. Maybe—just maybe—she could get away with it. The idea took root in her heart. She could do this.

She had to.

claire

@Pastor_Gavin: "Stand up, be brave, and confront your fears with determination. God's got your back. #StrongerWithHim"

Claire stared at her computer screen and sighed as she reread her tweet. It had been two weeks since she had spotted Gavin at The Saddle—a really long, hard stretch of time that she spent vacillating between righteous anger and fear for their marriage. She knew that she needed to talk to him, but something kept stopping her. It was as though acknowledging it would make it more real. In their three years of marriage, she and Gavin had fought, but it was about small stuff: whose turn it was to empty the dishwasher or who would get up at 3:00 a.m. when Sadie started crying. They'd always been on the same page for the big things, and she'd never once questioned Gavin's commitment to her. Maybe it was all a misunderstanding, like her mom said. But what if it wasn't? What would she do then?

She hadn't told her friends yet, and with every day that she didn't confront Gavin, she thought of how hard she'd pushed Gabby to come clean to Tony. It was hard to tell the truth, but as it turned out, it was just as hard to ask for it.

Taking her own tweet to heart, Claire said a quick prayer and walked down the hall, knocking on Gavin's open office door. "You have a second?" she asked, standing in the frame, her stomach in knots.

He looked up distractedly from his computer, his black frame glasses slipping down his nose. "For you, always."

"Wanna go for a walk?" Claire asked, holding her shoulders back and ignoring how her palms had begun to sweat. "I just need some fresh air."

"Sure, babe."

They walked through the quiet church gardens, shivering in the crisp November air, and settled onto a stone bench nestled in between pansies and geraniums.

"How's your day going?" Gavin asked, pushing his glasses up his nose.

She turned toward him, pulling her sweater closer around herself. "It's . . . it's fine. Look, you always say you need to practice what you preach, so I'm gonna do that, okay?" She took a deep breath.

Gavin cocked his head to the side. "Is everything okay?"

Claire scuffed her black-heeled boots against the ground, anxiety coursing through her veins. "Remember when I went to the Gumbo Fest with the girls? I was driving behind you and you didn't go home. . . ." A lump formed in her throat. "I saw you at The Saddle, Gavin."

Gavin's brow furrowed. For a long moment he just stared at her and bile rose in her throat. Then he put his warm hand on hers. "Why didn't you come to me sooner? This had to have been eating you up for days." He ruefully half-smiled. "Claire, if you would've just talked to me, I would've told you why I was there."

Claire pushed her wind-blown hair behind her ears, confused. "And why's that?"

Gavin started stroking her palm with his thumb. "One of the girls who works there has a kid and a drug problem. Her aunt asked me to intervene and help her." He squinted up at the sunny blue sky. "I should've just told you, but the girl's abusive ex is trying to get custody of the kid, so her aunt asked me to keep it a secret. If the ex found out, she could lose her son." He looked her directly in the eye. "I'm so sorry if you thought anything inappropriate was going on."

Claire's entire body went slack—she hadn't even realized how tense she'd been. *Of course* it was just for church outreach. Of course. "So, were you able to help the girl?"

"I hope so. It's a really sad situation." He shook his head. "But I think I was able to get through to her."

Claire felt like a fool. Her husband was such a good man, and all she'd done was jump to conclusions and throw accusations at him. "I'll pray for her," Claire said, squeezing his hand.

Gavin smiled and kissed her on the forehead. "By the way," he said, frown lines wrinkling his brow, "why did you follow me? Do you not trust me?"

Claire's stomach clenched. This whole time she'd thought Gavin was jeopardizing their marriage, when in reality, she had been. She'd created a problem where there was none, and gone as far as following him.

"Of course I trust you, Gavin. I was just so confused when you said you'd be at one place and ended up driving in another direction. But I never should've just assumed something without asking you about it." She buried her face in her hands. "I feel like I've failed our marriage."

Gavin wrapped an arm around her shoulders and pulled her in toward him for a kiss. "You could never fail me, Claire. I love you."

"I love you, too," Claire said.

"We should probably get back to work," Gavin said, checking the time on his iPhone. "I've got a couple coming in for premarital counseling in ten minutes."

Back at her desk, relief washed over Claire, followed by a twinge of guilt. Why did she even question Gavin? She'd known there had to be another explanation. That's why she'd been so mad at Madison in the first place. She flashed back to his wedding vows. Gavin had thanked God for putting her in his life, and had promised to Him, their families, and their friends that he would always treat her with love and respect. That he would always be faithful and believe in them, even when times got hard.

Claire thought about her accusation, how she'd doubted his faithfulness. That wasn't showing belief in him—or *them*, for that matter. But as awful as she felt about the whole situation, she was experiencing a renewed sense of their relationship. God worked in mysterious ways, and it was time she showed that she had as much faith in her husband as she had in Him.

With that, she pulled up Twitter and typed: *"When things get dark, remember that God is ready with the flashlight."*

madison

MADISON HAD BEEN on her best behavior in the months leading up to the Mardi Gras Ball. She had laughed at George's lame jokes, accompanied him on a few dinner dates, and even invited him to Christmas dinner with her family when she'd discovered he'd had nowhere to go. But now, strolling with him through the bustling streets of the Big Easy, Madison felt all the effort had been worth it. Within five minutes of walking outside their hotel on Canal Street, they had already stumbled upon a parade. As they turned onto Bourbon Street at one thirty in the afternoon, crowds of people were lined up on both sides, yelling and holding their hands out, begging for tacky plastic beads.

Madison had never been one for organized fun. She'd skipped every homecoming pep rally in high school, and ditched Toulouse's annual fais-dodo dance party to make out with Cash in the back of the Sea Shack. Something always felt so forced to her about these events, but now she couldn't help but get caught up in the revelry.

"Throw me something, mister!" she yelled at a middle-aged man wearing a glittery top hat. He was walking in front of her and carrying dozens of strands like a rainbow-colored wreath.

"*Show* me something," he said with a lewd gesture, dangling some cobalt baubles in front of her.

"Pfft," she said and motioned for him to move on. "Take your blue balls somewhere else."

George's mouth dropped slightly. "Well played!" he yelled into her ear.

"Thank you!" she said, dusting off her shoulder with her right hand.

A trio of toga-clad women sporting curly cotton-candy-pink wigs and purple masks walked past, followed by a marching band pounding on drums and blowing their horns. Then came a plump gray-haired woman who was Mardi Gras' answer to Big Bird. Gold feathers covered every inch of her dress and fluttered from her lamé headband. In her hand were heavy strands of metallic beads.

Her glitter-covered eyes caught Madison's. "You," she mouthed, pointing her perfectly manicured finger directly at Madison.

She pointed at herself. "Me?"

The woman stopped right in front of her. "You're too pretty not to have any beads, darlin'!" She draped a couple of purple and green strings around Madison's neck.

Madison flashed a smile, and then the lady was on her way.

George whooped. "Guess I'm gonna need to start catchin' up." He unbuttoned his navy Patagonia vest and started to lift his gray T-shirt, as if to flash the crowd.

"What the hell are you doing?" She laughed, gently hitting him on the shoulder before he could lift the shirt any higher. He was so dorky. "Here, take this." She put one of the strands around his neck. "There. Now you're one of the cool kids."

"That's one hundred percent not a true statement, but thank you anyway." He zipped his vest back up and leaned against the black column of the building behind them.

"Let's keep walking," Madison said. "We only have twenty-four hours in New Orleans, and I've got things to do." She'd been counting down the days to this trip since George invited her, making list after list of the places she wanted to see. She even had to tamp down her excitement in front of friends, given their misgivings about her relationship with George, but now that she was here—and none of her friends were around—she allowed herself to embrace it.

"What's on your list?" he asked as a person from the balcony above dropped a strand of beads on their heads.

"Getting assaulted by drunks. Check!" she said, looking up at the rowdy group of guys leaning over the ornate wrought iron railing and yelling "Flash! Flash!" at her.

"And welcome to Mardi Gras," George said wryly. "Let's get out of here."

They walked along Chartres Street, passing a restaurant called Napoleon House. "You hungry?" he asked. "The food here's great."

"Can we get it to go and sit in Jackson Square?" she asked. "It's on the list. . . ."

George nodded. "Sounds good to me."

They stopped in and grabbed their food—a muffaletta for him, a po'boy for her—and began walking toward the park. On the way they passed a streetlamp with a black and white sign that read RUE TOULOUSE. She pulled out her cell phone and snapped a picture of it to send to the girls.

"I can see why you come here so much," she said as they sat on the bench in the park. The Parisian-style square had manicured hedges and towering oak trees. St. Louis Cathedral loomed in the background, its dark spires stretching to the blue sky. It was the most beautiful place she'd ever been.

"Usually it's not so crowded, but it's one hell of a city." George shielded his eyes and looked out over the park. It was hot for February, almost seventy degrees, and the sun picked up reddish highlights in his dark hair.

She took a bite of her sandwich. "Oh my god, this is so good."

The fried shrimp was perfectly cooked and the bread was fresh from the oven. She smiled, remembering the time last year when Laura was craving a po'boy, so they attempted to make one for dinner. Laura burned the shrimp—along with a piece of her hair—then read the recipe wrong, putting half a cup of salt in the seasoning instead of half a teaspoon. Needless to say, it was inedible.

After they threw their sandwich wrappers away, George checked his phone. "So, we've got a couple of hours until we have to go back to the hotel to get ready for tonight. What's next on the list?"

Madison grabbed a handful of photographs from her bag and handed them to him. She felt suddenly shy.

"What are these?" he said, holding up a picture of a young Johnny Depp look-alike circa 1990 wearing a leather jacket and pair of torn jeans. A cigarette hung from his mouth as he posed in front of a red streetcar.

"Don't make fun of me," she said. "But I found these pictures of my dad's trip to New Orleans when he was my age, and . . ." She paused. "No, never mind. It's stupid."

George's eyes widened. "What? Really . . . tell me."

"Well, I had an idea to re-create some of these for his birthday present." She turned toward him. "It's dumb, right?"

"Not at all," he said, grabbing her hand. "Come on! I know where all these places are."

They first ventured to William Faulkner's house, across from the park. In the bookstore in the bottom floor of the house, she touched a copy of *The Sound and the Fury*, posing like her father had with his signature stoic look. She kept breaking into laughter, though, so George had to take a number of pictures before they got it right.

Next, they stopped in front of Marie Laveau's House of Voodoo on Bourbon and St. Ann. She mimicked Allen's playful scaredy-cat pose outside of the building. After the picture was snapped, she begged George to go inside and try out the voodoo dolls. "I've got some enemies I need to take care of," she said.

But he adamantly turned the invitation down. "Heck, no," he said, shaking his head. "I don't mess with voodoo—that's some serious stuff."

She laughed and held up another picture of Allen. "But you'll do cemeteries, right?"

He reluctantly nodded his head and walked her to St. Louis Cemetery No. 1 on Basin Street.

"Man, these have been around for a while," she said, turning through the maze of crumbling above-ground tombs.

"There it is," he said, pointing to a spot on the path that looked the same as the one in the picture.

She leaned on the black wrought iron fence, a deteriorating brick tomb standing behind her. Her expression was solemn and pensive, like her father's. It wasn't until after George took the picture that Madison thought about the morbidity of the whole situation. Her dad was sick with cancer, about to die, and she was making a photo album for him that included a picture of her in a graveyard.

Her throat tightened. "Let's go," she said gruffly, grabbing the picture out of George's hand.

"Are you okay?" he asked as they walked through the bustling streets back to the hotel.

She nodded her head and changed the subject. "I'm looking forward to tonight. Anything I should know before we go? Are there any weird rituals or songs I need to be aware of?" She couldn't help but feel a little nervous. Back at home, she knew what to expect at parties, and hell, she ruled them. But a few kegs and warm cans of Natty Light in someone's backyard were a far cry from a black tie event.

"It's a Mardi Gras krewe, not a cult," George said, opening up the door to the hotel entrance.

She laughed and stepped into the lobby.

"But if you must know, we all dress up in hooded capes and sing Latin ritual songs by candlelight. Newbies in the group—like yourself—have to dance in the middle."

"Pfft," she said, then paused. "Wait . . . really?"

George laughed. "I'll pick you up from your room at six thirty."

• • •

MADISON TOOK A long shower and then snuggled up on the king-size bed, wearing the white cotton bathrobe she found in the closet. She ate the overpriced cashews from the minibar and sipped sparkling water while admiring her room. Blue and burgundy silk drapes framed the windows, thick striped wallpaper covered the walls, and gold mirrors hung above an oversize mahogany desk. This was the type of hotel the folks whose houses she cleaned would stay in, not people like Madison Blanchette, and all this luxury was thanks to George driving his gleaming Porsche into her life.

"Be jealous, losers," she texted Claire, Gabby, and Laura alongside a picture of her hotel room.

After that, she dried her hair, put her makeup on, and walked over to the closet, where the old pageant gown she borrowed from Laura hung. The cut of the emerald strapless gown was simple, but the fabric shimmered with thousands of green sequins. She slipped into it, zipped it up, and admired herself in the mirror for a moment. Madison felt *classy*—an adjective she had never used when describing herself.

Back in the bathroom, she pulled her hair up in a neat bun like Laura had showed her. Her friend had packed an entire makeup bag filled with bobby pins and a travel-size bottle of hairspray. "Now, you're gonna have to spray the shit out of this to keep everything in place," Laura had said, bobby pin in mouth.

Madison wished Laura could be there to help her now. The bobby pins kept popping out of the bun and the spray made her hair look clumpy and stiff. She screamed with frustration after a third failed attempt to smooth it down, then furiously took the pins out one by one and flipped her hair over, letting the waves hover just above the marble tile floor. She scrunched the ends, then swung her head back up and looked in the mirror. Her hair was a bit wild, but it would have to do, especially since George was knocking on her door.

As Madison walked over to let him in, she almost tripped on the small train of fabric trailing behind her. She turned the doorknob and blinked.

George's brown hair was combed neatly back, and there was even a slight sheen to it (maybe *his* friend told him to spray the shit out of it, too). His tux fit him perfectly, emphasizing the width of his shoulders and the narrow V of his waist beneath his black cummerbund. His bow tie was jaunty, and his shoes gleamed beneath his slim-fit pants.

"Wow!" George finally said, his green eyes shining. "You look stunning."

"You're not so bad yourself," Madison admitted, impressed. She thought of his immaculate house and wondered if he was one of those guys who was actually more comfortable in black tie than in a T-shirt and jeans.

George cleared his throat, then held out his right hand. Nestled in it was a robin's egg blue square velvet box with the words *Tiffany & Co.* stamped across it.

"I thought you said there wouldn't be any *Pretty Woman* stuff happening this weekend." She kept her voice light and teasing, but she had to clasp her hands together to keep from reaching out and grabbing the present.

He chuckled and walked into the room. "Well, you don't have to give this one back." He opened the box, which held a long strand of pearls. "You'll get a lot of beads around your neck tonight, but I thought you should have at least one set that was just as special as you are." The words were rushed, like he had recited that line all afternoon and was hoping not to mess it up.

A knot formed in her stomach as Madison took in George's earnest expression and shining eyes. Sure, she had hoped George was going to start buying her things—hell, that was pretty much the only reason she started hanging out with him—but seeing the look on his face now, she couldn't help but feel a little guilty.

Snap out of it, she commanded herself as she ran her fingers over the smooth pearls. It wasn't like she was stealing from him.

"I love it," she said, doubling the strand around her neck. "It's the nicest thing anyone's ever given me."

• • •

"HAVING FUN?" GEORGE yelled, spinning Madison around the dance floor.

"Heck, yeah," she cried, flushed from the heat of the bodies swirling around her.

The event was in the ballroom of an old mansion in the French Quarter, where a ten-piece jazz band presided over an increasingly drunk crowd of dancers. Of course that was after the five-course meal, the crowning of the krewe king and queen, and the debutante portion of the evening.

Finally, the stuffy society people were letting loose, dancing with martinis and gin and tonics in hand. Madison was completely sober; every time George went to the bar, he came back with club sodas with lime. He took that whole under-twenty-one thing very seriously.

Still, she was having a great time. George had introduced her to the mayor and a famous local musician who was up for a Grammy. He seemed to know everyone in the room. Who knew that nerdy George could hold court at a ball?

"Want to take a break?" George asked breathlessly as the song ended. Madison nodded and they stood off to the side, sipping their seltzers. A moment later, a middle-aged couple they had briefly said hi to earlier approached them. Madison had already forgotten their names.

"So, George," the woman said, touching his arm. She wore a black satin gown with an elaborate bow on one shoulder. Her silver hair was in a neat bun, and teardrop diamonds hung from her ears. Madison tried not to eye them too hard; they could've paid for at least six months of her family's mortgage. "We were really shocked to hear about Henry—I just couldn't imagine him running off to St. Maarten to get married. It's a little barbaric if you ask me." She waved her white-gloved hand. "Why travel when he could have had his wedding at your beautiful family home."

Madison tipped her head, wondering who Henry was.

"How was it, George?" the man said, swirling his glass of bourbon. "St. Maarten?"

"Oh uh, I . . . I couldn't make it." George paled slightly and tugged at his bow tie. "Had to work."

"George, you need to remember to take breaks from work. Life goes by too fast." The lady put her hand on his arm. "He's your brother, after all."

As George coughed awkwardly, understanding dawned on Madison. Remembering what he'd told her about his family drama, she stepped in front of George. "I'm so sorry to interrupt," she interjected, smiling sweetly at the woman. "But, George, I've been dying to check out the exhibit at the front. Will you head over there with me?"

"Yes, of course," George answered, shooting her a grateful look. "Maggie and Mark, it was so nice to see y'all again."

As they walked to the front, George put his arm around her shoulder. "Thanks for that. Maggie and Mark were close to my parents, but they were always a little too . . . inquisitive for my taste."

"You mean nosey?" she said bluntly. "Yeah, I got that. So do you actually want to see the exhibit or should we call it?"

"I think I've officially had my fill," George said. "What do you say to one more adventure before we head home, though?" His eyes sparkled.

"I'm in." She nodded, and he took the club soda drink out of her hand, putting it on an empty table. They walked outside to a line of town cars. Madison hoped one of those was George's—her feet were killing her, thanks to Laura's sparkly gold heels.

He grabbed her hand and led her to the third one in line. Madison breathed a sigh of relief and crawled into the backseat. "So, where's this other place you want to take me?" she asked.

"You'll see," he said, his green eyes flashing with excitement.

The car drove through avenues and narrow streets, along the water, and finally pulled up next to a large café with a striped green awning and a large sign that read CAFÉ DU MONDE. George held up one last picture of her dad, where his nose was covered with powdered sugar at the famous beignet stand. Madison smiled at George's thoughtfulness. She'd never met anyone quite like him before.

They re-created her father's picture and sat for the next hour, eating beignets and drinking chicory coffee, laughing about how one of the debutantes had tripped on the way to the stage and the krewe king had gotten so drunk he threw up into an antique vase.

Before they knew it, it was almost midnight. They hopped in the town car and headed back to the hotel. As they approached the front doors, Madison paused.

"Thank you," she said genuinely. "Really. Today was so great." There was something about standing there in an elegant dress with a man in a suit, full of beignets and coffee, and surrounded by the sounds of the big city. She felt more sophisticated somehow. More interesting. More . . . *happy*.

"I had a really good time with you, too."

He walked her back to her room. Before she went inside, Madison leaned in to give George a hug. His arms wrapped around her and held her tight, almost for a beat too long. When he pulled away, he looked at her longingly, like he was about to kiss her.

"Well, good night, then," she said, stepping out of his embrace before he got the chance.

George looked down at his feet, a slight flush rising to his cheeks. "Good night, Madison," he said. He stood there for another minute, like he wasn't sure what to do next. Then with one last embarrassed smile, he went on his way.

Madison shut the door behind her and flopped onto the bed with a groan. She could just hear Claire asking her what the heck she was doing to that poor lonely man. She liked George. She did. She had more fun today than she'd had in a long time, but she'd been clear that it was just a friendship for her. Hadn't she? But the way he'd looked at her, then hung his head as he shuffled back to his room . . .

She pressed the heels of her palms to her eyes, trying to push all the guilt aside. Other than that last awkward moment, the whole day had been an amazing dream. Mardi Gras . . . Jackson Square . . . Café Du Monde . . . A ball . . .

She grinned, running her fingers over the gorgeous pearl necklace around her neck. This was the kind of life she could get used to.

20

laura

"I JUST FEEL like things are finally starting to get better," Laura said into the phone. She hadn't talked to her mom in over two weeks. Her parents had been on a Caribbean cruise to celebrate their twentieth anniversary.

"It sure does sound like it," her mom said. "I knew that boy was gonna turn things around. Sometimes they just need a lil' tough love is all. I still have to shake your daddy up every so often. They'll never be perfect, but you've just gotta accept that, as long as they're trying."

"Oh, he's definitely trying," Laura said as she lay on the bed, staring at the ceiling. Brian was playing Grand Theft Auto with Rob in the living room. As much as she loathed video games, she welcomed the excuse to have time to herself. "There's just a new side to him," she said.

"What's going on with the surgery? Any word from the insurance company?" her mom asked.

"Way to bring me back down, Mama. I'm still working on the appeal forms," she said, pouting her lip. The forms were unexpectedly complicated—they needed Brian's entire medical history and letters from the doctors and LSU's training staff. Between the sheer amount of paperwork and her work and school schedules, it felt like it was never going to get done. "But we're determined to do it, no matter what. I've saved about twenty-five hundred dollars from my work, and Brian's made a couple a thousand, too. We're just puttin' it all into savings right now."

"How much more do you need?" her mom asked with a concerned voice.

Laura sighed heavily into the phone. "Like thirty thousand more."

Her mom let out a laugh and then quickly apologized. "I'm sorry, hon. That's just an obscene amount of money. You sure it's worth it? Why don't you just convince him to just do the surgery the insurance will pay for? They have to believe it'll work if they're gonna cover the cost."

"No, that one will just fix his knee, but he most likely wouldn't be able to play again. He's determined to be back on the field next year, and I truly believe this surgery is the answer. I would pay a hundred thousand if I had to." Laura closed her eyes, picturing Brian back on the field in a Tigers uniform, sweeping to the right in a designed run play, the whole stadium roaring.

"I definitely support you, you know that," her mom said in a placating voice. "I'm prayin' for y'all and hope you can make it happen this year."

"Thanks, Mama." Laura opened her eyes. "It'll be so nice to just get on with our lives again. I'm so tired of this place."

"How's school going?"

"I'm still a little overwhelmed, not gonna lie. There was a lot of catching up to do to make up for missing that first month, and I think it's still hurting me." Just talking about school made her anxious. From the girls who talked about her behind her back to the stress of classes, she was ready for it to be over.

"What are your grades like?" her mom asked.

"Fine. As and Bs as usual." She shrugged. "I'm struggling in math a little, which is weird, because that's always been my best subject. We're just in a section that goes over my head a little."

"Well, I'm sure you'll figure it out." Her mom paused. "I don't think I say this enough, but I want you to know how proud I am of you."

Laura hadn't heard that in a while. "Thank you." She smiled. "I'm tryin' hard."

"I know you are, sweetie." Her voice trailed off. "Okay, I need to go. Your daddy is lookin' like a lost little puppy in search of food. A woman's work is never done, I tell ya."

"K, I love you both," Laura said, sitting up.

"Love you!" She tapped END CALL and jumped off the bed with a renewed energy. She knew she and Brian had a long road ahead of them, but Laura finally felt like they were on the same journey. He had quit drinking, was actually making money with the online poker, and together, they were getting closer to the possibility of surgery every day. It had been a struggle, sure, but Laura was beginning to feel proud of herself for everything she had been doing. For the first time in weeks, things were finally looking up.

● ● ●

"A 'D'?!" LAURA huffed under her breath. The red ink in the top right corner of her quiz looked like a nonsensical squiggle.

Vince leaned over and saw her grade. "Everyone has those days," he said sympathetically.

Over the past few months, Vince had become her only friend at school. After Laura had heard Riley, Rory, and Emma talking about her in the bathroom, she'd confronted them, and told them she didn't need their friendship if that was how they really felt about her. Unfortunately, that led to the cheer girls initiating an unspoken ban against her at all of their social functions and the cafeteria table, which made school a lonely place.

Vince, who couldn't care less about his social status, despite being a star on the football team, had stepped into their place, at least between the hours of seven thirty and three fifteen. But even though they'd become friendly, she could never quite get what he'd said to her in the library out of her head: *"You're obviously smart. Why'd you drop out?"*

"What'd you get?" she asked, not really sure she wanted to know the answer.

"It doesn't matter," he said, shoving the paper in his bag.

"Yes, it does!" she said, her competitive side coming out in full force. "Give it!"

The two fought over the paper for a second. Laura's giggles stopped abruptly when she finally got hold of it.

"An 'A'? You nerd!" she whispered, flashing a bright smile to hide her jealousy.

Mr. Leblanc had finished passing out the papers and was now back at the front of the room. "If you were less than happy with your pop quiz results," he said to the class, "I have good news. You have a whole week to study for the test next Tuesday."

Laura stifled a groan and resisted the urge to face-plant on her desk. Vince scribbled something down on a sheet of paper, folded it up, and passed it to her discreetly.

The note read: "I'll help you study."

Laura stared at the missive. It felt a little weird that he was swooping in with a "Don't worry, babe" attitude. It's not like she was his girlfriend. But that red D stood out like an ugly zit on her quiz, and she had to admit she needed help. Who else would do it? Brian? Ha.

"OK," she scribbled, and passed the note back to him.

After the bell rang, Vince walked with her to the south wing, where she had English with Mrs. Baldwin.

"So, when do you want to study?" he asked, fist-bumping a fellow football player as they passed each other. For a second, Laura felt like the clock had rewound to last year and she was walking with Brian again.

They stopped in front of her classroom, and she hugged her books to her chest. "Can we do today? I have to work the next two nights."

"Yeah, we can do it at my house." He rubbed his jaw. "Does that work?"

Laura nodded, even though she secretly felt a little uncomfortable going over to another guy's house. *Whatever.* She brushed it off. *We're just studying math.*

• • •

THE SMELL OF Hot Pockets wafted through the kitchen as Vince took the snacks out of the microwave. He put them on a plate and brought them over to the dining room table, where Laura sat surrounded by textbooks, notebooks, calculators, and pencils.

"My favorite!" Laura exclaimed. "Wait—" She glanced at the intricately patterned blue and white dish. "Is this your mom's nice china?"

Vince shrugged. "All of the other dishes are dirty."

Laura laughed. "Way to class it up."

He grinned and took a bite of his Hot Pocket. "Okay, let's get down to it. What'd you get wrong on the test? Maybe we can start there."

Laura took out the piece of paper, feeling somewhat embarrassed to show him all the red ink. He studied it for a second and nodded his head.

"Okay, it looks like you got the mean down, you're just getting messed up on the variance, and that's ruining your standard deviation results." He looked up at her with his gorgeous hazel eyes. "So, like, let's say you were trying to calculate the standard deviation of the bitchiness levels of girls like Riley, Emma, and Rory. . . ." He muffled a laugh and started scribbling down numbers on his notebook. "Riley's a ten, Emma's a seven, and Rory's a four."

"Hmm . . . I would have thought the numbers would have been much higher," Laura said, trying to sound serious, although cracking a smile. "But do continue."

"Well, for the purposes of this exercise, we're doing it on a scale of one to ten, because I don't want to use numbers that reach into the thousands." He tapped his pencil on the paper.

Laura twisted her hair and laughed.

"Okay, so you know the mean is seven, that's easy," he said, writing the equation down. "To find the variance, we square the group's total level of bitchiness, then square them individually and subtract that number from this one." He pointed his pencil to his scribble and looked up at her. Their faces were so close, she could feel the heat of his breath as he talked. He looked back down and continued. "Then subtract one from your data set, and divide these two numbers." She realized she was still staring at his face.

She shook her head to refocus her attention back on the paper. "Okay," she said, punching numbers into her calculator. "Eighteen divided by two is nine." On the paper it looked so hard, but all of a sudden she got it—it was so simple!

"Awesome!" Vince said, giving her a high five. "So, now just take the square root of that number and you'll have your standard deviation."

She didn't even need a calculator for this one. "Three!" Laura shouted the number out with excitement, sounding like a contestant on *The Price Is Right.* "The standard deviation of the bitchiness of Riley, Emma, and Rory is three!"

"Ding ding ding!" Vince raised his arms and shimmied a little. Laura blushed.

"Here," he said, pointing his pencil to a problem in his textbook. "Try this one."

Laura started entering numbers into her calculator. Minutes passed as they both tried to figure out the problem, scribbling digits into their notebooks. Sure, she could figure out a small number equation, but this had five numbers, all in the thousands. That D on the quiz had shaken her confidence.

Vince put his pencil down. "What'd you get?"

"Is the sample standard deviation two thousand and seventy-one point eight?" Her voice reached the high pitch it always did when she was unsure of herself.

Vince held his hand out, palm up.

"Wait—that was right?" Laura asked excitedly, high-fiving him.

"Well, that's what I got, too, so either it's right or we're both the same amount of stupid." He shot her a sly grin.

Laura grinned back and rewarded herself with a Hot Pocket.

"Should we try another one?" Vince asked, flipping the page. He pushed up his gray long-sleeve shirt, revealing his muscular forearms. Laura's eyes lingered on them a beat too long and she felt her face growing red. She averted her gaze. "Sure."

They raced each other, like they did in class. He scribbled; she scribbled. He coughed; she huffed. Finally they both yelled out "Done!" within mere seconds of each other.

"What you got, Landry?" Vince asked.

"Twelve," Laura said, more confidently this time.

Vince shook his head and dropped his pencil onto his notebook with a clatter. "You're a genius. What are you even doing here . . . just stealing my Hot Pockets?"

Laura let out a laugh. "Thank you. I feel like I'm finally getting it now. It's a shame I didn't do this well on the quiz."

"Maybe you were just having an off day. It happens." He leaned back, running his hand through his dark hair. "Like, just the other day, I accidentally said *coucher* instead of *cochon* to a question in French class. So instead of talking about a pig, I basically asked Ms. Bellerose if I could sleep with her."

She burst out laughing again. "Oh my god!"

Vince blushed. "Anywayyyy," he drawled. "Back to you. So, you're obviously smart. What college is going to be lucky enough to have you on campus next fall?"

This again? "No college," she said firmly.

Vince's eyebrows furrowed and he leaned closer. "Why, though? With your grades, you could probably get a scholarship."

"Why are you trying to plan my life?" Laura snapped. The truth was, she'd never given college much consideration. No one in her immediate or extended family had a degree, and they all seemed to be doing just fine. The only reason her husband was going was for football, and the idea of her applying felt disruptive, like even thinking about an alternate future could adversely affect her and Brian's life.

Vince held up his hands and gave her a placating look. "Okay, I'm *definitely* not trying to plan your life, and I'm sorry if you feel like I am." He paused. "I just think you have so much—and forgive me if this sounds guidance-counselory—*potential*."

"I'm pretty sure Mrs. Walker has a poster in her office that says that exact thing." Laura smiled in spite of herself.

Vince chuckled. "Sorry, forget it."

"So, what's your big plan, then?" she asked. "What are *you* gonna do when you graduate?"

"Well . . ." Vince blushed, looking proud and embarrassed at the same time. "I just signed with Duke. They gave me a full scholarship."

"Wow, seriously? How come you never said anything?" Laura was floored. When Brian signed with LSU, he made sure everyone in the whole town knew. It was literally headline news in the *Toulouse Town Talk*. Ricky even hosted a party at the Sea Shack to celebrate.

"I guess I just didn't want to make a big deal out of it." Vince shifted uncomfortably in his chair. "Don't get me wrong, I'm definitely excited."

"So, are you hoping to go pro?" she asked.

He leaned in toward her slightly, as if he had a secret. "Just between us, I'm only doing the football thing so I can pay for school."

Laura didn't know what to say to that. No one in Toulouse put education over football . . . not even the teachers. "Wow," she repeated. "Well, good for you."

As they dove back into their schoolwork, Laura kept sneaking looks at Vince from under her lashes. She'd never met anyone like him before, someone who actually valued getting an education. It made his words weightier somehow. He thought she had *potential*. That she was bright.

Brian constantly told her how beautiful and pretty she was. But it occurred to Laura that in all their years together, he'd never once praised her for being smart.

gabrielle

"WHERE ARE YOU taking me?" Gabby asked Tony as they turned down a gravel road in the small town of Vacherie. When she'd met him at his apartment earlier that day, he said he had a surprise for her, but they'd been driving for more than an hour and—while she relished getting to spend extra alone time with Tony—Gabby was starting to get antsy.

"Okay, I guess we're close enough," Tony said, keeping his eyes on the road. "Remember at Thanksgiving when you described your dream wedding? The antebellum mansion and old oak trees?"

In the two and a half months since Thanksgiving, she had let herself relax into her role as a bride. Her new method of handling her situation was willful denial—it was all tomorrow's problem. Willow had helped her set up her Pinterest board, which was now covered in floral arrangements and pictures of peach-colored brides- maid dresses. Gabby had even gone old school and bought up all the bridal magazines Walmart had to offer. There was still a little voice inside her head screaming that she was a fraud, but it grew quieter with each day that passed without anyone finding out her secret.

"Yeah." She looked out the window as the car turned onto a nar- row oak-tree-lined street.

"Well, I found it!" A large white house appeared in the distance. He glanced up at her and smiled, his dark eyes crinkling around the edges. "I thought we could check it out and see what you think."

Gabby gasped as they made their way closer. A path lined with towering, ancient live oak trees led to a large, majestic antebellum home straight out of *Gone With the Wind*. Imposing two-story Greek revival columns framed the mansion's wraparound porch and balcony. Moss grew on the oaks, the lawns were perfectly manicured, and green shutters bordered each window. She looked back at Tony, speechless.

"What do you think?" he asked, pulling into the small parking lot on the side.

"It's straight out of my dreams," Gabby replied. In fact, she had a photo of a home just like this in her wedding book. But that—along with everything in the wedding book—had always seemed like a far-off fantasy, a wedding for a different, luckier girl. Her heart swelled.

Tony grinned. "Good."

As they got out of the car, a petite young woman in a beige tunic dress and cowboy boots came briskly down the path, carrying a clipboard and iPad. "Tony and Gabrielle?"

"That's us," Tony said, shaking her hand.

"I'm Missy, the event coordinator. It's nice to meet y'all." She ushered them toward the mansion, sliding a headset over her sleek black bob as she walked. "We have a wedding tonight and the bridal party will be here in twenty minutes, but that should be enough time for you to get a feel of the place."

They followed her up onto the porch, and with a grin, Missy instructed them to turn around and look out onto the front yard. Gabby's jaw dropped. The view was even more beautiful from here. The lawn seemed endless, rolling across the horizon, and directly in the center of her view were the incredible, enormous oak trees. They bowed together as if kissing, forming a moss-laden path.

"So, this is where most of our wedding ceremonies occur," Missy said, gesturing to the porch and yard. "Gabby, you would walk down the oak alley from the back." Gabby could picture it already: she would be in an elegant, flowing gown, walking slowly down the aisle. Maybe Tony's father would agree to escort her and give her away. Tony would be waiting for her at the altar, flanked by his brother and all her best friends. "And then all of the guest chairs would be in the yard facing this porch." Missy put her hand on Tony's shoulder. "Tony would be waiting for you right here."

"Oh my god, it's perfect," Gabby said as she surveyed the setting. It was a dream she didn't want to wake up from.

Missy opened the large front door and they passed through the hall into an intimate seating area adorned with gold and silver antiques and a large chandelier. "This is where the groom's party would get ready and hang out before the ceremony." She nudged Tony's arm. "And indulge in some prewedding mint juleps if they'd like."

Across the hall was an even bigger room with a cozy fireplace. The chairs and sofa were covered in blue velvet, and the small round coffee table was set with floral teacups. "And this is the bridal party area." Gabby could see Claire, Laura, and Madison in there, helping her into her gown and toasting her with a glass of prewedding champagne. Willow would be a bridesmaid, too, and she'd fit right in with Gabby's friends. Maybe Tony's mom even would lend her a family heirloom as her "something old."

They followed Missy to a reception room in the back of the mansion, which must have once been a formal ballroom. It was decorated for the upcoming wedding, each table covered in white linens, gold dishes, and cutlery. The centerpieces were overflowing with lilies, and the dance floor glowed under soft lighting. Gabby put her hand on her chest. It was stunning.

"How many people does it hold?" Tony asked.

"You can comfortably fit two hundred people in the reception hall for a sit-down dinner," Missy said. "But if you decide to have the reception outside, we can set up a tent and easily triple that number." She turned her gaze directly at Tony, assessing him shrewdly. "I'm sure your family has a large invite list."

He nodded then turned to Gabby. "What do you think, babe?"

She looked around. This was exactly what she'd always pictured for a wedding and now she could reach out and touch it. "I love it."

"Great!" Missy started tapping on her iPad. "Well, I do want to let you know I'm pretty much booked solid for the next two years," she said. "But I *do* happen to have one spot available for April fifteenth of this year." She leaned in conspiratorially. "Big cancellation. It was supposed to be a five-hundred-person wedding, but the bride's mother was so controlling that the groom called it off, and the couple eloped to Vegas." She shuddered. "I know the date is only a little over a month away, but since it happened so recently, I would imagine that all their vendors are still available."

Tony's smile widened as he put his arm around Gabby's waist. "What do you think? Should we reserve it now?"

She looked around the room one more time. "It's so . . . perfect," she breathed.

Tony squeezed her gently. "Then it's done. We'll book it," he said, kissing the top of her head.

"Okay, great!" Missy said, tapping her iPad with a stylus. "We've got a lot of things to discuss, but unfortunately I've got a bridal party coming in five minutes, so we'll have to schedule another meeting to finalize all the details." She handed Gabby her business card. "I have the date saved—you just have to put down a nonrefundable five-thousand-dollar deposit by Monday for me to keep it for you guys. Sound good?"

Gabby nodded her head slowly, the word *nonrefundable* echoing in her mind. A deposit made the wedding feel real, and while this was what she wanted, the guilt she'd worked so hard to keep at bay since Thanksgiving came rushing back. What if something happened—what if Tony found out about everything—and they had to cancel it? A pit grew in her stomach.

"No problem," Tony chimed in. "We'll have it to you first thing Monday."

"Perfect!" Missy hugged them both. "We're gonna make sure this wedding is so magical, you're going to feel like you're living in a dream."

Gabby flashed a nervous smile. It wasn't the dream she was worried about. It's what would happen when reality set in.

22

madison

"SO, HOW WAS it?" Claire asked Madison as she chopped bell peppers for the seafood rice she was making for dinner. A country song played in the background on her laptop. A man with a deep voice sang, praising chew tobacco, bourbon, and the man upstairs.

"It was . . . it was really nice," Madison said, leaning forward on the counter to see Claire's chopping skills in action.

"Well, did y'all kiss?" Claire looked up and smiled.

"Oh god, Claire." Madison huffed. "You don't have to be awkward about it." She walked over to the fruit bowl and grabbed an apple.

"Um, when have you ever not kissed and told?" her cousin said. "I always have to hear about what you've done with Cash . . . at least let me have this one, where I genuinely care."

"Yeah right! You genuinely care only so that you can make me feel guilty . . . like I'm using this poor guy to get money. Well, guess what. I don't feel guilty." Madison flashed a sly grin.

At first the car ride from New Orleans had been filled with overly bright observations (*Oh! Look at that Tesla!* Or: *I think that truck driver is having a little too much fun by himself* . . .) and long pauses, as if neither of them could quite move past their awkward good-bye the night before. But by the time they'd hit Baton Rouge, Madison had George laughing so hard he almost drove off the highway. When he'd dropped her off at home, he'd given her a hug and invited her to Harvest, the nicest restaurant in Lafayette.

"Fine," Claire said, chopping the pepper harder now. "Well, don't come crawlin' to me for advice when this whole little plot of yours bites you in the butt."

Madison chomped down on the apple. The way things were going, she thought she'd need Claire's advice just about never. "You'll be the last one I call. Promise." She perched herself on the countertop.

"Why are you still here?" Claire said, looking up at her very comfortable house guest. "You're not stayin' for dinner are you? 'Cause I only got enough for me and Gavin."

"Nah, I'm gonna go home." She shook her head and dangled her feet. "I haven't seen my parents much since I've been home from New Orleans."

"What the heck have you been doing?" Claire looked up at her with judging eyes. "You've been home for two days now."

"I got busy." Madison shrugged her shoulders, thinking of how Cash had shown up on his motorcycle and taken her away to his parents' cabin, fake-casually asking how her weekend with George was before throwing her down on the futon.

She jumped from the counter, her feet landing on the floor, and kissed her cousin good-bye on the cheek.

"Love you," Claire said as Madison walked out of the room.

"Sure ya do," she yelled back with sass.

• • •

"WHAT ARE Y'ALL doing?" Madison asked when she walked into the den and saw her parents boxing up her mom's collection of porcelain dolls. She'd always found their round eyes and overly made-up faces creepy, but they were her mom's prized possessions.

"Oh, just doing some spring cleaning," her mom said in a high voice. She looked at her husband as if to say, *Did that sound convincing?*

"It's not spring yet," Madison pointed out. "Why are you getting rid of your dolls?"

"We're gonna have a garage sale," her dad said, taking a sip from his blue tumbler. There were dark circles under his eyes and his hands trembled slightly. "Out with the old, in with the new."

Madison processed this conversation for a moment. "Does this have anything to do with money?" She turned to her mom, who couldn't tell a lie. "Are y'all selling things because Daddy isn't working anymore?"

Her mom teared up but didn't answer.

"Daddy?" Madison asked, turning to her father.

He walked over to her and put his hand on her shoulder. "Gotta pay the mortgage somehow, darlin'."

Madison's stomach dropped. She knew times were tight but had no idea it had gotten *this* bad. "But, Mom. You love those things." Madison looked at her mother as she boxed up Bella, her beloved blond doll who wore a satin pink dress covered with bows. "There's gotta be something else we can sell, right?" She glanced at her dad.

He walked over to the glass sliding door and looked out at the old rickety boat.

"Don't even think about it," Madison begged. That boat was more than a possession—it was their memories, and something that would last long after her dad's illness had stolen him from them.

"That should give us a couple 'a thousand." He walked back over and put his frail hand on her head. "I'm sorry, sweetie, but we need to do this."

"I'll fix it," Madison blurted out. "I'll get the money. I promise."

She went to her bedroom and closed the door. A wave of sadness crashed over her, and she couldn't control the tears. The last time she had cried was when she got into a fistfight with Jenny Wiggins in seventh grade. That girl was a bitch. And strong. And probably still had that clump of hair she yanked from Madison's head stored in some weird collection she kept of her enemies' body parts.

Madison looked around her bedroom. It was pretty bare—there was nothing she could sell, save for the signed Black Keys poster Cash brought her from a music festival he played at last summer. But the money she'd get from that would be mere pennies. She looked at her white dresser and caught a glimpse of the Tiffany box sitting on top of it. Madison stood up, walked over, and opened it up. The strand of pearls felt heavy in her palm.

She shifted the necklace from one hand to the other, the pearls hitting against each other with a light clack. As much as she loved them, they didn't feel right in her hands. Pearls like these belonged to the rich ladies she and her mom worked for, not her. They needed to be in a velvet-lined jewelry box among other pearls and diamonds and gemstones, not next to a couple of faux leather-wrap bracelets and a cheap metal ear cuff from Claire's Accessories. She wasn't meant to have nice stuff, she convinced herself. Not when she had the chance to help her parents.

• • •

"I GET A cut, right?" Cash asked as they walked to the pawnshop on Main Street.

"Yeah, right," Madison said, holding the box tightly in her hand. According to the quick Google search she'd done before they left the house, she had to have been carrying a couple of thousand dollars. It would be enough to tide her parents over for a month or two.

"Pfft," Cash said. "You wouldn't even know what to say to ol' man LeRoy. I'm a regular pawner. He's good to me."

"You get me a good trade, and I'll give you something good," Madison said with a flirty wink.

"It better involve you being naked," Cash said, running a finger along her waist.

"Gross," she fired back at him.

"Hmm . . . you don't usually seem to think that," he said, grinning.

She turned to face the road, waiting for the crosswalk signal to turn. As they stood there, shivering in the cloudy weather, guilt settled in her stomach. She remembered how George had rehearsed his speech when he gave her the necklace and how eager he'd been to clasp it around her neck. But then she closed her eyes and thought about her parents and their house. She nodded, steeling herself—this was the right thing to do.

A line of cars began passing them, a parade of rumbling motors and exhaust fumes. One of the cars honked twice from up the street. Madison turned her head toward the sound and watched as a silver vehicle drove toward them. As the car slowly made its way across the intersection, she realized it wasn't just a silver car. It was a silver Porsche.

Her whole body went weak as the vehicle inched closer, coming to a gradual halt in front of her. The window rolled down and George flashed her a goofy grin. She forced herself to smile and waved with her hand that wasn't holding the necklace. *Maybe he won't see*, she thought, quickly hiding the box behind her back. But she was too late. He blinked twice and, as if in slow motion, turned his head to look across the street at the neon-lettered LEROY'S PAWN SHOP sign. Her heart sank as he glanced back at Madison and Cash, lowered his eyes, and waved good-bye. She stood there, mouth open as his silver Porsche drove away.

"What the hell was that?" Cash asked after the car was down the road.

Madison stood there speechless, looking at the blue box in her hands. She felt as though she might throw up, and it had nothing to do with that hot dog she had for lunch.

"Oh my god," Cash said. "Was that him? Was that the old guy?"

Madison dropped her head in her hand, not wanting to believe what had just happened.

Cash laughed out loud. "Oh man, this is great," he said. "Just great."

"Shut up," Madison said, punching him in the arm. "Just shut up, okay?" She tried to collect her thoughts and figure out what to do. For the first time in her life, Madison felt evil. Like, no-good, scummy, nasty evil, and she didn't like it.

"Geez, what's up your ass? It's not like you actually liked him," he said, turning to her. His harsh voice turned sweet, and he lifted her chin with his finger. "Want me to kiss you and make it better?" Before she could even answer, he bent down, and right in the middle of Main Street, he kissed her.

"Better, right?" Cash said when he pulled away.

Madison nodded her head. But of course she didn't feel any better. Cash of all people should know that she was just really good at lying.

23

laura

AS MR. LEBLANC handed back the graded tests, a mix of cheers and moans filled the room. Laura prayed that she wouldn't fall into the latter group.

"Nice work," her teacher said, tossing a paper on her desk. Her entire body relaxed when she saw the "A-" scribbled at the top in bold red ink. She looked over at Vince, who gave her a thumbs-up, then spotted the "A+" written at the top of his. *Of course.*

Vince and Laura left class together, passing Riley, Rory, and Emma, who were huddled around a desk, comparing their bad grades. Laura and Riley locked eyes, and both quickly turned away.

Laura smiled at Vince. "I think we should celebrate," she said as they walked through the hall. Lockers clanged open and shut, and a group of sophomore girls bumped into them, blushing when they saw Vince.

"What are you doing after school?" Vince asked. "Want to check out that new ice cream place that just opened up, Delicious-something or other?'"

Laura laughed. "You mean 'Udderly Delicious'?"

"Seriously?" Vince wrinkled his nose.

"Yeah. Tragic, right?" It was a family-owned shop. Horrible name, but according to the *Town Talk*, great ice cream.

"Completely. You in?" He adjusted his backpack on his shoulder, and Laura caught a whiff of his woodsy cologne.

"Yeah, sure," she said. "Oh wait. Do you mind if Brian comes, too? I forgot, he's picking me up today." Though Brian was still hobbling around with a brace on his leg, it was luckily on the left side; he was comfortable behind the wheel now.

They'd finally finished the insurance appeal over the weekend, and ever since they'd mailed it, Brian had almost been back to his old self. He whistled while he helped his mom make her famous crawfish soup, and they'd even managed to have sex yesterday morning without Janet walking in on them. Still, as much as she tried to push her unease aside, something was bothering her. Perhaps she was just worried about the appeal. It was one thing to send in the paperwork; it was another to get the green light on the surgery.

If she was being honest with herself, though, Vince's comment the other week had gotten under her skin. He'd said she had potential—but for what, exactly? She was working so hard in school, but she didn't know to what end. Was a diploma from Toulouse High as far as she'd go? And was it really enough to stand from the sidelines, cheering Brian on?

"That'd be cool," Vince said, snapping her out of her thoughts. "I'd love to finally meet 'The Legend.'"

Laura raised her eyebrows at the sarcastic edge to his voice, but Vince just winked and told her he'd meet her in the parking lot after school.

Before her next class started, she bent down in her seat to text Brian from inside her backpack. Mrs. Baldwin had a policy of making you read your last five text messages out loud if you were caught with a phone in class. Laura blushed thinking about the sexy selfie she had sent Brian from work the evening before. As she tapped the screen, she noticed he had already written to her.

Can't make it today, babe. You'll find a ride?

A strange feeling of relief washed over her. "No prob," she typed and then tucked the phone back into her bag just as Mrs. Baldwin called for attention at the front of the room. For some reason, she had a feeling she'd have more fun if he wasn't there.

• • •

"I'M SERIOUS!" LAURA squealed, laughing so hard that her face was probably the color of her red velvet ice cream.

The parlor was surprisingly modern, with Lucite tables, a blond-wood soda fountain bar, and brushed metal stools. The owner of the shop, an overweight middle-aged guy, hummed along to the zydeco music playing on the speakers. He crumbled up Red Hots and cinnamon into chocolate ice cream while shaking his shoulders along with the music. His moves reminded Laura of her dad, who was physically incapable of cleaning up after dinner without dancing to eighties music.

"You mean to tell me Mrs. Baldwin had *no idea* her skirt was tucked into her tights? I don't believe it!" Vince laughed. "Also, she's like a hundred. No one wants to see that."

"I know," Laura said. "Also, I can't believe none of us told her. That's kind of bitchy, huh?" She flashed a devious smile.

"Wasn't she the one who made Jack Robicheaux *cry*?"

"To be fair, she confiscated his vintage *Playboy* collection, and we all know how, um, special those are to him." Laura shuddered. "And he got two months of detention because of it. But yeah, that's her. The infamous Mrs. Baldwin."

"Karma, man . . ." he said, scooping out a chunk of his Tabasco jalapeño ice cream. "Okay, I'm gonna try this. Wish me luck." He took a bite and looked up at the ceiling with a thoughtful expression. "Not bad," he said. "Not bad at all." He pushed the cup toward her. "Here, try it."

She dipped her pink plastic spoon into his ice cream. "This is weird," she admitted as the flavors—somehow both spicy and sweet—dissolved on her tongue. "But I like it." Laura scooted his bowl back to him. "Can you believe there's only a few more months left of school?"

"Yeah, it's insane." He shook his head. "What are ya gonna miss the most?"

Laura considered the question. She'd already had the experience of leaving high school, so in many ways, she'd already made her peace with it ending. "Well, not the people, that's for sure. My three best friends are out of high school already, and as for everyone else . . . frankly, I'll be happy if I never see any of them again." She shrugged.

Vince grinned. "Really? You won't miss *anyone*?"

She snuck another quick bite of his ice cream. "Okay, fine. I might miss you, study buddy. But only because you share your snacks." He laughed again, and Laura felt a warmth bloom in her chest. "To be totally honest, though, I think I'm going to miss school-work. I know it's so nerdy, but there's something incredibly satisfying about doing a problem and getting it right."

He nodded slowly. "I completely agree. And not to keep poking at a sore spot, but that's part of the reason I'm excited to go to college."

She scraped the bowl with her spoon to get the last bits of her ice cream. "Well . . . I've been thinking about what we talked about the other day," she said. "You know, the whole me-not-going-to-college thing."

His eyes sparkled. "Oh yeah?"

"I even had a dream the other night where I was walking across a college campus with a bunch of heavy books in my bag," she confided. "Well, at first they were books but then they turned into spray paint canisters, and this guy wearing a leather jacket—who I think was supposed to be John Travolta—started serenading me." She took a sip of her Coke. "I had fallen asleep watching *Grease*," she explained.

Vince nodded with an "Oh, that makes more sense" kind of look.

"But when I woke up, that feeling of being on campus as a student lingered. It was nice to be there as something more than a visitor. It just felt—I don't know—*right*," she confessed.

"Maybe your dream was trying to tell you something," he said, resting his elbows on the table and leaning closer.

"I don't know. You think?" Laura looked up at him.

He nodded enthusiastically. "You're one of the smartest people I know." His voice softened. "You should go to college, kid." He playfully nudged her foot under the table.

"Thanks, man," she said, nudging him back. "I'm gonna look into it, I think." She knew that many of the deadlines had passed, but now that Brian's insurance appeal was finally done and submitted, she actually had time to do some research. Maybe she could even go to LSU with Brian when he returned for the next football season.

She tucked her hair behind her ear, suddenly a little embarrassed. "I just wanted to say thank you for encouraging me to do this. I know I was kind of a brat when you first brought it up, but the idea has grown on me."

Vince's eyes lit up. "Well, I'm happy I could help."

"Can I ask you something?" she said. "How long have you had your life planned out?"

He gave her a surprised look. "You think I have my life planned out?"

"Well, yeah . . . you've got a spot at one of the best universities in the country and they're actually *paying* you to go there. You seem like the type to have it all figured out." She paused and smiled. "You already know what you're gonna be when you grow up, don't you?"

Vince laughed and glanced out the window, where a woman wearing an LSU sweatshirt was pushing a stroller. "I'd love to be a surgeon, so I'm going to study premed in college. That doesn't mean my life is planned out, though. No one's life is. There are always gonna be things you didn't see coming, some good, some bad. Like, did my parents plan to live here? Nope. Did your husband plan on hurting his knee? No way. Did I think I was ever gonna eat Tabasco ice cream and like it?" He pointed his spoon into his empty cup. "Hell no."

Laura chuckled. "I get all that, of course." She lowered her head, and suddenly the uneasy feeling she'd been trying to keep at bay washed over her in full force. "But you gotta have some goals. The only thing is, I'm looking at my life and realizing—my goals are all for someone else. I've planned my husband's fantasy life and decided it was my own: *Brian* would go to college. *Brian* would get into the NFL. *Brian* would make us a lot of money. And I'd be along for the ride. Now, I'm not sure what to think." She squirmed a little in her seat. "I don't know why I'm telling you all of this."

"No, I totally understand." He nodded. "And I can relate, kind of. I was dating a girl pretty seriously back in Atlanta. We always talked about the future, and I'd even given her a promise ring," he said. "When my family left to come here, we tried to make it work—FaceTime, texting, the works. Then one night, she asked me point-blank what was gonna happen to us. And I just sat there, completely silent, unable to come up with an answer. In my heart, something had changed, and I no longer saw her in my future. So we broke up."

"Aw, I'm sorry to hear that," Laura said, wondering if that's what would have happened if she'd stayed in Toulouse to graduate when Brian went off to LSU. It had been her worst fear, and the main reason why she'd quit school in the first place.

"But that's the thing, Laura." He sat up in his chair. "Things change. And you can't regret anything that you've done. You make decisions based on what you can see in that moment. Sometimes the view shifts."

Laura raised her eyebrows. "That's deep."

"Yeah, I got that in a fortune cookie at the China Café on Main Street." He grinned.

She laughed. "Well, that's really deep for them. I got one last month that said, 'You have rice in your teeth.'"

As he chuckled, she started crumpling up bits of her napkin. "This whole thing with Brian's injury shook me up a little. Don't get me wrong—we're happily married, and I love him so much." She blinked, the backs of her eyes suddenly burning. "But it made the future seem less certain and made me wonder what I was doing for my own life. Like, career-wise. Even if I do become an NFL wife someday, shouldn't I figure out some of my own interests? I think I want to do something, though I don't have it planned out quite yet—at least not like you do, Dr. Williams."

He smirked. "Well, I have a feeling everything will come together for you. Even without a plan, you seem to be doing just fine. As I said, you're one of the smartest girls I know."

His voice turned serious and he held her gaze. She had never stared so openly at him before, and she noticed that his hazel eyes had little flecks of gold at the center. His full lips were curved up in a slight smile, and for a moment, she wondered what it would be like to kiss him. And from the way he'd begun to lean in to her, ever so slightly, she could have sworn he was thinking the same thing.

A customer came in, jingling the bell over the door. Just like that, the moment broke. Laura cleared her throat guiltily, sitting up straighter in her chair. Vince blinked and shook his head a little, as if coming back to himself.

"Thank you for the pep talk," Laura said, feeling a little unbalanced.

"Anytime," he said too loudly, before changing the topic to some prank a wide receiver had pulled on the football water boy.

Laura smiled along and soon the tension dissipated, as did the knot of guilt in her chest. It had just been one errant thought and Vince had caught her at a vulnerable moment during the rockiest time in her relationship. With Vince she had the luxury to be her freest self, away from the tension of filing appeals, saving money, and navigating nosey in-laws.

What she had with Brian was hard but real. And, she reminded herself, with the insurance paperwork in the mail and nearly ten thousand dollars in the bank, they were the closest they'd been to their dream life since he'd collapsed on the field all those months ago.

24

gabrielle

"I'M SO HAPPY you're here." Elaine reached her dry, cracked hands across the square table. The fluorescent lights of the visitation room made her mom's skin look dull and yellowed. Since the last time that Gabby saw her, the lines around Elaine's eyes had deepened, and her frown lines had grown more pronounced.

The room buzzed around them—families reunited, husbands and wives talking in hushed voices, visitors trying to cheer up their imprisoned friends—but Gabby tried to tune them out and focus on her mom.

"It's been months," Elaine said, lowering her eyes. "Why didn't you come for Christmas?"

"I've been busy, Mama." Gabby squeezed Elaine's hands. *Busy lying about you,* a guilty voice said in her head.

The prison guard walked past them, her boots clicking on the gray tile floor.

"You're glowing." Elaine's lips curled into a mischievous smile. "Who's the guy?" Her mother put her elbows on the table and leaned in eagerly.

Though Gabby hadn't visited recently, she and her mom had been keeping up with their regular biweekly calls, but Gabby knew she'd been distant on the phone. She hadn't told her mom about the engagement yet—hadn't even told her about Tony—and was afraid that she'd hurt her mom's feelings. Here, finally face-to-face with Elaine, she wouldn't be able to hide the truth.

Gabby took a deep breath. "Mama . . . I'm getting married next month." She leaned back, bracing herself for her mom's reaction.

Elaine's eyes widened. "Oh," she said softly. "I just thought you might be dating someone. But marriage? Wow. I can't believe . . . I can't believe I'm going to miss that."

Gabby paused, her shame intensifying. She didn't know what to say to that. "It all happened so fast," she confessed. "We just picked out the venue last week."

Elaine sat up straight and pushed her curly brown hair behind her ears. "Well, tell me about him." She was smiling, but it didn't reach her eyes. "Tell me about my new son-in-law."

Gabby lowered her head. "I'm sorry I didn't tell you sooner." *I'm sorry about so much more than I can tell you. . . .*

Elaine put her hands across the table, her eyes looking deeply into Gabby's. "I understand. This . . . it's hard. But I'm really happy for you." She softened her tone. "Tell me about him."

"Well, his name is Tony, and he's a lawyer," Gabby said, fidgeting with her engagement ring. "He's so smart, Mama. And funny." She smiled, thinking about him. "And kind . . . and has a wonderful family."

"That's great, darling. That's so great." Elaine swallowed, glancing away. "So, tell me about the wedding. Where's it gonna be?"

Elaine's words felt weighted, and Gabby realized that her mom might be jealous. She was spending time with another family, making memories that had nothing to do with Elaine.

Gabby took a deep breath, trying to squash her guilt. It wasn't *her* fault that her mom was in jail. "Tony found this gorgeous antebellum home—it's got huge oak trees and a ballroom. It's absolutely beautiful."

"Wow! Sounds so classy." Elaine paused, as if steeling herself. "Have you picked out a dress yet? Is . . . is his mom going to go shopping with you?" Tears filled her eyes. "I can't believe I don't get to be there when you pick out your dress."

Gabby's heart sank. She hadn't thought about how painful this would be for her mom. "I'm not going with his mom. No one will ever replace you, okay?" She swallowed, trying not to cry, too.

Elaine gave her a watery smile.

Gabby continued, "I'm going with Laura tomorrow."

"The girl who used to do pageants? Wasn't she Miss Maple Bacon Praline Pie or something like that?" Elaine laughed, wiping the tears away.

Elaine and Gabby had gone to that pageant to support Laura, and it was about the cheesiest thing they had ever witnessed. So much off-key singing during the talent competition, and one too many answers about world peace during the Q&A. Needless to say, Laura won by a landslide.

Gabby nodded, smiling nostalgically. "That's her. She's taking me to a store a half hour out of town that she used to get her pageant dresses from—she says they had a whole section of wedding dresses."

"Well, that's just lovely," Elaine said, looking like she meant it. "You're gonna be such a beautiful bride." She sighed. "I just wish I could be there to see it in person." She began to cry again.

"You'll be there with me in spirit, Mama," Gabby said, her stomach twisting.

"Well, it's my own fault," Elaine said, shaking her head.

Gabby couldn't deny that, but she felt for her mom. It was hard to imagine getting married without Elaine by her side—she couldn't even imagine what Elaine must be feeling. She reached out and grasped her mom's hand again, giving it a supportive squeeze.

"So, you'll come back here with Tony soon?" Elaine asked, brushing away tears with her other hand. "I'd like to meet him."

Gabby nodded slowly, but she knew there was no way that could happen. She'd been trying not to think about this. Eventually Elaine would be out of jail, and Gabby could only hope that she and Tony had been together long enough by that point that she'd have come clean to him . . . or that he would be so committed to her that he wouldn't care. It was a problem, she kept telling herself, for another day.

"Well, I can't wait to meet him." Elaine paused. "He's a *lucky* guy." She smiled.

Gabby lowered her head, unable to keep holding her mother's heartfelt gaze. *Something like that.*

• • •

"AND THEN AS the reception ends, they're gonna hand out sparklers to everyone, and Tony and I'll run through them to the car," Gabby told Laura as she drove them into the parking lot of Lilah's Gowns. After the visit with her mom, she'd been feeling down, but talking about the plans with Laura was getting her excited for the wedding all over again.

"That sounds gorgeous!" Laura said, unbuckling her seat belt. "So, what kind of dress are you hoping to find today?"

"I have some pictures," Gabby said, reaching for the wedding book in the backseat. She looked down at the black three-ring binder and pursed her lips in embarrassment. "Please don't make fun of me, but some of these might be a little outdated—I've been collecting pictures since I was eight."

"Um, amazing," Laura said, grabbing the book. She began flipping through the pictures and stopped on a three-tiered magnolia cake. "Beautiful!" She turned the page to a curly-haired bride wearing an A-line chiffon dress with intricate beading on the back. "Oh my goodness." She gasped. "Gorgeous."

"You think they'll have something like this here?" Gabby asked, looking up at the store.

"Let's go find out!" Laura said, opening up the car door.

Inside, pristine white carpet covered the floor, and racks of clear plastic garment bags holding sparkly dresses lined the walls. The store was bustling. A tween held on to a red rhinestone gown, crying, as her mother tried to coax her to try on something more conservative. Two older teens, spray-tanned an impressive orangé-brown, teetered around the racks in five-inch heels.

Laura took Gabby's arm and guided her to the wedding section in the back of the store.

"Oh, look—a sale," Laura said gleefully. "This one's only a hundred-ninety-nine. That's amazing." Upon closer inspection, the girls realized the hem was lined with dangling pom-poms. "Oh dear," Laura said, raising her eyebrows and sliding it back on the rack.

"Can I help you?" A tall slender woman with a pixie cut approached them.

"Aw, hi, Miss Kathie. Do you remember me?" Laura asked in her sweet high-pitched tone. Gabby recognized the voice she was using: it was one Laura saved for important adults and customers at the Sea Shack.

"Well, if it isn't Miss Maple Bacon Praline Pie herself!" The woman hugged Laura. "How are you, sweetie?"

"I'm good! Just shopping with my friend Gabby for a wedding dress." She grabbed her arm and pulled Gabby closer. "Can you help us find something?"

"I certainly can! Now, what style are you looking for?"

"Long, flowy, maybe a beaded sash or a sexy but classy cutout back." Laura turned to Gabby and put her hand over her mouth. "Sorry. I didn't mean to take over. This is your day. You should answer." She shook her head and let out a laugh. "Look at me pretending I'm the one getting married."

Gabby smiled, glad for the guidance. "Oh, please. That's why I brought you! You know more about this stuff than I do." She turned toward Miss Kathie. "Everything Laura said is right. I'm just looking for something simple but elegant, like this." She handed her the tear-out of the A-line dress Laura had admired in the car.

"Oh, wow—this is definitely a beautiful style," the woman said, looking at the model. "When's the big day?"

"Next month, actually." Her stomach fluttered with a mix of nervousness and excitement.

The woman's eyes widened. "Quite the time crunch. Well, that just makes it more fun, doesn't it?" She smiled and put her hand on Gabby's shoulder. "Don't you worry—we're gonna find you a dress today."

The three of them began pulling dresses off the rack that they thought might work: a sleek halter with a tulle bottom, a lacey off-the-shoulder, and Gabby's favorite—an elegant cap-sleeved with a sheer low back. As Laura assisted her in the dressing room, Gabby twirled and posed in front of the mirror, feeling as chic as Kate Middleton.

"Girl, you look amazing!" Laura squealed. "Now, for the final touch." She placed a veil atop her friend's head.

Gabby gasped. The deep sweetheart neckline—outlined in lace and beading—made her neck look long and regal. A belt covered in clear jewels hugged her slim stomach. Her back peeked through soft sequined netting, looking somehow both sexy and demure. And the veil, elbow length and dotted with fake pearls, completed the picture.

She looked like a bride, a *real* bride.

"Oooh! What do you think?" Laura asked excitedly.

Gabby studied herself in the mirror, proud of the girl staring back at her. Not just the dress, but everything. This was how Tony saw her every day—the perfect bride, the perfect future wife. Finally, that little voice in the back of her mind that chanted *fraud, fraud, fraud* went silent.

"So, how's it going in here?" the woman asked, popping her head into the fitting room area.

"I think this might be the one," Laura said with a beaming smile.

Gabby smiled and nodded slowly, awed into silence by her own appearance.

"It sure is beautiful," the woman said. "Now, do you want to try on any more? Or are you sure?"

Gabby kept her eyes on her reflection in the mirror and smiled. "I've never been more sure of anything in my life."

25

claire

"CHEERS!" CLAIRE, GABBY, Madison, and Laura cried as they clinked their glasses together, but for some reason, the energy seemed anything but cheery. Maybe it was the thunderstorm brewing outside, but Claire got the feeling none of them wanted to be there—including her, even though it was *her* belated birthday celebration. They were at Willy's Crawfish and Catfish, a small kitschy seafood restaurant that had just opened up near Darby Lake, toasting to her twenty-second year.

"So, did you have a good birthday?" Gabby asked, twisting the tail off the boiled crawfish.

"Not really," Claire admitted, looking out the window at the clouds over the water. "Sadie was sick, so Gavin and I stayed home with her. He cooked us breakfast for dinner—which was so sweet—but bless him, the bacon was burned, and the eggs and grits were too watery." She grinned. "I could have sworn it was Laura in the kitchen."

"Not funny," Laura said, throwing an empty tail across the table. Claire ducked just in time.

"Well, Gavin will just need to make it up to you," Gabby said. "Tell him to take you to that nice Italian place next to the used-car dealership on Stanley."

Claire slouched against the booth. "Gavin's been working like a madman lately. I don't think I'll get a rain check." She tried to pretend it was okay, but Gavin had always been one to go overboard for her birthday. Last year he had surprised her with a romantic backyard picnic under the stars, and the year before that a scavenger hunt around town with twenty small gifts—one for each year of her life. This time, nada. Just some burned food that gave her indigestion later that night.

"What's he so busy with?" Madison chimed in. "Aren't *you* the one writing his book and running his social media?"

Claire popped a crawfish tail in her mouth and gave the excuse he'd given her. "He's running the entire operation, though. We have a thousand members that he's taking care of."

Madison rolled her eyes. "Okay, well, you deserve a lot of credit, too. We know how hard you work."

"I don't need credit," Claire said, taking a sip of her sweet tea. She thought about all the retweets she got, and how preorders of the ebook were already flooding her inbox. People were inspired by her words, even if they were under Gavin's name. Her latest tweet— @Pastor_Gavin: *"A relationship with God can be the most fulfilling one in your life. #SwipeRight"*—already had three hundred favorites.

Thunder boomed outside as the storm began rolling in. Silence fell over the girls as they watched the rain start to hit the window.

Claire's cell phone whistled and vibrated from her bag. It was a message from Gavin.

> I'm gonna be later than I thought. Meeting the guys to watch the game right now, so 11 or 12.

Claire wanted so badly to believe him, but a warning bell went off in her head. After she'd confronted him about The Saddle, she'd been positive that he was telling the truth. She'd started working on herself and trying to be more present in their relationship. She'd asked her mom to take Sadie twice a week, so she and Gavin could have a few hours alone at night. She'd been reading his sermons, asking him about his day, and preparing his favorite meals, but she hadn't really seen any changes. There was still some sort of wall between them. And this text felt off. He rarely stayed out that late without her.

She bit her lip, debating what to do. She'd promised that she trusted Gavin, and she'd meant it. But she had to go with her gut here.

She threw her phone back in her bag. "I have to go. I'm so sorry. Y'all stay, finish your dinners."

Gabby glanced up in surprise. "What's wrong?"

"Yeah, you have to tell us," Madison demanded.

Claire took a deep, shuddering breath and decided it was time to finally come clean to her friends. After all, if she couldn't count on them, who could she count on? "I think you were right about Gavin, Mads. I caught him at the strip club." She looked up toward the ceiling, frustration festering inside her.

Laura grabbed her hand from across the table. "Oh, sweetie."

Claire sighed. "I asked him about it and he insisted he's going for work, as part of church outreach."

Outrage flashed across Madison's face. "Hold up—he really said that?"

"I believed him at first, but now I think he might be lying," Claire confessed. "I'm going to drive by the club. If he's not there, I'll know I was wrong and I'll never doubt him again. But if he's there—"

"We'll kick his ass," Gabby interjected, rising to stand.

"Obviously we're going with you," Laura said, grabbing her purse from her chair. Madison was already putting her jacket on.

Claire wanted to say no, that she needed to do this herself, but she couldn't bear to face this alone. "Thank you," she whispered.

After they paid the bill, they ran outside, dashing through the pouring rain to Claire's car. The drive to The Saddle was quiet. When they reached the parking lot, they scanned the vehicles looking for Gavin's truck. "Oh god, there it is," Madison said, pointing out the truck with the RON PAUL bumper sticker.

Claire felt her head spinning. Her stomach roiled like she was going to be sick.

"Wait, let's not jump to conclusions just yet," Laura interjected. "Maybe he's really helping that poor girl like he said he was."

"But . . ." Claire stared dazedly at Gavin's truck. "Now that I know about this supposed girl, why wouldn't he just tell me that was where he was? Why would he say he was watching the game with his friends?" A jolt of anger passed through her and she turned off the ignition in a swift move. "I'm going in."

"You got this," Gabby said from the backseat.

Claire threw open the door and stepped outside, running through the thunderstorm to the front door of the dingy club. Inside, the place reeked of cigarette smoke, and the tiled floors were sticky under her boots. The lighting was dim and anonymous. All she could see were the outlines of men watching a young brunette dance around the pole onstage to a rap song.

Claire's heart pumped in sync with the heavy bass. She slipped past one of the scantily clad women serving cocktails and scanned the room for Gavin. Nothing.

In the back of the bar, she noticed a VIP room with the black velvet curtain drawn closed. Maybe, just maybe, he was in there, counseling the stripper he'd told her about. If that was the case, she'd forgive him for all the lies. But, if she found him in there doing anything else . . . she didn't even know what would happen.

As she approached the room she realized the curtain was gaping open just enough for her to see in. Claire looked around the strip club, making sure that no one was watching her, and then peered through the curtains. There was a stripper on a man's lap, facing her. The stripper's obvious implants were pointing in Claire's direction, and Claire blushed. She couldn't see behind the girl's mass of blond hair; all she could see was her hot pink thong and the man's legs—he was wearing brown leather dress shoes and dark navy slacks. Claire leaned in a little closer, and at that moment, the girl flipped around toward the man. His face came into perfect focus.

Gavin.

Claire covered her mouth and stumbled back, tears beginning to stream down her face, and ran away from the curtain before either of them noticed her. In a daze, she wove her way through the dark club and out the door. For a moment, she just stood there, sobbing as the heavy rain poured down over her.

Then a car door slammed and Madison, Laura, and Gabby rushed toward her, surrounding her in a tight hug. Laura wrapped her arm around her waist and led her back to the car.

When they were all buckled in, Gabby finally spoke. "What do you need us to do?"

"We're here for you, Claire," Laura added. "Anything. Anything at all."

Her mouth was dry and she felt shell-shocked, but she mustered up the energy to respond. "Thank you. But there's nothing y'all can do right now. Just be there for me when I call."

• • •

"YOU LOOK LIKE hell," Jillian said, putting her iPad down on the coffee table as Claire walked in the front door. Her hair was wet and curly from the rain. "Come in, get warm." She grabbed Claire's shoulders and led her into the living room, wrapping a blanket around her. "Why do you look so upset?"

Claire began crying into her mom's shoulder.

Jillian rubbed her back. "What's wrong, sweetie? Gavin again?"

Claire nodded as her tears fell. "He lied to me," she said finally, shaking her head in disbelief. "I caught him at the strip club again." She closed her eyes, trying to get rid of the image, but all she could see was the stripper's hot pink thong and Gavin's face, his eyes locked onto that girl's implants.

"Oh, honey," her mom said. "I'm so sorry. I really didn't see this coming."

"You and me both, Ma." Claire slouched into the couch. She told her mother everything—how he'd lied and how she'd found him getting a lap dance. "He's strayin', and there's nothing I can do about it." Her mind flashed forward to her worst-case scenario, her life spiraling downhill. There'd be hard days and nights of raising Sadie by herself, just like her mom had done with her. And she was going to have to find another job, wasn't she? She couldn't work with Gavin anymore if they got divorced.

Jillian handed her a Kleenex. "You're really just gonna give up like that? Sweetie, there *is* something you can do about it. You just have to. He's the father of your baby, and she needs her daddy," she said with a steely look in her eyes. "Believe me—I've been there. I love being your mother, but being a single mom was so hard. You need to try to make it work—for both you and Sadie."

Claire blew into the tissue, her eyes burning from all the tears. "But how? I don't even know what went wrong in the first place. Why would he throw away our marriage like that?"

Her mom nodded. "Think about it, Claire. It's not necessarily his fault."

"I know, Mama. I know you think it's *mine*. But I've been trying, I swear."

"No . . ." Her mom paused. "Maybe it's *her* fault." She stood up and paced around the living room. "Gavin's a good Christian boy. I just don't see him doing anything to hurt your marriage on purpose. Maybe he did go there to help her, and maybe she seduced him."

Claire gasped. Suddenly, this whole confusing mess started to become more clear. "I could believe it," she said, throwing the flannel blanket off of her shoulders. She felt comfort thinking that it wasn't her fault—and it wasn't even Gavin's. It was someone else's entirely.

Her mom stopped pacing, turned to Claire, and put her hand on her hips. "You've tried talking to him. Maybe it's time you confronted *her*."

laura

LAURA'S HEART ACHED for Claire as she drove home from The Saddle. She couldn't wrap her mind around what Gavin had done. He and Claire had always seemed so solid and loving, and she would never have pegged Gavin as the straying type. He was a pastor, for goodness' sake, and the type of husband who always remembered their anniversary and enjoyed taking their daughter to the zoo. Why would he throw it all away over for a cheap lap dance at a roadside strip club? As much as it pained her to see her friend's marriage crumbling, it made her problems with Brian seem less severe.

The thought stayed with her until she was at home and found Brian sitting in their dark bedroom, staring at the computer. A virtual poker game was on the screen and a half-empty bottle of his dad's bourbon sat on the table next to him, a glass of it in his hand. Laura's stomach clenched. Shooting star be damned—he was breaking his promise to her already.

Brian's bloodshot eyes slid over to her as she walked in. "Hey," he slurred.

Laura put her hand over her mouth. "What happened?" she said softly, kneeling down next to him. "I thought you quit drinkin'?"

He stared at her, his hair sticking out in messy tufts, as if he had been pulling at it all night. "It's gone," he finally said, lowering his head.

"What's gone?" Laura's voice cracked in fear of what he was about to say.

"The money. I lost it all." He slammed his fist on the desk.

Laura's heart beat wildly as her mind spun to comprehend. "What do you mean, you lost it all?"

"*All* of it, Laura," he shouted. "All twelve thousand dollars."

She stumbled back, colliding painfully with the bed frame. He was joking, right? That was six months' worth of savings. Six months of no privacy, of dealing with his mom poking her head into their room every morning. *Dear God, let him be joking.* But as she stared at him and his desperate expression, she knew it had to be true.

"How?" she whispered.

"Poker," he said slowly. He buried his face in his hands. "I got a bad hand and tried to win it back but kept getting bad ones. I didn't mean to, I swear."

A cold numbness spread through Laura's chest. "You just have to win it back."

"How the hell am I supposed to do that without any money?" he asked, his voice shaking.

Laura glanced at the desk, where her plastic name tag from the Sea Shack stared back at her. So many nights of sweet tea spills on her clothes, the stench of crawfish in her hair, and Bible verses in lieu of tips . . . And for what? For Brian to give it all away to some faceless Internet jackass living in his grandma's basement in Idaho?

She let out a low scream and stood up, pacing back and forth.

Brian took another sip of the bourbon.

"Dammit, Brian. Stop it!" She grabbed the glass out of his hand and her voice raised. "Do you realize what you're doing to your life? To *mine?* I've given up everything to support you. I quit school and got married to you, moved back here, worked my ass off to help you pay for this surgery. And for what? You've thrown our future away." Her entire body trembled in anger.

"Oh really? It's all my fault? You're making it out that you're the victim, Laura." He took the drink out of her hand and put it down on the desk. "But guess what—I'm the victim. I'm the one who got handed the bad cards, literally. And if you can't support me through that, then what kind of wife are you?"

She felt like she'd been sucker punched, and her mouth fell open. He could accuse her of being unhappy at his parents' house, or of being overly focused on school . . . but that was over the line. "Are you freaking serious? You're really gonna say that I don't know how to support you? After all I've given up?"

"It's not a competition," he argued. "We've both made sacrifices."

She scowled at him. "What sacrifices have *you* made? Sitting around here all day playing video games? Getting drunk with Kenny? I know you didn't ask to get hurt, but what the hell are *you* doing to fix it?" The sternness in her voice surprised even Laura.

Brian lowered his head like a scolded dog. "Look, Laur—I'm sorry. I'm so sorry." He hobbled over to her and put his arms around her neck. "I love you so much. You know I can't do this without you."

She shoved him off of her. "Here's the thing, it's *your* surgery," she reminded him. "You can't have it if we don't have the money. It affects you more than me."

"I'm still holding out for the insurance appeal," he said hopefully.

Laura scoffed. "We haven't heard a peep since we filed the paperwork. There's no way we can count on that." For the first time, she felt a seed of resentment that he didn't just take the surgery the school would have paid for. Maybe he'd never play football again, but he would've been able to stay in school through the physical therapy and get his degree. And at least they wouldn't have been in this mess—living with his parents without a dime to their names.

"We'll come up with somethin'." He moved to kiss her on her forehead, but she sidestepped away.

She looked back up at him. "No—*you* come up with somethin'. You lost the money, now it's up to you to get it back."

With that, she stormed out to the bathroom to get ready for bed, her heart still pounding with fury. When she returned, Brian was passed out on the bed, his drunken snores vibrating the mattress. She sat next to him, wishing it weren't too late to call her mom.

She leaned her head back on the pillow and thought back to a conversation she and her mom had the night before her wedding. The two of them lay in her parents' bed, wearing matching floral pajamas that her dad had gotten them for Christmas the year before.

"How are you feeling?" Angela had asked as they ate leftover chocolate-covered pralines from the rehearsal dinner.

"A little bloated from those baked beans, but I think I'll be okay," Laura said, rubbing her belly.

Her mom laughed. "What bride eats a whole bowl of barbecue baked beans before her wedding day? Oh, sweet child . . . who raised you?"

Laura giggled and threw a praline that bounced off her mom's shoulder and onto the navy and white duvet.

Angela's smile slowly faded as she began fidgeting with the covers. It reminded Laura of that awkward "if you're having sex, you should be on birth control" talk she had given her when she was fifteen.

"I think moms are supposed to give the bride advice on her wedding eve night," she said, grabbing Laura's hand. "At least that's what that little booklet that came with my mother-of-the-bride dress said."

Laura snuggled into the bed and braced herself for a pep talk.

"I raised an independent girl, and I wanna make sure she stays that way, even though she's gettin' married." She pushed a lock of hair behind Laura's ear. "It's something I've made a point to do myself, and I'm so happy I did it. I know you're gonna take this the wrong way, but please don't. The best advice I ever got was from my crazy aunt Mary."

Laura smiled. Crazy Aunt Mary had died in a freak horseback riding accident on the family farm. She had only seen pictures and heard stories about her but knew her mom secretly worshipped this chain-smoking free-spirited hippie.

"Well, when I was fifteen, she pulled me aside at the Sugarcane

Festival Fais-dodo and told me that when I was married, I needed to have enough money in my savings to leave my husband if I ever wanted to."

"That's pretty bleak," Laura said.

Angela pursed her lips. "I think she was in a horrible marriage—her husband was a jerk to all of us, so I could only imagine how he was to her behind closed doors. But she didn't work, so it's not like she had any money to just pick up and leave him."

"But Brian's not a jerk," Laura said, narrowing her eyes and wondering what her mom was getting at.

"I think you're missing the point here." Her mom laced her fingers through Laura's. "It was always important that I work so that I could have my own savings account, just in case."

"But you and Dad have an amazing marriage . . . right?" Laura asked, confused.

"Heck yeah we do!" Her mom held her shoulders back proudly. "But there's a certain security and confidence to having my own money and my own worth. I love your daddy, but I also love feeling independent and capable. If the worst ever comes to pass, I'll be all right."

At the time, Laura hadn't been sure about her mom's advice. She understood wanting to feel independent, but somehow it felt like giving up before they even got started. But after everything that had happened tonight with Brian, she wondered if it wasn't a bad idea.

For the first time since they moved back to Toulouse, Laura admitted honestly to herself that the surgery wasn't a guarantee. What would happen if Brian's knee wasn't fixed and he didn't go back to college? Not only would his future be ruined, but so would Laura's. She'd hitched her star to someone else's wagon, only for all the wheels to fall clean off.

madison

"ARE YOU OKAY, honey?" Allen asked, joining Madison at the kitchen table. Her dad had caught her staring off into space, her Cheerios getting soggy in the bowl of milk.

She wanted to say no, to tell him everything about George. When she'd handed her dad that $2,500 last week, he'd been blown away and immediately asked where it had come from. She knew he'd never accept it if he discovered what she'd done, so she'd lied and said she'd pawned some of her thrift store jewelry and one of the necklaces she got for a dollar turned out to be real pearls with 18 karat white gold.

She hadn't seen or talked to George since the pawnshop incident. Every time she picked up the phone to text him an apology, her fingers literally felt numb, and she couldn't bring herself to do it. She wanted to tell her dad about Claire, too. She wondered if she did the right thing by telling Claire what she saw in the first place. Maybe she could have spared her cousin the pain.

"I'm fine," she said instead. After all, her dad had bigger things to worry about, like his next doctor's appointment and his latest test results.

Allen put a frail hand on her shoulder. "By the way, your mom and I ran into George last night at the grocery store."

Madison's eyes snapped up.

"He was in the frozen food aisle looking like kind of a wreck."

He crossed his leg. "Baggy eyes, disheveled clothes, messy hair . . ." Allen put his arm around her chair. "Reminds me of someone else I know."

She looked down at herself. "Who . . . me?" she asked defensively. "It's seven in the morning. What do you expect?!"

Allen snickered. "I don't know what happened between the two of you, but he asked about you."

"He did?" Her heart started beating faster. "What did he say?"

"I believe it was, 'How's Madison?'" He smiled.

She slumped down in her chair. "Oh, that doesn't mean anything."

"Why don't you go visit him today? It seems like he could really use the company." Allen patted her on the knee.

She dangled her spoon in the bowl. "What gave you that impression?"

"The fact that he was buying twenty frozen dinners for one." He took a sip of coffee and raised a brow at her. With a sigh, Madison stood up and threw her leftover cereal in the sink, the little mushy Os sticking to the scratched-up stainless steel, then kissed her dad on the cheek before trudging to her room.

After sitting on her bed, stewing over the possibility of going to see George for half an hour, she finally walked to the bathroom and took a shower. The scent of her eucalyptus body wash was relaxing, but she couldn't wash the guilt away.

Stop thinking about it, she kept telling herself. But George's face was still there, as was the memory of him driving away in his Porsche looking heartbroken. And beyond the guilt . . . if she was being honest, she missed him. Odd as it was, she'd really enjoyed his company. She'd liked his phone calls and how he'd always say, "Just callin' to say howdy." She liked sitting on his porch and hearing about his travels abroad, or making him laugh with stories about her epic fishing trips with her dad. She closed her eyes and shampooed her hair, the water and suds running down her cheeks. The pipe squeaked in the wall, causing scalding hot water to run from it and burn her skin. "Owwww!" she screamed out loud, jumping out of the water. "I deserve that . . ." she muttered under her breath.

As she dried herself off and combed her knotty hair, she stared at her reflection, her dark eyes looking back at her as if they, too, were judging her. And why wouldn't they? She was scum. No, she was that nasty mold that developed on top of the scum in her bathroom.

I can't take this anymore, she said to herself, running to her bedroom, stepping into a pair of ratty jeans, pulling on a black sweatshirt, and grabbing her keys.

As she drove into George's driveway, she noticed his silver car sitting in the open garage. Her mind reeled with nervous thoughts as she slowly got down from her truck and walked up the sidewalk to the front door. Her fingers trembled when she knocked on the door, then waited. Silence—save for the leaves rustling from the breeze. Madison sighed. *Guess he doesn't wanna talk to me,* she thought. *Who can blame him?*

She walked back to her truck with her head held low, started the rumbling engine, and began driving back home. But about a tenth of a mile down Egret Lane, she spotted George out walking Charlie. Her stomach twisted with nerves.

"Hey," she said softly through her open window, as she pulled up slowly.

George looked at her, his expression unreadable. "Hey."

Charlie barked and ran up to her truck, dragging George along with him on the leash.

She took a deep breath. "Mind if I join you?" she asked, turning the engine off.

"I guess not." He focused his attention on his dog, who was now greeting Madison with licks as she knelt down beside him.

Madison stood up and looked at George apologetically. "I just came to explain that day outside the pawnshop. I'm sorry it's taken me so long to come to you. I've just been really embarrassed." She shuffled her keys back and forth from one hand to the other.

George rubbed the back of his neck. "Yeah, that . . ."

"I know what's probably going on in your mind," she rushed on. "Hell, I know what you're probably *calling* me in your mind. But I promise I didn't *want* to hurt you. That necklace was the nicest thing anyone's ever given me, and I appreciated it more than you'll ever know."

"So then why did you pawn it?" He kicked some dried-up mud with his stark white Reebok tennis shoe. Charlie let out a sharp bark and strained at the leash as a squirrel ran up a nearby tree.

She lowered her head. "We're about to lose our house. I was tryin' to buy time." She took a deep breath, her eyes watering. Spring was officially only a day away, and pollen hung heavy in the air. "It's been a really shitty year, George."

George's expression softened instantly. "Oh, Madison. I had no idea it was that bad." He put his arms around her and pulled her to him. She felt herself relax in his embrace, the weight she'd been carrying around since she'd seen him outside the pawnshop abating slightly. "Here, come with us for a walk."

Madison wiped her eyes and started walking with them along the dirt path. "For what it's worth, I am really sorry."

"So, do you still need money?" He looked at her with concern, leaves crunching under his feet.

"We're making do with what we got." She put the keys she had been fidgeting with in her back pocket. "What I care more about right now is that you and I are cool. I know I really messed up and should have apologized sooner, but I'm . . . I'm just not good with this kinda stuff."

"You're doing an okay job," he said, urging Charlie away from a patch of wildflowers with bees buzzing around it.

She gave him a half-smile. "'Okay' is better than I expected."

He laughed before growing serious once more. "So, level with me. Are you gonna lose the house?"

She pushed her bangs out of her eyes. "I'm trying to pick up extra jobs cleaning houses. And we're having a yard sale next weekend.

You should come!" She put her hand on his shoulder and put on her best auctioneer's voice. "The animatronic singing bass and peeing angel fountain will go fast. Come early before they get snatched up by the little old couple who roam the town in their van."

"Ha!" He stroked his clean-shaven chin. "That sounds like a pretty good deal. Maybe I'll have to go."

"You should," she said, nudging his arm and smiling up at him.

They turned onto a paved path that ran along the lake. The sun shone brightly overhead, reflecting off the calm surface of the lake. A few ducks swam through the lily pads and patches of algae near the edge, honking loudly.

"I'm really sorry that you guys are going through this, especially when your dad is so sick," George finally said, running his fingers through his hair. "He's one of the nicest people I know."

"I feel like all the bad karma in my life is coming back to haunt me," she admitted. "Seeing my dad like this is heartbreaking."

George stopped to let Charlie poke in the underbrush. He leaned against a wooden post and regarded Madison. "I've been lucky to always have the money I need, but I know how hard it is to watch your parents slip away. I lived it myself not so long ago."

"Any advice, then?" she asked, blocking the sun with her hand. "What do you think I should do?"

"Marry me," he said calmly. Charlie barked, as if echoing his statement.

Her eyes widened. "*What*?" She playfully hit his arm and laughed. "You tryin' to get a rise out of me?"

He shook his head. "No, I'm serious. I know I sound crazy, and maybe I am, but this could work." He took her hand. "I can't make this time any less sad for you, but I can help make it easier. Your parents won't have to worry about losing their house or their medical bills, and you can quit cleaning with your mom." He smiled. "Madison, I have so much fun when I'm with you—I've never felt this happy with anyone else. Marry me."

She gently tugged her hand from his and started pacing, turning tight circles in the little clearing, her mind whirling. Even if she really considered it, what would marrying George *mean*?

"This is crazy." She stopped walking and faced him, taking in his green eyes, his fleece, and the jeans he wore a few inches too high on his waist. "*You're* a little crazy."

"I mean, yeah, a little," he said with a grin. "But just think about it for a minute." He took her by the shoulders. "I'm not asking you to love me. I'm just asking you to come live with me and keep me company."

"So, let me get this straight: You're cool with paying for my family's debt if I marry you and make you laugh sometimes?" she clarified. Even to her, who had admittedly started hanging out with George for all the wrong reasons, this sounded completely ridiculous.

"Forget it, you're right, it's stupid," he said. His cheeks flamed red and he bent down to wrestle a stick from Charlie's mouth.

But now that he had taken it back, something insistent tugged in Madison's chest. This incredibly insane, spontaneous decision could actually be the answer to all her family's problems. "Wait. I mean, maybe it's not stupid." She put her hands in her pockets and rocked back on her heels.

He looked up at her with wide eyes. "So, what are you saying, then?"

Madison shook her head. She had done some crazy things in her life, like the time she went skinny-dipping in a lake that most definitely had alligators in it, or when she and Cash broke into Nan's Diner at 3:00 a.m. to eat peach pie. But now she was officially about to do the craziest thing she'd ever done in her almost twenty years on Earth.

"Yes, I'll marry you."

28

gabrielle

AS GABBY OPENED the door of Dixie's Thrift Boutique on Main Street, she was hit with the smell of mildew, old leather, and dust. Madison had texted her urgently the night before, telling her to be at the store the following morning—"Eleven a.m. SHARP!"—but she wouldn't explain why, though Gabby hadn't heard anything from her since Claire's birthday dinner a week ago. Gabby walked through the rows of musty clothing, looking for her friend.

Madison popped her head out from behind a rack of dresses. "Hey!"

Gabby jumped. "Oh dear god!" She took a second to catch her breath. "What are we doing here?"

Madison emerged from the hanging clothes, holding a short white mesh dress. The gap in her front teeth showed through her beaming smile. She seemed infinitely happier and more energetic than last week. "Surprise! I'm a fellow bride!"

Gabby's jaw dropped and she quickly realized she was gaping. "What are you talking about?"

Madison shoved the dress at her. Gabby took it, bewildered. "I'm getting married, too!" She looked up at Gabby expectantly.

Gabby tried to morph her shock into happiness for her friend. "Oh my gosh, congratulations!" She leaned in, squeezing Madison in a hug. "I can't believe Cash went from noncommittal to ready for marriage. Men, huh?"

Madison wriggled out of the hug. "Actually, it's not Cash, but thank you."

She eyed the white dress that Gabby was holding. "Hmm, I want casual, but I think that's *too* casual, what do you think?" Madison grabbed the dress out of Gabby's hands and put it back on the rack.

Gabby felt like she was staring at her friend in a way that probably bordered on rude, but this was unbelievable, even for the typically impulsive Madison. "Um . . . sorry if I missed something, but if it's not Cash . . . then who are you marrying?"

"George!" Madison laughed, digging back into the rack. "Can you believe it?"

"Actually, I can't," Gabby confessed. She had never even met the guy—although to be fair, the girls hadn't met Tony either. She still had to get the courage to tell them they were going to have to keep her past a secret at the wedding in a few weeks. The thought made her a little nauseated. But this was different, right? She *loved* Tony. "I thought you insisted that y'all were just friends."

"We *are* just friends." Madison pulled out a long white dress that had some yellow stains on the skirt. She made a gagging face and quickly shoved it back in. "Funny how things work out, huh?"

Gabby leaned on the rack of clothes, more confused than ever. "How did this happen?"

"We were hanging out last weekend and it just came up. I know it sounds crazy—and it is—but it's one of those things I just can't explain." She put her hand on Gabby's shoulder and looked her in the eyes. "I'm doing the right thing for me, I promise."

Gabby wanted to tell her friend she was certifiably nuts and that this was the most insane decision she had ever made, but instead she said, "Well, I'm happy for you," and gave her a hug. After all, who was she to judge?

"So, I know your date is set for April fifteenth," Madison said. "Do you care if I do it the weekend after?"

Gabby cocked her head to the side. "Not at all, but what's the rush?"

Madison shrugged and began combing through the white dresses on the next rack over. "Why wait? It's not like we need a lot of time to plan. It's just gonna be a small party at his house." She pulled out a long cotton spaghetti strap gown and held it up to her. The material was soft and had a bohemian flare to it.

Gabby nodded at the dress. "That's gorgeous. You have to try it."

As the girls wound their way back to the dressing room, Madison grabbed a dress that was on one of the displays. "Ooh, you have to try this one on," she said, handing it over. "It's only five dollars! Bridesmaid dress?"

Gabby glanced down at the item in her hands and burst out laughing. It was a short corset dress made out of green camouflage material. Neon orange tulle peeked out of the bottom of the full skirt. It was like someone wanted to go to a formal dance but also wanted to show off her love of hunting. "This is ridiculous . . ." She paused, staring it down. "Ridiculously awesome!" She walked into the dressing room, closed the curtain, and shimmied into the dress.

"Oh, this is *special*," Gabby called out to Madison, who was in the dressing room next to her. For being hideous, the dress fit her surprisingly well. "I look like I'm going to Redneck Prom!"

"Okay, I'm ready," Madison finally called out. The two opened up their curtains and faced each other.

Gabby put her hand over her mouth. "Oh Mads, you're beautiful."

The cotton gown hung just to the tops of her feet, and even though Madison was skinny and angular, it gave her the appearance of soft curves. The bright white made her pale skin look pearlescent, and her long dark hair contrasted beautifully with it. Madison smiled as she looked at herself in the full-length mirror.

"It's great, isn't it?" She looked back at Gabby and her eyes widened. "But not as awesome as yours, that's for sure."

Gabby sashayed up to the mirror next to her, her brightly colored dress contrasting with her deep red curls. "Don't mean to steal your thunder and all, but I look *good*," she said sarcastically. "Maybe I'll wear this to *my* wedding."

"I will literally pay you a hundred dollars if you wear this for your wedding," Madison said, with an evil grin on her face.

Gabby looked up to the right and pretended to ponder it for a moment. "Nah, I think I'm good."

"Your loss," Madison said, twirling in front of the mirror. "Tony wouldn't be able to keep his hands off of you in that."

Gabby let out a snicker. "So, is this the one?" she asked, nudging Madison's hip with her own.

Madison smirked. "The dress or the guy?"

"Either!"

Madison looked at herself in the mirror again, an unreadable expression on her face. "They'll both do."

• • •

AS SHE PULLED into her apartment complex parking lot later that afternoon, Gabby prayed none of her neighbors would see her in the camo dress. When she'd tried to change out of it in the store, Madison had begged her to keep it on—"I'm buying, my treat"—and Gabby had let Madison's enthusiasm override her own good sense. It seemed funny at the time and they'd left the store laughing, but as she got closer to home, self-consciousness set in.

Gabby parked and almost got inside without anyone seeing, but as she turned the corner to her apartment, she was surprised to find someone waiting by her door. The tall man stood erect, as if afraid that touching the walls would dirty his neatly pressed khakis and button-down. He looked familiar. . . .

She squinted. "Congressman Ford?" Panic bubbled up in her chest. What was he doing at her *apartment* . . . the apartment she'd hidden from Tony for the past ten months?

Mr. Ford slowly looked her up and down and Gabby's cheeks went bright red. Her hands hovered over the dress awkwardly. Oh, who was she kidding? There was no hiding this ridiculous thing. She wanted to kill Madison.

"Hi, Gabrielle," he said, stone-faced. "Mind if I come in?"

She nodded and opened the door. As they entered her tiny apartment, her heart was beating so fast that she was afraid he could hear it.

He looked around the small dim room, his lip curling as his gaze landed on the old futon that acted as both her couch and bed. Gabby's morning coffee was still on the table, along with some candy wrappers and a half-burned vanilla-scented candle. Atop the cheap faux wood bookcase, a framed picture from Claire's wedding—where she and the girls posed with cake-frosting mustaches—sat next to a photo of her and her mom on her eighteenth birthday, taken just a few months before Elaine went to jail.

She imagined her apartment through his eyes and felt so small, once again reduced to nothing but a poor girl whose mom was serving ten years in prison.

"Can I get you something to drink?" she asked. At the very least, she always had her manners. "Sweet tea?"

His cold gaze met hers and her stomach dropped. "How long did you think you'd get away with it?"

Gabby swallowed the rising lump in her throat. She clenched her fists, her palms sweating. "What do you mean?"

Mr. Ford frowned. "Don't play stupid with me, Gabrielle. We welcomed you into our home, into our lives, and you—" He cut off, his face reddening, and took a breath, as if to steady himself. "You *deceived* him. You deceived all of us."

Gabby backed up toward the futon, afraid she might faint. "Listen, it's not what you think," she started, knowing the words sounded desperate. "It's all a misunderstanding."

"A misunderstanding? Can you tell me this—why does my son *misunderstand* that you're enrolled in college when you're not?" His voice got deeper and louder. "Why does my son *misunderstand* that your parents are dead when your mother is actually in jail?"

Gabby felt her breath leave her body and covered her mouth with her hands, trying not to cry. "How—how did you find out?"

Mr. Ford's dark brown eyes flashed like steel, and she could suddenly picture Tony looking at her that same way. She hung her head in shame and embarrassment.

"I've got a reelection campaign coming up, Gabrielle. I vet everyone. Of course I'd look into someone who was planning on joining my family."

That was it, then. It was over. She sat down on the futon, cradling her head in her hands. Gabby had imagined a million ways this would all fall apart, but never, ever thought it would happen like this. She felt wrung out and exhausted. "I love your son," she said quietly.

Mr. Ford cleared his throat and she looked up at him. His gaze was smoldering. "That may be true, but nothing else is."

Tears began streaming down Gabby's face. "Have you told Tony yet?"

He shook his head. "No." His eyebrows furrowed with disappointment. "My son means everything to me. He's a *good* person. Your lies would destroy him. I'd prefer if he never knew about this."

She looked up at him with wide eyes. Did that mean he was really going to let her get away with it? Was he going to forget all of this happened and let her marry Tony anyway?

He moved closer to her, looming over her. "So you have a choice here, Gabrielle. Break up with him—lie to him if you have to, you're certainly good at that—but don't tell him *how* you deceived him."

Gabby sat up straighter, her face feeling puffy and sore from the tears. "Or?"

Mr. Ford glowered. "Or I'll tell him everything. I know my son better than you, and I can guarantee he'll never speak to you again."

She flinched. "Mr. Ford, I just told you, I love Tony—"

He waved an arm at her, cutting her off before she could protest or try to think of an alternative solution. "You didn't hear all of my terms. Leave him—tell him nothing about what you did, but leave him—and I'll get your mom out of prison."

Gabby gasped, her mind reeling. "Why would you do that for me?"

"My son has a bright future ahead of him. He wants to go into politics, for god's sake. He doesn't need someone like you ruining his life. If freeing your mom is what it takes to make you go away, so be it." He paused. "I'll leave you to think about it. You've got one day."

He walked out the door, leaving her alone with nothing but a stupid dress, a broken heart, and an impossible decision.

29

claire

CLAIRE PULLED INTO The Saddle's parking lot, unsure what she was going to say when she confronted the stripper, but shaking with anxiety. Her mom's words had been replaying over and over in her head the whole week, but it wasn't until Gavin came home late again the night before that she finally got the nerve to do something about it.

Gathering her courage, she strode into the grimy building. The mood in the place was much more depressing than it had been on Saturday night, if that was even possible. An overweight bald guy was the lone guest, watching a brunette who looked to be about eighteen practicing her moves on the pole.

A petite blonde in a clingy red dress came out from behind the empty bar and walked over to Claire. "Can I help you?"

Claire quickly realized who was standing in front of her. She could never forget that long, bouncy golden hair or those perky breasts. There she was—the woman who was ruining her marriage. Up close, she was much prettier than Claire realized. Her stomach lurched. Had Gavin fallen for her?

Claire held her chin high. "Yeah," she said, taking a deep breath. "You were with my husband on Saturday night—I saw you giving him a lap dance." She shuddered at the thought.

The stripper's blue eyes grew wide. "Um, do you want to speak to my manager?"

"No, I wanted to speak to you," Claire said, pulling her shoulders back and hoping it made her look more confident than she felt. "I'm here to tell you to back off from my husband." She hoped she looked and sounded threatening.

The stripper cocked her head to the side and put her hands on her hips. "I'm sorry—I don't even know who your husband is. But I can tell you that nothing inappropriate happened. I was just doin' my job."

Claire laughed harshly and took a step forward. "'Nothing inappropriate?' I *saw* you grinding on him. You're really gonna tell me that's not inappropriate? You *seduced* him."

The woman rolled her eyes. "As I said, I was just doin' my job. It was a harmless lap dance . . . that he paid for. If there's anyone you should be yelling at, it's him." She looked around the bar, as if searching for backup.

Claire slammed her fist on the hostess stand and the woman startled. "That isn't like my husband. He wouldn't do something like this. You clearly took advantage of him."

The stripper shook her head and sighed, seeming exhausted. "You know what? You think your husband's an angel?" She took a step forward, fire in her eyes. "At least half the guys who come in here have wedding bands on." She paused. "You're not special."

You're not special. The words rang in Claire's ears and suddenly she felt light-headed. They cut through her posturing, her belief in her husband's goodness, her determination to lay blame elsewhere. This happened all the time. Gavin wasn't some man who'd been seduced by another woman, and she wasn't his beloved wife—she was just some pathetic woman whose husband's attention had strayed. Her knees wobbled and she leaned against the hostess stand. Why was she here? What was she doing?

"Look, are you okay, lady?" the girl asked, softening.

Claire bit her lip and nodded, trying not to cry. She wouldn't be *that* pathetic.

The woman put her hand on Claire's shoulder and sighed. "You look like you're gonna pass out. Come on," she said, grabbing a packet of cigarettes and lighter from behind the hostess stand and leading her outside.

Claire and the woman sat down on the bench outside the building. She looked younger in the daylight, about Claire's age—in another life, she could've been one of Claire's friends. Claire put her head in her hands. "What am I doing?" she moaned.

The woman patted her on the shoulder. "It'll be all right, hon."

Claire sat back up. "What's your name?"

"Kimmy," she said. "Yours?"

"Claire."

Kimmy offered her a cigarette, but Claire shook her head. "Look, Claire," Kimmy said in an even and understanding tone. "I get that you're upset. You're not the first wife to come stompin' in here looking to start a fight. But we're all just trying to pay the bills here, not steal husbands." She inhaled her cigarette.

Claire nodded, a lump forming in her throat. She took her engagement ring off and began fiddling with it. The small solitaire diamond stared back at her. She thought about all the good, thoughtful things Gavin did: How he always had a cup of coffee ready for her each morning. How he'd make sure her cell phone was charging before she went to bed because she always forgot. How he'd sometimes take her car to be filled up with gas so she didn't have to make an extra stop. She paused, trying to figure out why someone who did all those things would be coming to a strip club. Did he not find her sexy anymore?

"I'm sorry I blamed you," she said finally. "You're right—it's not your fault he's coming here. It's definitely his. But maybe it's also mine."

Kimmy glanced over at her, her brows raised. "What in the world are you talking about, *your* fault?

Claire sighed, feeling defeated. "He's obviously not happy in our marriage, and I have to partly blame myself," she confessed. "It's a two-way street."

Kimmy scoffed. "That's bullshit, you know that, right?" She ashed her cigarette. "If the wives were to blame for every single married man who comes in here, I'd lose hope in our gender." Kimmy shook her head and then took another drag. "Seriously, don't take this personally. Be mad, fine, but don't beat *yourself* up over it."

Claire lowered her eyes to her tightly clasped hands. It was easy for this girl to tell her it wasn't her fault, but Claire didn't know what else to think. She was furious with Gavin, of course, but a part of her felt sure that if she'd just spent more time working out, or doing her makeup, or trying to spend intimate time with him . . . things would be different.

She got an idea and grabbed a piece of paper from her bag, scribbling her phone number on it. Before Kimmy could say anything, Claire pulled out her phone and showed her the lock-screen picture of her family, taken in the church parking lot. Their faces smiled as brightly as the sun that was hitting their eyes. She sighed and pointed to Gavin as she said her next words. "Will you call me if this guy comes back?"

Kimmy stared down at the pink and green monogrammed sticky note and winced. "I feel for you, Claire, but I can't do this," she said, trying to hand it back. "It's against club rules."

"Please?" Claire begged. If she knew the next time Gavin was here, maybe she could confront him in a more meaningful way. And maybe, just maybe, if she concentrated for real on improving their marriage, Kimmy would never have to use that number.

Kimmy looked at her hesitantly, then sighed and grabbed the piece of paper.

"Thank you," Claire said. She stood up, brushing off her jeans.

Kimmy folded up the piece of paper and held it tightly in her hand. The girls nodded at each other, and Claire walked to her car, shaking even more than when she first arrived. With trembling fingers, she opened her phone and fired off a tweet.

@Pastor_Gavin: "You want real change in the world? Look in the mirror and start with yourself. #BeTheDifference."

laura

"WHERE ARE YOU taking me?" Laura asked Brian as she threw her backpack in the backseat of Rob's Ford F-150. "Your text was so cryptic."

He had messaged her during lunch that day as she and Vince were having a heated debate about the best snow cone flavors (Laura insisted on wedding cake, Vince was a root beer guy). Her phone buzzed just as she was about to propose a taste test at Sal's Sno-Cones that afternoon. It was almost as if Brian knew she was making plans with another guy. . . .

"I just wanted to spend some alone time with my girl," he said, his muscular arm draped over the steering wheel.

Laura looked out the window and rolled her eyes. They'd barely talked all week. She'd taken to stopping at the local library when she wasn't working at the Sea Shack to finish her homework, not heading back to the Landrys' until she knew Janet and Rob would be in bed. Then she'd slip under the covers and turn off the lights before Brian could ask her how her day was. She'd also gone to Gulf Coast Bank and opened her own bank account. There was a measly $131 in it, but it was all hers.

The ride was quiet, save for the country music on the radio. She gazed out the window, watching as they passed sky-high cedar and pine trees. They turned down an unmarked dirt road, the loose bits of gravel hitting the bottom of the truck with steady metallic *ping*s.

"Here we are," he said, slowly getting down from the truck.

Laura opened the door and realized they were at an access point for Darby Lake. Rob's fishing boat was docked a few yards away, bobbing in the light waves. Laura felt a sudden rush of nostalgia; this was the place where Brian had proposed. She glanced up at him. He was staring at her nervously, his dirty blond hair newly cut, his hands in his back pockets. It was a smart move, reminding her how happy they'd been that day.

"Are we going fishing?" She looked down at her outfit—a red silk blouse, a pair of light blue jeans, and the expensive ballet flats her parents had gotten her for her birthday. "I'm not really dressed for this."

"Come on, it'll be fun." He took her hand and laced his fingers through hers. His blue eyes were pleading, the same color as the clear sky. "Please? You've got to talk to me sometime."

Despite her anger, Laura still felt a little thrill as Brian rubbed his thumb along her palm. She felt herself softening. "Okay. But I've got to get to the restaurant by six."

Brian grinned. "Deal."

● ● ●

TWENTY MINUTES LATER, they were floating in the center of the lake. They were the only boat in sight. A crow circled overhead and a lone fisherman was casting his line on the far shore.

Brian grabbed a piece of uncooked bacon and put it on the hook. "I know you're really mad at me."

She paused as she put her hair up in a ponytail. The wind was turning it into a tangled mess. "Of course I am," she said bluntly. "Can you even comprehend how hard I worked to make that money?"

He threw his hook and line into the water. "I can," he said. "And I'm sorry. I was just tryin' to help us. I know this whole thing is my fault, and I was just tryin' to fix it."

"I appreciate that." Laura pulled her notebook out of her backpack and looked for a pencil. She might as well study while they were out here. "But what happened is still real shitty, Brian. I have every right to be mad." She found the chewed-up pencil and gripped it tightly.

"You do," he said, grabbing a can of Coke from the cooler. "If it makes you feel any better, I'm probably more mad at myself than you are at me."

She gave him a flat look. "I highly doubt that."

"No, I am." Brian rubbed his forehead and blew out a loud breath. "I've played football from the time I could stand up. It dictated everything: Every wake-up time, every meal, every workout . . . nearly every hour of my day revolved around football in some way. Without it, I'm . . . lost." He groaned. "And now I feel like I've thrown my only chance away. This has been my dream for so long, and I *blew* it."

His chin trembled slightly, and Laura felt a pinch in her stomach, her anger beginning to ebb. He hadn't handled the last few months well—at all—but he'd been living a nightmare, too.

He shook his head and turned his attention back to the water. "Anyway, whatcha studyin'?"

"Math," she replied.

Brian half-grinned. "Ugh, math. That was my worst subject."

She rested her feet on the cooler across from her. "I know . . . I did your homework for you. Don't you remember?" she joked.

"Well if you've already done it, why do you need to study?" he said, missing her tone.

She erased an equation from her paper and blew the red eraser specks off the page. "You were in general-level classes. This is advanced—all of my classes are, if you didn't know—and I'm tryin' to get an A."

"Why are you tryin' so hard, babe?" He pulled his line out and recast it. "I thought that going back to school was just something to distract you during the day."

Laura shifted uncomfortably on her seat. Before Brian had lost all their money, she'd started looking into the LSU admissions site, wondering if she could join him there next year. Her grades were good enough, though perhaps not high enough for a scholarship. For some reason, though, she couldn't bring herself to talk to him about it quite yet. Not when his own future was so uncertain.

"Well, I'm just trying to keep my options open, you know? It'll look good to have my high school diploma if I want to apply to any other jobs." She looked back down at her notebook, afraid he'd realize there was more to her words than she was saying. "Besides, I kind of like it. . . ."

Her gaze caught on a doodle Vince had drawn on the top right-hand corner of her paper and she smiled. It was a cartoon version of Mr. Leblanc with the words, "Math jokes. If you get them, you probably don't have any friends." The quote was from one of their teacher's many inspirational posters plastered on the walls—the same posters that Laura had confessed to Vince that she actually loved.

"You're a nerd," Vince had said, his grin giving him dimples.

Laura had laughed, a little too loudly, trying to cover her embarrassment. "Oh, like you don't secretly enjoy them a little."

He'd leaned back in his chair. "Talk nerdy to me, girl."

"A-ha!" She pointed at him triumphantly. "That's the one by the window in the back! *You* love them, too!"

Brian's phone rang, cutting through the silence, and Laura lifted her eyes from the doodle.

He answered it quickly. "Hell-o," he said. After a brief pause, he said, "Yes." Brian looked over at her as he listened, his eyes slowly widening. A grin spread across his face and he shot her a thumbs-up. "That's awesome! Thank you so much, sir." Immediately after he hung up, he threw his phone down in the tackle box and let out a whoop. He moved toward Laura, picking her up and spinning her around. The boat bobbed with their movement.

Laura laughed, feeling weightless. "Good news?"

"That was the insurance company. They're gonna pay for my surgery. We did it, Laura!"

"What?" Laura screamed, giving him a hug. "That's amazing!"

His arms tightened around her and she squeezed him back, filled with elation. Brian kissed her, slowly and passionately, and warmth filled her from her head to her toes. Eventually he pulled away, resting his forehead on hers. "It's gonna happen, babe—we're finally gettin' back on track."

"I'm so happy for you," she said softly, trying to just live in this joyful moment.

"For *us*," he corrected her, grinning.

Laura smiled back. "For us."

Brian put his Oakleys on top of his head. "And see, we didn't need that money anyway."

A vice of anger wrapped around her again. "I don't know about that . . ." she said, trying not to let her frustration ruin the moment. But she couldn't help thinking that if Brian hadn't been reckless, they would have twelve thousand hard-earned dollars saved up right now, money they could have put toward building their life together—or for her college tuition.

The two sat down on the bench and Brian wrapped his arm around her shoulders. For a moment, they just sat there, basking in the warm spring weather. All of the anxieties of the past few months melted away. Finally, *finally*, she knew that everything would be okay.

So why, when Brian kissed her, had she been thinking about Vince?

• • •

"I DON'T GET it—isn't this what you wanted the whole time? Why do you sound so sad?" Madison took a sip of red wine from the long-stemmed glass in her hand and set it down on the hot tub ledge. Between the two of them, they had already drunk three-fourths of the bottle of 2012 Château Margaux they'd found in George's wine cellar earlier that night. He was out of town on a business trip, and judging from his large stock, he'd probably never even notice that one—or a couple—bottles were missing. After the first sip, they both agreed this was exceptionally better than the Sutter Home they usually downed on girls' nights.

Laura leaned her head back on the ledge and sunk down into the water, dampening the loose hair at the nape of her neck. Her face felt numb, which was usually the first sign that she was drunk. Once, during junior year, she'd poked a fork into her cheek to prove that she'd lost all feeling there. Now every time she had too much to drink, Madison would go around yelling, "Hide the forks, y'all—Laura's drunk!"

She pulled her knees to her chest. "I guess I'm just . . . confused?"

Madison poured the rest of the bottle of wine into Laura's glass. "Tell me everything," she said, handing the goblet to her friend.

Laura took a long sip. "You know those movies that show what a person's life woulda been like had they done something slightly different? Like, how one decision changes everything?"

"Yeah," Madison said, adjusting the black strap on her bikini. "I totally understand. You're wondering if you woulda won Homecoming Queen if you hadn't worn that feather dress." She shook her head. "Honey, we've all contemplated that one, too."

"Oh, shut up!" Laura said, splashing water into Madison's face. She giggled as her friend exaggeratedly wiped the water from her eyes. "Seriously, though . . . I love Brian, I do. But what if we hadn't gotten married when we did? What if we had waited?" She took another sip of her wine. "Lately, I've just been going down this tunnel of what-ifs? Would I have been happier if I'd just stayed in school in the first place?"

Madison put her glass down and leveled a stare at Laura. "Laur . . . are you not happy?"

A cloud moved over the moon and an owl hooted loudly in a nearby tree. Finally, Laura spoke. "I just wonder how my life would be different if I'd waited. If I'd thought more seriously about it . . . I'm not sure I would've made the same decision."

Madison's eyes widened. "Did something happen? What made you feel this way?"

Laura sighed. "It's just been the hardest year of my life."

"So, there were a few bumps, but he's getting the surgery now, and things will be back to normal. What's the big deal?" Madison took another sip of wine.

"The big deal is that I was happy for him—*so* happy. But I realized I wasn't happy for me." She sighed. "He gets his dream, but is it enough? I want more than to just to follow him around like a little puppy dog."

Madison shook her head. "I'm so confused—isn't that what you wanted to do? Wasn't that your plan? You were so set on getting married. Brian's dreams *were* your dreams."

"I was seventeen, Mads. I don't think I knew what I wanted," she admitted quietly.

"Does this have anything to do with that Vinny guy?" Madison grabbed her cigarettes from the ledge.

"Vince?" Laura asked, massaging her forehead. The wine was starting to give her a headache.

"Yeah, that nerd that you always hang out with at school." Madison lit her cigarette, the end glowing a bright red in the darkness.

Laura thought about Vince for a second, his supportive nature and the ability to make her laugh on cue—she couldn't remember the last time Brian had said something funny. Being with Vince did make her wonder sometimes what life would be like had she ended up with someone other than Brian. "Do you worry that George isn't who you're supposed to be with?" Laura asked instead. "Do you wonder what your life would be like if you were to marry Cash instead?"

Madison inhaled deeply, letting the smoke trickle from her mouth in long tendrils. "That's a different situation," she said, not quite meeting Laura's eye. "And Cash Romero's never gonna be able to give me the things George does."

Laura looked up at the starry night, her eyes focusing in on the Big Dipper. "But what if he could one day? What if Cash becomes a huge rock star and makes ten times more money than George? Are you still going to be happy with your decision to marry George?"

Madison squirmed in the water. "Listen, I don't know what you're so worried about. Brian's set—he's gonna be rich and famous. You made the right decision."

Laura leaned her head back. "I'm not worried about Brian's future." She sighed. "I'm worried about mine."

gabrielle

GABBY SAT IN her car as the rain poured down, pummeling her roof. In front of her, the Barton Correctional Facility stood under a gray-colored sky. She had driven all the way out there this morning, positive that she'd be able to make a decision about Tony if she could see her mom in person. But instead of going inside, she'd been sitting here for hours, lost in thought.

Gabby knew Elaine was miserable in the prison, even more so than she let on. Elaine always had a habit of pretending things were better than they actually were. Like the time when Gabby was in third grade and their car had broken down, but Elaine didn't have the money to fix it. She spent three months walking Gabby a mile to school, under the guise of trying to get in some more exercise. Or when they heard that Gabby's dad, who split almost right after she was born, had settled down two towns over and was raising a new family. Instead of getting upset about it, Elaine had simply lifted her chin, said, "Sure do feel sorry for that woman," and never discussed it again. So, in all likelihood, when Elaine said everything inside the prison was "fine," she probably meant, "hellish, but I'm getting through it." And Gabby had the ability to change that.

But on the other hand, did Elaine deserve to be released six years early? *Mom's in jail for a reason*, she reminded herself as thunder rumbled in the distance. She had committed a serious crime and was paying the price for her actions. What she did was wrong, and it had cost Gabby her college career, so why should Gabby sacrifice more of her life to get Elaine out of there? Gabby rested her head on the steering wheel, thinking about the first time she'd gone to visit her mom in jail.

Gabby had been so livid with her mom that it had taken her six months to go see her. The meeting had started out awkwardly, neither of them really knowing what to say. Gabby's last words to her mother after the sentencing had been, "I'll never forgive you," and the words seem wedged between them now. She and Elaine had been so close. It was always the two of them against the world, so the distance felt disorienting. Gabby, trying to fill in the silence during their first visit, had started talking about the weather.

Elaine had cut her off, grabbing her hand across the cold metal table. "Gabby, I know you'll never be able to forgive me, but I need to tell you that I'm sorry . . . and that while it was wrong, my intentions were good. I did it all for you."

Gabby had scoffed, yanking her hand back and crossing her arms over her chest defensively. "Are you serious, Mom? I worked *so* hard to get into Tulane—" She felt tears growing behind her eyes and sniffed, looking up toward the fluorescent light above their heads. She refused to cry over this anymore. "I worked so hard. And now all I can do is try to get by."

Elaine started to weep. "I just . . . I just wanted you to have a better life. I felt like a failure as a mother because I couldn't give you everything you deserved." She wiped the tears from her cheeks. "What I did was wrong—believe me, I know it was wrong—but I saw an opportunity for a better life and I took it. And then things got out of control and I couldn't undo it. Even if you can't forgive me, I hope you can someday understand."

Now, Gabby actually *could* understand, and she sympathized with her mother. While Gabby hadn't committed a crime, wasn't her situation similar? She, like Elaine, had seen an opportunity for a better life and she'd taken it. And now she, like Elaine, was going to have to deal with the consequences.

As the rain continued to beat down on her car, Gabby closed her eyes and considered her options. She could break up with Tony and get her mom out of jail. And honestly, she had missed Elaine desperately. Her friends were wonderful, but there was nothing that could substitute for the counsel of your own mother . . . trying to plan a wedding without her was proof of that. She didn't want to continue going through life's big moments without her mom.

On the other hand, Gabby could wait and watch as Tony's father told him the truth. Elaine would serve her sentence like any other criminal, and Gabby would have to pray Congressman Ford didn't know his son as well as he claimed . . . that even after knowing everything, Tony would still love her and want to be with her.

But was that the right decision? Could she trade her mother's life for a chance at her own happiness?

A tapping noise on the window made Gabby jump. A prison guard stood outside, peering in her window. She rolled it down, the rain splattering into her car.

"Ma'am, you've been sitting here for a while," he said, looking into her car suspiciously. "Do you need any help?"

"No," Gabby said, a resolution forming in her mind. "I was just leaving."

"All right, have a good day, then." He walked back toward the prison.

Gabby started the engine and looked down at her phone. She typed a message to Tony: Meet me at King's Cafe at 1?

He immediately wrote back, OK!

Gabby drove away from the prison, trying not to look back. If she thought much more about this, she was sure she would crumble.

• • •

GABBY HAD PICKED a busy café, thinking Tony wouldn't make a scene if there were other people around. As they sipped on Mello Joy coffee, she finally got the courage to do what she should have done months ago. "I have to talk to you about something," she said, shifting uncomfortably in the metal chair.

Tony looked up from his steaming yellow mug, his long lashes framing his beautiful dark brown eyes. Gabby wanted, so badly, to reach out and kiss him one last time. "Sure," he said. "What's up?"

She took a deep breath, trying not to tremble. "I can't marry you."

Tony paused, looking at her quizzically, and then laughed. "That's not funny, babe." He grabbed her hand, interlacing her fingers in his own. "So, I was thinking about a road trip for our honeymoon. Have you ever driven Route Sixty-Six?"

"No—Tony," Gabby said, her voice quiet and direct. She pulled her hand away, her stomach churning. Tony's brows furrowed, confusion flitting across his face as Gabby rushed to get the rest of the words out. "I can't marry you. It has absolutely nothing to do with you, but I'm going through something personal right now and I have to deal with it on my own."

Tony's face blanched and he leaned back in the seat. "Gabby, stop that. Whatever it is, we're a team now. I'll help you get through it."

Gabby looked around the coffee shop at all the people laughing and talking around them. For her, time had slowed to a crawl; it felt like her world was ending. Tony stared at her in concern, like he was trying to figure out how to help. He wasn't getting this, so she needed to make it clear to him. She couldn't look at him as she pulled off her engagement ring. "I'm sorry," she said. "I wish things were different." She placed the ring on the table and stood to leave, her stomach and chest aching with pain.

"Wait . . . where are you going?" He grabbed the ring and scrambled out of his seat, following her out of the coffee shop. "I'm so confused. Are you actually breaking up with me?"

Outside, the rain had stopped and the sun was out, illuminating the puddles in the parking lot. The world looked like it was glittering, a cruel contrast to the hollow feeling inside of her. Gabby turned to face Tony, finally looking him in the eyes. His gaze was desperate and wild—disoriented, even—and his mouth hung slack.

"You're a good guy," she said softly. "You'll find someone better than me."

"Gabby . . ." He reached for her, trying to wrap her into a hug, but she disentangled herself from his embrace. An angry red bloomed across his cheeks, and he stepped back, hurt.

She walked briskly to her car, his footsteps splashing on the wet ground behind her. As she opened her door, he grabbed her arm and spun her around. The look in his eyes was pleading and heart-wrenching. "You have to talk to me," he said, starting to tear up. "You can't just . . . end it. Not like this. What did I do?"

It's what I did, she wanted to say. But as painful as this was for him, his dad had made himself clear: keeping silent about her lies was part of the deal of getting her mom out.

"It's over, Tony. I never want to see you again," she said, lying to him one last time before slamming the door in his face.

madison

MADISON STARED AT herself in the bathroom mirror, her surprisingly mature reflection looking back at her. Her skin was dewy and bronzed. Her eyes, outlined in black kohl, were wide and luminous, and her lips were painted a light pink.

Claire stood behind her, creating soft waves in her dark hair with a curling iron.

"I still can't believe you're doing this," Claire said, clamping down on her hair with the hot tool. "Marriage isn't something you should take so lightly."

Madison stared at the scowl on her cousin's face. "Just because you're having problems doesn't mean it's going to be hard for everyone else."

Claire laughed. "Oh, sweet child, you're so naive. Bless your heart. If two people who love each other can have problems, a fake marriage is in for a world of trouble."

"Shhh," Madison said, glancing around to make sure her parents weren't within earshot. Perhaps it wasn't a conventional wedding, but the only people who knew that besides George were her friends . . . and Cash.

When she'd told him, he'd gaped at her. The two sat outside on the stoop of his trailer as the sunset gave off a purple glow. The sky was eerie and calm at the same time, which wasn't too different from how Madison felt as she broke the news about marrying George. "I'm actually in shock," he said, looking as though he was trying to process the information. Madison felt the same way.

"I just thought you should hear it from me first," she said, nervously shaking her knees.

"Is this what you want?" He looked at her, his eyes lowering.

She thought about it for a second. Sure, it wasn't exactly what she had in mind when she first started hanging around George. Claire and Laura had married their "one true loves" and didn't seem any better off for it. At least she knew that George would never hurt her. And besides, their marriage would practically be a business arrangement.

She twirled her hair as she locked eyes with Cash, wondering what he was really thinking. Was he plotting to win her back? She fantasized about him grabbing her hand and begging her to ditch George and run away with her. They'd find another way to help her parents with the mortgage and the medical bills and they'd finally be together for real, a true couple. But she knew deep down none of those things would happen. She had been fantasizing about that for years, just like she did with those lottery tickets she and Allen scratched off—addicted to the fantasy and hope of winning, but always disappointed in the end.

"Is it what you want?" he asked again, digging his Chucks into the dirt.

She looked off into the sunset and nodded her head slowly. She had finally won the lottery—it just wasn't the prize she was originally hoping for.

"Oh, my baby!" Madison's mom cried now as she poked her head in the bathroom door, bringing Madison back to the moment. "You look beautiful." The tears were already starting to flow and the ceremony hadn't even started yet. It was going to be a long day for Connie Blanchette.

"Thanks, Mama," Madison said, greeting her mom with a very careful cheek kiss so as not to mess up the makeup Claire had just spent an hour applying.

"K, yer all done," Claire said with one final curl. "Let's get the dress on." She peeked out the tiny bathroom window at the backyard of George's lake house. "Guests are already startin' to come."

Madison walked over to the dress that was hanging on the back of the bedroom door. The sunshine from the large windows was shining directly on it, although nothing was sparkling, because, well, it was Madison after all. She slipped on the dress, and Claire placed the floral wreath they made that morning on her head. For the first time all day, Claire smiled.

"You really do look beautiful," she said, hugging Madison.

"She's ready," Connie called out into the hallway, and Madison's dad appeared in the doorway.

"Aw, Daddy," Madison said, running over to Allen. He was wearing his only suit—the one he had worn to nine funerals in his lifetime. "At least this baby gets to attend something happy," Madison joked, smoothing his lapel.

He laughed. And then something happened that Madison never thought would: he broke down and sobbed.

"I'm just so . . ." He trailed off, smiled, and handed her a small wooden box.

"What's this?" she asked, holding it in her hand.

"I heard that you were supposed to have something blue," he said, wiping the tears away.

She opened it. A silver bracelet with a large beautiful blue charm sat in the box. "Oh, Daddy," she said as she held it up and looked it over. "It's perfect!"

"Do you recognize it?" he asked, looking proud of himself.

Upon closer inspection, Madison realized what it was: the blue fishing lure they had used on their epic fishing trip where the catfish tugged her dad into the water. "Oh my gosh." Her eyes began watering. "How did you do this?"

"Hold it in!" Claire yelled, running to get some tissues. "Don't you dare mess up your makeup!"

"Your mama's friend Mrs. Ashley helped me," Allen said. "I gave her the lure, and she turned it into a charm for me."

Madison handed it to him to clasp onto her wrist. "It's my favorite thing ever," she said, her heart overflowing. "Thank you." She kissed her dad and then her mom. "I love you both more than anything."

"The feeling's mutual, m'dear," Allen said, taking her by the hands. "We're both so proud of you, and we know that George is a good man. He's gonna take good care of you long after we're gone." He paused as his eyes filled with tears once more.

All of them were now crying, even Claire, who was clutching the box of tissues to her chest.

"Well, we should get out there," Connie said, looking at her watch. "It's time!"

The four of them walked out into the backyard where forty guests and George waited eagerly for the bride. The solo violinist played a moody melody that gave Madison chills. Claire walked first down the path in between the white wooden chairs that were lined up in a row. Madison, flanked by her parents on either side, gracefully followed.

George and Charlie stood at the end of the path, greeting her with a beaming smile and a wagging tail, respectively. As she stood under the floral arch with her groom, she paused to think about her friends, all so unhappy in their own relationships. She couldn't help but feel like her marriage was going to be different—after all, it was love that ruined everything. She and George didn't have to deal with that; they'd just be good friends, sharing a life. She took a deep breath as Gavin began officiating the ceremony.

Madison swallowed and pushed her hair behind her ears. She and George looked at each other, smiling.

"You ready for this?" he whispered.

"Yes," she said with a grin and was surprised to realize she meant it.

• • •

"TODAY WAS ONE of the best days of my life," George said as the two lounged on the large comfy sofa in their PJs that evening. Most girls would wear white lacy lingerie on their wedding night, but Madison had a different way: navy blue sweatpants and an old

Toulouse High T-shirt that had a bleach stain and some holes in it.

"Yeah, it was pretty awesome," she said. "I've never gotten so many gifts in my life!" Granted, they were mostly useless things like crystal candlesticks and a melon-baller, but she knew she'd have fun exchanging them for better stuff . . . or for some cold, hard cash.

"Well, I'm gonna go to bed, *bride*," George said, looking at the clock. It was already midnight. "It's been a long day."

"Yeah, I'm pretty tired, too," Madison said, letting out a loud yawn.

"So, we never talked about this, but I guess you'll want your own room," he said awkwardly.

She stared blankly at him and then it clicked: the whole *wedding night* thing. "Yeah," she agreed. "I'll take the guest room." She felt a twinge of guilt about it, but after all, he'd offered.

George leaned in and kissed her on the forehead. "G'night, Mads," he said, getting up to head to bed.

"Hey, George . . ." she said as he walked up the stairs.

He glanced back at her, an almost-hopeful look in his eye.

Madison swallowed, looking down at her hands. "I know this is a really unconventional marriage, but I just wanted to let you know I'm excited to be your wife."

He smiled, and went upstairs alone.

Madison considered her options for the night: she could check out the pay-per-view channels on George's TV, or she could take a dip in the hot tub, or she could rummage through the kitchen and eat a couple more slices of cake. But before she could make a decision, her phone buzzed. Cash.

U up new wifey? Wanna smoke?

Her heart lurched. She hadn't realized how much it would hurt to have Cash call her "wifey" . . . and not mean that she was his own. She shook her head, as if to disperse those thoughts, and picked her phone up.

Yeah, meet me at the dock in an hour?

Once she was sure the house had gone still, Madison snuck out. The evening was cool and dark, and she pulled her sweatshirt closer to her body as she walked to the dock. About a half mile down the road from George's house, Madison sat down on the wooden planks. After a few minutes, she heard them creak with the weight of some-one's footsteps. She looked up, smiling.

"I cannot believe you went through with it," Cash said with a laugh. The full moon illuminated his grin. "And I can't believe you actually snuck out to meet me on your wedding night. You're one devious little girl." He sat down next to her on the dock and lit up a cigarette, wrapping an arm around her shoulders.

Madison shrugged. She wondered if she should have felt guiltier for what she had done. *But it's not like George would really care*, she tried to convince herself.

"Why *did* you meet up with me?" Cash asked.

She stared at him in silence for a moment. "I don't know, really." *Intrigue . . . the fact that I've never been able to say no to you, perhaps.*

"Second thoughts?"

The crickets chirped and the lightning bugs glistened. She'd been trying so hard to not think about Cash. But once he'd texted, she remembered what Claire had said earlier—that she was being naive. She thought of Gabby, who put on a brave smile at the recep-tion, but Madison had seen her wipe tears from her eyes when she thought no one was looking. Not being able to be with the man she loved had turned her into a shell of herself. Would Madison feel that way, too? Would she feel trapped in a dead-end marriage with a person she didn't love?

"No," she lied, her attention returning to Cash. "No second thoughts."

He leaned back on the post and looked up at the starry night, his long hair brushing his shoulders. "So, what about us?" Cash asked. "What's going to happen to us?"

She stared back at him and bit her lip. "I really don't know."

33

claire

"SO, HOW ARE you holding up?" Claire asked Gabby. "You put on a good show, but I could tell you were kind of upset last night." The girls sat side by side in plush leather pedicure chairs at Winnie's Nails and Spa on Frontage Road. Somewhere during their third glass of champagne at Madison's reception the night before, they'd made plans for this catch-up date—though neither had anticipated what awful headaches the bubbly would give them.

"Kind of?" Gabby said, her sunglasses still on. "I'm a hot mess, Claire. Every time I force myself to stop thinking about him, Tony texts me, asking to meet up."

Claire's whole body tingled as the pedicurist tickled her feet with a scrub. "So, why don't you?"

"What would I even say?" Gabby said under her breath. "I'm not allowed to tell him the truth."

Claire glanced over at her friend. "Well, if you'd been honest in the first place . . ." She trailed off. *Honest. Ha!*, she thought to herself as she flashed to her problems with Gavin. *Good one, Claire.*

"If I'd told him that in the first place, I would've never been with him at all. Guys like Tony don't date girls like me." Gabby fanned herself with a copy of *Us Weekly*.

Claire leaned her head back on the vibrating neck rest. "He did date a girl just like you—and he asked you to marry him. I don't think you're giving yourself enough credit."

"Well, it doesn't matter," Gabby said. "My mom is getting out of jail soon and we can concentrate on trying to be a family again."

"I guess just learn from this and go into your next relationship with complete honesty," Claire said.

The technicians began painting the girls' toenails—hot pink polish for Gabby, ruby red for Claire.

Gabby pushed the sunglasses on top of her head and squinted in the fluorescent light. "So, how's that whole honesty thing working out for *you*? You talked to Gavin about everything?"

There it was. Claire squirmed. The technician steadied her foot with a firm grip and gave her a stern look. It had been almost a month since she caught Gavin at the club and, no, she still hadn't confronted him about it. "It's a completely different situation," she said evasively. The last thing she needed was gossip spreading about her and her husband around town.

"You're right," Gabby whispered back. "But I don't see how pretending like that didn't happen is going to solve anything."

Claire crossed her arms. She knew she couldn't ignore what she'd seen forever, but confronting him could lead to things she wasn't ready for—like the truth . . . or divorce. "I'll do it when I'm ready."

Gabby frowned and began massaging her temples with her fingers. "So you're just pretending like nothing's wrong?"

The technicians placed the plastic sandals on Gabby's and Claire's feet and motioned for the girls to follow them.

"Nothing is." Claire walked over to the manicure table, wishing with all her heart that what she said was true.

• • •

@Pastor_Gavin: "Decluttering isn't just for closets. Clean out your life. There's no room in it for people who bring you down." —3 hours ago

Claire stared at her phone as she got into her car at the nail place, her French tips tapping on the notifications from her tweet earlier that morning. She had gotten the idea for the line from Gavin's sermon that day. He had talked about the importance of choosing the right people in your life.

The Twitter followers were eating it up—105 retweets and 240 likes. As she sorted through some of the replies, a call from the 337 area code showed up on her caller ID.

"Hello?" She rested her hand on the steering wheel.

"Claire?" a high-pitched woman's voice asked.

"This is she," Claire responded, unsure of who it was on the other end.

"It's Kimmy . . . from The Saddle." Her voice sounded hesitant.

Claire's heart sank. "What is it?" she asked, her voice shaky. Her palms began to sweat. She'd been praying that Kimmy would never use her number.

"Hey, don't worry. I haven't seen your husband or nothing like that." She paused.

Claire relaxed slightly. "Then what?"

"I've been thinking a lot about our conversation last month. And, well, I have an idea." Her voice sounded confident.

"What kinda idea?" Claire hesitantly asked, watching a group of women walk in front of her parked car at the spa.

"Can you meet me for coffee right now?"

She looked at the clock on the radio. Her mom could keep Sadie for another hour, she supposed. "Okay," she said.

"Great!" Kimmy cheered. "Meet me at the Chicory Coffee House in twenty minutes?"

"Okay." Claire ended the call, the Twitter screen popping up again. She paused, feeling inspired to tweet a follow-up message: @Pastor_Gavin: *"Each person comes into your life for a reason— it's up to you to figure out why."*

• • •

"THANKS FOR MEETING up," Kimmy said as she held her iced coffee with both hands across the table. Her nails also looked freshly painted, although they were neon orange. "I have a proposition for you."

"I'm listening," Claire said, blowing on her hot cup of coffee.

"So, you know how we were talking about your marriage and how you wanted to feel sexy again?" she whispered.

Claire blushed as she looked around the coffee shop, hoping that no one heard that. She nodded quickly.

"Okay, so this is something I've wanted to do for a while. And talking with you, I got even more inspired to do it," Kimmy said, fiddling with the straw of her iced coffee. "My grandma passed away a few months ago."

"Oh, I'm so sorry to hear that," Claire interrupted, putting her hand over Kimmy's.

"Don't be—she was old and crazy—like, swears she was abducted by aliens-crazy." She quickly made the sign of the cross. "May she rest in peace." She looked back up and smiled. "But she left me an inheritance. And, well, I'm ready to be done with the club and be a boss lady, but my real talent is stripping. So . . ." She smiled and ran her fingers nervously through her bleached blond hair. "I want to open up one of those aerobic striptease studios to help women like you get their groove back. What do you think?" she asked, beaming at Claire.

Claire leaned back in her chair, thinking about Kimmy's idea. Claire had recently read an article in *Glamour* about pole fitness being a hot workout trend. "I think you might have something there," she said, nodding her head. "But, what do you need me for?"

Kimmy stretched her hands across the table. "I want you to be my first client."

"Um, I dunno about that." Claire shook her head, thinking about the brunette she'd seen writhing on the pole when she'd caught Gavin with Kimmy. There was no way she could move like that.

"Ah, come on!" Kimmy cocked her head to the side. "You wouldn't even have to pay me. I just want to make sure this is what I want to do and that it works before I throw all of Granny's money into the studio." She took a big sip of her drink and flashed her wide eyes at Claire. "Please let me practice with you," she begged. "Please?"

Claire fanned herself with her napkin. She could feel herself getting hotter and more uncomfortable.

"We'd have a blast, I promise!" Kimmy continued, smiling at her.

She contemplated the offer for a moment. As far as she knew, Gavin hadn't been to the club in a month, but it's not like their sex life had improved. They were still stressed and busy. The one time she'd tried to initiate, Gavin had said he was too tired and ended up falling asleep in front of the TV. Claire looked down at her outfit— a boring gray pencil skirt she had gotten before they were even married. The hem was fraying and the back zipper didn't go all the way up, a casualty of the extra pounds she had put on after Sadie. The dark satin blouse was a more recent purchase, a quick pickup from Talbots after her baby had spit up on the top she had been wearing that day. But she had to admit it made her look frumpy. Most of her postbaby clothes did.

"Please?" Kimmy said again, her blue eyes pleading.

Claire could feel herself softening. It couldn't hurt to try, right? Maybe it would help her get her sexy back. And at the very least, she'd be helping Kimmy get out of stripping.

"Sure," she finally said. "Why not?"

Kimmy clapped her hands and yelled out a loud "Woo!" The young couple sitting one table over turned their heads and stared at the two of them. Claire put her elbows on the table and rubbed her face with her hands, wondering what, exactly, she'd just agreed to.

• • •

THE NEXT DAY, Claire drove to Kimmy's apartment on her lunch break, downing a Moon Pie and an RC Cola on the way. Her nerves jumped in her stomach as she pulled into the small apartment complex on Sugar Mill Road, fifteen miles from the church.

Kimmy opened the door with a beaming smile. "Come in! Come in!"

Claire's eyes widened as she entered the studio. "Wow, your place is so . . . beautiful."

She was surprised at how nicely decorated it was. A twin bed sat in the far right corner, covered with a plush floral duvet and chunky knitted afghan. Hardcover books and picture frames filled with images of Kimmy and her family were placed on a white vintage bookcase. A lavender moth orchid perched atop a rustic wooden side table, and a sprawling peace lily stood in the opposite corner. The kitchen was small but well organized. A buttercup-colored Kitchen-Aid stand mixer sat on the counter next to a homemade three-tiered strawberry shortcake in a glass dome.

"You can just throw your stuff right here," Kimmy said, pointing to a Tiffany-blue chaise lounge by the door. She was wearing a pink sports bra and black leggings.

Claire couldn't help but be jealous of Kimmy's rock solid body. *Goals* . . . she thought to herself as she dropped her bag and ran into the bathroom to change. She stared in the full-length mirror on the back of the door, looking at the old white tank top and faded blue yoga pants that were wrinkled from being crammed in the back of her drawer for at least a year.

"Okay, you ready?" Kimmy greeted her as she came back into the main room. "I know you only have an hour, so let's just jump into it." She walked over to the stereo. "Since I don't have a pole in here, we're just gonna have to do some warm-ups and a sexy little dance, but I want you to really be honest with me about everything, okay, Claire? Like does this work and do you think I have a good idea for a business and all that."

Claire nodded. "I'm ready." She clapped her hands, trying to pretend that she had no qualms about what she was doing there.

Kimmy grabbed Claire's waist and positioned her in the middle of the room. "Stand up straight. You're slouching. And take your hair down." Kimmy tugged at her ponytail. "You'll feel sexier."

Claire loosened her rubber band and shook her short ponytail out.

Kimmy yelled out, "Beautiful!" then hit a button on the stereo. A hip-hop instrumental song started blaring from the surround-sound speakers.

"Okay, we're just gonna get loose right now," Kimmy said, touching Claire's shoulders with a firm grip. "You're so stiff. Relax!"

Claire let out a deep breath and shook her body out a little, trying to unwind a bit. She figured if she was going to do this, she might as well *try.*

"Now, let's just warm up. Do what I do." Kimmy stood in front of her and moved her head in a circular motion. Her long curly blond hair swayed in a seductive way, sending whiffs of grapefruit and almond from her fragrant shampoo with every swing.

They did a couple of bends, shoulder rolls, and chest pops. Claire's didn't go as far as Kimmy's did, although the more they moved, the more into it she got.

"Let's move our hips, now," Kimmy said over the music. She put her hands on Claire's waist and began guiding her body with the rhythm. "You go, girl!" she said.

"I feel ridiculous," Claire shouted, laughing uncontrollably.

"Well, you look fierce!" Kimmy said, jumping up and down with excitement.

The two girls started dancing with each other, and Claire's awkwardness began fading away as the beat grew stronger and her moves became more fluid.

Maybe Kimmy was right, she thought to herself as she popped and twirled her body around the room with an energy she hadn't felt in almost a year. *Maybe this could help Gavin find me sexy again.*

madison

Dear Claire and Gavin,

Thank you so much for the crystal vase. Immediately after opening up your gift, George and I ran to the backyard and chopped a couple of roses from the garden to put in it. The flowers died within a couple of days, but that's not because of your vase—I'm just not good with plants. But I'm determined to be! Thank you for helping me become one of those girls who always has fresh cut flowers in her house. Love you!

Madison (and George)

Dear Laura and Brian,

Thank you so much for the fun box of kitchen goodies you gave us for our wedding. I can't wait to open up beers with the deer antler bottle opener, and George is super excited about baking a turkey with the roaster you gave us. Plus, we're already fighting over who gets to use the salad spinner when we cook! We'll have to have you guys over for dinner soon— let me just learn how to cook first (Laur, wanna give me lessons? ☺). Love you both.

Madison (and George)

Dearest Gabby,

*You really shouldn't have gotten us those bathroom towels—
all I want to do now is take showers every minute of the day
so that I can use them! They're beyond perfect—just like you
are. Thank you so much for helping us celebrate our big day.
Love you.*

Madison (and George)

MADISON PUT HER pen down and shook out her hand. Writing
thank-you notes was such a bitch, but she knew Connie would kill her
if she didn't do it. It was only a week after the wedding and Madison
wondered if she'd get bonus points for sending them out so quickly.

She looked across the kitchen table at George's pile of beige note
cards. "How are yours coming?" she asked.

"Almost done." He took a sip of his coffee. "And yours?"

"Two more." She shook her hand again and walked over to the
sink—it was full of dirty dishes from breakfast. Madison had made
her famous scrambled eggs (famous in the sense that she watched a
Martha Stewart how-to video on YouTube and then made them her
own), and George had whipped up his delicious fluffy pancakes (his
secret ingredient was sour cream). "You know, we're already acting
like an old married couple," she had joked earlier as they shuffled
past each other in the kitchen, busy with their food preparations.

"Do you remember who gave us this?" George asked, holding up
a navy and white paperback book called *101 Questions for Your First
Year of Marriage*. On the cover, a cartoon couple sat at a table drinking wine and eating pasta.

Madison walked back to the table, her plaid pajama pants dragging on the wood floor, and studied the book. "Aunt Jillian." She
sighed. "Make that three more notes I have to write." She yawned
loudly. "I'm done for now."

"Tired?" George asked.

"Uh-huh," she said, sitting back down at the table.

"Out late last night?" he asked casually, not looking up from his note card.

Madison's head snapped up. "Uh, what do you mean?"

"Oh, I thought you went out with Cash . . ." he said quietly, finally looking at her. "I heard his motorcycle on the street and saw you get on it."

Madison's heart beat faster as she put her water glass down on the table. Cash had taken her to a concert, then back to his place to hook up, before dropping her at George's a little after 4:00 a.m. She tried to come up with some kind of excuse that wouldn't make her sound—or feel—like the biggest bitch in the world, but nothing came to mind.

"You don't have to hide it," George said, blinking a few times. "You should feel comfortable hanging out with whoever you want."

"I'm sorry," she said guiltily. As she stared at him, taking in his weary green eyes and the light stubble that lined his chin, she tried to figure out what was going through his head. When they'd decided to get married, George had asked for her companionship, but not her heart. Still, did he truly not care about her sneaking out with another guy? Or did he care for her so much that he was happy to take what he could get? The thought tugged at her and she laid her hand over his.

"George, I know what we have isn't exactly normal, but I want you to know that I am happy and I really like spending time with you. I'm sorry if I betrayed your trust by lying."

He shook his head. "You haven't. I know what I signed up for. And the feeling's mutual by the way." He gave her hand a squeeze, then pulled out of her grip and pushed his thank-you notes pile to the side.

"So, I can think of about a million things I'd rather be doing than writing these, including removing my own front teeth. How 'bout you?"

She laughed, feeling the tension between the two of them ease. "Same."

"How about a drive?" He stood up and started clearing the table.

"Sounds great," she said, brushing her hair out of her eyes. "Where do you wanna go?" She stood up and placed her water glass in the sink.

"It's a surprise," he said. "Meet me back here in ten minutes."

The two went upstairs to their respective rooms to change. After throwing on a clean T-shirt and swapping out her plaid pants for a pair of jeans, Madison slid down the wooden staircase railing and joined George by the back door. He was waiting patiently with his keys in hand, wearing a blue-and-white-checkered button-down and khakis. His hair was also neatly combed with a little bit of gel.

"You clean up nice," she said, gently punching him in the arm. "How the heck did you get ready that fast?"

"Time machine," he said, waggling his brows. "Let's go!"

They drove with the top down on the quiet oak-tree-lined back roads, letting the cool springtime breeze float over them. She hummed along to the Milky Chance song on the radio while George tapped out the beat on the steering wheel, the silence between them easy and comfortable.

After about twenty minutes, George turned into a long gravel driveway that led to a large antebellum mansion.

"What's this?" she asked, lowering her sunglasses.

"My childhood home," George answered.

Madison's mouth dropped as she looked at the gorgeous structure standing before her. It was painted yellow with black shutters and had imposing white columns. A large porch wrapped around the entire home and a wrought iron Juliet balcony was situated just above the front door.

"Who lives here now?" she asked in disbelief.

"No one." He parked the car in the paved semicircle in front of the house and got out.

She opened up her door and followed him. "Why don't you live here? It's unbelievable."

"It's complicated," he said as they walked up the front steps.

Madison continued gawking as he unlocked the front door. They stepped inside, and the smell of cedarwood, dust, and cardboard hit her. The first floor was empty, save for a few boxes, a large armoire, and a vintage leather trunk.

She ran her hand along the mahogany banister that lined the grand staircase inside and came away with a light coating of dust.

"My brother and sister and I would slide down these when we were little," he said, gesturing to the steps. He pointed to a tiny scar on his forehead. "Christmas day, when I was five." He chuckled. "Parents made the mistake of buying us new sleeping bags, so I used mine to slide from the top of the stairs to the bottom. It was the best moment of my life until I hit the last step and fell face-first onto my brother's new toy bricks."

"Oh my god, I have a matching one." Madison lifted her bangs and pointed to a small scar on her forehead. "When I was four, Claire chased me around our grandma's house with a remote control, saying she was going to control me, and I ran right into the corner of a glass coffee table."

"Ouch," George said, running a finger lightly over the raised skin.

Madison shivered under the unexpected touch. To cover, she gently punched him on his arm. "Whatever, I think it makes me badass. And you, too."

He laughed. "Something like that."

"So, why don't you live here?" Madison walked into the kitchen, which had a large brick fireplace on one wall. "Not that your place on Darby Lake isn't great, but this is *spectacular*."

He leaned his elbows on the wooden island as she looked through the cabinets. "Family drama."

She joined him at the island and bumped her hips against his. "You can't keep teasing me with that. What's the drama this time?"

He shrugged. "It's a long story, but after my parents' accident, my siblings and I inherited this place, split three ways. Henry and Chelsy wanted to sell it—they made a big fuss about needing the money, since they weren't given the family business like I was."

He coughed. "The house stayed on the market for months, and it was looking like we weren't gonna get what it was worth. So, I just bought them out to try and appease everyone."

"I take it that didn't work," Madison said.

He chuckled and shook his head. "Nope. They thought I was rubbing my wealth in their faces."

"So, is that why you're not living here? Because your brother and sister made you feel guilty about it?"

George was silent for a moment, staring out the kitchen window to the manicured backyard. Madison followed his gaze to a set of wrought iron benches and tables positioned around a mossy fish pond.

"And because being here reminds me that I don't have a family anymore," he said finally.

Madison's heart wrenched at his words and the deeply sad look on his face. She could tell that once his family had meant everything to him. She put her arms around his shoulder. "That's not true," she said softly. "I'm your family now."

He looked at her and smiled, pushing a lock of hair behind her ear. His silver Rolex caught the sunlight from the window, casting a rainbow on the cream-colored walls.

"Thanks," he said, giving her a brief hug.

"So, show me the rest of this place," she said when he pulled away, walking out of the kitchen and heading up the stairs.

They entered a small bedroom to the right of the landing, which George admitted was his. The walls were covered in map wallpaper. Upon closer inspection, she noticed there was handwriting over some of the locations. Madison leaned in and read one of the scribbles. "Florence, Italy: August 20. Had the best sandwich I've ever tasted—prosciutto è buono." Above it, a city in Germany was circled. The writing read, "Stuttgart: February 7. Visited Porsche Museum—I will have one of those one day."

"Um, this is the most adorable thing I've ever seen," Madison said. "You kept a diary of your travels on the wall?" She walked over to him in the doorway and pinched his cheeks. "I can just see little George Dubois writing on his wall after every vacation."

His face turned red. "You shoulda seen how mad my mom was when she caught me doing that."

"Why? It's so cool," Madison said, running her fingers along an entry over Provence. "If I woulda ever traveled, I would have totally done something like this."

"Well, I'll make you a map room if you want. We'll be traveling to all sorts of places." He turned back to her. "Which reminds me, we still have to plan a honeymoon."

Her stomach jumped with excitement. "Yes! I've narrowed it down to twenty places. The list is at home—maybe we can go over it tonight."

He laughed as they walked into another room. It was larger than George's and painted a soft lavender. A set of French doors led to a balcony overlooking the backyard.

"This was Chelsy's room. She was the princess. Andrew and I were so jealous of this balcony—she got a rope ladder and used to sneak out at night to meet up with the boy who lived down the road." George walked out onto the veranda. "You see those old oaks?" He pointed ahead. "There was this story about a guy in the eighteen hundreds who brought in a million spiders and set them loose on his oak trees so that they would make all these webs. His two daughters were getting married on the same day, and on the morning of the wedding, he had the servants spray the trees and cobwebs with gold dust."

"Oh my god, the famous Gold Dust Wedding—was that this house?" Madison interrupted.

"*Hell*, no," he said, laughing. "But Chelsy was obsessed with that story, always telling my dad that's what she wanted for her wedding. So on her wedding day, that sucker brought in hundreds of pounds of gold dust and had it sprinkled everywhere on the grounds as a surprise." George shook his head. "It was a mess! Everyone had that shit on them for weeks. Hell, sometimes I still see it on my clothes."

She gazed out over the oak trees, and for a moment she could have sworn she saw them glistening with gold. They stood there, leaning on the railing and watching the day go by until the afternoon sun slanted in the sky and slowly sunk beneath the tree line. It reminded Madison of all the times she had sat with her dad on the back porch, shooting the shit or just being together.

Madison glanced at George out of the corner of her eye, taking in his neatly combed hair and the jeans that came up a little too high above his sneakers. She'd never pictured having a husband like him. Heck, she'd never much thought about being married at all. But standing in this house, she could imagine what it'd be like to raise their kids here. They'd have map rooms and build forts in the oak trees. They'd slide down the banister on Christmas morning and make s'mores in the kitchen fireplace.

This was what she was supposed to want. Ease. Comfort. Happiness. And a part of her *was* truly happy. But she couldn't stop the voice in the back of her mind that wondered whether it was enough.

35

laura

"ARE YOU SURE you don't want anything else to eat?" Laura asked Brian, looking at their hotel's room service menu. They were sitting on the large king bed, and Brian was flipping through the seemingly endless channels on the TV. It almost felt like they were on vacation, and not waiting anxiously for Brian's surgery in New Orleans the next morning. "Doctor says you can't eat past midnight, and you've only got an hour before then. Spring rolls? French fries? Chocolate cake?"

Rob and Janet had taken the two of them to Copeland's earlier that night, splurging on Brian's last meal before his surgery. He had ordered cheese fries, a rib eye, mac and cheese, and a slice of turtle cheesecake. She had figured he couldn't possibly still be hungry, but Laura had learned over the years to never underestimate the power of Brian's insatiable hunger.

Brian wrinkled his nose. "I'm good."

"Okay!" She closed the menu, put it back on the nightstand, and cuddled up next to her husband on the bed. "Can you believe this day has finally come?"

He wrapped his muscular arm around her shoulders. "Babe, I know this hasn't been a good year for you—*for us*—but I want you to know how much it means to me that you stood by me through it all." It made her happy hearing that—like he finally understood and appreciated all the sacrifices that she had made for him.

She nuzzled her head into his neck, breathing in the familiar musk of his aftershave. "Well, we're in this together. That's what marriage is." Sure, they had their setbacks this year, and maybe she had her own doubts, but she reminded herself they were married and she needed to give their relationship everything she had. Maybe neither of them had grown up completely yet, but they were gonna grow up together.

Brian softly stroked her hair. "So, you'll still love me if this surgery doesn't work?"

Laura's stomach twisted into a knot. She'd spent so much time worrying that he wouldn't be able to even get the surgery that she'd barely considered the possibility that it wouldn't work. "Why would you be worried about that?"

He turned on his side and faced her. "What? You not loving me anymore . . . or the surgery not working?"

"Both," she said, sitting up, her eyes narrowing in on Brian's face. "Of course I'll still love you. And of course the surgery will work. Why would you even say that?"

He sighed, lacing his fingers behind his head and staring up at the ceiling. "You'll be at the hospital the whole time, right?" Brian sounded nervous. He was *never* nervous, not even when Toulouse High had played their rival in the playoffs junior year. They'd been down by twelve in the fourth quarter, but Brian managed to turn the game around and win it on a last-second quarterback sneak.

"Of course I'll be there," Laura said, kissing his forehead and forcing herself to calm down. She had to be strong for the both of them . . . because if she thought about what would happen if the surgery didn't work, she might fall apart. "Now, are you sure you don't want the chocolate cake?"

Brian grinned, his mood instantly lightening. He reached around her to grab the room service menu, "Well, maybe just one slice."

• • •

IT HAD ONLY been twenty minutes into Brian's operation when Janet opened up her purse and pulled out three sandwich bags filled with powdered sugar-covered Chex. "I made some puppy chow for us," she said handing Laura a bag. "I always get hungry when I'm nervous."

Laura, Rob, and Janet were sitting in the hard green faux leather chairs in the waiting room. Laura had been studying but was finding the waiting room too distracting. Two young kids kept tugging on their mother's sleeve to show her their drawings. An elderly man with a smoker's rattle coughed on cue every five minutes, and a woman with a faux-hawk and a snake tattoo on her neck kept checking her watch and sighing. Everyone was restless, which in turn made Laura restless.

Laura smiled and took the bag from her mother-in-law, grabbing a handful of the sugary snack. "How's your knitting coming?" she asked between bites.

Janet held up a big square of knitted yarn featuring a gray and yellow geometric design. "Well, I just started. It's gonna take me a while to finish it."

"It's beautiful," Laura said, admiring the piece. "What's it gonna be?"

Janet blushed. "A baby blanket."

"Aw, that's sweet." Laura paused. "Whose baby?"

Janet looked back down to her work, as if she didn't want to make eye contact with Laura. "Yours."

Laura suddenly felt like the powdered sugar had congealed in her throat, and started to cough. She doubled over, and Janet patted her on the back. She waved her mother-in-law off. "I'm fine . . . wrong pipe."

"Don't worry," Janet said, sitting back. "I know you're not pregnant, dear. But I hope that you and Brian are able to start your family soon, and thought I may as well get this done so when I do get a grandbaby, it'll be ready."

Laura's stomach roiled and she felt her face growing hot. She was only eighteen—did Janet really want her to become a teen mom? She fought to keep her cool and stay polite.

"Well, that's just the sweetest," Laura lied, twisting her wedding band around her finger anxiously. "I'm gonna go get a Coke—do either of y'all want anything?"

"No thanks," Rob grunted from two seats down, not looking up from the issue of *Outdoor Life* in his hand.

"Could you get me a Diet Coke, sweetie?" Janet reached into her pocket and pulled out a wad of ones.

Laura pushed Janet's money away. "Of course, but it's my treat. Y'all paid for our hotel room. It's the least I can do."

As Laura made her way to the vending machine area, she began to feel dizzy. She stared at the glowing soda machine, remembering her conversation with Brian the night before. What if he had complications with the surgery? What if he couldn't play football again, and they were stuck living with Rob and Janet forever? What if Brian, like Janet, just expected her to get pregnant and pop out three babies by the time she was twenty-five?

As she pushed the Diet Coke button, she felt a wave of frustration pass through her. Janet expected Laura to focus her whole life on Brian. It was selfish. But honestly, hadn't Brian been a little selfish, too? Brian had let her quit high school to be with him. Yes, she had wanted to do it, but he'd never even questioned that decision, never encouraged her to think about what she might be giving up.

Laura grabbed the soda from the machine and she pushed the button for the Cherry Coke, startling as her phone vibrated in her back pocket.

It was a text from Vince.

Missed you in class today. Mr. Leblanc may or may not have been stoned. I'll tell you everything when you're back. Hope the surgery's going well.

Laura smiled and started to write back, her stomach fluttering a little. Then Madison's words from the night in the hot tub popped into her head: "Does this have anything to do with Vince?"

She stared at the screen for a second, her heart beating out of her chest. Maybe Brian was being selfish, but if Laura was being honest, she was in the wrong, too. She'd developed an emotional connection with another guy. She looked forward to seeing Vince in class and laughing with him over lunch. Hell, she'd talked to him about wanting to go to college when she hadn't worked up the courage to tell Brian that yet. She clicked the lock screen on her phone and put it back in her pocket.

Anxiety bubbled up inside of her, and she tried to fight it off. Brian was her *husband* and he needed her right now. He was in surgery and his career was on the line. That was where her attention—her *heart*—should be. Not with some other guy.

She headed back to Rob and Janet, and spent the next few hours with her headphones in, focusing solely on her schoolwork—something that she could actually control.

• • •

BY DINNERTIME, THEY were allowed to see Brian. The doctor had told them the surgery went perfectly and they had high hopes for his recovery. After Rob and Janet fussed over their groggy son, they left Laura and Brian alone in the room.

"How's the food?" Laura asked as he took bites of the roasted chicken, rice, green beans, and carrots the hospital delivered to his room.

"I can't believe I'm gonna say this . . ." His voice was hoarse from the breathing tube they'd used during the surgery. "But I'd rather have your cooking than this crap." He smiled and patted the cot. Even though the joke was at Laura's expense, she appreciated his attempt at humor. She sat down next to him, being careful not to touch his leg.

She grinned back. "You're a jerk, you know that?" She pushed his blond hair off his forehead and stroked his cheek.

"I can't wait to get back onto the team and move back to Baton Rouge with you," he said, a little slur in his voice thanks to the painkillers coursing through his system. "Maybe we can get a house off campus next year, with a backyard and a puppy."

Laura kissed his cheek. "Can we name him Gumbeaux?"

"We can name him whatever you want." He squeezed her hand. "Just as long as he's, like, a hearty dog . . . like a bulldog or a Lab."

Laura laughed. "Works for me."

Brian focused his bleary eyes on her. "I love you so much. Thanks for being here for me."

"I love you, too, babe," she said, kissing him again. They had been through a lot this year, but it would only make them stronger.

"From here on out, it's all gravy. Red carpet events, private jets, a mansion . . . baby, I'm gonna make you so happy," he went on.

Her phone buzzed. She stood up from the bed and read the message from Vince.

When are you back?

She held her phone close to her heart as Brian continued talking about the life they were going to have. Laura closed her eyes and imagined it, too. A happy marriage, a successful husband . . .

She looked back at her phone and stared at Vince's text again. She hovered over his contact information, then with a deep breath, pressed DELETE. A few seconds later, Vince was no longer in her contacts. She put her phone down, smiled at Brian, and took another deep breath.

For better or worse, in good times and bad, she'd committed herself to Brian. They were married, and Laura for one believed in keeping her promises.

gabrielle

IT HAD BEEN a little over a month since Gabby had broken up with Tony and shattered both of their hearts—a long, miserable month. Tony's father, of course, had been gleeful about the breakup, but true to his word, immediately started the process of getting her mom released. It had been agonizingly slow but Gabby kept telling herself that waiting a month for her mom was a million times better than waiting the remaining six years of her sentence.

First she'd had to fill out a petition for her mom, which Mr. Ford submitted to the governor, who in turn passed it along to the parole board. She knew that Mr. Ford being best friends with the governor had everything to do with the pardon getting the green light, but Gabby also liked to think that the board felt empathy for Elaine's circumstances and could see that she was a good person.

Now the day of her release was finally here. Excited as she was to have her mom back, Gabby wondered if she'd think of Tony every time she saw Elaine, of the life she could've had?

As she stood outside the penitentiary, waiting for Elaine to exit through the barbed wire fence, Gabby scrolled through her messages from Tony. It'd become a habit over the past few weeks, as if rereading his words could somehow bring him back into her life. The last text was sent on April thirtieth, and it was the most excruciating of all: I just need to talk to you. Do you know how hard it is to not have closure on something like this?

Since then, there'd been radio silence. The fact that he'd stopped reaching out made her sad, but relieved. She couldn't blame him. After all, she hadn't been responding to him. Who'd want to have a one-sided conversation? Gabby stared at his name on her phone and wondered if he was over her yet. He'd fallen in love with her so quickly; maybe he'd already met a new girl to dance with in the kitchen . . . in the bedroom . . . in the living room. The thought made it hard for her to breathe.

Just as she was debating erasing his contact information, the prison doors creaked open, and for the first time in four years, her mom stepped out into the world. Elaine had cut her hair since the last time Gabby saw her, and her normally dark locks were streaked with gray. Instead of the orange jumpsuit, she wore a purple cotton blouse and high-waisted faded blue jeans. Gabby used to make fun of her for wearing them, but they were now actually back in style.

Her mom stood at the top of the steps, taking a deep breath of fresh air, clearly savoring her freedom. Her head tilted back, her eyes closed, and she smiled. Gabby, through her heartache, found herself smiling, too.

"Mama!" Gabby called out. Elaine's eyes fluttered open and she looked around, finally spotting Gabby at the bottom of the steps. The two women squealed as Elaine ran down and into her daughter's arms.

Gabby hugged her mom as tight as she could. "Dang, Mama," she said, eventually stepping back from the hug and taking a look at the woman before her. "Freedom looks good on you."

Elaine did a little shimmy of excitement. The two grasped hands and didn't let go until they got to the car.

• • •

"YOUR PLACE LOOKS great," Elaine said as they walked into Gabby's apartment. "You're cleaner than I am!"

"Well, I knew the queen of clean was gonna be stayin' with me, so naturally I tidied up." Gabby walked over to the air conditioner and turned it on. It was only early May, but it was muggy already. "Sorry I couldn't keep our old place. It was just too expensive."

"It's lovely," Elaine said, looking around the room. "What's this?" she asked, walking over to a small pink and white Easter basket from Gabby's childhood that sat on the futon. Gabby had filled it with her mom's standard toiletries, like Rembrandt toothpaste and Pantene Pro-V shampoo and conditioner.

"I just picked up some of your favorite things." Gabby pulled her hair into a ponytail and sat on the couch. "I figured you'd probably wanna pamper yourself, now that you're out."

"Look at you taking care of your mama," Elaine said with a proud smile. "I should be the one taking care of you." She put her hands on Gabby's cheeks, and the two of them awkwardly stood there in the middle of the room for a moment. Gabby had made space for Elaine in her home, but she still wasn't sure how to make space for her in her *life*.

"I'm gonna order some pizza for us," Gabby said, breaking up the silence. "Pepperoni from Giovanni's?"

Her mom nodded enthusiastically. "Sounds delicious."

Later, as they indulged in the pizza, they caught up on the past month.

"So, are you ready to talk about why you broke off your wedding with Tony?" Elaine asked as she blotted the grease off of the pizza with a paper towel. Gabby had mentioned the breakup during their visitation in April but hadn't gone into detail. She didn't want her mom to know the truth about why she was being released early—she knew Elaine would feel guilty, and this was supposed to be a fresh start for them. Plus, if Gabby was being honest, it was easier for her not to talk about it.

"Um, it just didn't work out. We were two different people." She took a big bite of pizza, trying to stave off any further conversation.

"I'm so sorry to hear that." Her mom put her hand on her shoulder. "It's better that you found out before you actually got married though. Saves both of you a lot of pain." She shook her head. "You will find somebody great one day. . . ."

"I sure hope so," Gabby said, attempting to figure out a way to steer the conversation elsewhere. "So, what's your plan now that you're out? What's on your agenda?"

"Well, for starters, I'm gonna make up for lost time with you," Elaine said, her eyes shining. She put her pizza crust on the paper plate and wiped her hands with a napkin. "I'm gonna make things right, okay? I'm gonna get a job and help you pay for college. I owe you that."

Gabby put her plate down and frowned. "Mom, I'm almost twenty-two. I've made it okay on my own and you don't owe me anything. Besides, looking out for me is what got you in trouble in the first place. . . ."

Her mom sighed and then hung her head.

"Sorry, that came out wrong." Gabby bit her lip. "Listen, today marks a clean slate for both of us, okay? No more lies . . . no more guilt. Let's just put everything in the past and start over—what do you say?"

Elaine took a deep breath. "I'd like that."

"Okay, great!" Gabby grabbed her half-eaten pizza crust and held it up. "To new beginnings," she said, tapping her mom's crust with hers.

"To new beginnings!" Elaine smiled. "Hey, you know what I'm craving? Ice cream! Want to go to Dairy Queen for dessert?"

Gabby's eyes lit up. They used to go through the drive-thru all the time. A cookie dough Blizzard was her mom's reward for good grades and a pick-me-up when either of them had a bad day. One time they both got the giggles so hard as the car pulled up to the speaker that Elaine couldn't even get the order out. When she finally did and they pulled up to the takeout window, tears of laughter were streaming down both their faces. The employee's confused look only made them laugh harder.

"I'm in!" Gabby said.

As Gabby drove them toward the outskirts of town, she scanned through the radio stations until she found her mom's favorite—the classic country music station. But instead of it making Elaine happy, her mom started to cry.

"Oh my gosh, what's wrong, Mama?" She kept her eyes on the road but reached her arm out to comfort Elaine.

"I'm sorry," she said, drying her tears. "It's just—being out. It's incredible! I'm so thankful. And being back . . . with you." She put her hand on Gabby's leg. "I know you said I don't owe you anything, but I'm gonna be a better mom. I promise, Gabs." Elaine looked out the window as a semi-trailer truck passed them on the interstate. "Prison changed me. It made me realize what life was really about."

"And what's that?" Gabby asked, slowing the car down as she took the exit for Dairy Queen.

"Family—*you*." She leaned her head back on the headrest. "You're my world, Gabs. You're the best thing that ever happened to me." Her voice grew angry. "And I was so stupid and so focused on giving you material things that I ended up missing out on *years* of your life."

Gabby turned the car into the parking lot and shut the engine off. "Listen, Mama. I know you were just trying to help me. You were in a tough situation, and I get that you were putting my happiness first." She flashed back to her deal with Mr. Ford; she understood the feeling of putting someone else first all too well. "I want you to know that I forgive you," she said, realizing that she meant it.

"You do?" Her mom smiled through the tears.

"Yes," she said, leaning in for a hug. "I love you. And I promise I'll help you get back on your feet."

As she and Elaine sat inside the Dairy Queen, catching up and eating their cookie dough Blizzards, Gabby thought about everything that she had gone through to get to this point. Maybe she and Tony weren't supposed to end up together, after all. Maybe he and Mr. Ford were put in her life to get her mom back, to help her forgive Elaine for what she'd done, to understand how quickly one lie could snowball into another. And as painful as it was that she'd never be with Tony again, there was something comforting about knowing she got a second chance with her mom. She'd wanted so badly to be a part of his family . . . but now, against all odds, she had her own back again.

madison

"SO, WHY AREN'T you wearing one of those sexy lil' black and white uniforms?" Cash asked as he greeted Madison with a nuzzle on the neck and welcomed her into his trailer.

"What the hell are you talking about?" she asked, raising an eyebrow and tossing her backpack of cleaning supplies on the floor.

"You know—like those French maids." He opened the fridge and handed her a cold can of Budweiser.

She rolled her eyes. *"Je ne suis pas française."* It was one of the phrases she remembered from high school French class, and the only one she could think of off the top of her head that was actually relevant to this conversation.

"Ooh . . ." Cash smiled. From the look on his face, it was clear he had no idea what she had said to him. "Talk dirty to me, baby."

She laughed, then took a sip of the beer.

"So, remind me why this rich husband of yours is making you work again?" He propped himself up on the kitchen countertop in the one spot that wasn't covered in empty boxes, beer cans, or dirty dishes.

She walked over and sat down on the hideous orange couch—he had taken it from his parents' den when he moved out after high school graduation. Madison had helped him hoist it from the house and get it to their backyard, where his new home was parked.

"I'm just helping my mom make some extra money." She leaned back. "George is already paying my dad's medical bills and their mortgage. I can't really ask him to give them an allowance every month. . . ."

"I dunno." Cash swung his feet from the counter. "It sounds like you got him wrapped around your finger."

She gave him a look. "So, what was so important that you needed me to come here immediately?"

Cash had texted her an hour before while she was cleaning the home of Ms. Benoit, an eighty-nine-year-old woman with four cats. Madison knew the only reason the old lady paid for the service was so that someone would check on her at least once a week to make sure she didn't die and get eaten by her felines. And Madison couldn't blame her—she had seen those kinds of stories on the five o'clock news, too.

Cash jumped off the counter and walked toward her. "Guess what!"

She had never seen him so excited—save for the time when he and his brother successfully stole the NO SEMIS ALLOWED sign from Caldwell Lane. "What?" she asked.

"We're going on tour with Pistols and Pops!" He threw his arms out so excitedly, she half expected him to break into jazz hands. "It's a full U.S. tour—all the big cities like New York, Los Angeles, Austin. . . ."

"No way! That's awesome!" She stood up and gave him a hug. She was so proud of Cash; all of his dreams were finally coming true. "When does it start?"

"We're heading out next week, starting in Mobile, Alabama." His smile revealed his slightly crooked teeth, the ones she for some reason found so sexy.

But as thrilled as she was for him, a lump was forming in her throat. "That's so great," she said, trying to sound like she meant it. The idea of Cash going on a cross-country road trip without her made her heart ache.

"Ditch your sugar daddy and come with me," he said, kissing her.

Madison pulled away from him, wondering if she heard him right. "What?"

"You heard me, baby," he reassured her, flashing a devious grin. "Blow him off. Come with me. You know you wanna."

She stared at him, processing his words. For years, this was all she ever wanted. Exploring the country together. Standing in the crowd, cheering him on. Flashing her backstage pass and walking past all the jealous girls. Now it was finally happening, and she couldn't go. A wave of dizziness washed over her, as she sat back down on the couch heavily.

"Why aren't you saying anything?" he asked, sitting down next to her.

"I just wish this would have happened a few months ago," she said, pushing her hair behind her ears. "I'm married now, Cash. . . . I can't just pick up and leave."

"Oh come on, we both know it's not a real marriage." He laughed. "Dude would probably pay for you to come."

She shook her head slowly. "Cash, it's more complicated than that," she said, thinking of her parents. How could she let George pay for their mortgage and medical bills while she was riding around the country with another guy?

Cash narrowed his eyes. "Are you in love with him?"

"No." She nudged his foot. "But you and I are complicated, too. I mean, we've been hooking up for years and you can never even tell me what I mean to you."

He pushed her bangs out of her eyes. "I love you, babe. I don't say it, but you know that."

She put her hands on his muscular chest. "I love you, too," she whispered. So long she had fantasized about him saying those three words—so long—and *this* is when it actually happened? When she was a married woman? "But that's not what I'm asking."

"Look, I don't understand why you're so obsessed with the idea of settling down." He leaned back. "How can I know if you're the one I want to be with for the rest of my life? It took me like a year to pick out my guitar, and I still stay awake at night thinking I should have gone with the Fender." He rubbed her thigh. "I love you. I'm happy when I'm with you. Isn't that enough?"

She lowered her eyes. It was always a game with Cash. But she was guilty of it, too—after all, she always had it in the back of her mind that George was a way to get under Cash's skin. And she knew he would crack one day. She just wished it would have been before she got married.

"I want to go . . ." She paused. "But I can't. Not right now."

Cash shook his head in disappointment. "You can't or you won't? There's a big difference there."

"You know in any other circumstances I would do it," she said, massaging the back of her neck. "But I can't afford to ruin this right now."

Cash stood up and faced her. "You know, I thought this whole George thing was just one of your weird little evil plans, and I was fine with it for a little while. Hell, I even supported it," he said sternly. "But I think it's changed you, Mads. You're not the same girl I knew before. You're weak now."

How dare he? If Cash saw doing something like this for her family as weak, then he was a bigger asshole than she'd realized. She stood up, grabbed her backpack, and headed to the door. "Well, I'd rather be weak than an ass like you," she hissed, her eyes flashing. "Good luck on your tour, Cash."

At every stoplight Madison checked her phone, hoping she'd see a missed call or text from him saying he was sorry and that he didn't mean what he said. But her phone remained silent the whole drive home.

• • •

"HOW YOU FEELIN', Daddy?" Madison asked softly as she walked into his bedroom. He was sitting in his bed under the covers.

"Like poison," he said, scooting over so she could sit in bed with him.

"Me, too." She sighed. "I'm sure for different reasons, though."

"What's wrong, darlin'?" He let out a hacking cough.

She leaned her head back on the pillow. "Nothing. Just a long day." She turned to the TV, noticing two familiar little girls on the screen. "Oh my god, it's me and Claire!"

"Ha-ha, yeah. Yer mom found these old videos when she was cleanin' out the scary closet." He was referring to the coat closet in the front hallway. It had gotten that nickname after it had become a storage place for all the things they couldn't find a place for in the house. Every once in a while, Madison would throw something in there: her flowered Doc Martins, a stuffed monkey she was too old for but couldn't bear to throw out, a faded jean jacket. Over the years, she'd seen a beef jerky machine, a broken dart board, a rusty old bait-casting reel, a turkey fryer. . . .

She focused on the home video. "Oh, is this the one where we're at Uncle Mason's wedding?" He was Connie and Jillian's little brother who had moved to Grand Isle to be a fisherman.

"Yeah," he said with a sentimental grin.

She cracked a smile and focused in on the TV. "The bride is wearing a lovely white gown wrapped in a big pink bow," little Claire announced on camera, mimicking the red carpet reporters she watched on TV. "She looks like a present. . . ." She pushed her short brown hair behind her ears. "Absolutely gorgeous."

"Yeah," little Madison chimed in, scratching the big white bow in her hair that her mom had made her wear. "She's pretty."

"I can't wait to get married!" Little Claire beamed, twirling around in her frilly pastel pink smock.

"Who are ya gonna marry?" Madison asked with a wide grin.

"Someone who makes me feel like a princess," she answered matter-of-factly. "What about you?"

Young Madison turned her head straight into the camera and looked up to the right, biting her lip in excitement. "Cash Romero," she said with a giggle.

Madison put her hand over her mouth.

"Is that the boy who always steals your glue?" Claire continued on the video.

"Shut up," little Madison said, laughing, her knotty brown hair blowing in the wind.

"Um, let's turn this off," she said to her dad.

He hit the remote, and the screen froze. He turned to her with a smile before taking a sip from his blue tumbler. "Aren't you happy that didn't actually happen?"

She wanted to agree with him—she really did. But for some reason, all she wanted to do was hug that little girl in the stupid pale blue dress and cry.

claire

"AND TURN . . . AND shake . . . hips to the side . . . one, two, three, four . . . and crawl . . . crawl . . . bend . . . snap . . . and pose!" Kimmy pushed her messy hair out of her eyes and studied Claire's stance. "Finger to the mouth! You can't forget that! That's the sexiest part."

"Oh, sorry," Claire said, biting her pointer finger in the seductive way Kimmy had taught her just a couple of minutes before. "I feel so stupid," she finally admitted.

"But you're doing so great!" Kimmy shouted above the loud music. "Seriously . . . when you were shaking those hips, I got a little turned on." She gave Claire's butt a playful smack, similar to the one they had been practicing on themselves in the last routine.

Claire's eyes widened, and she blushed.

"Here, let's take five," Kimmy said, turning off the music. She sat on the floor and began stretching out her legs. "So, I looked at a potential studio space today. It's an old car garage, but I think I could convert it easily."

"That's fun," Claire said, joining her on the floor. "So, it's really happening?" She was excited for Kimmy to start her own business; it made her wish she had something she was so passionate about.

Kimmy nodded eagerly. "I think so."

"Have you thought about teaching other kinds of workout classes beside strip?" She stretched forward, grabbing her feet with her hands. "I just feel like you'd get a bigger client base that way." Claire left out the part about also being too embarrassed to take the class in a public setting.

"Aw, but I love the whole concept," Kimmy said. "Don't you just feel empowered after you do it?"

"Um . . ." Claire looked up to the side and pondered the question. "I like doing this, yes, but I don't know if 'empowered' is the word I would use." She unscrewed the cap of her water bottle.

Kimmy tightened her ponytail. "You don't have to answer this if you don't want to, but have things with your husband gotten any better?"

Claire thought back to her and Gavin's relationship over the past month. She had been reading a lot of Christian self-help books, mainly about forgiveness and building a stronger marriage. She had pushed the whole strip club memory to the back of her mind and tried to instead focus on keeping her husband happy and interested in her. He had apparently stopped going to The Saddle—at least that's what Kimmy had told her—and they'd even had sex a few times, but she couldn't help but feel like their relationship was still stagnant. "I mean, if you're asking me if these classes made Gavin look at me differently, then no," she finally said.

"Well, that's not the point of them," Kimmy said, standing up. "Do you think I stand up onstage every night dancing for those gross guys at the club? Hell no. I'm dancing for myself."

Claire took a gulp of her water, feeling perplexed.

"I know you think that you're doing it for your husband to turn him on, and maybe that's a perk, but that's not the goal with this stuff." Kimmy grabbed Claire's hands and pulled her up off the ground, placing her hands on her shoulders. "It's about *you*. You need to feel sexy and confident for anyone else to think that. And trust me . . . when you do feel that way, you won't even care what anyone else thinks because you'll be so high." Kimmy did a twirl, striking a pose at the end with a hip pop.

Claire clapped and smiled. "Okay, I'll try."

"Take it from the top!"

• • •

"NOW, BEND . . . SHAKE the hips . . . crawl . . . crawl . . . five, six, seven, eight . . . and pose!"

After Kimmy's pep talk and half an hour of practicing, Claire was feeling sexier with each move that she did, her hip cocking in the proper position and her mouth as pouty as it could ever be.

"Nailed it!" Kimmy said, giving her a high five. "So, how do you feel?"

Claire wiped away the sweat on her forehead with a towel. "I feel good," she said.

"Just good?" Kimmy looked disappointed.

"Great!" Claire clarified. "And maybe a little sore because I bent too far down on that last beat—but yeah." She smiled.

Kimmy laughed. "All right, so then I'll see you next week for our last session, right?" She walked over to the kitchen sink to refill her silver water bottle.

"Yep! Looking forward to it." Claire grabbed her bag and slung it over her shoulder.

On the drive back home, Claire decided to make a last-minute detour, stopping off at Geauxchamp's Department Store downtown. Kimmy's words rang in her head—if *she* could feel sexy again, maybe Gavin and her marriage would benefit from it, too.

In the lingerie department, she made her way over to a display of lacy black things. Some slow jazz played on the department store's sound system, setting the mood. She picked up what looked to be panties, but her eyebrows shot up as she realized they were missing the crotch part. She quickly dropped it and moved to another display.

A pile of red satin items was spread out on a white shelf. She rubbed her hand across the material—it was so smooth and soft. No wonder why guys loved this stuff.

Something royal blue caught her eye, and Claire turned to find a mannequin wearing a beautiful, soft satin set similar to the red one she'd just been admiring. Gavin always said he liked her in that color. It was perfect—sexy without being overly revealing—and she quickly spotted the set hanging on a rack nearby. Claire shuffled through the sizes until she found hers.

As she headed toward the checkout counter, a voice called out, "Well, is that you, Mrs. Claire?"

Claire froze, glancing down at the satin lingerie in her hands. Her gaze slid over her shoulder, where she found a petite little old lady with silver hair looking up at her expectantly.

"Oh, hi, Mrs. Rosa," Claire said. She could feel herself turning bright red. "How are you doing?"

The woman, one of the oldest members of their church, stared at the lingerie in Claire's hands, raising an eyebrow. In Mrs. Rosa's hands was a green pair of cotton granny panties and some packages of the type of stockings she wore to church every Sunday, even when it was ninety degrees. "Now, I'm doing lovely, dear," she said, clearly trying to not seem like she was staring at the blue pieces.

Claire thought about shoving the lingerie behind her back, hiding it from Mrs. Rosa's judging eyes, but she decided not to, in fear of seeming too obvious. And also, if there was anything that Kimmy had taught her in those lessons it was that she needed to be confident in everything that she did. Claire held the nighty and thong in her hand as they chatted about the upcoming church potluck and Mrs. Rosa's successful attempt at spicing up her deviled egg recipe with a dash of Worcestershire sauce and Tabasco.

"It gives it quite a little kick." She put her tiny frail hand on Claire's arm and lowered her voice. "After so many years of the same recipe, they were gettin' kinda boring." She flashed a toothy grin.

Claire laughed out loud. "I understand, Mrs. Rosa."

"Well, I'll see you soon, darlin'," the old woman said. "Have a good night."

She could have sworn Mrs. Rosa winked at her. "Bye, now!" Claire giggled to herself as she headed to the checkout register.

● ● ●

"SADIE'S ASLEEP," CLAIRE said softly to Gavin as he put away the last of the clean dishes from their dinner earlier that night. She had made seared scallops and lemon orzo from her *Living Skinny Cookbook*, and her husband had all but licked the plate clean. She stopped him from putting their wineglasses in the dishwasher. "Hey, let's just be bad and finish the bottle of wine."

Gavin looked up with wide eyes. "Well, I'm not gonna argue with that." He walked over to her, still in that day's work clothes—a simple white button-down shirt with his sleeves rolled up and his preppy salmon-colored chinos—and poured them each another glass.

Then he went into the living room and picked up his iPad before settling into the armchair. Claire took a large sip of the wine, and then snatched the device from his hands.

"We're gonna go technology free tonight," she purred, sitting on his lap.

"Are you drunk?" he whispered, smiling mischievously. He wrapped his arms around her waist.

"Nope," she whispered. She took another sip of her wine and set the glass down on the side table, then scooted off his lap. She stood up and pulled her brown hair out of its ponytail, shaking it out like Kimmy had showed her.

Gavin leaned back on the couch with an appreciative grin. She shimmied down and then back up again, and swayed her hips from side to side. As Gavin's eyebrows shot up, Claire slowly unbuttoned the top button of her shirt.

He let out a low whistle, and she smiled, feeling more confident.

"I'm buying this wine every time from now on," he said, his eyes not leaving her once.

She leaned over and nibbled on his earlobe. "This is just the appetizer."

He immediately put his wineglass down on the table next to hers and stood up, grabbing her hand and leading her to the bedroom. Claire's whole body tingled with excited anticipation.

As Gavin headed to the bed, Claire ducked into the closet to put on her new lingerie. As she came out, revealing her new purchase to him, she ran her hands down the silk fabric. Gavin lay on the bed, in nothing but his boxers.

"Come here," he said with a grin. As she got into bed with him, Gavin put his hands around her head and pulled her in close for a kiss. She could taste hints of the wine on his tongue.

"You are so sexy," he said in between kisses.

She smiled. It felt so good to hear him say that. As they twisted and turned in the sheets Claire felt like something was different. They hadn't had this much passion in a very long time. She felt like she did when they had just gotten married—beautiful and loved.

After it was over, they both lay breathing heavily in each other's arms.

"That was amazing," Gavin finally said, brushing her matted hair from her forehead. "What's gotten into you?"

"I dunno," she said with a laugh. "I guess you just inspired me."

Gavin fell into a contented sleep shortly after, and Claire lay awake, reveling in her victory. With a smile, she grabbed her phone, and send out a missive to Gavin's followers:

@Pastor_Gavin: Life is good! #hallelujah — Just now

madison

"CAN I GET two of the Lucky Day scratch-offs, please, Mr. Gary?" Madison said, fidgeting with the blue fishing lure charm bracelet on her wrist. The air-conditioning in the gas station was on full blast, making her shiver even though it was eighty degrees outside. "And two coffees," she said, handing him a twenty-dollar bill. As Mr. Gary turned around to get the lottery tickets, she glanced down at the Snickers bars. "Oh . . . and these, too," she said, placing two of the candy bars on the counter, feeling a sudden twinge of guilt at all she'd stolen over the years.

"How's your daddy doing?" he asked, pushing his Coke-bottle glasses up on his nose.

"I'm actually goin' to see him right now," she said, grabbing the paper coffee cups he handed her. "He just got done with his chemo session so I'm gonna keep him company while Mama's workin'."

"That's good of ya, darlin," Mr. Gary said over the Shania Twain song playing on the background speakers. "These tickets for him?" He pointed to the two scratch-offs sitting on the grimy counter.

"Well, yeah," she said, pouring the sugar into her cup and tightening the lid. "You know that's the only way to *actually* cheer that man up. I'm just his puppet really. He says, 'Mads, I wanna see you,' but that's really code for, 'Mads, bring me my lotto tickets.'" She smiled because as much as her dad loved her, it wasn't completely far-fetched.

Mr. Gary chuckled, rubbing the front of his black and gold Saints T-shirt. "Okay, wait," he said, turning around again. "Take another one on me. Tell 'im ol' Gary hopes he strikes it rich."

"Thanks, Mr. Gary!" She put the tickets in her bag and zipped it up. "He'll be thrilled."

He waved good-bye. "Drive safe, ya hear?"

Madison nodded. "Bye now!"

She started up her truck and hit SHUFFLE on her phone's iTunes. As she backed out of the parking space, the first song to play was Cash's acoustic song, "Hurricane." It was the one that he wrote and recorded when they were sophomores, shortly after they started hooking up. Even though Cash would never admit it, she knew the song was about her. He had written it after their first breakup, a result of some drunken argument at Billy Prejean's sixteenth birthday party.

> *You shoulda come with a warning / Strong, fierce, wild in the*
> *   morning*
> *I never thought I'd survive / but oh, oh, baby, you make me feel*
> *   so alive*
> *We got one chance to get through this night*
> *And if the tears don't dry out tomorrow*
> *Will we give up this fight*
> *For I'll take the thunder strikes and all the rain*
> *If we can make it through, if we can make it through*
> *This hurricane . . .*

The song stopped just before she turned down her parents' street. She put her hand on her chest, hoping the aching feeling there would go away, but it didn't. She took some deep breaths and opened the truck door slowly. In a few seconds, she'd be sitting with a man who was literally fighting for his life—she needed to forget about Cash and her own problems just this once. Connie said Allen needed some cheering up, and that's what she was going to do.

"Hello?" she said into the empty house, walking through the living room to her parents' bedroom. Allen was lying in bed, staring at the ceiling. He looked miserable—even more miserable than the time when she was ten and he snipped the tip of his middle finger off with the chain saw while cutting down a tree in their backyard. He'd been in so much pain, but she still managed to cheer him up: "At least when you flip people off, it'll be even more gnarly," she'd said.

"Hey darlin'," he moaned.

"Daddy," she said softly, kneeling down. His skin was pale and his lips were cracking. Her stomach went sour seeing him in this state. "You look terrible."

He put his frail hand delicately on her face. "You don't look so good yourself," he said, pinching her cheek. "What's wrong with you?"

"Don't even get me started," she said, shaking her head. "How are you feeling?"

"Awful," he said quietly. "This stuff they put in me isn't natural. I dunno if I'm gonna do any more."

"Um, yeah you are," Madison said with a strict tone in her voice. "That's the only way you're gonna get better."

"Hell, I was doin' fine until your mama made me go see the doctor in the first place. It's been downhill ever since." He let out a hacking cough. "Just look at my dad—lived 'til he was ninety-three, and that man didn't go to the doctor a day in his life. Smoked a pack a day, drank his gin like it was water, completely fine 'til he just up and died from old age. He said, 'I've had it with this place, I'm gonna go to sleep now.' And that's the way to do it."

"But you're not ready to go to sleep yet," Madison said, touching his arm. She was trying to be strong, but his words pained her. "Mama's not ready for that yet and neither am I. You've gotta fight it."

"I am," he said, lowering his head. "I'm here, aren't I?"

"I brought you coffee," she said, handing him the warm cup that she had placed on the bedside table when she walked in. "And these . . ." She pulled the three scratch-offs from her bag. "Gary sent you an extra one."

"Well, that's awful kind of him," Allen said, struggling to sit up.

Madison plopped on the bed next to him and gave him a quarter. "Go for it," she said, handing him the first ticket.

He scratched off the golden horseshoes, which gave him numbers eight and seventeen. He tried desperately to find a match, but with each scratch-off, all he got were the little gold flakes that fell onto his white cotton undershirt.

"Try this one," she said, handing him the one Mr. Gary had sent over. Allen continued with the scratching, but their hopes waned with every nonmatching number he uncovered.

She sighed and began scratching off the last one. With every horseshoe she uncovered, it became clearer that they weren't even going to win a dollar. As Madison scratched off the final horseshoe, a weird squiggle began to appear—something that didn't look like a number. Her heart jumped and she scratched harder.

"Oh. My. God." Madison could barely speak.

"What?" Allen looked over at the ticket.

She pointed to the final slot on the card, which contained a symbol neither of them had ever seen in their lottery-playing career.

"Is that the pot of gold?" her dad screamed with excitement.

She nodded as disbelief raced through her. "We just won fifty thousand dollars!" she said, giving her dad a long hug.

Winning the lottery was something Madison had fantasized about happening since she was a little girl, but through the years with every unlucky scratch, her dreams faded. This win, though, seemed like proof that good things could happen to her—that she wasn't destined for a life of bad breaks and misery.

"I can't believe it!" he cried.

She stared down at the ticket in her hands. It was one of the most beautiful things she had ever seen. And suddenly, she knew what she had to do.

"Daddy, this is enough, right?" she asked, continuing to stare at the little cartoon drawing to make sure it was real. "It'll pay off the rest of the house and cover the medical expenses?"

He nodded. "This will certainly get us back on our feet."

"Good!" she said, handing him the ticket. "I want you and Mama to have it all." Her heart felt warm.

He looked up at her with wide eyes. "How are we so lucky to have gotten such an amazing girl?"

"You musta done somethin' right," she said, kissing him on the forehead and saying good-bye.

She'd set his life right. Now she had to take care of hers.

• • •

"HEY," SHE SAID, poking her head onto the back porch where George was sitting with Charlie. She smelled steaks on the grill as soon as she stepped out.

"Hey! How was your visit with your dad?" he asked, putting down his copy of the *Wall Street Journal*. He was the only person she had ever met who read his newspapers at night. Actually, he was the only person she had ever met who still read newspapers.

She ran her fingers through her hair. "I have to talk to you about something," she said nervously, joining him at the bistro table.

He gave her a worried glance. "What's up?"

She wished she could just press FAST-FORWARD and skip this whole scene, but she knew she had to do it. Madison swallowed, her mouth dry. "I have to leave, George." All the happiness she felt from the ticket earlier that day drained away as she tried to find the right words.

"What? Is something wrong with Allen?" He sat up straight, his eyes widening with fear.

"No, no." She shook her head. "He's okay, I think." Her knees began bouncing up and down under the table. "I have to leave . . . *this*." She waved her hand between the two of them.

George face's fell and he slumped back into his seat. "Was it something I did?"

"It's something we both did, George," she said. "We entered into this thing knowing full well it was a marriage of convenience. I mean, who's to say it couldn't work for some people, but I think I'm the kind of girl who needs something else."

"I can give you what you want," he said, his voice low and urgent. "Just tell me what you need."

She shook her head and leaned back, her heart aching for him. "George, I'm not the right one for you. I want you to find someone who is."

He stared at her for a second. "But you are the right person for me, Madison. I like what we have, and call me crazy, but I think you like being with me, too."

Madison put her hand over his. "I think we both really care about each other in a weird way," she admitted. "But what we have is friendship, not love."

His eyes flashed. "So, you're just gonna leave now? After all that I've done for you?"

"I will pay you back, every penny," she promised in a hard voice. "But don't say I took advantage of you when you know you had your own agenda in mind. You knew I was vulnerable and you offered to swoop in and save my family. What was I supposed to do?"

He straightened his shoulders but he had the decency to look ashamed. "I never made you do anything you didn't want to do."

"It's true, you didn't." She paused. "But I didn't either."

George pushed away from the table and leaned against the porch railing, looking out over the grounds. The pool she'd joked about so many months ago now glistened in the distance, and the restored flower beds were in full bloom.

"Look, I don't mean to hurt you, and I know that it's going to—it's hurting me too." She took a deep breath. "But this is just something I have to do. I need to go out on my own."

"Then go," he said quietly, not turning to face her.

She stood up and touched his shoulder. "Good-bye, George." She took a deep breath and felt a mixture of relief, freedom, and heartache.

Madison went into her room, stuffed her backpack with as many of her clothes and belongings as possible, and headed back downstairs. She peeked out the sliding glass doors in the kitchen and saw that George was still sitting in the same position, looking up at the sky. Her stomach and chest hurt even worse than the time he caught her with the necklace in front of the pawnshop, but she tried to shake it off. This wasn't her real life and it never had been.

She headed through the front door and onto the driveway where Cash Romero waited for her. As she lowered her sunglasses over her eyes, she reminded herself that this is what adventurous girls like her were meant to do—ride off into the sunset with the bad boy on the motorcycle.

40

laura

"YEAH, BABY!" BRIAN hollered from the bedroom. Laura was in the kitchen, helping Janet chop bell peppers for the gumbo while Rob was preparing the sausage. The three of them looked up from their tasks as Brian hobbled into the kitchen on his crutches, beaming.

Laura felt herself smiling back. Brian had just called Coach Perkins to update him on his recovery, and based on his response, it had to have been good news.

"What'd he say?" Janet asked excitedly, moving toward her son.

"I get to keep my scholarship, *and* they're gonna work with me on physical therapy this year!" Brian exclaimed. "They want me to come back to Baton Rouge as soon as I can so we can get started. Coach said I can train with the team, and if everything's good, I should be back starting the year after—maybe even sooner." He grabbed a piece of the pepper off of Laura's cutting board and threw it in his mouth, then kissed her on the cheek.

"That's amazing!" Laura cried. A sense of relief rushed over her, as well as gratitude. They'd been through hell this year: moving back to Toulouse, living with Janet and Rob, losing all their money. But they'd done it all for this moment, when Brian could return to the team with the hopes of getting back on the field and leading the Tigers once more.

Janet crossed her arms, looking worried. "You're not gonna jump into training too fast, are you? I don't think you're supposed to put that kind of pressure on it for a while."

"Don't worry, Mom," Brian said. "They won't make me do anything too major for a while." He paused. "I can't believe they're actually taking me back!"

"So proud of you, son," Rob said.

Laura walked over to Brian and gave him a hug, nuzzling her face into his light blue polo shirt. "I'm really happy for you."

But even as the words came out of her mouth, contradictory thoughts spun through her mind. The idea of moving back to Baton Rouge with Brian worried her. Sure, she could apply for LSU's spring semester, but she wondered if they moved back, would she go back to waitressing at the coffeehouse again, doing her husband's homework at night, and spending game days hearing people talk about all the great things he was doing with his life?

The real question was, what was she doing with hers?

• • •

"YOUR HUSBAND IS the man," Kenny said to Laura as he opened his front door and gave Brian a one-armed hug.

Laura squeezed past them and entered the cozy front room of his parents' camp at Mossy Pointe, a small man-made beach twenty miles from Toulouse. Kenny had it for the weekend and was hosting a party to celebrate his best friend's successful surgery.

"Where should I put these?" She held up a bag of tortilla chips and a medium plastic container filled with homemade cowboy caviar.

"Ooh, what's this?" Kenny asked, lifting the lid and greedily eyeing the mixture of black-eyed peas, tomatoes, corn, and avocado. He looked up at her, worry flitting across his face. "Did you make this?"

Brian answered for her. "Don't worry, man—it's a Janet Landry contribution." Laura rolled her eyes. Kenny had experienced one of her cooking mishaps a couple of years back—she had made Brian a yellow cake with chocolate frosting for his seventeenth birthday, and everyone at the party realized within the first bite that she had used baking soda instead of baking powder.

"I'll just put these in the kitchen," she said, flashing a polite smile.

The guys followed her, and Kenny threw Brian a beer from the fridge.

"Should you be drinking with the painkillers?" Laura whispered in his ear as he cracked open the can. She wanted to remind him that he'd promised to stop drinking entirely, but held her tongue. After all, this was a celebration.

"Nah, I'm good," Brian said with a laugh. "I didn't take any today—knew I was coming here."

As people started arriving, remarking over Brian's surgery and congratulating him on being back on the team, Laura snuck outside to get some fresh air and set up for the party. She covered the long picnic table out back with old issues of the *Toulouse Town Talk* and set three rolls of paper towels on top. Through cabin windows, Laura watched everyone huddle around Brian, focused in on his every word. She wondered if he was telling them that he couldn't have done any of this without her; how she'd helped save money for him before he lost it; how it was her idea to file the appeal for the insurance; how she missed four days of school to be by his side at the hospital in New Orleans. And if he wasn't saying it out loud, did he at least appreciate it?

As Laura was putting the plastic forks and knives in a mason jar, everyone finally started coming outside. She looked up to see Claire and Gabby in the crowd.

"Hey, girl!" Claire said, carrying a bottle of wine.

"Why are you setting up Kenny's party?" Gabby asked, giving her a hug.

Laura laughed. "Do you really think Kenny Fontenot knows how to set up for anything? For his Super Bowl party last year, he filled the washing machine with ice and put the beers in there."

"I dunno," Gabby said, grinning. "That sounds pretty genius to me."

The girls sat down at the end of the bench as the rest of the partygoers gathered around the keg. "You doing okay?" Claire asked, eyeing her shrewdly.

Laura shrugged. "Just a little stressed with finals and everything, but holding up fine."

Gabby uncorked the wine and poured it. "Well, tonight we celebrate." The three girls raised their red Solo cups. "To Brian's recovery!" she shouted.

Laura flashed a closed-lip smile, clinking her cup with theirs. "Cheers."

• • •

A FEW HOURS later, the party had consumed a total of thirty hamburgers, twenty-three hot dogs, six bags of chips, four twelve-packs of beer, and six bottles of wine. The party had moved over to Kenny's fire pit, and Brian was drunkenly holding court, detailing every painstaking moment of his recovery.

Laura, Claire, and Gabby sat on a log away from the crowd. "So, has anyone talked to Madison since she left with Cash?" Laura asked, pouring some more seltzer water into her cup. She had stopped drinking wine an hour ago, since she was Brian's designated driver.

"We texted a little a couple of days ago," Claire said. "I think she's feeling guilty about George, but as much as I hate Cash, I told her she had to do what felt right. Otherwise she's going to have too many lingering doubts and questions."

"Is it weird that I actually really liked George?" Gabby confessed, straightening her legs out on the grass.

"No," Laura agreed. "I thought he was good for her . . . in his own odd way."

"I actually liked him, too," Claire said. "But she's been in love with Cash since they were kids. I can't blame her for wanting to give that a chance, I guess. I just wish he wasn't the worst."

Laura sighed. "Maybe she's in love with the idea of him, and doesn't see the bad stuff." She leaned forward on the log, her elbows propped on her knees. "Maybe she'll wake up one day and realize he doesn't make her as happy as she thinks he does." As she said the words, she couldn't help but wonder if she was projecting her own insecurities on her friend.

"Well, as much as I don't like him, I'm all for her doing this." Gabby cradled the red cup in front of her. "If I learned anything this year, it's that it's important to be with the one you love."

Claire put her hand on Gabby's arm. "Has Tony reached out any more?"

She shook her head. "Nah. I mean, I wouldn't have kept texting either if I wasn't getting a response. It's for the best, really."

"I don't know why you don't just tell him everything," Claire said. "Your mom's out now. Mr. Ford can't put her back in or anything."

"We don't know what he's capable of," Gabby said, shaking her head. "And I'm afraid to find out."

"You could take him," Claire said, waving her away. "Do I need to remind you about the time you made Collette O'Conner cry in front of everyone at the prom?"

"Well, she shouldn't have talked about my mom like that." She shook her head.

The girls laughed, then fell silent. The crowd had gotten progressively drunker as the night wore on. The group was now making s'mores and having a sing-along, like they were at some adult summer camp.

"Should we go over and be social, y'all?" Laura asked. She couldn't see Brian in the crowd, but knowing him, he was the closest to the fire. Brian loved to roast marshmallows, and they'd always argue over whether they were best browned or blackened.

"Meh," Gabby said, but nodded.

The girls stood up, and Laura brushed the back of her shorts to get rid of the dirt and leaves that stuck to them. As they walked over to join the rest of the party, she noticed that the bag of marshmallows was empty. "I'll go grab some more," she said. "Be right back!"

Inside, she searched the kitchen counter but found only empty beer bottles and plastic food containers scattered across it. She headed over to the walk-in pantry and twisted the doorknob. As the hinges squeaked, a woman's voice squealed inside. By the time Laura realized someone was in there, it was too late.

Tanya Pothier, one of the seniors on her cheer team last year, peeked out from the doorway. Tanya's dark eyes were a little unfocused, her brown hair mussed and her lips red.

"Oh my god—I'm so sorry," Laura said, backing away from the door. "Carry on!"

Tanya covered her mouth and hiccupped, stumbling out of the closet. The door swung wider, and Laura's mouth dropped when her eyes locked on Brian.

"I'm sorry, babe," he slurred. "I can explain."

Laura felt like she was going to vomit. She turned to Tanya, who at least had the decency to look embarrassed. "Out. Now," she said, pointing to the door to the yard.

After Tanya slunk away, Laura focused her rage back on Brian. She grabbed his arm and dragged him into the den, slamming the door behind them.

"What the hell is wrong with you?" she screamed, not even caring who heard.

"Calm down . . ." he mumbled, sitting on the green-and-red-plaid couch. Brian tapped the cushion next to him, inviting her to join him. Was he out of his freaking mind?

She scowled at him and paced around the room instead. The den's wood-paneled walls were covered with animal mounts, all of which were staring at them. "How could you do this to me, Brian?" It felt like her heart was beating a thousand times a minute. "And at a party with all of our friends? I just cannot believe you."

He leaned heavily against the couch. "It was an accident."

"So, you just *accidentally* went into the pantry and started making out with another girl?" She paused her pacing, her head pounding like she'd been the one drinking all night.

Brian frowned, clearly trying to think through his excuses. "I'm drunk, babe. I didn't know what I was doin'."

How many times in her life was Laura going to hear some lame justification for Brian's bad behavior? All of a sudden she felt exhausted, like she'd been holding up a wall for months and it finally was collapsing around her. She sat down on a worn armchair across from him and knew what she had to do.

"Brian, I can't do this anymore," she said.

"No, don't say that," he begged. "You're overreacting. I just messed up."

Laura took a deep breath and held her shoulders back, looking directly into his glazed eyes. "Brian, this is so much more than an argument about you kissing some girl. I know you're drunk right now, and maybe you won't remember any of this tomorrow, but I need to say this."

He sat back and stared at her.

"Since we've been together, everything I've done has been for you. Our whole relationship has revolved around what our lives are gonna be like once you go *there* and when you do *that*." She looked down at her hands, clasped tightly in her lap, and spoke the truth she'd been feeling for months. "I don't feel like you ever encouraged me or even supported me." Her mind flashed to Vince, who always pushed her to do better.

"That's so not true," Brian interrupted.

"Brian, you told me to quit high school!"

"That's not fair—you wanted to do that," he said, his face growing red.

Laura bit her lip and looked away from him. "I thought I did . . . but everyone makes mistakes, right?" She pointed in the direction of the kitchen, reminding him why they were arguing in the first place. "This year, going back to school, I realized that what I really need is to focus on my plans, not yours."

Brian swallowed and lowered his head.

Laura took a deep breath, her stomach clenching. She couldn't believe what she was about to say—that it had come to this, after everything they'd been through this year—but she knew it was the right decision. "I don't think that we should be together any-more."

Brian's eyes widened as his face went slack with shock. "Oh baby, you don't mean that," he slurred. "You love me." He held out his hands toward her but didn't move from the couch. "C'mon. I'm gonna make you so happy. It's what we both wanted."

Laura stood from the armchair. "Brian, I've always loved you. I will probably always have a place in my heart for you. But this is something that I need to do for myself." She looked him in the eyes. "There will be other girls who will cheer you on. But it's not going to be me anymore."

"Stop it," Brian hissed, leaning forward so suddenly that he al-most toppled off the sofa. "Don't say that. We can get through this, I promise."

Laura glanced back at Brian. He was now sprawled across the couch, his beer-stained T-shirt straining over his belly. His drunken-ness only reminded Laura of all the promises he'd made her over the past year and how few of them he'd actually kept.

"I just don't think you're ever gonna change. But the thing is . . . I have."

As she walked out of the room, Laura fought back tears. Leaving Brian was the scariest thing she'd ever done, and the hardest. But she couldn't deny that it felt like a huge weight had been lifted off her shoulders. She'd spent so long carrying his dreams for him. And now, finally, she had the freedom to find her own.

gabrielle

"MAMA, HOW ABOUT this one?" Gabby asked, holding up a beige silk top.

"Oh, that's nice," Elaine said. "See, I told you it was worth comin' all this way. This mall is way better than Geauxchamp's."

Gabby laughed. For a forty-five-year-old, her mom had quite the trendy taste. Everything she'd seen at the Toulouse department store was too "old lady" for her style. And that's why they were twenty miles away at the Lafayette mall, shopping at places like H&M and Forever 21, which Gabby had to admit had some seriously cute work clothes.

"Does this one say 'Hire me!' or 'Take me to the club?'" Elaine asked, holding up a little black dress.

"Ooh, I like," Gabby said, giving it the once-over. She walked over to the rack and grabbed a gray blazer. "Pair it with this for the interview," she said, holding them together. "And take it off when you go dancing," she said, moving the blazer away.

"My daughter's a genius," Elaine said, laughing. "Add it to my pile."

They collected dozens of skirts, tops, shoes, and belts until finally Gabby reined her mom in. "Why don't you go try these on?"

"Something's bound to work, huh?" Elaine sighed and headed into the dressing room.

Gabby sat outside on the plush white leather bench, watching all the people scurry around the store. A tween was rolling her eyes at her dad as he told her the shorts she had picked up were way too short. A couple holding hands perused the lingerie section, shooting each other shy grins. Gabby spent a moment checking out a handsome guy looking at belts in the men's section . . . and then he turned around.

Oh my god. Tony. Every muscle in her body froze up. She looked away quickly, trying to hide her face and hoping he hadn't seen her. A few seconds later, she heard a familiar voice right behind her.

"Hey." Tony stood next to her, wearing dark blue jeans and a gray T-shirt. Gabby's heart stopped in her chest and her stomach felt like it was turning over. He was even more gorgeous than she remembered him. She felt torn between looking for somewhere to hide and wanting to reach out and touch him.

"Hi," she said softly, resisting the urge to do either. She pushed her hair behind her ears and stood up. "How, um, are you?" she asked awkwardly.

"Well, I really wish you would have called me back," he said, scratching his head. "But I'm surviving, I guess."

"I'm sorry," she said, lowering her gaze.

He shrugged his shoulders. "What do you want me to say to that, Gabby? I'm sorry, too. It's a real shame that you ended things like that."

She swallowed, not knowing how to respond. If he was standing here, still wondering why she broke it off, his dad had held up his end of the bargain and not told Tony that she'd lied to him. But that meant she couldn't tell him, either. She had to get out of here before Tony saw her mom. "I've gotta go," she said, feeling suddenly panicky and grabbing her bag.

But it was too late. "Gabby!" Elaine came out of the dressing room wearing a navy dress. "What do you think about this one?" She ran her hands down the pleated cotton dress.

Gabby's hands began to sweat, her heart beating as fast as the store's blaring techno music. "Looks great," she said, nodding her head. She prayed that her mom would go back into the dressing room immediately.

"Great!" Elaine smiled and then turned her gaze to Tony. "Oh, who's this?"

She wondered if she could make a run for it—just distract both of them by throwing her bag on the ground and sprinting out of the store, through the mall, and into the parking lot, where she would get into her crappy little car and drive far, far away. Surely that would be easier than what she knew she had to do. With a pit in her stomach, Gabby answered: "This is Tony."

Elaine's eyes widened. "Oh Tony, yes," she said. "I've heard a lot about you. I'm Elaine, Gabby's mom. It's nice to meet you."

Emotion flitted quickly across Tony's face—his brows furrowed in confusion, his jaw clenched with anger. No doubt the pieces clicked into place. He coughed and glanced at Gabby. "I've heard *so* much about you, too," he said, slowly drawing his gaze back to Elaine and plastering on a smile that Gabby recognized as fake.

"Well, you kids catch up." Elaine waved her hands at them. "If you'll excuse me, I've got forty other outfits to try on!" She bustled back into the dressing room.

Tony turned to Gabby, his eyes narrowing. "Your *mom*?" he hissed.

She bit her lip. "It's . . . complicated." Her body temperature shot up. She could only imagine what was going on in Tony's head. She wished she could explain it to him, explain *everything*—how things spiraled, and her deal with his dad.

He paused and raised his arms. "What the hell is going on, Gabs?"

She looked around at all the people surrounding them—the women in line waiting for a dressing room . . . the employees folding tank tops and T-shirts . . . the little girls spraying each other with vanilla-scented body mist. She'd imagined this moment—when he'd catch her in a lie and she'd have to be honest—so many times, but she'd never imagined it would be in such a public place.

"What's going on?" he repeated, leaning toward her, the scent of his familiar cologne making her heart wrench. "Were you lying to me this whole time?"

Here we go, she thought to herself, taking a deep breath for confidence. It was time. "You assumed my mom was dead, and I never corrected you." She lowered her head, knowing she'd have to come clean. "I figured it was easier than telling you the truth. She was in jail for four years, and I lost everything when she left. Her. Our house. My chance to go to college. She just got out. I tried to tell you the truth so many times, Tony, I really did." Her voice cracked with emotion. "But then I fell for you and I just couldn't do it. Once the wedding date neared, I realized I had to get out of your life."

"I can't believe you," Tony said, his dark eyes flashing with anger. "How could you lie to me? We were weeks away from getting married!"

She lowered her head. "I'm sorry." A lump formed in her throat. No doubt he hated her as much as she hated herself right now. "I never deserved you, and I'm sorry." Her voice began to crack as she held the tears back. "But for what it's worth, I want you to know every stupid lie I led you to believe was only because I was madly in love with you."

He crossed his arms over his chest. "That's supposed to make it acceptable?" His voice got angrier. "This entire situation is so unbelievable. I just can't even process this right now."

"Oh, there you are," a tall girl with short black hair shouted to Tony from across a display of neon-colored bikinis. "I've been looking for you. We're late!" She looked at the silver watch on her tiny wrist. "Are you ready to go?"

"Yeah," he said, turning around and glancing back at Gabby. His gaze was cool and unfamiliar. "I'm done here."

She watched as the two of them walked away. The girl linked her arm through Tony's, throwing her head back in laughter at something he said. Gabby could only watch as the man of her dreams walked out of the store—and her life—for good, with another woman at his side.

Elaine came back out of the dressing room, gripping the navy dress tightly. Gabby withered under her mom's appraising gaze. "So, that was *the* Tony, right?"

Gabby stood there in silence. Every muscle in her body was tight as she replayed that painful conversation over and over again in her head.

"Are you okay?" Elaine asked, putting her hand on her shoulder.

She let out a long sigh and closed her eyes, trying to get rid of the image of Tony . . . except that when they were shut, the picture of him was even clearer. She couldn't forget any of the amazing moments of their near-perfect relationship. And now, alongside all of the good—the laughs, their conversations, the feeling of his arms around her—would be the memory of how his face looked when he'd realized what a liar she'd been. Gabby thought her mom's arrest was the worst moment of her life, but this was right up there. It was a different kind of low, though, with a deeper cut in her soul. Perhaps because she had only herself to blame.

42

madison

THE NEON COCKTAILS sign at Dre's Dive Bar in Birmingham flickered in and out. Madison found the sign ironic. The bartender could barely make a gin and tonic. She shoved her ice cubes with the skinny black straw and shuddered, thinking what one of his martinis would taste like.

"Did you see that guy crowd surf during 'Raise Your Voice?'" Cash yelled over the loud music. He was standing a few feet away in a closed circle consisting of one of his bandmates and a group of eager fans who had cornered him after the show. He held his longneck beer bottle tight—tighter than he had held Madison the entire week they had been on the road together.

Madison let out a sigh. It was induced by boredom and anger, both directed at her no-good boyfriend who had recently told her to give him some space and let his fans think he was single.

"It's better for the appeal of the band," he had explained earlier that day as they shoveled cheap Thai food into their mouths five minutes before they had to set up for the show. Little did Madison know when she had ridden off with Cash that she'd be free labor for the band. The guys were constantly asking her to help do things like pick up their food so they could get some last-minute practice in. They even had her hook up some of the instruments before the shows, like she was their roadie or something.

"The only thing I came here for was to be with you, and that's the only thing I'm not actually doing," she had said, stabbing her green curry chicken with a chopstick.

"You know . . . you've been a real downer since this trip started." He squeezed his lime over his pad thai.

"Excuse me! My boyfriend spends every day in these amazing cities sleeping off his hangovers instead of exploring with me like he promised," she said. "And then he spends the nights flirting with groupies, telling me to pretend I don't even know him. I'm sorry, but do you really expect me to be all bright and cheery?"

"Oh, c'mon . . . it's not like you didn't know this was how it was gonna be." He chugged his can of Coke. "You wanted an excuse to get out of Toulouse and away from that weird shit you had going on with that guy. I saved you. . . ."

Madison rolled her eyes. "Whatever!" She had stood up, closed the Styrofoam container, and stormed out of the bus, taking a deep breath of the Alabama air. She perched herself atop a fence surrounding the parking lot as Cash's words replayed in her head. *"It's not like you didn't know this was how it was gonna be."*

Actually, that wasn't true at all. She had naively envisioned them eating at restaurants written up in *Time Out* and TripAdvisor, not living on takeout from restaurants that were *this close* to failing their health inspection.

She'd thought they'd check out the aquarium in Atlanta—she had always wanted to see a shark up close—but Cash had insisted on getting high and playing games on his phone. She had pictured them strolling hand in hand as they checked out the botanical gardens in Mobile, but instead she ended up just lying in the uncomfortable tour-bus bunk bed as the guys practiced their new song, "The Worst," for what felt like the hundredth time.

And now, she sat alone in the dive bar sucking down the most awful gin and tonic she had ever tasted, wishing for the night to be over already.

Her phone vibrated, shaking the sticky round-top table she sat at. HOME showed up on the caller ID. She didn't really want to talk to her parents—they were already disappointed with her for how she'd handled things with George. But she figured talking to someone, even someone who was mad at her, at this point was welcome.

"Hiya," she answered as she walked outside in the dimly lit parking lot. "What's up?"

"Sweetie, I think you should come home," her mom said without preamble.

Madison let out an audible sigh. "How many times do I have to tell you—I needed to do this, Mama!"

"No, darling. You don't understand . . . you need to come home to see your daddy." There was a long pause. "He's not doin' so well."

"What do you mean?" Panic gripped her chest.

"Well, he was having trouble breathing this morning." Her mom's voice sounded shaky. "I took him to the emergency room, and the doctors found some fluid around his lungs. They thought about draining it, but since the chemo's not working, it would just come back."

"Oh my god." Madison put her hand over her mouth. "So what's the next step? What do we need to do now?"

"He's been through so much and hasn't been feeling good for a while." She took a jagged breath. "Mads, he's decided to go to hospice."

"What's hospice?" Madison asked, tensing.

"It means the doctors are gonna make him comfortable for his final days. . . ." Her words slowly trailed off. "It'd be good if you could get back here soon. We're not sure how much longer he has."

A lump formed in Madison's throat. She'd watched her dad waste away for the past year, the poison slowly seeping through his body. But he'd borne it all, still laughing at her jokes when they sat on the porch and still taking his morning walk. And now he was choosing to let go? It hurt her heart to think how miserable he must be to come to that decision.

"I'll get on the first bus I can," she told her mom, her voice cracking. Clouds moved over the half-moon, casting an eerie haze over the parking lot.

"Okay," Connie said softly. "Just keep me posted on your timing. I'll come pick you up at the station."

"I'll look up the schedule right after I talk with you and call you back tonight." She paused. "Mama?"

"Yeah, darlin'?" the sweet voice on the other end said.

"Whatever happens, we're gonna get through this together." The tears started welling up in her eyes.

"I know, baby." Connie sniffled. "I love you."

"I love you, too." Madison wiped her cheeks dry. After she ended the call, she took a moment to gather her thoughts. She'd known this was coming for months, but nothing could have prepared her for this moment. She choked back a sob, then pushed her hair out of her face and headed back inside the bar.

The group of girls was giggling at something Cash had just said.

"Cash, I need to talk to you," she said, pulling on his arm.

With narrowed eyes, he whispered, "I'm busy," then turned his attention back to his fans.

"It's important." She tugged at him again, and he begrudgingly walked with her over to one of the high-top tables.

"My dad isn't doing well, and I have to go back home." Her eyes welled up. "He doesn't have much more time left."

His face dropped. "Dammit. I'm sorry, Mads." He put his arms around her and gave her a hug.

"Thank you," she said, resting her head on his muscular shoulder, inhaling the familiar scent of his cedary cologne. His hand moved in a circular, soothing motion on her back.

"So, how are you gonna get back?" he finally asked as they pulled apart.

"Well, I was thinking we could take a Greyhound. I have to look up the schedule, but would you be able to leave first thing in the morning?" She pulled her phone out of her back pocket to begin searching for tickets.

"Babe, you know I can't do that." He sighed. "I'm really sorry about your dad and all, but I can't leave the band. They need me."

He looked over at the guys, who were now doing body shots off the girls.

Her eyes widened. "Are you serious?"

"This is a once-in-a-lifetime opportunity for us. I can't just leave." He shook his head and gripped his beer bottle tighter.

"I don't think you understand the situation," she said, her eyes narrowing. She slowly emphasized each word: "My dad is *dying*." Her voice broke on the last word.

"And I told you I'm sorry, babe. I really am." He put his hand on her shoulder. "But you can't expect me to just pick up and leave right now, can you?"

"Oh my god . . ." she said, shaking her head. "Oh my god." She stared at him, and for the first time she saw what everyone else around her did: an arrogant, narcissistic guy who only cared about himself.

"What?" he said, pushing his long black hair out of his face.

She scowled at him. "I just can't believe I wasted so much time on you." She thought back to all of their arguments and breakups, and the moments she put up with his rude, cavalier behavior. She had forgiven him and taken him back more times than she could count. And for what? To just keep getting hurt like this?

He just shrugged and took a swig of his beer, completely unaffected; after years of fighting, it was like he'd become immune to her anger.

She'd been in love with Cash for so long. But was it love? She shook her head. Love wasn't fighting and crying and wondering how many other girls he was sleeping with on the side. Maybe she didn't know what love was, but she knew it wasn't Cash.

Madison grabbed her bag and turned to him, putting a hand on his chest one last time. "Don't call me." She walked out of the bar and didn't look back.

43

claire

"NO REGRETS?" KIMMY asked Claire, sitting on the floor of her living room. The girls were stretching their legs after their final workout session.

"I'm gonna admit," Claire said, touching her toes, "when you first suggested this, I thought you were crazy. Heck, I thought *I* was crazy when I said yes. But it's been really fun." She smiled at Kimmy. "Your studio is gonna be amazing."

"Thanks," Kimmy said. "That really means a lot to me. I just hope the rest of the town feels the way you do." She sighed. "I mean, it's not like I can advertise on the church bulletin board."

Claire laughed, imagining how that would go over. "Maybe not, but I have some social media tricks we can use to get the word out." The night before, she'd brainstormed creative ways to market the place. She'd even researched starting a YouTube channel where Kimmy could teach the workouts to girls all over the world.

Kimmy's eyes widened. "You'd do that for me?"

Claire nodded. "Of course. I'm grateful for everything you did for me. I know we only did this for a few weeks, but I really do feel a lot better about myself, and I think that's helping my marriage, too." Ever since the night she'd seduced Gavin, things had been different between them. She kept catching him looking at her out of the corner of his eye, and last weekend after she'd put Sadie to bed, he'd taken the dirty dishes right out of her hand and led her to the bedroom.

"Oh my god, I think I'm gonna cry," Kimmy said, leaning over to hug Claire. She pulled back. "Thank you for even agreeing to do this and letting me practice with you. I probably wouldn't have had the courage to do this on my own."

Claire smiled and stood up. "What are you up to tonight? Gavin's at softball practice until eight, and my mom's picking my little girl up from day care. Want to go grab a celebratory drink?"

Kimmy looked up at the clock on her phone. "I have to leave for work soon." She frowned. "Actually—I should call a cab now." She stood, and started scrolling through her contacts.

"Where's your car?" Claire asked, putting her water bottle in her bag.

"In the shop. Overheated yesterday. It's like, do I really need that in my life right now?"

Claire hitched her bag over her shoulder. "You want a ride?"

Kimmy glanced up. "That'd be great! Give me one sec, I'll change there."

As Kimmy gathered her things, Claire pulled out her phone and tweeted from @Pastor_Gavin: "*So many times we ask ourselves what someone else can do for us. Instead, we should be asking, how can we be the answer to THEIR prayer?*"

The girls drove to The Saddle with the windows down, the breeze ruffling their hair. When they got there, only a couple of cars sat in the dusty lot. "Well, I guess I'll see you soon?" Claire asked. She was surprised to feel a pang of sadness. She wasn't sure when she'd see Kimmy again, now that their lessons were done.

Kimmy paused as she opened the car door. "Wait . . . why don't you come in? Try out your new moves onstage?"

Claire burst out laughing. She was joking, right? "No way! You're crazy, girl."

Kimmy put a hand on Claire's arm, a sly grin on her face. It reminded Claire of Madison, who was always so good at talking her into doing things. "Remember what you told me like thirty minutes ago?" Kimmy asked. "How you thought I was crazy with the lessons, but you were glad you did it after all? I'm just sayin' . . . it'd feel pretty great to try those moves with an actual pole."

Claire put her sunglasses on top of her head, squinting into the sunlight. "It's one thing to practice a couple of moves behind closed doors, but there's no way I'm gonna do it in front of strangers."

"Oh my gosh. Look around!" Kimmy gestured at the nearly empty parking lot. "It's five thirty on a Wednesday. There's *no one* here. C'mon . . . you know you wanna. It's an adrenaline rush."

Claire could just hear her friends—especially Madison—telling her to do it. *"You've got nothin' to lose,"* they'd say. They'd be so proud of her. And as much fun and confidence-boosting as the workouts were, she could only imagine what being onstage would feel like.

"So?" Kimmy nudged her.

Claire took the key out of the ignition and shook her head in disbelief. "I can't believe I'm gonna do this."

Kimmy grinned. "That's the spirit!"

Inside, the strip club was dim and hazy, the only light coming from a rainbow-colored string of Christmas lights above the stage and the small red lanterns on each round table. A twenty-something girl with short black hair and dark skin was dancing, but there was no one in the audience. Her body gyrated to the heavy bass in ways that Claire only wished hers could.

Kimmy grabbed her hand and led her to the stage. "See, no one's here, so don't be nervous." Still in their yoga pants and tank tops from their workout, they joined the girl onstage. The dancer studied Claire for a moment, then grabbed her waist and led her to the pole.

Claire looked out from the stage. She felt like she'd slipped on someone else's skin . . . someone else's life entirely. Kimmy grabbed the pole and did one of the moves she'd taught Claire, a super-low dip that Claire had never been able to get right. Maybe it was the setting, or the pole, or the extreme confidence that washed over her, but as she tried it this time she was able to replicate Kimmy's move exactly. And it felt powerful. *She* felt powerful.

As Claire twirled around the stage to the thumping music, she got lost in a trance of happiness. Kimmy was right—dancing up there on that stage was an adrenaline rush. Kind of like that time when she was performing on the Toulouse High dance squad at the senior pep rally and caught Gavin staring at her from the bleachers. His eyebrows were raised the entire time. They'd been dating for a few months, but it was the first time he'd looked at her like *that*. Gavin would later tell her that there was just something about her that day that was different. Maybe it was the glitter eye shadow, he joked. Or the way she kept shaking her hips right at him . . .

But Claire knew it wasn't just her looks. It had been her confidence. Her happiness. Standing up there on that stage at The Saddle, dancing and feeling free, she'd finally recaptured that confident feeling. She laughed and dipped on the pole and spun around it.

After a moment, Claire realized the other two girls had stopped dancing. She raked her hair out of her eyes. "Why'd y'all stop?" she asked.

Kimmy nodded her head into the audience, her lips in a tight, flat line.

The door to the strip club was propped open, the sunlight streaming in. A team of three police officers stood in the middle of the room, talking gruffly to the owner, and periodically glanced up at the three women onstage.

Claire leaned against the pole for support, her knees suddenly weak as one of the officers shoved the owner against a table and handcuffed the man.

"Oh my gosh," Claire murmured, her hand over her mouth. Kimmy stepped back, her eyes wide. She reached out and squeezed Claire's hand. Behind her, the two other officers headed toward them. Claire's heart started racing.

The officers stopped at the foot of the stage, glaring up at the women. "We need to take y'all down to the station," said the one with the mustache. "Please come with us."

• • •

THE ROUND WALL clock ticked slowly as the hands reached eight. Claire's heart continued to race, as it had been doing for the two hours she'd been there. They had taken away her cell phone and put her in a room by herself so she couldn't talk to Kimmy or anyone else in the group. An officer had told her something about a drug ring at The Saddle and that he needed to ask everyone there some questions.

Finally, the door opened and a stout cop came in, staring at a folder. A name tag over his breast pocket read MARSHALL. "Claire Thibodeaux?" he asked, then looked up. "Hey, wait a second—aren't you Gavin Thibodeaux's wife?" He stared at her with wide eyes.

"Uh, yeah," she said, putting her hand on her forehead. "This is all one big misunderstanding."

"Well, I can't wait to hear it." Officer Marshall stroked his beard and grinned. "What's a preacher's wife like yourself doin' at a strip club?"

Claire blushed. This was *humiliating*. "I can explain everything," she said, fidgeting with her wedding band. "One of the strippers— Kimmy—I was tryin' to help her." She swallowed. "She wanted to get out of stripping."

He shuffled through some papers. "But it says here you were dancing onstage?" He looked up. "Can you explain that?" He grinned again, like he was getting some kind of enjoyment out of this interview.

She gestured to her workout clothes. Gray yoga pants, an orange tank top, and dirty hot pink Nikes. "Do you really think I was stripping, Officer Marshall?"

He laughed. "No, no. Of course not. So, do you know the owner, Jonny Bernard?"

"No." She shook her head.

"Has anyone tried to sell you drugs while you were there at any time?" He clicked his pen.

She frowned. "No."

"This Kimmy girl that you were helping . . . did she ever talk about drugs or give you any indication she was a part of a drug business?"

"No. *Was* she a part of it?" Her heart sank at the thought of Kimmy lying to her this whole time.

He shrugged his shoulders. "Not sure. That's why I'm asking you."

Claire shook her head again. "I don't think Kimmy was aware. And either way, she was planning to quit soon. She had an idea for a new business, and I was helping her put it together."

"Well, that's awfully nice of you," Officer Marshall said. "Was it a drug business?" he asked, his lips twitching.

"Goodness no!" Claire put her hand on her heart.

"I'm jus' givin' ya a hard time, Mrs. Thibodeaux." He chuckled. "Go on, call your husband. He can come pick you up now. You're clear."

Claire closed her eyes for a second and thanked God for getting out of this mess. When she opened them, Officer Marshall was handing her the phone on his desk. She gulped. Gavin was going to find out sooner or later. *Might as well get it over with now*, she thought.

She picked up the clunky black receiver, and punched in the numbers, her hands shaking.

"This is Gavin." His voice sounded so professional and serious on the other end, probably because he didn't recognize the number.

"Hey," she said nervously. "It's Claire. Don't freak out, but I need you to pick me up from the police station."

"What happened?" His voice got louder, panicked. "Are you okay?"

"I'm totally fine," she said, trying to sound calm. "Will you just come and get me, and I'll explain everything in the car?" She could only imagine what was going through Gavin's head.

"I'm on my way," he said.

She hung up and gathered her phone and purse from the front

desk before walking outside with her head down. She spotted Kimmy sitting on a wrought iron bench in front of the station. The sun had already set, and the old streetlamps in the parking lot were on.

"Oh my god," Kimmy said, standing up and hugging Claire. "You're out. I'm so sorry about this. I feel like it's all my fault. I had no idea Mr. Bernard was doing that kind of stuff, I swear, Claire." She pulled out a packet of cigarettes from her bag. "Are you okay?"

Claire shook her head slowly, thinking about everything that had just happened—it had been an emotional few hours to say the least. And soon, Gavin would be there, and she'd have to explain everything. She sat down on the bench and put her head in her hands. The scent of Kimmy's cigarette smoke engulfed her.

What am I doing? Claire asked herself. As much as she enjoyed spending time with Kimmy, it had been one big distraction from what she needed to do: talk to Gavin. Even though things had improved with him, she still had never confronted him about the fact that he was going to a strip club and lying to her about it. And look where all of this denial had gotten her. Their marriage wasn't fixed. It simply had a Band-Aid on it.

"Claire?" Kimmy asked, sitting down next to her. "Are you okay?" she asked again.

Claire massaged her temples with her fingers, wishing she could just go back to that night two months ago when she saw Gavin getting the lap dance. She wished they'd had an honest conversation then and that she'd never gotten caught up in all this.

Claire looked out into the parking lot and saw Gavin's truck pull in. She looked over at Kimmy and put her arms around her.

"Thank you for everything. You've been a real friend." With Kimmy's eyes heavy on her, Claire stood up, grabbed her bag, and walked away.

• • •

CLAIRE CONFESSED EVERYTHING in the truck to Gavin— how she'd seen him getting a lap dance, how she'd confronted Kimmy, and how the two girls found a way to help each other. Gavin sat in silence, his jaw clenching harder at her every word. She told him how she happened to be at the strip club at the wrong time and how the whole thing was a big misunderstanding.

He continued to drive in silence. Claire nervously asked, "Aren't you gonna say something—*anything*?"

Gavin finally turned his head toward her and slammed his hand on the steering wheel. "You want me to say something?" he asked, livid. "Here's what I have to say: I am so disappointed in you, Claire. We have a reputation to uphold in this town and you almost ruined everything for us."

A reputation to uphold? Just like that, Claire broke, her months of frustrations coming to the surface. "You're being so hypocritical, Gavin! You know what you did, but now you're holding me to a different standard than you hold yourself?" She scoffed. "What you did was *way* worse than what I did. You betrayed me and our marriage. I, on the other hand, was trying to help us—I wanted you to feel attracted to me again." Her heart thumped quickly in her chest. "But you know what? I don't care what you think anymore."

For the first time, she understood completely what Kimmy was talking about when she said it wasn't really about what the guys thought—it was about *her*, it was about how she felt about herself. And right then, as she called out Gavin on what he really was, she felt empowered, just like Kimmy said she would.

They stared at each other in heated silence. Finally, Gavin spoke, an eerie calmness in his voice. "I'm willing to work on it if you are."

She knew what he was saying. But could they do it? Forgive each other and move forward? It wouldn't be the same naive relationship. She thought about their perfect daughter, their perfect house, and the congregation she loved so much. She didn't want to disrupt all that she had worked so hard to build, did she? But deep down, she knew the answer, the one she'd been trying so adamantly to deny. "I'm tired of working on things for you. I'm ready to work on things for myself."

"What are you saying?" His tone was urgent.

With a heavy heart, she said, "I think we need some time apart." The words echoed throughout the quiet truck.

"Do you want . . . a divorce?" Gavin asked, his voice breaking.

"I don't know," Claire said. "But I do know we can't go on like this. If we have any chance to make it, we both have to look hard at ourselves and figure out if this is what we still want."

Gavin stared at her with barely contained rage. She knew how it would look to his parishioners when word got out that they'd separated, and he wasn't used to her standing up to him. But he must have seen the resolve in her eyes, because after he dropped her off to get her car at The Saddle, he screeched out of the parking lot.

Later that night, after Gavin had packed a bag and left for his parents' house, Claire pulled out her phone and tweeted her last message from Gavin's account: *@Pastor_Gavin: "The sun will rise tomorrow, and you will, too."*

44

madison

MADISON CURLED UP with her Chucks on the seat and leaned her head on the window. The stench of a fellow passenger's onion sandwich made her want to vomit, or maybe it was Cash . . . or the fact that her dad was dying . . . or the gin and tonic from the night before. She didn't know for sure. But her stomach roiled as she sat watching the rain pour down outside. A bird flew by, dropping its business on her window.

"Shit just follows me everywhere . . ." she said under her breath, shaking her head.

Her phone buzzed on the seat next to her. In the split second before she picked it up, she secretly hoped she'd see Cash's name. *Maybe he realized what an ass he was being,* she thought. *An apology would be nice.* She took a deep breath and braced herself. But it was just a weather alert.

She scolded herself for being foolish and holding out hope where there was none. Then she shut her eyes, wishing her mind would quiet itself enough to sleep. She hadn't gotten any the night before. Her mind had spun restlessly, churning up old memories of her dad, like how when she was little, she'd walk behind him as he mowed the yard, fascinated by the little path of freshly cut grass he left in his wake. Or the time when she was six, and they made a dollhouse out of a refrigerator box. He let her use his camo duct tape for the wallpaper, and they made curtains out of one of his old black T-shirts.

"This is the most interesting dollhouse I've ever seen," he had told her, scratching his chin and admiring their work.

He was such a good man. He gave to charity even though he didn't have a lot, he went to work, even when he was feeling bad, and he never missed an opportunity to make Madison feel special, even when she felt like she didn't deserve it.

She wondered what he was doing now, if he was thinking of her and remembering the same things she was. She didn't know what to expect when she got to the hospice center. Would he be on his last breath? Hell, would she even make it in time to say good-bye? *God, please let him see me and know I made it.* She didn't want his last memory of her to be her leaving.

As the bus rolled down I-59, Madison tried to understand why someone like him would be taken out of this world when such mean and selfish people got to stay. It just didn't make sense.

She leaned her head back on the plush seat. *Death isn't fair.* But she knew it was inevitable. She couldn't help but wonder what her life would look like when she neared the end. Would she be old? Would she be married? Would she be looking back on a life spent with someone like Cash, who caused her so much anger, or someone like her dad, who made her feel loved?

George. Her mind flashed to him. She wondered if she hadn't left him, would he have been by her side right now, holding her hand, supporting her through all of this? She closed her eyes, her heart heavy with all she'd already lost and everything she still had left to lose.

• • •

"DADDY?" SHE SAID quietly as she tiptoed on the hardwood floors into his room at the hospice house. Her blue fishing lure charm bracelet jingled softly. The room was painted a warm yellow. A lush tropical evergreen sat on the mahogany dresser. The last bit of sun slanted in through the windows along the far wall. Everything about this place seemed lively, happy, and healthy except for Allen, who lay still in the twin-size bed with his eyes closed.

Her mom lingered by the door as Madison sat down on the bed and held her dad's fragile hands in hers. He didn't stir and his pulse was weak beneath his paper-thin skin.

"Daddy," she cried, her voice breaking. "Daddy," she tried again, struggling to breathe through her tears.

"I'm gonna leave you," her mom said, putting her hand on her shoulder. "I've said my good-byes, so take your time."

Madison nodded and watched her mom shut the door behind her. "Daddy," she said one more time, gripping his hand harder. The words finally loosened themselves from her tongue. "I have so much to say right now, but I don't even know where to start." She took a deep breath. "I want you to know that you're so much greater a person than I'll ever be, but I'll always strive to live like you did. With passion. And love. And kindness." Her eyes blurred as the tears came faster. "Thank you . . ." Her voice cracked with emotion. She took another deep breath to compose herself.

"Thank you for all those fishing trips where you taught me much more than fishing. Like how to be funny and how to swear and how to dream." She wiped her tears away, the fishing lure charm chiming on her wrist. "I just can't imagine life without you. . . . I truly don't know how I'm going to get through it. . . ." She trailed off, the weight of the moment pressing down on her. "But I promise—I vow right here, right now—that I will keep your spirit alive with me for the rest of my life." She broke down and cried into his chest. "I'll try to keep laughing, and loving, and seeing the good in people like you do." She squeezed his hand again. "And I want you to know Mama and me'll be fine. I'm gonna take good care of her and make sure she's happy and comfortable and everything else you want her to be. I don't want you to go, Daddy, but I understand that you have to—I don't want you to suffer anymore."

She kissed his forehead and hugged him once more. "I love you, Daddy."

And though he lay still, his breath ragged and pulse slowing, she could have sworn she saw his lips curve up in one last ghost of a smile.

45

gabrielle

THE BLINKING CURSOR stared back at Gabby, taunting her as she searched for the right words for her college scholarship essay. After the long day working at the day care, her brain felt like mush, but the deadline loomed—forty-eight hours to be exact—so she grabbed a root beer, pulled up a chair at the office desktop, and tried to come up with something . . . *anything*.

As nice as it was being in the day care when screaming sticky kids weren't all up in her face, it was eerie being in the church complex after hours, when it was so quiet and empty. This was how so many of those horror flicks she watched on Netflix started, after all. But she knew staying after hours was the only way she'd be able to write her essay in peace. Her mom, while a very pleasant houseguest, couldn't stop talking or humming, bless her heart. Despite the quiet, Gabby had spent the last two hours staring at that screen, trying to come up with the perfect answer to the seemingly simple question: "Which experience in your own life has influenced you the most?"

A few things had come to mind. She started to write about her experience growing up in Section 8 housing. How she and Claire would play "Fancy House" and pretend they lived in mansions. But she wondered if that really influenced her life, other than teaching her to pretend things weren't as desperate as they seemed. Then she tried talking about growing up with a single mother, and how she and

Elaine had to be there for each other, but she didn't want the scholarship committee to think she was trying to win with a sob story.

The cursor kept blinking. She kept thinking. Finally, she started to type:

Have you ever wanted something so bad but were told you couldn't have it? I've often felt like I'm the poster child for this. Time and time again in my life, I've dreamed and worked toward something only to hit the big wall of "no." One of the hardest moments of my life was when I was told I couldn't go to college— not because I couldn't get in, but because I couldn't afford it.

I know you asked for one single experience, but I'd like to lump together all of the "no's" and "you can't do that's" into one. They, as a whole, have influenced me more than anything else. Without these individual setbacks throughout the years, I don't know if I would have finally gotten to the point where I am right now, saying, "Enough is enough! It's time to make things happen."

After twenty-one years of being told I can't have these things I've wanted so badly, I've finally learned my lesson: I'm not going to take no for an answer anymore.

I am writing this essay in hopes of getting financial help so that I can finally go to college. Of course you can say no (and you might), but for the first time in my life, I'm happy to say that I plan on doing it even if someone tells me no—because in my heart, I believe that dreams should come true and some things are worth fighting for.

Gabby looked at the essay and took a deep breath, starting to edit bits and pieces of it. The day care's doorbell rang, the shrill sound echoing through the empty room.

Her eyes shot toward the door, her heart beating fast. Who would be trying to get into the day care at 8:00 p.m.?

The doorbell rang again. Gabby grabbed a baseball bat from the sports closet and walked cautiously to the front door. She peered through the glass and her heart leaped into her throat. There, on the other side of the door, was the most unexpected sight of all: Tony.

She wanted to collect her thoughts, but it was too late—he'd already seen her. He raised a hand in greeting. She sighed in nervous anticipation and slowly opened the door. "What are you doing here?"

Tony stood there with a serious expression, his hands in the back pockets of his Levi's. "Can we talk?"

"How did you find me?" Gabby crossed her arms over her chest, as if holding herself together.

"I have my ways," he said, attempting a half-smile. "Can I come in?"

She nodded slowly and opened the door wider. They stood in the entrance, a small hallway covered with the kids' drawings on one wall, and the other covered in chalkboard paint. She leaned her shoulder against the blackboard wall, the now familiar shame and embarrassment resurfacing. "Why are you here?" she tried again. It'd been a week since they ran into each other at the mall. Maybe he wanted to tell her off, or rub it in her face that he'd moved on.

Tony leaned his head against six-year-old Jacob Marston's monster artwork. He had written the words "I smell" in big letters above it, an arrow pointing to the drawing, and it now appeared as though the arrow was pointing to Tony's head. She bit back a small smile, then took a deep breath and braced herself for what he was about to say.

He shook his head angrily. "My dad told me everything. . . ."

Her heart stopped, not expecting to hear that. Why would Mr. Ford make such a big deal out of not telling Tony . . . and then tell him? Was it to hurt her even more? To prove that she was so devious that she would use him for a trade? To let Tony know just how trashy her family was? Anger festered inside her, making her palms sweat.

"I'm so ashamed, Gabby." Tony lowered his eyes. "I'm so . . ." He paused. "I'm so sorry."

She looked up in confusion. "Wait, what?"

"Can we sit down?" He started walking into the main playroom. "There's a lot I have to say to you."

Gabby led him to a small kids' tea table in the middle of the room. "Have a seat," she said, still thrown by his words. They both sat down, their knees bending so much they almost touched the floor.

"My dad did a horrible thing," he said, fiddling with the tiny teacup in front of him.

She grabbed the other teacup, needing something to fidget with. "No, Tony, *I* did a horrible thing."

"Okay, true," he said with a soft smirk. "You both did horrible things, but I'm here to apologize to you on his behalf."

"Why did he tell you what happened?" She leaned forward and put the teacup in the saucer.

"Seeing you at the mall the other day . . . man, that really screwed me up." Tony rubbed his neck and glanced up at the ceiling.

She nodded. Seeing him again had haunted her, too. As much as she tried to put the relationship to bed, to be thankful to have Elaine by her side, she couldn't stop thinking about him. When her car had gotten a flat the other day, her first thought had been to call him. And when she'd decided to go to college, she'd wanted to run to him and say, "Look, I can be the girl you fell in love with." But then she'd remembered the withering look he'd given her and knew she'd never be anything but a liar in his eyes.

"I went home and told my parents I was gonna try to get you back. I didn't know how I was gonna do it, but I was gonna fight for you, Gabs." He held the teacup by the handle, moving it as he spoke, as if to punctuate his words.

She stared at him, disbelieving. "Why would you want me back after finding out that I lied to you? Aren't you mad at me?"

"Of course." He put the teacup down and grabbed her hand from across the table. "But I think I know you better than you realize. So, maybe I missed a couple of things. . . ." He chuckled quietly. "But I know that what we had was love and I don't think you actually meant to deceive me. I remember those conversations with you at the beginning, and I remember making assumptions." He pulled back his hands. "That doesn't make what you did right." He paused. "But I could understand why you might have done it."

"I *never* meant to hurt you," she said. "I hope you know that."

Tony frowned. "When I was telling my parents I wanted you back, my dad ended up telling me about your deal." He shook his head. "He refuses to admit that what he did was wrong, but it was . . . it was awful." Tony's brown eyes stared deeply into hers. "I'm so sorry that he put you in that position. I feel betrayed by him."

She picked up the teacup to fiddle with. "It's not his fault. It's mine, Tony. He wouldn't have done all of this if I hadn't lied in the first place." She lowered her head.

"Look, I don't care whose fault it was." He clenched his jaw and then softened his voice. "I got the facts wrong but the person right. Can we just start over? With honesty—the way we should have done in the first place?"

Gabby raised her head. Was he really saying what she thought he was saying? "But what about your new girlfriend?"

Tony's brow furrowed in confusion. "Who?"

She bit her lip. "The girl you were with at the mall."

He laughed. "That was my cousin, Mary-Anne."

A knot of jealous tension unraveled in Gabby's chest. She looked into his dark eyes and then at the nervous smile on his face. "So . . . you're serious?"

"I'm very serious." He stood up and reached for her hand, pulling her close to him between the tea party table and the jungle gym. "The girl I fell in love with is *you*." He looked deep into her eyes. "I fell in love with your intelligence." He touched her head. "It had nothing to do with you pretending to be enrolled in school. You didn't fake your ideas or passion in our conversations." He paused. "I fell in love with your heart." He touched her chest. "The same one that chose to help her mom find a better life—and who could blame you for that? No other girl has made me feel the way that you do, and that is real." He lifted her chin with his hand. "So what do you say? Can we just start fresh? I just want to be with you again. I love you, Gabby."

Gabby's heart fluttered, but questions kept popping into her mind. She wondered if Tony would be able to trust her moving forward, and whether this sense of embarrassment would fade or stay with her throughout the rest of their relationship? She also thought back to her college scholarship application on the desktop in the other room. She finally had plans—would her dreams fit into Tony's life? But when she looked into his eyes, she knew what the answer was. They would figure it out . . . together. "I love you, too, Tony."

His smile widened, and he kissed her. Gabby kissed him back, pouring all of the longing of the past two months into it. When he pulled away, she felt like she was standing on solid ground for the first time in months.

Tony's eyes crinkled as he smiled at her. "You just make me so happy." He kissed her again and lowered himself onto the ground, bending on one knee.

Gabby's heart stopped. "When you said start over I thought—"

"Shhh," he interrupted her, laughing. "I have a speech."

Gabby blushed and nodded for him to continue.

"You're the most important person in my life, and I don't want to spend another day without you. I wanna try this again and do it right." He pulled out the diamond engagement ring, the one she had given back to him at the café when they broke up. "Gabby Vaughn, will you marry me?"

Gabby put her hand on her heart. "Of course I'll marry you!" She couldn't say the words fast enough.

He slipped the ring on her finger. She looked down and admired it. Even though it was the same piece she had worn for six months, it looked different this time around. Somehow it was even more perfect. She wrapped her arms around Tony's neck and held him close. "We should go celebrate."

"Where do you want to go? For a drink? Out to dinner? You name it."

Gabby pondered it for a second. "Actually, I've got a few people you need to meet." She pulled her cell phone from her back pocket and texted her friends to meet them at the Sea Shack in thirty minutes. "And is it okay if we pick up my mom on the way there?"

He kissed her on the forehead. "That sounds perfect."

"I'll be right back!" Gabby ran into the office and saved her scholarship application essay to work on in the morning. She grabbed her bag, and they began walking out of the day care.

"So, there's just one more thing . . ." Tony said as they reached the hallway.

Gabby stopped and looked nervously in his eyes. "What?"

"With my whole dad situation, I'm not asking my parents to help pay for the wedding anymore, so we can't afford your dream wedding."

She took a deep breath and then pulled him in closer for a kiss. "I don't care about a stupid wedding anymore," Gabby said. "All I want is *you*."

madison

MADISON SHIFTED UNCOMFORTABLY at the podium in the church auditorium, staring out at a sea of expectant faces. She normally didn't mind public speaking, but giving the eulogy at her father's funeral was even harder than she'd imagined it would be. She found her mom in the front row and met Connie's eyes, red and puffy from days of crying. Connie nodded at her and Madison took a deep breath, and then began.

"Thank you all for being here today. As I look out and see how many people are here to say good-bye to my dad, I'm overwhelmed with love." Her hands were shaking and she gripped the podium tightly. "And I know he's looking down and loving all of this, too—probably with a drink in his hand, a cigarette in his mouth, and that huge smile he got when he was happy, like when the Saints scored or when he'd catch a monster fish."

The crowd laughed, loosening the vise around Madison's heart. She attempted a smile and started again, the words coming more slowly. "If you knew my dad—which I'm assuming you did because why else would you be spending your Saturday morning here?—you know that he was a great guy. What I've seen throughout my life—and what I've heard from a lot of you over these past few days—was that he always had a way of making everyone around him feel special. When he listened to you, it felt like you were the most important person in the world to him. Everyone loved talking to him because he gave the best advice—in his straight-shootin', no-nonsense kind of way, of course. So, with that in mind, I'd like to share a few of my favorite Allen Blanchette words of wisdom."

Madison looked back into the crowd and saw Claire, Laura, and Gabby seated together in the second row. They gave her encouraging smiles. Her eyes shifted to the row behind them, and that was when she saw George, wearing the same dark suit he'd worn to their wedding. After everything she'd done, he was here, paying his respects to her father. Gratitude welled up inside her and she cut her eyes away from him and back to her speech, clearing her throat.

"One. You get what you pay for. This especially applies to fishing gear and lawn mowers." The mourners laughed again and Madison smiled along with them.

"Two. Find the good in everyone. People come into your life for a reason, even the ones you can't stand. He recited that one over and over again during the season Tommy O'Hare was traded from the Cowboys to the Saints.

"Three. Be kind to others. But if someone's not kind to you, it's okay to give them a taste of their own medicine. This one goes out especially to that mechanic who thought it'd be cool to rip him off in '97. May his business rest in peace.

"And four. Family is the most important thing in your life. Not money. Not career. Not that shiny new boat, however much happiness it will bring you. If you can go home every night to people who support you and love you unconditionally, you've won at life. And that, my friends, is why Allen Blanchette is wearing a gold medal up in heaven right now."

• • •

AFTER THE FUNERAL, Madison stood helplessly in the kitchen, looking around at all the deviled eggs and casseroles and cellophane-wrapped loaves of bread on the counter. People were starting to come over for the reception, and it was nice of everyone to bring food, but no amount of carbs or sweets or comfort meals would bring her dad back to life.

"Hey, you," Claire said softly as she, Gabby, and Laura entered the room. The girls were all wearing black: her cousin had on a cap-sleeved frock and a simple pearl necklace; Gabby wore a long cotton halter dress and covered it with a gray cardigan even though it was ninety degrees outside; and Laura had donned a dark tea-length skirt and top.

"Gosh, you all look beautiful," Madison said, hugging each of them. "You should go to funerals more often."

The girls smiled awkwardly at her joke.

Laura pushed some things around on the counter to make room for her large bowl. "How are you doing?"

"It's tough," Madison confessed. "But luckily I have enough fried okra to get me through the rest of my life," she said sarcastically, pointing to all of the containers of food.

"Well, when you need a break from the okra, I brought some homemade chocolate chip cookies," Claire said, holding up a silver tin wrapped in a black bow.

"And peanut butter brownies . . ." Gabby said, setting an aluminum pan on the counter.

"Yeah . . . and a vat of homemade mashed potatoes," Laura said guiltily. "And by homemade I mean like six boxes of the instant kind."

"Thank you girls so much for coming. Even if your goal is to make me fat." Madison smiled. They had been there for her every day with texts and hugs; Madison didn't know how she would have gotten through this without them.

Claire put her head on Madison's shoulder. "The funeral was beautiful. How's your mom doing? I only got to say hi to her briefly."

"You know . . ." Madison shuffled her bare feet on the floor and tugged her black shift dress. "She's handling it as best she can." She paused and leaned on the counter. "It just . . . it just doesn't seem real. I feel like he's in the other room, entertaining everyone with his stupid jokes." She cracked a smile and then frowned. "But he's not. He's gone. And there's nothing that can bring him back. It's like a nightmare." She paused, tearing up. "I feel like I'm living a nightmare right now, but I'm never going to wake up."

"Oh, sweetie," Gabby said, rubbing her arm. "We're here for you. Anything you need."

"Thank you," Madison said, forcing a smile and rubbing the tears away. She'd always had a hard time being vulnerable, even with the people she loved most. "You don't know how much it means to me, y'all being here and all."

"We wouldn't have missed it for anything," Laura said softly. "Like Gabby said, we're here for you."

Madison nodded and tried to shake the tears off. "Okay, I just need a moment. Why don't y'all go on in," she said, pointing to the living room. "And I'll be out there in a few."

The girls nodded and walked away, leaving her completely alone with her thoughts and the five hundred thousand calories sitting on the counter. She grabbed a strawberry from the Edible Arrangement Mr. Gary had sent over and walked outside to the porch, wiping her tears away.

A gust of warm air hit her as she stepped out into the muggy, overcast afternoon. The leaky tin awning above her head was dripping noisily and a small bird splashed around in the puddle of water on the blue tarp covering her dad's boat. Madison swatted away a mosquito. Cigarette smoke wafted toward her and she turned.

On the lawn, his back toward her, was George, puffing pensively. Madison's heart lurched. Since spotting him in the church, she'd wondered if he'd make it to the reception but figured that he didn't want to be anywhere near her.

"You know those are bad for you," she said.

George turned around, his green eyes lighting up at the sight of her. "Hey," he said softly. He looked down at the cigarette in embarrassment. "Uh, yeah, you know I don't really smoke that often—"

"Can I have one?" she cut him off, meeting him halfway on the concrete.

He nodded and handed her a cigarette, lighting it with his stainless steel lighter.

She walked over to the porch swing, and he followed. They sat down, neither saying anything for a few seconds. Instead, they just listened to the repetition of the swing creaking up and down.

After a few calming drags, Madison finally spoke. "How long have you been here?"

"Not long, just a few minutes," George said, his voice deep and soothing. He put his arm around the back of the swing, his silver Rolex clunking against the wood. Madison resisted the urge to move closer to him, bury her face in his jacket, and let him comfort her. "Your eulogy was great. It was perfect."

"Thanks." She exhaled some smoke. "I'm . . . I'm happy you're here. You don't know how much this means to me."

"I just wanted to tell you I'm so sorry, Madison." He touched her shoulder, and the warmth of his hand made her heart clench.

She looked up at him, wondering what he was apologizing for. Her dad? Their relationship? Something else?

"You were right—the things you said when you left. I took advantage of your situation and it was wrong." He crushed his cigarette into the concrete with his polished loafer. "You may have picked up on this over the past few months, but I don't always make the best social decisions." He sighed. "You were so much younger than me and in a desperate situation, and after you left, I did a lot of reflecting and realized that I shouldn't have put you in that position."

She leaned her head back on the swing and thought about what he was saying. He might feel guilty, but she took advantage of the situation, too. "I never felt pressured, though, so don't feel like that happened, okay?"

"I never wanted to hurt you," he said looking up at her. The earnest look in his eyes made her stomach ache.

"And you never did." She blew on her cigarette, realizing he sort of had the situation twisted. "But I know I hurt you. And I'm really sorry about that, George."

He stood up and walked over to a glass of scotch that was sitting on the windowsill. He must have set it down earlier when he came outside. "We both made mistakes, Mads," he said, taking a sip of his drink.

As she stared at him, she noticed for the first time how confident he was. George had never played mind games with her, or waffled about what he wanted. He made decisions—about her, about his life—with certainty, and followed through on them. It was an attractive quality. How had she not realized that before?

"You know why I loved being with you?" he asked, pacing in front of the window. "When I first met you, I had this need to comfort you, to take care of you. But the more I got to know you, the more I learned all the good in you that, quite frankly, I don't think you even knew you had. I stopped wanting to take care of you and started falling in love with you."

"You fell in love with me?" she said softly.

George stopped his pacing and locked eyes with her, a determined set to his jaw. "You made me laugh, and see things in a different way. Even though I knew what you were doing, what we were, I felt like you were being genuine when we were together."

Madison sighed. "I was." The times that she'd spent with George were always, surprisingly, some of the most fun she'd ever had. He made her feel heard and funny and adventurous. All he'd ever asked was for her to be herself.

He joined her on the swing again. "For the first time in my life, I allowed myself to be happy. I don't know—it's like you brought out things in myself that I wasn't even aware of. . . . I went thirty-two years without ever letting someone into my life, and I was starting to think that it was never gonna happen." He took another sip of his scotch. "Now, it hurt when you left." He put his hand on his heart. "But the pain was just a reminder that for the first time, I had let myself fall. And that was a good thing." He frowned thoughtfully. "I didn't see you leaving to go with Cash as something cruel. You might, but I don't. . . ."

Guilt tore at Madison. "Then what did you see it as?" she asked, leaning toward him.

"Something you needed to do." He put his arm around the back of the swing again. "You needed to see that you deserved better than that. You're a good person, Mads. Just like your dad."

A lump grew in Madison's throat as she thought about her father. Being compared to him was the highest compliment she could think of.

"All that stuff that you said in the eulogy about him—you got all of that from him," George continued. "And that family of yours that you'll go home to every night one day, they're gonna be the luckiest people in the world." He took another sip of his scotch. "There's something so special about you, and I know that you're going to find someone just as special as you are."

Madison considered his words. She'd been in love with Cash for years, and the whole time she'd been waiting for him to commit, for him to see her as special, as enough. But in a strange way, it'd never been about him, not really. He'd never let her get close enough to see if they'd actually work. It was like those Snickers bars she used to steal—a cheap thrill, or a bad habit she couldn't kick. But since she'd left Birmingham, she hadn't thought of Cash once.

"George, thank you for understanding. Going off with Cash *was* something I thought I needed to do." Her mind flashed back to Cash, and how dismissive he'd been. She frowned. "But you're right. When I was there, I realized it wasn't what I wanted or needed in my life." She sat back against the swing. "This whole thing with my dad—it made me realize that I wanted someone who would be there by my side through everything. When I'm looking back on my life, I want it to be filled with laughter and adventure—not tears and drama."

George put his arm around her and rubbed her shoulder. She leaned into his touch.

"What I'm trying to say is . . . I think that person is you." She took a deep breath. "If you would give me another chance, I'd like us to start over again and see if there's something real here."

He looked deep into her eyes, pulled her close, and kissed her. It felt surprisingly natural being in his arms. And for the first time, Madison felt genuine love for George—not because of his money, but because of the person he was . . . and who she was when she was with him.

laura

AS LAURA WALKED into Claire's tidy, sunlit kitchen, she was greeted by a cooing Sadie and a table full of pancakes.

"Happy last day of school!" Claire said, wiping off Sadie's face. Sadie and her high chair were both covered in blackberry applesauce. "Come join us! I made you breakfast." Claire pointed to the pancake plate on the table.

Laura couldn't believe this day was actually here—that she was actually graduating high school. She felt a strange sense of déjà vu. A year ago, she'd experienced what she thought was her last day of high school, and she'd been so proud to be leaving Toulouse behind. But one year later, everything had changed. Now she was just happy to have her diploma and her future—whatever it held—ahead of her.

She pulled out a chair, the scent of deliciously browned batter welcoming her as she sat. "Ooh, chocolate chip! My favorite. And you made 'em into a smiley face . . . that's how my mom used to do it." She grinned up at Claire, touched by the effort. "Thank you so much."

"You're very welcome."

Laura poured syrup over the pancakes. "You've been so wonderful to let me stay here." After she'd left Brian that night at Mossy Pointe, she'd packed up her things at Rob and Janet's and moved into Claire and Gavin's guest bedroom . . . although Gavin was no longer there. He'd been staying with his parents while he and Claire met once a week for counseling. She hated having to impose on her friend, especially when Claire was going through her own problems, but being together had helped them both get through these past few weeks.

She took a bite of the fluffy pancakes, thinking about how lucky she was to have such supportive friends. Her emotions had been in a constant flip-flop since leaving Brian. Sometimes she'd feel thankful that it had happened the way it did, that Brian was the one who clearly messed up and betrayed her. In a weird way, she felt like it gave her permission to break up with him, even though she was already unhappy in the relationship. But then other times, she would start crying as she mourned the good parts of their marriage, from the seemingly insignificant stuff like how comfortable she was singing music in the car with him, to the more significant things, like how he was the only guy she had ever loved.

"So, have you decided what you're gonna do after you graduate?" Claire asked, taking a handful of Cheerios and feeding them to Sadie.

Laura shook her head. With the stress of the breakup, making up all of her schoolwork so she could graduate on time, and taking on some extra shifts at the Sea Shack, she hadn't had a chance to sit down and actually plan her new future. After she graduated, she'd probably head to Arlington to live with her parents . . . but after that, she had no idea. Not having everything planned out was scary and exhilarating at the same time.

Claire stood up and put the dirty dishes in the sink. "Well, just know that you can stay here for as long as you need to while you figure it out."

"I appreciate it, Claire—I appreciate everything. I don't know what I would've done without you and your hospitality."

"Love you! We're so proud of you." Claire turned to her baby.

"Isn't that right, Sadie?" The little girl giggled and nodded her curly blond head.

As Laura headed off to school, she realized that she was proud of herself, too.

• • •

"CHEERS!" LAURA AND Vince sat outside of Sal's Sno-Cones, a tiny shed on Dupont Road that sold fifty different flavors of shaved ice. They had snuck away during their lunch hour and managed to snag the last available table outside, which happened to be right next to the speakers that were blaring Cajun music.

"I'm glad we're doing this," Vince said, cracking a smile. He bit into his cone. True to their argument all those months ago, he'd gotten root beer, but Laura had decided to go with a wildcard: blue moon.

"Me, too," she said, trying not to feel guilty. Since Brian's surgery, Laura had neglected her friendship with Vince—not answering his texts, declining his offers to study, and studying in the library during lunch to avoid having to talk to him. "I'm sorry I've been so MIA recently."

Vince set his sno-cone down, his hazel eyes widening. "Listen, you don't have to apologize. I understand why we stopped hanging out. You know, I'm not married, but I could see where it would be weird to make new friends of the opposite sex." He blushed and adjusted his blue Duke baseball hat. "And as much as I liked hanging out with you, I don't wanna make things complicated in your relationship."

Laura took a deep breath, shifting on the wooden bench. "Vince, I left Brian a couple of weeks ago," she quietly admitted.

Too quietly, apparently, because he cupped his ear and said, "What was that?"

Laura cleared her throat. "I left Brian," she said more loudly, practically shouting. She glanced around the packed outdoor area, afraid that someone from school was around and had overheard—so far she'd only told her parents and her closest friends.

Vince's mouth dropped open and he leaned across the table, lightly touching her arm. Laura felt a spark of heat at his touch. "I'm so sorry," he said.

"That's why I've been so weird," Laura continued. "I've just been doing a lot of reflecting. I won't get into everything, but I really wanted to thank you."

Vince gave her a confused look.

Laura shyly tucked her hair behind her ears. "I feel like you pushed me this year. You made me feel smart, like I wasn't just this dumb girl who lived in the shadows of her husband."

"But you are smart," Vince said incredulously. "And you know that."

"It's always good to be reminded." She shrugged, feeling her face turning red. "Anyway . . . you've been amazing this year, and I'm excited about your future."

"You know, you're not the only one who got something out of this," Vince said.

Laura glanced back up, and they locked eyes. Her stomach flipped.

"Thanks for making me feel welcome here," he said with a chuckle. "It was hard coming into a new school for my senior year— especially such a small, insular school—but you made everything feel easy."

They grinned at each other for a moment. Laura wondered what high school would have been like if she'd fallen for someone like Vince instead of Brian, someone who encouraged her to seek her own spotlight, though maybe the better question was who she would have been if she'd focused on herself instead of on a boyfriend. But she couldn't dwell on questions like that. She couldn't change her past, and as hard as this year had been, she'd come out the other side and she felt good about where she'd landed.

"I hope we can keep in touch after graduation," Vince said. "I'd love to hang out this summer." He looked down, his cheeks reddening slightly. "And I know you and Brian just broke up, but maybe—when you're ready—I could take you on a date some-time."

Laura's heart fluttered. "Definitely," she said with a smile. "I'd love that."

. . .

THEY GOT BACK to campus with five minutes left before lunch was over, and Laura used that time to stop by the guidance coun-selor's office.

"Well, hello, m'dear!" Mrs. Walker said as Laura entered her of-fice. "What can I do ya for?"

Laura sat down in one of the scratchy chairs in front of Mrs. Walker's desk. "I wanted to talk about college."

Mrs. Walker's eyes lit with excitement. "Oh, have you decided to apply to LSU? I heard that Brian was headed back—such a great idea to join him in school." She opened up her drawer, pulling out a brochure and sliding it across the desk to Laura.

Laura stared at it for a second and then gulped. "Um, actually, I was thinking somewhere else."

Mrs. Walker stared at her in silence for a moment, as if digest-ing the implications of that statement, and then clapped her hands together. "All right, sweetheart. Now, most college application dead-lines have passed for a fall start, but with your grades, you can get into just about anywhere you want for spring semester. So where are you thinking?" She pulled out some more brochures from her desk drawer. "University of New Orleans, University of Lafayette, Loui-siana Tech . . ." She spread the pamphlets out on the paper-covered desk. "What's your dream school?"

Laura paused. She didn't have a definite answer. "Somewhere far away from here."

Mrs. Walker nodded and put together a stack of folders on var-ious schools. Finally, she handed them to Laura—they weighed about as much as her history textbook.

"We can go over these anytime you want. I know it's summer, but send me an email and we can set up an appointment," Mrs. Walker said.

"Thank you," Laura said, standing to leave. Before she headed out the door, she looked at Mrs. Walker again. "I'll make you proud." And as cheesy as that sounded, she was finally ready to make that happen.

As the school bell rang and Laura went back into the hall, she looked down at the informational booklets Mrs. Walker had given her. There were so many options, so many possibilities.

Laura grinned, and her smile only grew bigger as she met up with Vince, who'd waited to walk her to her next class.

"It's so weird that this is almost over," Vince said, sounding nostalgic.

Laura glanced around the halls, at all her excited peers. "I don't know," she said. "It feels like everything is just beginning."

gabrielle

"WHAT'S GOING ON?" Gabby asked as Claire, Madison, and Laura sat her down on Claire's beige couch. Sadie was staying with Gavin so Claire could host Gabby's last night as a single lady. "Why do you guys look like you're up to something?"

"It's a slumber party—we have to watch a movie, duh," Madison said casually, braiding her hair on one side. The girls were wearing matching pink short-sleeve silk pajama sets, compliments of Claire.

"Okay, popcorn's ready," Claire announced from the kitchen, pouring it into a mixing bowl. The scent filled the room as she brought it to the coffee table.

"So, what are we watching?" Gabby asked, throwing a piece of buttery popcorn into her mouth. The other girls stood giggling in front of the flat-screen TV. "What in the world are y'all up to?"

"We couldn't agree on a movie to watch," Laura said, throwing the other girls a conspiratorial grin, "so we decided to make one."

Gabby put her hand over her mouth. "Oh. My. God." Her stomach flipped with excitement.

"Please turn off all cell phones . . ." Madison said, funneling her voice with her hand.

"And enjoy the show!" Claire finished, pressing a button on the remote control. The overhead lights dimmed, and the girls plopped back on the couch with Gabby, scooping handfuls of popcorn as the film began.

A title card appeared:

THE YOUNG WIVES CLUB

Gabby wiggled her feet in front of her with happiness. "You guys!" she shouted as the first scene began.

It opened with the three girls sitting outside in Claire's backyard, looking into the camera as they huddled close to one another.

Madison spoke first: "So, one of our best friends is getting married tomorrow."

"And we're really happy for her," Laura said.

"But we can't let her do it without first sharing our advice," Claire added. They giggled, their heads pressed close together.

It cut to Claire in her home office, the one that the girls had helped her redecorate a few weeks ago. Since Claire had separated from Gavin and left her job at the church, she was now working from home on her own projects. She was finishing up the ebook she had been writing for Gavin and planned to publish it that fall—under her own name.

On-screen, she sat in her desk chair and smoothed the lapels of her black blazer. Her hair was pulled back into a sleek ponytail.

"Hottie alert!" Gabby yelled out. "Ow ow!" The girls laughed.

On-screen, Claire's blue eyes focused in on the camera as she began her confessional. "My dearest Gabs," she said. "I want you to know how happy I am for you. I know things with Tony had a rocky, unconventional start, but isn't that how all the greatest love stories begin?" She winked. "I've known you for most of my life, and your eyes have never lit up quite like they do when you talk about him. I remember playing fairy-tale games with you when we were little— you always did believe in them—and I'm so happy that you finally found your prince."

On the couch, Gabby reached over and squeezed Claire's hand.

"But just like a knight wears shining armor to protect himself,

I want to arm you with advice that will hopefully prepare you for what's to come." She took a deep breath and leaned forward on the desk. "Gabs, marriage isn't easy, and anyone who tells you that is a liar. No one is perfect—not you, not him—and the more you live together, the more you'll realize that."

Gabby nodded in agreement. She knew she sometimes put Tony on a pedestal—especially when they first started dating. She was so focused on being good enough for him that she wasn't able to be herself, which ultimately led to their downfall. Instead of focusing so much on either of their mistakes and flaws, she knew she needed to spend that energy nourishing their relationship.

Claire continued. "The bottom line is that marriage takes work on both sides, and you both have to be willing to make sacrifices." She paused. "That being said, you shouldn't have to make too many. Put yourself first . . . be selfish sometimes. You should never feel guilty about doing things for you. When you love yourself, it'll be so much easier for you to love someone else." She flashed a soft smile. "I love you so much, and hope you have a lifetime of happiness." She blew a kiss into the camera.

Gabby smiled. "I love you, too, Claire. That's great advice." She leaned her head on her friend's shoulder.

Claire squeezed her hand as they watched the next scene unfold.

"Hey, Gabby," Laura said, waving as she sat in front of the camera at her new desk job. After graduation two months ago, she'd moved to Arlington to be with her parents and got a position at a local insurance agent's office, a temporary gig until she could start college in the spring. "So, first off, congratulations on your big day. I'm so happy for you. Now, I'm supposed to give my advice." She scrunched her nose. "As someone going through a divorce, boy have I got some tidbits for you!" she said sarcastically. "But really, I learned quite a bit from my marriage and hope you can benefit from my mistakes. Number one, don't ever live with your in-laws, however desperate you might be . . . but I don't think that's gonna be a problem, considering Tony hates his dad as much as you do." Laura smirked.

"Ha!" Gabby laughed. Tony's relationship with Mr. Ford was definitely still strained, but thanks to some intervention from Mrs. Ford, they were slowly working things out. And though Gabby was skeptical that she'd ever have a great relationship with the congressman, she did have her mom back thanks to him, so there was a part of her that was grateful for everything they'd gone through. Besides, if she learned anything from her experience with Tony, it was that everyone deserved a second chance. But Laura was right: no moving in with Mr. Ford—or any parents, for that matter.

Laura continued. "Number two, keep a separate savings account just for you. Someone gave me great advice before: have enough money in there so that if you have to leave, you can. I hope that you never have to use it, but just have it there, and you won't ever feel trapped."

"I have to *get* some savings first," Gabby said, thinking about how empty her account was. Her goal this year, though, was to keep applying for scholarships and save up enough money for tuition by next fall.

"And number three—this is the big one, okay?" Laura said on the screen, with an even more serious tone. "Remember that you are not Mrs. Tony Ford, and you will never be Mrs. Tony Ford. You are *Mrs. Gabrielle Vaughn* who happens to be married to Mr. Tony Ford. Do not let yourself get lost in this marriage, and don't forget to follow your own dreams."

"Hell yes!" Madison shouted in the living room, giving Laura a high five. The girls all laughed.

Gabby looked over at her friend and smiled. She had always seen a lot of herself in Laura—so much ambition but sometimes a lack of confidence. She felt like they were both probably going through similar changes right now, not only with their relationships but also with getting their personal lives and goals back on track.

Back on the video, Laura said her final wishes. "I hope that this marriage is everything that you hope it will be and more. You deserve nothing but the best. Love you, Gabs!" She waved good-bye.

"You guys, I can't take this! This is the sweetest thing ever," Gabby said in between scenes.

"Shhh!" Madison said. "The best part is coming up!"

On the screen, Madison sat in George's leather recliner with a glass of whiskey in her hand as a fire roared in the background.

"Yes, in case you're wondering, Mads did build a fire when it was ninety degrees outside," Claire interrupted.

"I just wanted George to take his shirt off," she said with a wink.

"Oh gross!" Claire said, laughing and hitting her cousin on the butt as she lay next to her. The girls turned their attention back to the screen as Madison began talking.

"Sweet Gabby. Congrats on your big day! You're going to make a beautiful bride, and Tony's a lucky man to be able to call you his wife. As someone who has been married for only five months with a break in the middle, I know what you're thinking—what do I know about marriage? Well, I'm not going to bore you with details of my and George's relationship." She leaned into the camera and whispered, "Even though it's awesome!" She leaned back in the chair. "Instead, I'm going to tell you what I know based on the purest marital love I've ever witnessed: my parents'."

Gabby put her hand on her heart. "I love this so much."

"Shhh, I'm still talking!" Madison joked, pointing to the TV.

"My dad once told me the secret to their marriage was, quote, 'workin' as a team just like the Saints or the Tigers would.' He went on to give all these football analogies, and I'm probably gonna mess 'em up, but let me see if I can remember them. . . ." She swirled her glass in her hand. "One: you have to have good on-field communication to make sure you're making the right plays together. Two: you have to defend yourselves against outside forces working against you. Three: your relationship needs cheering on—find people in your life who will support it, not bring it down. And, my favorite: have victory dances as often as possible." She tilted her head to the side. "You can interpret that however you want."

Gabby laughed. That reminded her of the old man's advice at the

Cajun dancing restaurant back in the fall. She was looking forward to dancing with Tony for the rest of her life . . . in the living room . . . in the kitchen . . . in the bedroom.

"Good luck, my sweet friend. I'll be cheering you on from the sidelines the whole game."

As the scene faded to black, Gabby put her hand on her heart, wondering how she was so lucky to have such amazing friends. "I love you girls so much," she said.

"Welcome to the Young Wives Club," Claire said, raising her glass. "We know you'll be able to give us advice later on, too. And just know we'll be here for you throughout your adventure."

"Cheers!"

Gabby looked around the room and smiled, confident that whatever happened with Tony, these girls would be by her side through it all.

epilogue

TWO THOUSAND, ONE hundred and fifty-four people live in my town. Each of them with their own hopes, dreams, and story. The streets may not be bustlin' with crowds and the buildings may be more run-down shacks than skyscrapers, but we've got a community, and it's stronger than any on the Upper East Side or in Beverly Hills. Everyone here's still got their troubles, don't get me wrong. We cry just like the rest of 'em—only we don't pat our tears dry with an Hermès handkerchief. We use our friends' shoulders, and I'll tell you, it's the most luxurious feeling in the world. Because in my little corner of Louisiana, your friends are your life. Love may come and go, but they'll be there for you 'til the day you die.

acknowledgments

A PROPER THANK-YOU is in order to all those who helped me during the process of this book. Sticking with my southern upbringing, I'll make sure you all receive handwritten notes as well.

Thank you to my editors, Eliza Swift and Lanie Davis, for your brilliant ideas and hard work, and to my publisher, Emily Bestler, and your wonderful team, including Lara Jones, Tory Lowy, and Hillary Tisman, for helping me share my words with the world. Thank you, Les Morgenstein, Josh Bank, Sara Shandler, and Joelle Hobeika for believing in this project and giving me this opportunity, and to the entire Alloy Entertainment team for all your work, support, and friendship through the years.

Albert Tang and Laywan Kwan, thank you for designing a gorgeous cover delicious enough to eat.

To my mom, Sandy Boot, thank you for being my biggest cheerleader. This book would not have happened without your constant encouragement. I love you, your positivity, and your use of exclamation marks!!

Thank you to my husband, Christopher Pennell, for allowing me to talk about this book nonstop and supporting me throughout this adventure. I'm so lucky to have said "I do" to you.

A big shout-out to my sister, Jill Dressel, for all of the hilarious moments we've had together through the years, which may or may not have inspired some of the funnier anecdotes in the book.

Thank you to my dad, Richard Miller, for teaching me how to be a Cajun girl and buying me my first computer, which inspired me to begin writing; Ryan Schlenger, for teaching me about football; Amy Seder, for your photography skills; Kathie Rowell and the staff of the *Shreveport Times*, for giving me a column—and subsequently a voice—when I was fourteen; the Louisiana Tech journalism department, for teaching me how to bring my writing to life and the importance of showing, not telling; and Atoosa Rubenstein, for mentoring a nerdy girl with a dream.

To the clique—you know who you are—thanks for being a great example of a close-knit group of girls. The strong bond and relationship of these characters wouldn't have been nearly as deep without you in my life.

And thank you to everyone who picked up this book and read it—I am filled with gratitude.

about the author

Julie Pennell grew up in Shreveport, Louisiana, where she ate her weight in crawfish, used the word "y'all" a lot, and wrote a weekly "Teen Scene" column for the local paper. After graduating with a degree in journalism from Louisiana Tech University, she moved to New York City to work at *Seventeen* magazine and later at Alloy Entertainment as a digital editor. She lives in New York City with her husband and is a regular online contributor to *Teen Vogue*, *TODAY*, and the *Nest*, among other publications. *The Young Wives Club* is her first novel. You can connect with Julie on Twitter and Instagram @juliepens or at juliepennell.com.